Obsession

By
Ann Mayburn

The unauthorized reproduction or distribution of this copyrighted work is illegal. Criminal copyright infringement (including infringement without monetary gain) is investigated by the FBI and is punishable by up to 5 years in federal prison and a fine of $250,000.

Please purchase only authorized electronic editions and do not participate in, or encourage, the electronic piracy of copyrighted materials. Your support of the author's rights is appreciated.

This book is a work of fiction. Names, characters, places, and incidents are the products of the author's imagination or used fictitiously. Any resemblance to actual events, locales or persons, living or dead, is entirely coincidental.

Obsession
Copyright © 2016 by Ann Mayburn
Published by Honey Mountain Publishing

All rights reserved. Except for use in any review, the reproduction or utilization of this work, in whole or in part, in any form by any electronic, mechanical or other means now known or hereafter invented, is forbidden without the written permission of the publisher.

DISCLAIMER: Please do not try any new sexual practice, BDSM or otherwise, without the guidance of an experienced practitioner. Ann Mayburn will not be responsible for any loss, harm, injury or death resulting from use of the information contained in this book.

Dear Beloved Reader,

If you've read my work before you already know that I'm a filthy, dirty bitch in the bedroom and you're ready for the ensuing sexy times. For my first time readers, please be aware that my sex scenes do not fade to black, and my characters are not big into missionary under the sheets with the lights off for procreation while thinking of England sex. That said, Leo is a kinky, kinky bastard and even though he's into Daddy/princess play, in no way-shape-or form does it ever become pedophile/incest role playing.

  Instead, the 'Daddy Dom' dynamic is one of love and trust, where the Dom enjoys caring completely for his baby girl, helping her grow into a stronger person, making her happy, while giving her the discipline she both needs and desires. This is a consensual relationship between two adults, and in my opinion, Daddy/princess play is a very loving form of BDSM that is caring and full of lots of open affection. Like everything else in life it means different things to different people so what I may find kinky you may find vanilla, and vice versa. ☺

  So, get your seatbelt on and your vibrator handy, 'cause you're in for a heck of a ride.

Ann

A true friend is someone who lets you have total freedom to be yourself - and especially to feel. Or, not feel. Whatever you happen to be feeling at the moment is fine with them. That's what real love amounts to - letting a person be what he really is and loving him for it.

~Jim Morrison

Prologue

Leo – Age Eighteen
Tucson, Arizona

There are few emotions that I experience with any intensity, and fewer still that are what ordinary people would consider "nice", but of those occasional bouts of negative feelings I have to endure, sorrow is by far the worst. Once it sinks its poisoned claws into you, it debilitates your body, steals your will to function, drains your life, and leaves you hollowed out and blistered raw inside. The only thing I've found to combat the choking depression of sorrow is violence, but my grief at this point is so absolute I couldn't fathom anything but pain.

Usually I'd be multi-tasking, touching base with the various members of the cartel I belonged to as we went about our daily business and shit like that. But with my mother dying in a room not too far from me in this barren medical wasteland, I could barely function enough to breathe.

My sweet, gentle, kind mother, who always smelled like cherries and vanilla, was pumped full of strangers' blood in a vain attempt to keep her heart beating and replace the liters she'd lost as I'd held her in my arms, trying in vain to stop the bleeding as she clung to me with the last of her strength.

Guilt and sorrow battled for supremacy in my chest, my lungs tight with the need to cry out against the injustice of it all.

If it wasn't for my mother's unending patience and kindness, her generous nature, I may have grown up having no idea what it felt like to care for another person, to have any form of compassion. If that had happened, I'm sure I would have become a monstrosity in the truest sense of the word. Instead, I've managed to channel my taste for the high violence gives me into a profession that had, ever so briefly, given my mom the kind of life she'd always dreamed of.

Tears burned my nose, but I turned my head up to the ceiling and closed my eyes, willing them away.

My dad had died not long after I was born, and my difficulties with processing the world like everyone else would be a challenge to anyone, let alone a single mother with only a high school education. Still, she'd always been there for me, helping me understand people and their emotional motivations like an interpreter translating a foreign language. It was through her that I learned to mimic the unspoken rules of our society, how to blend in. At least as much as I could ever blend in. I'm one of those people you look at and just know something is wrong, different. Nothing overt, nothing you can put your finger on, but when people meet my gaze, some animal part of their brain screams that I'm dangerous.

And I am. I carried within me the ability to do great violence without balking. If I had any respect for authority, I might have gone into the military; they tried to recruit me, but I had other plans. In the rough neighborhood I'd grown up in, violence was a fact of life and boys aspired to work for the biggest drug cartels, not the government. It was survival of the fittest, and I was born a predator, so it didn't take me long to move up through the ranks, even when I'd joined the Cordova cartel at the tender age of fifteen.

I'd grown up poor, but over the last few years had managed to move us into a decent house north of Tucson, the result of my working for the Cordova cartel as one of their enforcers. Turns out they had a use for a man of my talents, and while being sadistic would never serve me in the world occupied by offices and people standing in never-ending lines, it did allow me to flourish in the deep underbelly of society. The money was good, but the release of tension I felt after killing someone was even better, and because of my willingness to do gruesome work without a blink, for the first time in her life, my mom didn't have to work two jobs to support us.

Unfortunately, my activities had blown back on me—and my mother had paid the price. Someone had done a drive-by on our house and she'd been standing directly in the line of fire, getting ready to go bowling with her girlfriends.

She'd been so excited to show off the two-carat diamond pendant I'd gotten her for her birthday, hadn't been able to stop touching and admiring it. She had to have known my money wasn't legal, but she allowed me to think she bought my lie about working as an errand boy for a local construction company the cartel owned. My mom was brutally practical, and I'm sure she knew better than anyone I wasn't meant for the nine-to-five world.

A smile tugged at my lips as I remembered catching her standing in front of a mirror last night and touching the pendant with a soft, dreamy expression that took years off her lined face. At one time, Carla Brass had been a beautiful woman, but life had ground her down, aged her before her time. She deserved a break after all her hardship, and I felt a great sense of pride that I could take care of her, give her luxury and comfort. Her happiness was *my* happiness, and there was nothing I enjoyed more than the satisfaction of making her world a better place. I'd felt so full of gratitude that I could provide for her like that, ease her burden and give her the things she'd always wanted, but sacrificed when she'd decided to marry my dad after she got pregnant at eighteen.

Then the bullets had torn through the house, piercing her in the lung, stomach, and leg.

Blood…so much of it that I knew the chances of her making it were slim as I held her in my arms, screaming into the phone for the ambulance to hurry.

Now she was in critical condition and they were trying to stabilize her enough to do more surgery.

I knew, deep in my gut, she wasn't going to make it—and the knowledge made me furious.

Acid boiled in my veins and adrenaline surged through me as I thought about the men who'd done this.

I would find them and they would pay.

A family entered the waiting room, an older man with graying black hair and his pale, sickly looking wife, along with their daughter, jerking me from my dark thoughts. They were a nondescript family, the mother's blonde hair showing about an inch of brown and gray roots, the father's clothing wrinkled and worn, but something about them caught my attention. They were clearly grieving as they sat in the uncomfortable chairs filling the waiting room, the woman's loud weeping annoying me.

I almost looked away…until I noticed the girl. She was young, probably no more than ten or eleven, and she had the biggest, saddest golden-brown eyes I'd ever seen. Even rimmed with red they were beautiful, and filled with so much sorrow. I've never met someone with such expressive eyes, their rich amber depths revealing a wounded soul that was old beyond her years.

Something seized up in me, pierced through my grief and made me focus on her. Next to the girl, her parents clung to each other and wept, ignoring her pain in favor of their own. It made me furious that they were so selfish, that they could sit next to someone as young and innocent as that little girl and not even see her. Didn't they realize how short life was? That she needed them? I was pretty much emotionally fucked, but even I felt a flicker of compassion for the hurting kid who looked like her world was shattering around her.

I watched them for a little while longer, waiting for either the father or mother to even acknowledge their kid, but they didn't. She just sat there, staring down at her feet clad in a pair of red Chucks, her jean shorts loose and baggy, revealing pale, bony legs and knobby knees. As she looked up again to stare at the television, I noticed further how frail she was, her arms slender to the point I wondered if she was even eating. Dark circles shadowed her eyes and there was a look of such hopelessness on her narrow face that I couldn't help but raise my hand and wave until I had her attention.

She sat up straighter and glanced over at her parents, who were still wrapped up in each other, then back to me before easing out of her chair and walking hesitantly across the empty room to sit next to me.

Her parents never looked up, so I ignored them and glanced over at her, hoping my tattoo and size didn't freak her out. "What's your name?"

When she licked her puffy, chapped lips, I noticed she had braces as she whispered in a light and melodious voice, "I'm Hannah."

I held my hand out. "Hi. My name's Leo."

Looking at me from beneath her long lashes, she bit her lower lip, then tentatively took my hand in her own and said in the sweetest, softest murmur as she blushed bright red, "Nice to meet you."

Poor kid, she was going through that fucked-up, awkward stage of adolescence where your body seems to be growing out of sync. Her nose a little too big for her heart-shaped face, her chin too pointed, mouth too wide, and her mouth was puffed out by the braces she wore, giving her fish lips.

But there was something about her that made me take a second look. The more I studied her, the more I realized in a few years, she'd grow into her features and she'd be stunning, beautiful in an unusual way that wouldn't just draw a man's gaze, but hold it. I'd never seen a person with skin as pale as hers before, so milky smooth that I could faintly see the blue veins beneath if I stared hard enough. You don't see a lot of pasty people in Arizona, and I watched with fascination as her cheeks flushed a deeper red all the way to her ears.

Looking away, she muttered, "What are you staring at?"

"You're going to break hearts someday."

Instead of smiling, like most girls would at a compliment, she jerked back and hissed, confusing me. "You don't have to be mean. I know how I look. I'm plain, nothing special. My sister's the pretty one…or at least she was. She was so beautiful. Now, after battling leukemia for so long, then slipping into a coma three weeks ago, she's…she's like a dried-out husk. I have nightmares about her turning to ash and just floating away."

"That's fucked-up."

She gave a sharp laugh, and looked over to her parents before returning her gaze to mine. "Yeah, it is," she whispered, so softly I could barely hear it and I knew this girl wasn't used to swearing, "totally fucked-up."

"Is that why you're here? Your sister?"

Nodding solemnly at me, she took in a shivery breath. "Yeah."

I didn't know how to comfort her, so I tried to make her understand that I knew how she felt. In a way. While she held no responsibility for her sister's death, my mother's blood was on my hands, even if I didn't pull the trigger. Those bullets were meant for me and I failed to keep her safe.

"My mother's dying in a room that smells like medicine and piss," I blurted out. "It's bullshit."

She surprised me, anger burning on her innocent face as she whispered, "It is. I hate this place. My sister wanted to die at home, in her room so she could look out the window and see our tree house, but my parents made the doctors try everything to cure her, no matter what. She was in so much pain, crying all the time, trying to be brave. She wants to die, I heard her begging them to let her go to sleep and not wake up, but they won't. They say they believe in God, and pray to him all the time to cure Tiffany, but they don't really believe in him. If they did, they'd know Tiffany is going to Heaven where it doesn't hurt anymore. Where she can be happy. It's..." She looked around then lowered her voice to barely a whisper again. "Everything is bullshit."

Big tears rolled down her now blotchy cheeks, and I grabbed her some tissue from one of the boxes around the room. She gave me a watery smile then blew her nose.

When I looked over to where her parents had been sitting, the faded chairs were empty. "Where did they go?"

Her narrow shoulders rose to her ears as she shrugged, looking away when I sat next to her again. "Who knows?"

"Aren't they worried about you being in here alone and talking to me?"

"No. I think...I think they're mad I'm okay and Tiffany isn't."

"What do you mean?"

She held my gaze, something most people couldn't do. "I don't blame them for loving her more. I mean, I'm nobody and she's amazing. Tiffany isn't only my sister, she's my best friend. Kind, sweet, and awesome. She was so funny, always pulling pranks and making our parents laugh. I know they ask themselves why God would take Tiffany and not me, I heard them talking when they thought I was in bed, and I wonder the same thing. If I could trade places with her in a heartbeat, I would."

And people thought I was fucked-up. Anyone who could do this to their kid, mess with their head this badly, deserved nothing but contempt. She scuffed her feet on the floor and I reached out, taking her hand in mine, aware of how tiny the bones of her hand felt. Something, some unknown emotion, made me want to give her hope, needed to make her feel better.

"Do you believe in destiny?"

"What?"

"You know, fate."

"No. Do you?"

"Absolutely. Think about it, from the moment of conception to right now, how many things had to go exactly right to bring you here? How many close calls did you survive? What were the chances that your parents would even meet? If you look at the big picture of your life, you can see the divine pattern. You're here for a reason, a purpose, we all are, which means you're special." I inadvertently squeezed her fingers as the reality of what was happening down the hall hit me again. "My mom taught me that."

Even though I must have hurt her fingers, she placed her other hand on top of my tanned one, tears spilling down her cheeks. "I'm sorry about your mother. She sounds really cool."

"She's the best."

Movement through the glass windows by the door

drew my attention and I stood right away, recognizing the pretty older doctor who'd been taking care of my mom.

She motioned to me when she reached the doorway and my heart sank. I knew by her face my mom didn't make it. A high ringing filled my ears as everything inside of me screamed in agony, in denial. I didn't need to hear the words to know she was gone.

I stared with unseeing eyes at a window, looking out into the dark night, the thoughts of how I was going to torture those responsible for her death soothing me.

Chapter 1

Leo – Age 28

The darkness within my cold heart held no pity for the once beautiful woman trapped in the dog cage bolted to the floor, dirty and beaten. If anything, I wish we'd had longer to torture her, longer to keep her in the same pain her young son, Jason, had experienced at the hands of his kidnappers. Kidnappers his mother had hired to hold him for ransom.

I've always known Nina was a no-good ruthless bitch, but Fernando, one of my best friends and the son of the Cordova cartel leader, loved and married the bitch when she'd turned up pregnant, so I'd tolerated her. But now the sight of her disgusted me so much, I spat on her cringing form, fury sending a throbbing rush of strength into my clenched hands, urging me to dole out a richly deserved punishment.

"You wanna know how we found him, your beloved son?" I snarled. "Beaten, filthy, tied up with wire that had cut his wrists so deep it was embedded in his flesh, missing three of his fingers and one of his ears—*dead*, having choked to death on his own vomit because they gagged him too tight. So fucking tight the corners of his mouth were ripped open. All for fucking *money*."

I wanted to kick the cage again, to have another

hour to draw more pain from her body, but Nina's mother-in-law, Judith Cordova, was about to arrive, and she was going to demand her pound of flesh from the treacherous cunt whimpering in her own filth.

The hermetically sealed door behind me hissed open and I tried to calm my breathing as I went over to one of the industrial sinks in the corner of the interrogation chamber and began to wash Nina's blood from my skin. Normally I protected myself against any contamination from other people's bodily fluids; I dealt with too many nasty fucks who'd stick their dicks in any pussy offered to them. But I wanted to feel Nina suffer, to feel her tremble and writhe from the pain I was inflicting while trying to purge from my head the memory of Fernando's screams as he held his son's battered body.

Tears and heavy emotions were something that seldom bothered me, but I understood the loss of family enough that it awakened my rarely felt compassion. So while Fernando had been unable to personally deal with his betraying wife, I had stepped in for him, trying to ease his burden in any way I could by making sure she paid.

Unfortunately, I hadn't come close to slaking my blood lust, but I had to step aside as hushed voices spoke quietly behind me, the sound of Nina's moans and sobs almost drowning them out, but one woman's strained voice I recognized.

Judith was here to collect the debt Nina owed Fernando's family.

Dressed from head to toe in a stylish black pantsuit and decked out in tasteful diamonds, for once Judith looked like shit. Her normally carefully styled, short silver hair that framed her wrinkled but classically beautiful face was in disarray, the deep lines around her mouth betraying her grief. But her eyes, her dark eyes—much like my own—glittered with pure insanity. Not many people were aware of it, but Judith could sometimes lose her grip on reality and do some crazy shit in her rage. I had a feeling I was about to witness the demon that lived inside the wife of the head of the cartel I worked for come to life.

Behind her, two of her nephews came in, along with her son Ramón. Her other son, Diego, was no doubt with Fernando and their father, Jose. Diego and Fernando were twins, so they tended to rely on each other in times of crisis, and Jose was there to help keep Fernando from trying to take his life—again. A shudder ripped up my spine as I remembered the sound of my friend screaming in complete and total agony until his voice broke.

Judith strode to the middle of the large concrete room in the basement of one of the popular and trendy restaurants she owned, the drain in the floor stained with drying blood. The door hissed opened again and more high-ranking members of the Cordova cartel moved in, until there were around twenty of us circling the room, pressed shoulder to shoulder, all focused on the cage situated beneath the bright floodlight overhead.

My stomach clenched as I realized Judith was about to make an example of her daughter-in-law, one none of us would ever likely forget.

A heavy metal cross let out a teeth-clenching screech as it was dragged across the floor, both men pushing the weighty piece softly grunting beneath its bulk.

In short order, Nina was bound, nude and covered in bruises and cuts, to the X shape, almost incoherent pleas for mercy falling from her lips, saying that she didn't mean for it to happen, that the men she'd given Jason to had double-crossed her. Pleas for compassion mixed with her now panting breaths, her one good eye madly roving the room, looking for a hero, for someone to save her. She'd find no forgiveness here.

We'd all loved Jason, Jose and Judith's first and only grandchild. While Nina had been a mostly absent mother, Fernando had lived and breathed for his kid. Jason's birthdays were already legendary at the age of five and I'd been assigned to his bodyguard detail at various times over the years, enough that the kid always greeted me with a hug and a smile.

A deep pang of sorrow reverberated through me, my chest aching like someone had beat it with a sledgehammer, breaking ribs and sending deadly shards of razor-sharp bone straight to my heart. I could remember the earthy smell of his little boy hair warmed by the sun, the sweet ring of his laughter. Such a bright light, gone forever.

The tips of Judith's shiny red heels clicked across the floor as she slowly walked up to Nina, the rest of the room having disappeared for her as her focus narrowed on the evil bitch. Back in the day, before Judith married Jose and semi-retired to focus on being a good mother, Judith had been the Cordova cartel's torture master, and she made inflicting pain an art form that she greatly enjoyed practicing. Not that she got off on it in any sexual way, but breaking down an enemy, dishing out well-deserved punishment, satisfied her in a way I understood all too well. It fed the beast without breaking whatever particular moral code we subscribed to.

But this—this was personal.

Cocking her head to the side, Judith studied her daughter-in-law's once supermodel-perfect face. "You have committed the worst crime a mother possibly can, something so heinous it sickens me down to my soul. My grandson, *mi dulce bebe*. He died alone and in agony because of *you*."

A rare tear traveled down Judith's ashen face while Nina continued her hysterical pleading, saying she was innocent, lying out her ass even though she knew we had video proof of her talking about how she let the kidnappers into her house and poisoned her bodyguards.

I shook my head, seeking out the rage that lived inside of me as I stared at Nina, allowing my own crazy to surface and chill these emotions seething within me. The muscles along my back and hands twitched as I barely restrained the need to join Judith. She'd mentored me during information-gathering sessions with our enemies many times, I was her apprentice of sorts, but this moment was entirely hers.

The breathing in the room picked up as Ramón moved to stand next to his mother, the hatred and disgust on his face making Nina sob anew.

Two of the Cordova cousins moved behind the metal X and together they held Nina's head in place, their grips digging no doubt painfully into her bruised cheeks.

Ramón handed his mother a knife then pulled a device out of his pocket that I was familiar with.

A mouth spreader.

In short order, Nina's mouth was held wide open, her shrill screams making it hard to hear what Judith was saying, but I could easily read her thin lips.

"I'm taking your lying tongue, with which you told your baby you loved him." She swiftly did as she'd said, then closed her eyes and inhaled slowly as one of her bodyguards helped her put on gloves and a white hazmat suit that would soon be red, her cold voice almost clinical in its detachment above Nina's garbled shrieks. "I'm taking your breasts, a symbol of the motherhood you shit all over. Your fingers will be next, so you can feel what Jason went through when they took his. After that, I'll slice out your womb, then your eyes—and last of all, I'll cut your vile heart from your chest. Don't look forward to death to rescue you from the pain. If I were you, I'd try to hold on to life for as long as I could, because a special place in hell is surely waiting for you. *Espero que te pudras en el infierno.*"

And so it went, for a long, long time, until Nina finally died in agony.

The entire room was hushed yet still ringing with Nina's screams, and so very still as Judith turned to us, using a wet wipe Ramón had supplied her with while the cleanup crew got busy.

Judith's dead gaze locked on mine, and I noticed a fine spray of red droplets in her hair, glittering like rubies. "Leo, come with me, please."

A faint tremble threaded her voice and most people would dismiss it as being from shock, but I knew it was just the adrenaline leaving her body, the hard-addictive rush of a prolonged torture session coursing through her bloodstream.

I followed her, grabbing my shirt and jacket from a hook near the doorway and shrugging both on. Normally I would have paused to make sure I didn't have anything incriminating on me, but it was well past two a.m. and the restaurant above us was empty and dark. It was only below ground that the Cordova cartel continued to thrive. This basement area of the building the restaurant was situated in was normally used as a warehouse for moving illegal goods, but tonight it was unusually quiet, a sense of mourning hanging thick in the air, like the humid fog in New Orleans.

We reached her office at the end of one of the hallways, the normally pristine place littered with broken glass and wood. It took me a moment to realize that Judith had probably smashed all the pictures of her daughter-in-law and only grandson in a rage, the images too painful to handle. I know after my mother died, it took me years to even glance at a photo of her, the sense of loss still too great.

"Out," she snapped at whoever had followed us in.

The door shut behind me, but I didn't take my eyes off her as I carefully walked over the smooth oak floors to the long, tan leather couch that stretched out against the wall near her desk. This was my preferred place, out of the way if she was dealing with business and comfortable enough to rest if I had to wait.

After my mother's death, Judith had understood my need for revenge and had assigned her son Ramón's crew to help me find my vengeance. It was her contacts that had found out which rival cartel murdered my mother, and her top bodyguards had helped us plan out my revenge.

Of course, we got the extra help because Ramón was her son and this was his first big job, but she also did it because even then she'd recognized something twisted in me that she felt a kinship with.

When she slumped back onto the couch next to me, I knew what her silent request was. Leaning in, I pulled her to my side and hugged her to me, internally sighing as I felt how delicate she was becoming. At fifty-four, Judith had led a hard life as the wife of a cartel boss, and the loss of her beloved grandson seemed to have struck her a physical blow. Her entire body shook as she sobbed, and I held her, letting her get her grief out. I understood what an honor it was to be there for her like this, to provide her with the comfort she needed. She couldn't show this pain to her sons and husband, not when they needed her strength.

After a few minutes, she quieted, taking yet another wad of tissue that I handed to her. She hated being messy and quickly wiped her face. Her breath came out in a ragged sigh then she visibly wilted.

"I can't do this again, Leo. I can't bury another baby, can't watch my son beg me to let him bleed out after he cut his wrists, to let him die and join Jason."

Unable to think of any way to sooth her, I took her hand in my own and gave it a squeeze. "I understand."

"No, you don't." She pulled her hand away then stood, beginning to pace, her heels crunching against the floor when they hit a piece of broken glass. "There has to be some way to protect my boys from women like that bitch. Some way to make sure the girls they love will never betray them, will remain loyal and be good mothers to their children."

Not sure where she was going with this, or if she was just venting, I watched her as she ran her hands through her hair, attempting to fix it. "And how are you going to make that happen? Interrogate them? Blackmail them? None of that will work, and both your sons and their women will end up resenting you. Even if you could order them around like robots, your sons won't love Stepford Wives. They're probably even more paranoid than you now about trusting the wrong women, and will be constantly on alert for any odd reactions. Plus, you can't force love."

Her shoulders slumped. "No, you can't. But will you think on it for me, Leo? You never know what that unpredictable, brilliant mind of yours can come up with."

For once I had a clear insight into her feelings — and I knew she needed something to cling to, something to hope for. "I promise you, Judith, I will."

"That's all I can ask." She sighed then moved over to her desk, her gait slightly hitched and her head bowed. "I need to be alone for a while. Can you take Ramón to get something to eat? I don't think he's done anything but drink coffee and whisky since this whole sordid affair started."

"Of course, anything you need, Judith."

"Thank you, Leo."

Dismissed, I numbly made my way through the underground labyrinth until I found Ramón talking with some of his father's men. No doubt there would be some power restructuring within the cartel; Fernando was the heir apparent, but he was in no shape to do anything but breathe right now. There were rumors that he would be leaving the area for a while after his son's funeral, and I couldn't blame him. Too many ghosts haunted his house, and everywhere he looked, he would be reminded of what had happened, what he used to have.

With a deep sigh to announce my presence, I put a hand on Ramón's tightly muscled shoulder and squeezed. "Your mom ordered me to drag your ass out to eat, though I have no idea what in the fuck is open at this time of night."

Instead of fighting me, Ramón shook his head. "I know a place, not too far from here, but I don't know if I'll be able to eat anything."

"How's their coffee? New day's starting and it looks like you and I are shit out of luck about getting any sleep."

The men around us laughed softly, our lives so saturated in violence even the atrocities we'd witnessed started to roll off our backs faster than it would for normal people. We were killers, all of us, born and bred, so what happened with Judith and Nina was par for the course. It was the boy's death that haunted us and kept us from our beds. No one wanted to lay their heads down and close their eyes, only to see Jason's mangled form burned onto their lids.

Ramón slapped my back, hard, no doubt reading my grim expression. "Come on. I need to get the fuck out of here."

After I finished cleaning up, we walked through

the service exit and into the deep of night, that ultra-dark and quiet time right before dawn, with a blend of exhaustion and the hope of a new day twisting in the air. The world felt old, used up and dull as I waited for the first hints of dawn to break the horizon and paint the sky crimson and the mountains in shades of lavender. Even though it was warm, the evening still held a blessedly cool tinge that felt good on my skin, refreshing me as we approached a brightly lit diner done in a retro theme.

I'd passed it many times, admired the old fashioned and elaborate neon sign out front, but had never gone in. Now as we pushed the door open, the smells of good, greasy food mixed with coffee and a hint of sweetness filled my nose, rinsing away the residual smell of blood from my mouth and mind. I took a deep breath, not really paying attention as we were led to a booth toward the back of the restaurant. The place was fairly busy and it took us a minute of shuffling to get to our seats.

Thankfully, the circular booth we were seated in was situated so both Ramón and I had a view of the door. Neither of us liked having our backs to the room and I didn't feel like flipping him to see who sat where. The booth was high enough that it gave us a sense of privacy and I let the chatter of humanity wash over me.

I felt restless, edgy, as I contemplated Judith's words. Some people may think just because I'm able to view a human being as nothing more than meat, it meant I didn't or couldn't have the desire for a loving family of my own someday. I wanted to find a nice girl, somehow con her into marrying me, and spend the rest of my life making her and my children happy. I'd always taken it for granted that I would find a good woman worthy of my devotion and we'd grow old together.

Now, after Nina's betrayal, I wondered how I would ever be able to trust another woman again.

"Morning, gentlemen, my name's Hannah and I'll be serving you today." A young female's incredibly sweet voice rolled over my skin, stroking me from the inside out. "Can I start you out with some coffee?"

I turned to see who the enchanting voice belonged to, and was struck dumb by the leggy beauty smiling at Ramón as he placed an order for coffee, then added some pancakes and sausage to it.

Her long, long black hair was held back from her face in a high ponytail that still fell midway down her back, and she had the most delicate features I've ever seen on a woman. Big golden-brown doe eyes full of warmth and light, high cheekbones that curved down into a narrow, pointed chin, and lips so full they looked like they belonged on a porn star. Add to that a slender body with curves in all the right places, and even though she was dressed in a pair of loose brown pants and wearing a god-awful yellow apron over her white shirt, she struck me dumb with lust.

"Leo," Ramón growled.

Realizing I was making her uncomfortable, and that the smile was fading from her lips, I gave her the grin women always fell for. "Coffee, black."

She blinked and I had the strangest sense of déjà vu as our eyes met. "You got it. I'll be right back with your coffee."

As she quickly strode off, stopping to check with

her other tables on the way, I watched her.

"What's your deal?" Ramón asked in a low voice. "You know her?"

I squinted, trying to place her. I was usually very good at remembering people, and I swore she was familiar, I just didn't know how. It wasn't her looks — I'd have remembered those — but her voice and eyes that struck me. "I think I do, but I'm not sure."

"Well, if you happen to remember she has a bounty on her head, don't kill her until after I've eaten." He grimaced as he scanned the room. "What did my mom want to talk to you about?"

I didn't bother lying to him or trying to hide it. "Your mom needed a moment to deal with everything."

Ramón's long dark hair fell over his forehead and into his eyes as he looked down at the table top. "Thank you for being there for her. You know she thinks of you like a son."

Something deep inside of me eased the slightest bit. "She's a good woman."

He laughed and rubbed his face, his hands rasping over the dark bristles of his unshaved face. "Fuck…she's batshit crazy, but I love her to death. What else did she talk about? Something's on her mind. I don't know what but I recognize the conniving look on her face. She has a new resolve around her that scares me. Bad things can happen when my mother decides to do something."

"She's trying to figure out a way to make sure whatever woman you chose for your wife is loyal to you."

A flash of pain went through Ramón's hazel-brown

eyes before he smiled. "Lemme know how that works out for her."

"That's what I said, but she's got me thinking."

"You wanna know what I'm thinking?" he growled in a low voice. "I'm thinking that normally I'd be fucking away my pain with one of the cute pieces of ass smiling at us from across the room. But as soon as I even consider having one of them suck my dick, I get this sick feeling inside of me like someone's kicked me in the gut, so you don't have to worry about me looking for a wife anytime soon. Fuck, I'll be lucky if I can even jerk off anymore. Maybe you can brainwash me into forgetting that any woman I fall in love with could stab me in the back at any second."

A burst of laughter came from across the room, and I followed the slim line of our waitress's back as she practically danced through the growing crowd, her infectious smile and good nature making even the most surly patron grin back.

Tapping my finger on the cool tabletop, I pursed my lips as I thought. "Or maybe I could brainwash *them* into being loyal."

"Yeah, right."

"I'm serious."

Ramón leaned forward, the creases around his mouth deepening with his frown. "Even if you did, where am I going to find a good girl who's into my particular brand of kink? Not every woman is into the kind of dominance and submission we enjoy."

"This is true."

"I mean, how many women giggled the first time you told them to call you 'Daddy'."

For a moment, everything felt normal between us, our usual banter putting me at ease. "Not a single fucking one. Hard to laugh with a cock down your throat."

"I'll take your word for it."

I gave him a dry look, which he ignored while taking his phone out of his pocket. A second later he cursed, then stood and moved out of the booth. I went to do the same, but he waved me back. "Sit, eat my pancakes. I have to go deal with some family shit."

"What happened?"

Looking incredibly weary, he rubbed his face. "Nothing to concern yourself over. Dad's worried about me and wants me back home."

"If you need anything—"

He clasped my shoulder, his voice hoarse as he said, "You were there for me, for *mi familia* today, in every way we needed, and I'll never forget it."

After he left, I found my mind drifting again, the combination of exhaustion, too much caffeine, and lack of food dulling my wits.

Our waitress spoke from nearby, and I realized she was talking to the people in the booth behind me. I didn't mean to eavesdrop, but the soft cadence of her honeyed tone lulled me, soothed me, and melted through my bones like caramel. She was comforting whoever was in the booth, and as they talked with the waitress about their loved one in the hospital across the street, something clicked—and I remembered where I knew her from.

Hannah. The girl in the waiting room that I'd spoken with the night my mother died. It came back to me slowly, the braces, her awkward gait, the infinite sadness in her wounded gaze. I'd thought about her now and again over the years, wondering how she was doing, if her parents ever pulled their heads out of their asses.

When Hannah came back with the plate of pancakes, she glanced around before looking back at me. "Did your friend leave?"

"Yes, but I'll take his food."

It took everything I had just to get those words out, and as I stared at her, I marveled at the beauty she'd grown into. Her big eyes, now sparkling with life, had a slight tilt at the corners, and that mouth…Jesus it looked so soft, perfect for pushing my cock between. She'd put some kind of pale pink gloss on her lips and it reminded me of the way a woman's pussy looked when she was aroused, puffy and slicked with her desire.

My gaze must have revealed more than I'd intended, because she got flustered as she smiled at me. "Can I get you anything else?"

"No, thank you."

She smiled again, her gaze already on another table, where they were trying to get her attention. As I watched her, slowly eating my food I didn't taste, I wondered how her life had been since that fateful night and what she was doing now. I wondered if she was happy, if she had a man who thought the sun rose and set on her brilliant smile, even though her ring finger was bare.

The more I watched, the more curious I became, and by the time she dropped off my check, I was already making plans to find out more about Hannah with the soft, sweet voice and generous heart.

Chapter 2

One year later
Hannah

The hard pounding of bass from the nearby club reverberated down the street as I linked arms with my two best friends and strutted my stuff down the concrete of the still-hot sidewalk.

Well, I strutted what little stuff I had. When God had been handing out tits and ass, I must have gotten the bottom of the barrel because mine were barely a handful. Still, I added a swing to my hips and a lift to my chin as we approached one of the hottest bars in Phoenix on a warm spring night. A few days ago it had been my birthday, I was finally officially twenty-one, and I was super excited that we were on our way out to party in style, instead of at the crappy pub down the street from my apartment.

Unlike my regular bar, where they'd been serving my fake ID for years, with its faded brick front and windows layered with decades of grime in the corners, this dance club was less than two years old and reeked of wealth. Three stories high, the bar dominated the block, and inside was a massive adult wonderland of three clubs in one. On the first floor was mostly techno and dance music, while the second floor was divided up into a large bar area and a VIP lounge filled with semi-private alcoves. The third floor was officially admin, but there were rumors that there were private rooms up there as well, that could be rented for a night of debauchery.

I'd researched the club as soon as I'd found out I won three VIP tickets in some contest I didn't remember entering, and couldn't believe my good luck.

On my right, Joy, my curvy blonde roommate and best friend who'd gotten an extra, extra helping of boobs from God and angelically cute dimples to match, gripped my hand then squeezed. "I can't believe we're going to Obsession! Thank you so much for bringing me, Hannah."

"Me neither," Kayla chirped as our heels struck the pavement almost in sync. She had dark hair like mine, but hers was cut into a razor-sharp bob that accentuated her lean face. "You're so lucky you won those VIP passes. There's no way you could afford even a drink in this place if you hadn't."

"Can you *not* be a bitch for one evening, Kayla?" Joy growled, and I resisted the urge to roll my eyes.

Unlike myself and Joy, Kayla came from money and her family was influential in the Tucson business community back home. Sometimes she could be a spoiled brat, and I've had to break up more than one fight between her and Joy, but we've been friends since were kids, so I'm used to her antics and usually just ignore them. It was easier to just give Kayla her way and move on.

Smiling brightly at Kayla, and pretending I didn't see Joy glaring at her, I acted as though I didn't hear the implied insult and instead said in a bright voice, "You got that right. I don't even remember entering the Facebook contest."

"You probably did it while you were drunk." Kayla grinned, her new designer olive green silk dress flashing a good deal of her toned thigh as she walked. "Remember that time you ordered those god-awful beaded and rhinestone-encrusted duck sweaters off eBay?"

"Do I ever," I groaned while tugging at the hem of my dress as it tried to creep up. "I learned the hard way not to get wasted and go one-click shopping. Those things were expensive! A hundred and sixty dollars for a duck sweater. I had to pick up extra shifts at work to cover it."

My grin died off as we crossed the street, heat rising off the black pavement while we negotiated the slow-moving traffic. As the temperature dropped, more and more people had come out. An almost visible wave of excited energy rose off the long line of people winding around Obsession, all dressed to impress and waiting to get in. A wait we could skip, thanks to my lucky win.

People in line watched us as we dared to strolled past them up the white marble steps leading to the domed entryway, probably wondering what the hell we were doing. When we approached the purple velvet ropes guarding the club entrance, I gave myself a little pep talk and tried to appear confident. Any other night of the week and I'd be stuck at the back of the line, waiting to maybe get inside. But tonight...tonight I was somebody. Kind of.

Two of the four bouncers watching the entrance tilted their heads to watch us approach, then turned and spoke to each other in voices too low for me to hear. They were both very handsome Latino men who wore pitch-black suits, and in the deep purple-tinged lighting of the club's exterior, they were intimidating as hell.

The guard on the left, a gigantic guy with buzzed black hair and a hard expression, took us in with a small twist to his thick lips.

With large diamond studs glinting in both his ears he was an intimidating sight, "Ladies, how can I help you?"

"Um...I'm on the list," I said as I clutched my purse and tried to keep from withering beneath his surprised look.

Okay, so me and my friends weren't supermodels or wealthy socialites, but we weren't gutter trash either. The stares of the crowd grew and a couple women near the front of the line openly ridiculed Joy's breasts as being porn star implants and instantly labeled her a whore. As they began to cut my friend down I was having a hard time not going over there and putting my foot up their pampered asses. Joy's self-esteem wasn't the best, nowhere near as bad as mine, but she was very sensitive and uncomfortable about her figure due to a lifetime of men ogling her admittedly sexy as hell body. And lets not forget how Joy's older sister loved tearing Joy down. I know her sister is just jealous of Joy, but it still hurts my friend and has made her hyper aware of how other people see her.

Listening to those women cut Joy down added a snap to my words, "Hannah Barnes. That's my name."

He pulled out his phone and checked the screen for a moment before looking at me with raised eyebrows and said something. I missed the first part as the doors to the club opened and some gorgeous, laughing women stumbled out with their arms hooked around their male handsome counterparts, music booming from the club within.

It wasn't until the doors closed again that I heard him say, "...gold-level VIP?"

Distracted by the sight of the model-perfect people going down the steps, I said, "What?"

"Why didn't you tell me you were a gold-level VIP, Ms. Barnes?" He smiled, suddenly all charming and attentive.

"But I'm not. I mean, I won a contest."

"Says here you're a member." He took a step closer and lowered his voice. "Ms. Barnes, please believe me when I say if by some miracle you accidentally got gold VIP status, don't fight it. We're talking free food and drinks for life."

Shit, I'd eat here five days a week if I could and save a ton of money on grocery bills.

I wondered if they served breakfast.

"Wow...okay."

"Excellent." He winked at Joy, and I thought she might pass out as he unhooked the purple velvet rope for us next to a small gold sign that said "Elite Member Entrance Only". "Please go inside, ladies. A hostess will be waiting for you. Enjoy your night."

The women who'd been making disparaging remarks stared with open jealousy and I couldn't help but give them a catty, smug smile as I strutted past them with my girls. Yes, it was petty of me, but it wasn't every day I got to be a VIP anything. He must be wrong about the whole gold-level whatever, but for one night I was going to pretend that I was indeed a very important person, and that people knew I existed.

Though I wasn't proud to admit it, I craved positive attention the way a drug addict craves their next fix, and I'd put up with a lot of bullshit to get it. I've gotten better, Joy has had to give me a couple "come to Jesus" speeches about letting people use me without giving anything back, but it's a constant battle to keep from settling back into my default people-pleaser mode.

For a while after my sister's death, I'd wondered if *I* hadn't been the one who'd died, because my parents treated me like I didn't exist. If it wasn't for Joy's family basically adopting me, I don't think I would have survived my parents' cold silence without losing my mind.

After graduation, I'd moved from Tucson to Tempe with Joy and Kayla to go to college. I was at the University of Arizona on a full scholarship I'd busted my ass for, and worked at a diner to make ends meet, which sucked but I had to do what I had to do. Unlike Kayla's, my family didn't send me money, and I didn't have any trust funds, so my lifestyle was a lot more frugal than that of most college students. I've certainly never been able to indulge in going to a club where the mixed drinks cost close to fifty dollars apiece, and where everyone seemed so adult and sophisticated. Winning this night, getting to spend one evening pretending I'm someone other than a student and a server at a diner, was totally awesome, and I wasn't going to waste it.

Plus, even though it was also petty, it felt good to

be able to get us into a club that even Kayla, with all her dad's influence, couldn't.

A dark-skinned bouncer with a brilliant smile held the inner door open for us with a smooth, "Good evening, ladies."

We giggled—he was really cute—then a tall, sultry brunette in a pale mint-green jumpsuit greeted us in the dimly lit entryway with a big smile as soon as we stepped inside. Her hair was back in a sleek ponytail and she was perfect from head to toe, but her blue eyes were friendly as she said, "Ms. Barnes, welcome to Obsession. My name is Tina and I'll be your hostess for the evening. If you'll please follow me, I'll lead you to your private VIP area. It's been fully stocked, compliments of the club. I hope you like it."

I nodded, trying to act casual and hip instead of gawking at the huge dance club, the spectacular light show pulsing in perfect rhythm to the sensual, almost Latin beat of the techno music. "I'm sure we will. Thank you."

Joy and Kayla trailed behind me as we walked through the busy club and I tried to keep from ogling the crowd like a tourist. Despite the long line outside, the inside was full but not packed, and I didn't have to shoulder my way through the throng like I did at some of the local college bars. The feel of the place was certainly more cultured than the other clubs I've been to, cool and edgy with a hint of sensual darkness. Crazy beautiful women, and men, strutted their stuff on platforms around the club and moved like professional dancers. They wore impossibly tiny, sexy, sparkly, and obviously professionally made costumes that would have fit right in on stage at a glamorous Las Vegas review.

The whole vibe of this place was seductive, and I blushed as I stole a quick peek at a couple on the dance floor who were grinding and kissing passionately beneath lavender and indigo lights.

We took the stairs to the second level after passing a stainless-steel-topped bar, and I focused on keeping from falling on my ass. I didn't normally wear heels, but these shiny ruby red stilettos were so sexy and I got them during a clearance sale for a steal. Plus, I'd rarely had anywhere worthy of wearing them to before so they'd been sitting in a box on my shelf for a while now.

They went perfectly with my thrift store little black Chanel dress that showed off a lot of leg and dipped low in the back. I'd kept my eyes simple with just an extra two coats of mascara and some eyeliner, but my bright red lipstick perfectly matched my shoes, drawing attention away from my stick-figure body and to my mouth. While my hair is a boring black, my eyes an even more boring light brown, I had inherited a set of full lips that I've been told even Angelina Jolie would envy. Of course, as a kid, they'd been just another feature to make fun of, so I was still kind of self-conscious about drawing attention to them, but guys seemed to like my mouth so that was a small ego boost that I desperately needed.

The music on the second floor was a little lower in volume, giving me the ability to easily hear Tina point out different aspects of the club as she led us through the crowd to a big, white, U-shaped couch with a low ebony table in the center, along with a bucket of ice and a bottle of champagne. Three streamlined champagne glasses glittered in the warm lights and a cool breeze came from overhead. Tall cut-glass vases filled with purple and pink orchids flanked the couch and a few throw pillows done in black velvet were artfully flung here and there. It was a space that managed to be modern and edgy, but also comfortable enough to make me sigh as I got off my already throbbing feet.

"This is your area," Tina chirped with a smile as she expertly poured the champagne for us before handing out the glasses. "If you press the red button on the edge of the table, that will summon your server, Michelle. Anything you want is on the house, and Michelle's tip has been taken care of. If you need anything at all, just let her know."

Picking up my glass, I smiled and tried to play it cool when inside I was bouncing around like a kid who had too much sugar. "I will, thank you."

"Enjoy your evening, Ms. Barnes. It was a pleasure meeting you."

"Uh, you too."

"Wow," Joy said as she leaned forward, her ample cleavage squeezing together in a way I envied. "They're treating you like you're somebody important. I mean, Tina seemed ready to fall down at your feet and kiss your ass if you'd snapped your fingers."

Kayla snorted. "Trust me, having people fawn over you gets old after a while. Everywhere I go, people see my black credit card, or know my father, and they start sucking up."

"Seriously?" Joy said as she glared at Kayla.

"What?" Kayla looked away with a bored

expression as she sipped her champagne.

I rolled my eyes then lifted my glass in the direction of Tina's retreating perfect ass, trying to diffuse the tension between my friends. "Please, she's just a professional. Look at this place. Do you think they'd have anyone working here who wasn't an expert at kissing ass?"

Joy tossed her curly blonde hair over her shoulder. "Yeah, but she smiled at you like you were Santa Claus and the Easter Bunny all wrapped up in one."

"Oh my God," Kayla interrupted us. "Shut up and admire the scenery, ladies. There are some very, very hot men here tonight, and I, for one, don't plan on giving up the opportunity for some VIP dick."

We all laughed then Joy nodded as she tapped her lips with a pink-painted nail. "I wonder if there's anyone famous here tonight."

"Well," Kayla said with an arched brow and a smirk, "I think I see the mayor over there with someone who isn't his wife."

"What? Where?" I turned to look but Kayla hit my leg.

She gave me a disdainful sneer that made me feel dumb. "We aren't going to blend in if we sit here openly staring at people like we're on a safari and they're the wild animals. God, at least pretend to fit in."

Joy raised her glass and took a hefty drink while glaring at Kayla. "Anyway, I think this place is awesome. Thank you, again, for bringing me along."

"You're welcome, sweetheart." We exchanged air kisses while Kayla was busy on her phone.

Joy guzzled another gulp of champagne while I

laughed. "Slow down there, champ."

Narrowing her pale green eyes at me, Joy licked her lips then lowered her glass. "Please, you're the lightweight here. It'll take me more than a glass of champagne to even get a buzz going. Besides, this stuff is amazing. Live a little, drink up. We're cabbing it home so if you're going to get trashed on the good stuff, now's the time to do it."

"Good point."

I took a big drink of my own and was pleasantly surprised by how delicious it was. Certainly better than any champagne I've ever had, even the expensive stuff at my cousin Silvie's wedding. Savoring the tingling liquid before it slid down my throat, I enjoyed the way the bubbles exploded on my tongue and tickled my mouth. The drink had a sweet tinge to it that reminded me faintly of raspberries. Tart and delicious. I took another long drink, noticing Joy and Kayla had drained their glasses as well.

Smirking, Kayla took the champagne bottle out of the ice bucket and studied the label. "I thought it seemed familiar. My parents have a couple bottles of this at home, the reserve edition, of course."

"Of course," Joy muttered before she took another drink.

Ignoring their bickering, I eagerly looked around and studied how the other half lived. Or at least partied. Our little section of the room was partially concealed behind long, flowing and sheer white drapes that had an almost mother-of-pearl-like gleam to them. They undulated in the gentle breeze coming from the vents at the top of the walls and made it almost feel like we were outside.

Despite the crowd, the club wasn't sweltering and I shifted on the couch, trying to tuck my short dress beneath my butt as I turned to steal a quick glance at the surroundings. Hot guys were indeed everywhere and I wondered if maybe it was time to break my self-imposed celibacy streak. I'd sworn off men after the last guy I dated nine months ago accused me of being a stage-five clinger with stalker tendencies…and my friends hadn't disagreed.

Evidently he didn't appreciate me stalking him on social media while we were apart, and then I "just happened" to show up at the restaurant where he was having dinner with his friends like a desperate loser.

With a sigh, I downed the rest of my glass, pushing away my past regrets that clung to me like tar.

After returning from the restroom in a bouncy mood, Kayla grinned her perfectly white smile and launched into a detailed breakdown of what kind of dick random guys in the crowd had.

Laughing at my friend's antics, I leaned back into the comfortable sofa and did some people watching, one of my favorite pastimes. Back before I got over my shyness, I'd often been the quiet kid in class, absorbing everything around me while trying to blend into the scenery. My mother developed a hairpin temper after my sister's death and I learned to watch her every move, to read her every expression and base my day off of her temperament. It was only after I got out of their house for good and into college that I began to see how fucked-up my family was, and how much they'd messed *me* up.

Eager to distract myself from my negative thoughts and worries, I sat up straighter on the couch and took a good look around while Kayla carried on about some portly guy having a big one. As I scanned the dance floor, I was surprised by how many couples were dancing so close you couldn't slip a feather between them. The sexual energy was thick, and I squeezed my legs when a pulse of blood rushed between them. My nipples tingled and I shifted on the couch, tugging my skirt again to make sure I wasn't flashing anyone.

"Hannah," Joy said as she elbowed me in the ribs. "That guy is totally checking you out."

"What guy?"

"That scary-looking one with the sexy hair and psycho eyes."

"Who?"

"Heavy brow, broad forehead, square jaw, and hair that Thor would be envious over."

I followed the direction of Joy's pink-painted fingernail and it didn't take me long to figure out who she was talking about.

I'd always inwardly snorted when I'd read the description of a woman being struck dumb by the sight of a man, but I wasn't anymore—'cause I could barely breathe.

He was fascinating, and I found myself unable to look away.

Dressed in a pair of faded jeans that fit his athletic figure like a glove, his body was bigger and stronger than that of any other man around us, including the bouncers. As best I could tell in the club lighting, he had long, thick golden-brown hair that fell to his broad shoulders in messy waves, framing an unusual face that was roughly masculine, all carved cheekbones and thick jaw. Not a pretty boy by any means, or even a boy at all. No, this guy was one hundred percent confident man. His chest appeared impossibly broad and his torso tapered down to a trim waist. Everything about him seemed to reek of health and vitality.

While my gaze wandered his body, my attention was drawn to his solid right wrist, which had a black leather band wrapped around it. I found the sight of that black band incredibly sexy and wondered when the hell I'd developed a fetish for men's wrists. My breasts grew heavy and this odd…carnal urge began to burn in my belly.

The air around me thickened as our gazes met and he strode through the crowd to our table, drawing people's attention like a magnet. He wasn't conventionally attractive, his features too heavy, the lines going across his broad forehead too thick, and his nose broken too many times, but he was charismatic in a way I've never experienced. I couldn't blame the crowd for turning to watch him as he stalked towards us. He prowled like a beast and his intense, direct stare turned me on even as his approach made me increasingly nervous.

"Bet he's got a really thick dick," Kayla whispered as we all silently watched him.

By the time he reached our couch, we were full-on staring at him, but it was Kayla who spoke first with a flirty little, "Hi."

Ignoring her, he held out his hand to me and commanded in a deep voice, "Dance with me."

It wasn't a request, it was an order, and I felt a sense of almost relief that I didn't have to worry about making the decision of saying yes or no. How odd. I must be drunker than I thought because I wasn't alarmed by his domineering manner in the least. Instead, a fuzzy warmth tingled through my body as he kept all of his attention solely on me, despite Kayla's obvious pouting at being ignored.

After a quick glance at my friends — Joy was staring at him as if he was Channing Tatum doing a full strip tease in front of us — I placed my hand in his, and then tried to jerk away as an electrical charge zapped between us.

The mysterious man gently led me out of the seating area with his hand resting lightly on my lower back, his good manners a direct contrast to his rough image.

Alcohol obliterates the filter between my mind and my mouth so I found myself blurting out, "Why do you want to dance with me?"

He drew me closer, then dipped his face down to nuzzle my ear as he said, "Because you're the most beautiful woman I've ever seen. What's your name?"

I desperately wanted to believe him, but a lifetime of being told I wasn't good enough reared its ugly head and twisted his words inside of my mind, making me hear them as a mocking insult.

"My name's Hannah, but you don't have to give me a line. Why did you really ask me?"

He jerked back and looked down at me with a curious expression. "You don't believe me?"

Anger, mixed with a disconcerting desire, had me tugging away from him. "I don't want to dance with you anymore."

When I tried to let go of his hand, his gaze cleared

and, for the first time, I felt like he looked at me, *really* looked at me—then he gave me an utterly charming smile that flooded my panties with desire.

"I guarantee you do."

Holy hell, I think a small climax fluttered through my clenching sex.

Examining him closer, I was once again reminded that he was a solid man with a presence as big as his frame, drowning me in his heat. When he placed his hand gently beneath my chin and forced me to meet his gaze, I couldn't find the strength to resist his unspoken control. We studied each other for a moment in the flashing lights of the club, desire curling low in my belly as I drank in his harsh good looks. This was a confident, powerful, intimidating man. The exact opposite of my usual type of guy. I liked smart, quiet, and nerdy. Or at least I used to. My throbbing clit assured me that my tastes in men had changed.

Big time.

Now, mature, dangerous, and built like a professional wrestler seemed to be my preference.

In a way, he did actually remind me of a professional wrestler my cousin used to watch, Triple H. Same heavy brow and deep-set eyes, along with a good dose of menace. The man holding my face as gently as could be was the kind of men others feared, but not me. I had the strangest sense that he'd protect me, if I let him.

He raised my hand to his lips and gently brushed them over my skin, then, when his tongue flicked out to taste me, my nipples became so hard they ached. "One dance. Let me show you how good things will be between us."

"*Will* be?" I rolled my eyes even as my panties were wet with desire and my pulse throbbed with growing need. "You sound awfully sure about that."

"Baby girl, one thing I can promise you is that I've never been as sure about anything in my life. Enough talking, I've waited what seems like an eternity for this moment. I need to touch you."

A tremble of need raced through me and the thought of rubbing my drunk and horny body against his seemed to be the best idea I'd had in ages.

He led me to the dimly lit VIP dance floor, already packed with people dancing close—really close. I was pretty sure we passed a couple where the woman had her hand down her dance partner's pants, but we'd moved on before I could get a good look. When he came to a stop, we were near the middle of the dance floor and the bass was intense, shivering through my body like my skin was being kissed by snowflakes. My breasts ached and I hoped it wasn't too obvious I wasn't wearing a bra. Normally with my little lady humps, I didn't have to worry about support, but one glance down at my ridged tips sticking out like pencil erasers made me rethink my stance on backless, and braless, dresses.

That is, until my dance partner stroked his finger down my bare spine, sending a flurry of want cascading into my body, making me moan. Thankfully that wanton sound was hidden by the music, but when he moved fully behind me, grasped my hips and pulled me back into his thick erection, my moan must have been audible to everyone in a ten-foot radius. It felt so good that I'm not ashamed to say I ground my ass against him like a randy slut.

His hands were firm, strong, and they almost spanned my waist as he slowly ran them up my sides, barely grazing my breasts. Instead of stopping there and copping a feel, he traced his hands up the suddenly sensitive skin of my arms, raising them above my head as I followed his lead, then clasping them behind his neck, where I instantly tangled my fingers into the thick silk of his hair.

His responding growl had me arching into him and I swayed my butt against his solid shaft, gratified by another rumble vibrating through his chest behind me as we danced in perfect harmony.

The strong beat of the music guided our hips while we slid against each other as if we were fucking with our clothes on. He controlled my every shift with a familiar ease, like we'd been dancing together for years. The more he touched me, the more I fell into his overwhelmingly sensual presence while he guided me with his fingertips.

My pussy ached and when he ran his hands down the sides of my ribs again, I shuddered with burning desire. On the way back up, he brushed each hard tip of my breasts just the slightest bit, the feeling racing straight to my clit like erotic lightning. His touch was just enough to tease me, to make me ravenous for more. I tried to arch into his hand, but he wouldn't let me, and I wanted to cry with frustration that he didn't give me more.

"Sensitive, aren't you?" he murmured into my ear. "I knew you would be. Perfect."

He turned me in his arms and I sank my hands into his lush mane of hair again as one song transitioned to another, the strobbing lights following the music as I stared at this mystery man.

"What's your name?"

The side of his mouth quirked. "You can call me Leo."

"Leo? Is that short for Leonardo?"

"No, my mom had an Uncle Leo that she loved, so I got his name."

"It suits you, I like it."

He brushed my hair back from my ear then leaned forward and said, "I'm glad. I can't wait to hear you scream it while I fuck you. Bet your puffy pussy gets really wet, doesn't it? Are your panties soaked right now? Are you as hungry for my dick as I am your swollen little cunt?"

I stumbled as the carnality of his words hit me right between the legs, but he was strong enough to support my entire body, using it as he wished while he rocked my hips forward and made my erect clit press against his leg.

Like someone had flipped a switch inside of me, I shuddered, my nerves overwhelmed by how good the contact felt on my sex, how much it relieved the growing pressure.

"Oh my god, Leo. It's too much."

"Take it," he growled. "Don't fight me; take the pleasure because I want you to have it."

Grasping my ass, hard, he continued to rock me as I held on to him for dear life, my nails sinking into his back, making him groan.

My head fell back and I stared up at him with dazed eyes only to find him watching me intently. "Do you like that, sweet girl?"

It took a great deal of effort for my tingling lips to form the word. "Yes."

He ground my hips in a circle on his thigh and I shuddered in his arms. "I can feel you, feel how hot and wet your pussy is. I need to taste it. Will you give me that, sweet Hannah? Will you let me lick between your legs, suck on your clit, and fill you with my fingers?"

"Absolutely."

In response, he leaned forward and brushed his curved lips ever so lightly against mine, the action incredibly tender, and it had me melting into him. "Such a good girl. Do you want me to fuck you, Hannah?"

The thought of his erection pushing into me, the mental fantasy of taking someone as thick as he was, had me saying without thought, "So bad."

"Come home with me."

"Okay."

Wait...okay?

Hold on drunk, horny brain. Remember stranger danger.

While I'd had a one-night stand or two, like any girl, I normally didn't have sex with strangers. Then again, I've never had a man like Leo interested in me before. The empty ache between my legs urged me to go wherever he wanted and I don't think I'd ever been this turned on in my entire life. My whole body felt sensitive, needy, and I had a hard time thinking past the craving to get him inside of me as quickly as possible. Maybe I was passion starved after my nine months of self-imposed celibacy.

As we moved through the crowd, I came to my

senses enough to say, "Wait! My friends."

He paused then pointed over my shoulder. "Relax. They've found dance partners of their own."

Sure enough, Joy was dancing with a very handsome black guy with a shaved head, all but humping him as they swayed, while Kayla had herself twined around a tall, brown-haired man as he grabbed her ass with both hands.

"See, they're fine. Let's get your stuff and go."

I wanted to leave with him, but the tiny portion of my sensible brain that I had left insisted it was dangerous to leave a bar with a strange man. All the stories I'd ever heard about girls getting killed by some psycho warred with my overwhelming attraction for Leo. If I looked past my carnal fascination, I had to admit there was something different about him, and not necessarily in a good way. He was menacing—I knew it, everyone around me knew it—but I didn't get a sense that he was any danger to me.

Then again, I thought guys were in love with me who clearly weren't, so my read on things might not be the most reliable. I wished Joy wasn't busy grinding on that guy so she could tell me how to handle this situation. We were off the dance floor and had grabbed my purse by this point, and were approaching the stairs when I tried to stop again, teetering on my heels before Leo caught me.

"I can't just leave with you. It's not safe."

His dark eyes glittered in the club lights playing over us, bathing his solid jaw in sapphire light and shadows. "Would you believe me if I said I would never harm you? That I'd rather suffer than have anything bad ever touch you?"

I licked my lips, caught up in his steady gaze. "I...I don't know. I'd like to believe you, but that wouldn't be very smart."

He considered this for a moment, then nodded. "Understandable. I think I have a way to reassure you."

Going downstairs, he pulled me over to the front door where a pair of bouncers stood, and approached a tall, good-looking blond and freckled bouncer who had a country-boy vibe to him.

Leo still held my hand, and the bouncer respectfully nodded his head. "How can I help you, Mr. Brass?"

There, at least I had a last name to add to my limited database of knowledge about the man I was seriously considering fucking into next week. The lighting was better here and I stared up at him, fascinated by his heavy bone structure. My gaze traveled lower and I took in the curve of his ass again. He had a bubble butt, and as I'd trailed behind him through the club, I'd wondered what it would be like to sink my teeth into all that tight muscle.

"Hannah, this is Greg Dawson. He's a Tempe police officer who does security for the club on the weekends."

Snapped out of my perving, I smiled. "Um...hello."

"Hello, gorgeous." Greg gave me a slow appraising look, then smiled at Leo. "She's absolutely lovely. Those legs, they go on forever."

Looping an arm around my shoulders, Leo pulled me tight to his side and snarled, "She's mine."

Holding up his hands, Greg laughed but also looked a little scared. "Understood, Boss. No offense meant, ma'am."

I shifted on my heels, not liking the aggressive tension filling Leo. "None taken."

Leo continued to glare at the man, who paled. "Hannah came in with two friends, make sure they know she left, and that she's safe, and make sure they get home all right."

"Of course, Mr. Brass."

My feet were starting to hurt and I shifted in my heels again, the champagne wearing off and all the dancing I'd done catching up.

Leo must have noticed because before I knew it, he had me swept up in his arms and I had to bite back a squeal.

"We're leaving."

I was tempted to argue with him but I couldn't help relaxing in his hold, a feeling of complete safety coming over me in a warm rush. "How will they know who my friends are?"

"You were seated in the VIP area. All they have to do is check the security cameras to find out who you came in with."

"Oh, I didn't think about that." The cool night air kissed my cheeks as he carried me out the front door of the club, his muscles flexing while he scanned the crowd with a grim look. The line to get in was still as long as ever, and people flat-out stared as Leo strode past, but he paid them no mind. I had a feeling he was the kind of man who did his own thing, damn what other people think. Looping my arms around his neck, I lightly skimmed my finger over his stubble, wanting to know what it would feel like against my lips.

"Where are we going?"

He hesitated a moment, then said, "My place. Unless you'd rather go to yours?"

"Um, considering I share an apartment with two other girls, with super thin walls, no."

"That might be a little crowded for what I have in mind."

"Yeah. It's a decent three-bedroom apartment with plenty of space, but I can hear my roommate Joy singing to herself at night." When he set me on my feet at the curb out front of the club, I didn't want to let him go, so I babbled on. "Don't get me wrong, it's close to school, mostly clean, and cheap — three essential things. There's no way I could afford to live that close to school on my own, so it's either share a place or live in a not-so-safe part of town. Gotta save money where you can, you know what I mean?"

A pure white two-seater Jaguar pulled up to the curb, and I tried to keep my jaw from dropping as the valet got out and rushed around to the passenger side to hold the door open.

Staring at the car, I muttered, "No, you probably don't know what I mean."

"Actually, I do. I grew up in a rough area of Tucson and we didn't have a lot of money."

"You're from Tucson?"

"Yes."

"Get out of here! So am I." I couldn't help but beam at him, tickled at the thought that we both had the same hometown.

"Imagine that."

With a slight quirk of his lips, Leo helped me into the car, then said something to the valet and came around to the driver's side. After he slid into the tanned leather seat and shut the door, he leaned over and put my seat belt on me. It was a protective gesture that sent a little ember of warmth burning through me, chasing away my doubts and fears. His woodsy cologne filled the small space and my pussy clenched at the memory of his hands on my nipples.

I really wanted his long fingers there right now.

"Hannah?"

Snapped out of the naughty thoughts I had about Leo pinching my nipples, I turned to find him considering me intently. "Yes?"

His midnight eyes captured mine and I matched his breath as he said in an authoritative voice, "I want you to think about your sexual fantasies and pick one for us to indulge in tonight. This is your chance to let go, to be free of inhibitions and tell me what you really want. I won't judge you, and I will give you anything you desire."

"Wow, that's kind of forward."

"No, that's being honest. Games are for children, Hannah. I don't have time to pretend to be anything or anyone other than who I am. You give me the gift of being able to be myself around you, and I'll do the same."

I could only blink at him as my mind whirled with the implications of his words, but I said nothing. I was at battle with myself, my inner hussy vs. the potential embarrassment of telling this stranger some of my kinkier fantasies, then having him laugh at me. Or even worse, be disgusted by some of my more uncivilized daydreams.

The streetlights briefly illuminated the road as we pulled up to one of the newer apartment buildings, a beautiful structure made of black glass that seemed to absorb the night around it. We parked underground and took an elevator in the garage up to his place. The entire time my mind was strangely disconnected, caught between erotic dreams, and feeling ashamed and embarrassed by the taboo nature of the majority of my steamy fantasies.

It wasn't until we were in his apartment that the reality, or should I say unreality, of my situation began to kick in.

I was with an incredibly hot stranger, alone, in his luxury apartment that rivaled anything I'd seen on TV.

And he had a huge dick.

Leo may have grown up poor, but that wasn't the case anymore. This man had money, big money, and I suddenly felt awkward standing in the middle of all this wealth. My entire outfit combined came up to under sixty dollars, and I'd bet one of the navy-blue velvet curtain ties holding back the silver curtains across the room cost more.

The large and bright gray-toned kitchen looked out over a breakfast bar into the vast, sunken living room that faced a wall of windows. The floors were made of pale wood and the furniture was done in shades of cream, green, and blue. A vast painting of a rocky ocean coast hung above a dark stone fireplace and the kitchen boasted what I was sure were top-of-the-line appliances. As far as I could see, the entire place was spotless, neat to the point I was afraid to touch anything.

"You live here?"

Leo, who'd been watching me closely, nodded. "I do."

"But it's so…nice." He appeared offended and I quickly added, "I mean, I don't know anyone with stuff this nice. I'm afraid to touch anything in case I break it."

I slapped my hand over my running mouth and Leo smiled, moving closer to me until one of his hands rested on my hip while the other gently drew my hand away from my lips. "Don't be. With all the money in the world, I could never buy anything as precious as you. You're priceless. These things? They're inanimate objects, nothing more than material possessions that are hollow and cold. You…you breathe warmth into my world like sunlight on my soul. That makes you irreplaceable."

Sure I was blushing beet red, I ducked my head then bit my lip. "That's one of the nicest things anyone has ever said to me; crazy, but nice."

Grasping my chin, he made me look at him as he said, "I promise you that someday you'll believe my words, that you'll know your worth."

Drawn into the spellbindingly deep tone of his voice, I licked my lower lip. "You don't know me. I could be a horrible person."

I liked the way his eyes crinkled when he laughed. "Is that so?"

"Yeah. I could be one of those people who steal money from the animal shelter donation jar at the pet store."

"Are you?"

"Well—no. But I could be."

"Hannah, I am a very, very good judge of character, and I can say with complete confidence that you have never stolen money from anyone, animal shelter or otherwise."

"You're missing the point—"

"No, *you're* missing the point. Stop trying to convince me you're less than what you are. I see you, more clearly than you see yourself. And what I see is beautiful."

"Whatever," I muttered, secretly pleased as punch by his compliments, even if I had a hard time believing them.

He ran his hand down my bare back, a tender exploration of my skin that reawakened the pounding between my legs. I was so wet, my panties were pretty much useless at the moment. Unable to help myself, I leaned forward and rested my head on the swell of his hard chest, looping my arms around his waist and absorbing his warmth.

"Cuddly, aren't you?"

"Yeah. I didn't get a lot of physical affection as a kid." Jerking back, I wanted to pretend I hadn't said those words. What the hell was up with my sudden bout of being overly honest? "Just kidding."

Leo didn't say anything, instead letting me wiggle out of his arms. "You need to relax. Come, do a shot with me."

"That's the last thing I need."

He merely smiled at me and took my hand, leading me over to the couch. "Sit, beautiful girl."

I watched his ass bunch and flex beneath his tight jeans, each long stride poetry in motion.

When he turned around and caught me staring, I flushed and looked away, pretending to be absorbed by the painting of the ocean. Up close, I could see hints of pink and purple in the sky, along with the distant bright blue ribbon of a clear horizon. It was thin, barely noticeable from far away, but it cut through the boiling storm clouds like a stroke of light. "I like this picture. Kind of rough and turbulent, but if you look on the horizon, you can see calmer skies are on their way."

In the middle of pouring a drink, Leo froze and stared at me with an odd expression. "Is that what you see?"

Fidgeting beneath his intense regard, I licked my lips, which only made his interest in me sharpen. Setting the bottle down then picking up the glass, he strode across the room and sat right next to me, his heat saturating the side of my body. I tried to put some space between us, but soon reached the end of the couch. Still, it was enough room that I could breathe without pressing into all that hard, male bulk. His thick thighs were the size of two of mine together and I wondered what it would feel like to be able to explore the body of someone as fit as Leo.

Handing me a cut-crystal glass with about half an inch of amber liquid in the bottom, he said, "Drink."

"Where's yours?"

Instead of answering me, he gestured to the painting. "Would you like to know what I see when I look at it?"

I swirled liquid in my glass, the faint scent of honey reaching my nose through the heavy veil of alcohol. "Of course."

"I used to see rage in the form of water, powerful destruction that even the rocks can't hold back." I gaped at him and his cold expression thawed, warmth melting his dark eyes to molten chocolate. "But now I see the coming of the dawn. The promise of safe harbor."

I swear, this was one of the most overwhelming moments of my life. I stared at him, seeing only confidence and honesty in his face—along with a good dose of lust. Unable to handle this…whatever it was going on between us, I slammed the shot glass and gasped. "Holy crap!"

His white teeth gleamed as he smiled at me. "Are you all right?"

"Yes, that was strong stuff."

"Not a whisky drinker?"

"Uh, no. I'm more of a sangria kind of girl."

"Noted."

Not knowing what to do with myself, I balled my hands together in my lap, clasping my fingers so tightly they hurt. Was he going to kiss me? Was I supposed to kiss him? A quick glance at his face revealed his expression had once again shut down as he stared at my bunched hands.

I quickly unclasped them, stretching my fingers slightly and almost sighing with relief when he looked away. He crossed his legs and I realized for the first time he'd removed his shoes at some point, leaving his feet clad in black socks. I flexed my own bare feet against the floor, trying to think of something witty, something urbane to break the silence. My comment about the painting had pretty much used up my pool of small talk. If he didn't say or do something soon, I'd start talking about the freaking weather just to hear something other than the pounding of my heart.

"Do I intimidate you?"

"Yes."

"Do I scare you?"

"No."

"Not even a little bit? I'm a very big man, and you're a delicate girl."

I scoffed at him. "I'm not as fragile as I look."

"You remind me of Audrey Hepburn."

Without my permission, my inner insecure preteen self peeked out and said, "Really?"

He nodded solemnly. "You have the most graceful neck, and your eyes are as large and captivating as hers were. But your mouth…I am obsessed with your mouth. I think about it all the time, all the things I want to do to your lips, all the ways I want to corrupt you. Would you enjoy that, Hannah? Being corrupted by me?"

"Absolutely." I blinked rapidly as my entire body heated. "It's hot in here."

He took me in his arms and cradled me to his chest, my body going limp with relaxation as my thoughts became disconnected, drifting.

The last thing I remember is Leo tracing the side of my jaw with his thumb, a look of triumph gracing his hard face.

Chapter 3

Leo

Her eyelids fluttered shut over her extraordinary honey-brown and amber-flecked eyes, the naturally dark lashes sweeping to the curves of her high cheekbones, drawing my eyes to the unlined, almost childlike perfection of her ivory skin.

A thrill ran through me as I rubbed my nose along her cheek, savoring the feeling of her like an addict taking his first hit of opium. Having the woman I'm obsessed with close enough to smell, to taste, drives me crazy. My dick couldn't get any harder, and I had a difficult time remembering why she's here with me tonight. How much work has gone into this moment.

Once again I lost myself in leaning down so I could rub my lips against her fine hair, the softness making me think of what it would feel like to wrap all that silkiness around my cock.

There wasn't a part of Hannah I didn't want to both defile and revere.

To be honest, I'd all but forgotten about the girl I'd talked with in the waiting room of the hospital other than a random thought now and again, but some part of me had remembered the cadence of her words, the color of her eyes. When she'd waited on me at that diner a year ago, she was shy, sweet, funny, and when her hand brushed mine as I held my coffee cup steady, a flurry of sparks raced through my body, lighting up previously unused pleasure centers in my brain. Yes, I've had sex, and yes it has been pleasurable, but I've never felt the instant, enslaving blow of the need to own a woman that has made men stupid since the dawn of time.

At least until I saw Hannah.

In disguise, I'd visited her twice more at her job, an addict desperate for the fix of her soothing presence, the melody of her voice.

Briefly touching her as she'd handed me my food was both heaven and hell, her skin baby smooth and her sweetheart-shaped face graced with a small smile.

She invaded my thoughts, then my dreams, and finally I began my own reconnaissance in earnest, a yearning growing inside of me for a future I didn't deserve. The more I watched her, the more fixated I became, unable to believe a person as good-hearted as Hannah really existed. But time and time again she proved that she was just…nice. She was loyal to her friends, kind to strangers, and sweet to the point that people like her rich bitch roommate took advantage of her.

She was a treasure waiting for the right man, a man like me, to recognize her potential.

I'll give her everything she needs to be happy so even when I break her heart—and I will, the nature of my job almost guarantees it—she'll love me enough to let me put it back together again, because I'll be the only person who can.

If this works, I will have her absolute loyalty, and she'll be the one person I can fully trust in this whole world.

In my arms, Hannah's light weight rested easily

against me and I couldn't resist leaning forward and brushing my lips over her incredibly full, slightly parted ones before drawing away with great reluctance.

Now it was time to see if all my planning, all my work with the Cordova cartel's scientists would pay off, and if Judith would have her miracle.

The modified truth serum I'd put into Hannah's drink should be taking affect by now. A perfect blend of chemicals that would open her mind, relax her, while making her totally honest and open to influence. The serum we'd devised was powerful and could only be used sparingly without harming her, so I would make sure I used this time wisely. Not only did I to ensure she never betray me or our eventual family, I also needed to find out what she really wanted from a man. While I would do everything I could to make sure she wanted me, that she enjoyed submitting to me, I needed to fulfill her desires as well. Even the dark and kinky ones, way down deep, beneath the bullshit of society's influence trying to tell her what's right and wrong.

Once I knew her true desires, I was one step closer to owning her.

At our core, human beings are animals, and we all have certain needs that must be met in order to keep us content, one of the strongest being our sex drive. Having hacked into her computer and tracked her reading habits, I knew she tended to favor books with a dominant man, light BDSM, and taboo D/s pairings, which worked out well for me and my particular tastes in the bedroom.

It's amazing what you can find on the internet

these days and how willingly people put their personal information out there. Hannah was no exception, and thanks to her frequent activity on Pinterest, I knew everything from her favorite type of reading chair, to her favorite breakfast, to all the places she wanted to visit in the future. There were also over two dozen boards featuring clothes she liked, and I'd already stocked a closet full of items at our new home. There were also over four hundred photos in her "future living room" folder; Hannah pinned just about anything that caught her eye, so I didn't think she'd recognize the fact that my new home had been built to her specifications.

In many ways, I feel like I already know her, that she's confessed her greatest desires to me and let me into her glorious heart.

I wanted that, wanted her to allow me into the private parts of her soul, wanted her to confide in me and share her dreams. She fascinated me with her emotional delicacy, and I was afraid I might break her in my zeal to own every inch of her graceful frame. Like most aspects of my life, I needed to have complete control in the bedroom and, to a somewhat lesser degree, outside of the bedroom as well, something most women didn't enjoy to the extent that I did. I couldn't help but wonder if she'd find it odd that I wanted to dress her every day, that I got off on seeing her wear clothing and jewelry I provided her with.

I couldn't take the risk that Hannah wouldn't be turned on by my preferred sexual lifestyle, so tonight I would mold her mind, awaken desires in her she was unaware she had, give her subconscious permission to be as open and wild with sex as she wanted, without guilt. Through my careful training, Hannah will soon learn that giving me that control will be to her great benefit, that I will take care of her in every way and love doing it. She may be starved for affection, but I hadn't had anyone to love in over ten years. My need to cosset her was compulsive, and building her dream home had been an act of worship to a woman oblivious of how much her life was about to change.

    I wasn't like the men she usually picked to fixate on, spineless and weak boys who reminded me of her father. He was a pathetic man, still living in thrall of his bitch wife while ignoring his daughter. At some point one of them would get sick, or lonely, and I'd bet my Rolls they would suddenly want to reconnect with Hannah. Fuck that. They didn't deserve her and I planned to keep them out of her life, and mine. I had such a good future planned for Hannah, one that would give her everything she needed to be happy, and she would reward me with her love while I rewarded her with painful pleasure.

    When I hurt her, when I spanked her ass red or tied up her breasts until they were almost purple, I needed her to get off on it. From my studies of Hannah, I suspected she might be a masochist, so my hypnotic suggestion would have a greater chance of taking root. Unlike in the movies, hypnosis can't reprogram people like robots; the human brain is too complex and messed up for anyone to be able to do that. However, a trained hypnotist can influence the subject, plant little suggestions that the subject's mind can absorb as its own truth.

I've trained with the best in the world on using hypnosis during interrogation, and I've experimented extensively with mind control during interrogation sessions, but I've never used the knowledge I gained to fuck around with the mind of an innocent before.

If I was a better man, I would have felt guilty about what I was about to do, but the only emotions rolling through me were anticipation and satisfaction.

This would work, I knew it would, and it would give the Cordova brothers some desperately needed hope. Since Nina's betrayal, none of them had taken a woman for anything other than fucking, and they always had their bodyguards with them, even in the bedroom. Their trust in any female outside of their family had dwindled to zero, and I know it hurt Judith to see her boys so emotionally cut off. It hurt the cartel as well; the brothers' ruthless behavior was bordering on psychopathic and causing problems. They needed the anchor of a good woman to hold them to their sanity, to give them something to live for. They needed the bright light of a girl adoring them, and they needed to be able to trust that her smile didn't hide a pair of poisonous fangs.

But beyond helping the Cordovas, if my experiment with Hannah worked, I would have my baby girl, the greatest prize in the world, and no one could take her from me.

Not even my fucked-up self.

"Hannah," I said softly, loving the ethereal, breathy feel of her name on my tongue. "Can you hear me?"

Her eyes opened the slightest bit, the pupils huge from the drugs coursing through her system, her mind unguarded. "Hi, Leo."

"Hi, sweetheart. I'm going to ask you some questions. Do you think you can answer them for me?"

"Sure."

The word was slurred, but I understood her. "I asked you earlier to think about what you wanted from a man. Can you tell me what you thought about?"

She shifted in my lap, the highly specialized truth serum I'd given her earlier in her whisky still coursing through her, encouraging her to be honest in a way she'd never be while fully conscious. "I want someone to love me, *really* love me. I want someone to think I'm amazing, I want to make them happy, I want them to take care of me and I want to take care of them."

God she was sweet, pure in a way I'd never encountered. I almost felt bad for what I was going to do to her. "That's good, tell me more. What do you want your life to be like ten years from now? What would make you happy?"

She licked her full lips and sighed. "I want a family. I want to be a mother, to have a husband who loves me, a nice home, a dog…I want a house filled with kids who are happy and cherished. I want to go to school plays, and complain about driving to their sporting events when secretly I wouldn't miss one second of them. I want a husband who will help me go crazy decorating the house for Halloween and hold me at Christmas while we watch our children tearing into their presents. We'll spend the rest of our lives together, loving each other, sharing the joys of growing old together. I want to never be alone again, because loneliness is like cancer, it kills you a little at a time until nothing is left."

The heart some thought I didn't have ached even as my cock pressed into the nicely rounded curves of her ass. The sudden image of her pregnant, with *my* child, sent a visceral shock of yearning through me. Her body would change after she had children, soften with the curves of motherhood, and I already looked forward to licking drops of milk from her swollen breasts. Nothing would be off limits between us; we'd do anything that brought us mutual pleasure. Our life would be good, so good together, but only if I could guarantee her loyalty. If I couldn't, it didn't matter how perfect we were together. I'd have to leave the cartel that I considered my family if I wanted to have Hannah as my wife.

Then again, I don't think Judith would let me leave. I knew too many secrets.

Trying to focus past the worries that plagued me, I stroked her cheek as I asked, "What is it you want out of a relationship? What could your man do for you that would please you and make you happy?"

"I want him to take care of me. To love me. To praise me. I want to be his good girl. I'll be so good, I promise. If you love me, I'll be the best."

It didn't take my genius-level IQ to figure out Hannah's childhood had scarred her deeply, but witnessing the evidence of it made me more determined than ever to heal her.

Then she said something that had me wishing I could break her parents' necks. "I have so much love to give, but nobody wants it."

"I want it."

"You do?"

"More than anything."

"You seem like a nice guy, and you smell really good. You can have it." She patted my chest before loosely curling up in my lap. "I'm sleepy, Leo."

"One more question, then you can go to sleep."

She yawned then stretched. "Okay."

"If you needed punishment, correction for your actions, how should you be punished? What would make you really sorry?"

"If you ignored me. I hate that. Makes me feel so cold inside."

"What about a spanking?"

Barely looking at me, she gave me a smile so seductive I would have done anything she wanted just to keep the warmth filling my chest, chasing back the empty cold. "Spanking turns me on. At least I think it does. I've never tried it."

My throbbing dick ached beneath her slight weight and begged me to fuck her, to give the greedy bastard just a taste of the no doubt sweet little pussy between her slender thighs. "What else turns you on?"

Her eyes closed all the way. "You. So big, strong. Reminds me of a Viking warrior. Commanding. Even when you're mean I find you sexy. Is it wrong that I like it when you scare me? That I'm horny when I should be afraid?"

"Nothing wrong with that, baby girl."

"I want to be your baby girl, Leo. So much."

I could only pray she would feel the same way after she learned about who I really am. The muscles in my thighs and around my groin tensed, and I bit back a groan of frustration. The need to fuck her was already hard to resist, but combine it with her chiming voice and I was a goner. This girl had no idea the power she held over me.

A beep from my watch let me know I didn't have a lot of time left before the truth serum ran its course and her mind closed to my influence once again.

A rumble of pleasure escaped me in the form of a groan. "I want to fuck every inch of your body. No part of you will be unmarked by my seed, inside and out. But right now, you need to sleep. Just let your body go limp, nothing matters but feeling good…content…just drift."

After she fell into a deeper trance, I began to lay the groundwork for addicting her to me, mind, body, and soul.

I'm not a good man, in fact I may be an evil one, but I'd bind this angel to my wicked life any way I could.

After I was done with setting the mental triggers in her subconscious, I'd take a vial of her blood and send it overnight to El Salvador. The potent aphrodisiac the Cordova cartel made, D128, would be ready after being custom altered to her body chemistry and mine, then shipped up from our El Salvador lab. The complex chemical mix would increase Hannah's sex drive to the point of her going into heat, of her body demanding sex the way most female animals do when they're fertile—though the drug won't force ovulation. She'll beg for my cock and I'll give it to her, sooth her need, and bind her to me forever. The more I fuck her during those first few essential days, gave her endless orgasms and drowned her in my filthy desires, the more she would crave me and my admittedly kinky brand of sex until no other man would do.

The Cordova cartel first developed this particular combination of chemicals by accident, but when they figured out what they had made, the cartel's wealth had exploded overnight as everyone wanted a taste of the aphrodisiac.

Unfortunately, it didn't work for men — we were always in heat; always fertile and ready to create life — but for women…it was a miracle.

D128 was obscenely expensive because each batch had to be custom made for each individual woman, and took a team of highly trained chemists to produce, but the results were worth the time and money. While the drug couldn't force arousal — female desire comes as much from their minds as from their bodies — the blend of chemicals would increase a woman's physical response and sensitize her body so that when she did naturally become turned on, the results were…overwhelming. Strong enough to release her sexual inhibitions and allow her to blossom into the erotic creature she was meant to be, before society's bullshit opinions weighed her down.

I couldn't wait to see Hannah's reaction.

She would become insatiable and I'd give her everything she needed, addict her to my touch, to my rough brand of sex, to my cock.

Was it immoral to drug a woman and basically brainwash her? Maybe. If I was a cruel man with cruel intentions towards Hannah, I could see the point that such an action was an outrageous violation of her basic rights as a human being. But turning her into a slave wasn't why I was doing this. I needed her to be so happy she'd never leave me. I wanted her to enjoy every aspect of our lives together and share her pleasure with me. Including our sex lives. Maybe especially. While I'd never be the kind of man who would be what society envisions a picture-perfect husband, I *was* the kind of man who could satisfy her sexually in a way no other man ever could. It's not bragging, it's simple fact. I've studied women, what they like, how they respond, and I've used that knowledge to punish them into submission with agonizing pleasure.

Those past sexual encounters had been physically satisfying, but emotionally empty. The equivalent of jacking off with a woman's body. The thought sounded crude even to me, but I didn't lie to myself. Slipping into Hannah's no doubt exquisite pussy would be an entirely different experience, the addictively positive feelings I had for her surging at the thought of finally having her beneath me, stuffed full of my dick while I rutted into her.

Marked her.

Filled her up until my cum flowed out of her well-fucked cunt.

But first I had to open her mind to the type of dirty fucking I liked best.

Still speaking to her in a persuasive, unhurried voice, I told her that my pleasure was her pleasure, that when I was aroused, she would be aroused, and she would orgasm on command for me. I conditioned her mind for my needs and desires, shaping her own naturally submissive soul for my particular brand of kink. I couldn't drastically change who she was at her core, or make her suddenly love lemons when she truly hated them, or even love a monster like me, but I could mold some of her responses with a butterfly touch to her psyche. I could plant the seeds of trust and absolute loyalty deep inside her mind and pray they took root.

Though I wanted to keep her here with me, I'd take her home instead. She'd wake up and realize she couldn't remember anything after her second glass of champagne, would forget she'd ever met me, only to learn from her roommates that I had gallantly driven her home, untouched, after she'd had too much to drink. Then, when I reentered her life in two weeks with her dose of D128, I'd have an excuse to talk with her, and an in with Hannah for being a good guy who'd returned her safe and sound. Her roommates — who I would make sure to charm into liking me — would encourage Hannah to see me again.

Running my fingers through the heavy silk of her hair, I let the shiny black sheet flow over my scarred knuckles. Touching her felt good, so good I was reluctant to let her go, to take her safely home, along with pastries from an exclusive bakery and gourmet coffee. It was my way of apologizing to her for the wicked hangover she'd experience. I didn't want her to suffer, and wished I could be the one to care for her, but the time wasn't right.

No, I'd have to content myself with stalking her from afar for the moment.

There were cameras already set up in the public areas of her apartment, and Hannah's bedroom, but not the bathroom. I had no desire to see either of her roommates naked, and since Hannah slept only in a long t-shirt, I'd had plenty of time to admire her pussy as she'd kick off her covers in her sleep. Watching Hannah while she lived her safe, normal little life had become one of my favorite pastimes when insomnia plagued me late at night. Sometimes, when I had a particularly stressful day, I'd watch her for hours if she happened to be home, fantasizing about what it would be like to spend my day with her. The sharp curves of her face fascinated me, her laughter made me smile, and now that I finally held her in my arms, the urge to own her, all of her, threatened to overwhelm my iron control. Without that control I'd become a monster, so it was absolute.

But oh, did she tempt me.

I still had enough time for the final phase of my plan, the real reason I'd put her under tonight. Her breaths came light and even as I said what I hoped would be magic words in her ear, ones that would enable her to fully embrace her potential as my wife.

By the time the beeper on my watch alerted me that the drug had worked itself out of her system, my voice had gone hoarse, but I'd managed to repeat my instructions three times. Hopefully it would be enough.

It had to be enough.

Soon her personal dose of D128 would be ready then Hannah would be mine, forever.

Chapter 4

Hannah

At three a.m., the twenty-four-hour diner I worked at was populated with an odd mixture of the late-shift crowd from the hospital across the street, drunk students from the bars one block over, and random people who had a craving for greasy diner chow in the middle of the night. The smell of frying food hung heavy in the air, mixed with the ever-present aroma of coffee and a hint of cigarette smoke that had seeped into the walls long before the city banned indoor smoking. Those smells mingled in an oddly comforting blend I'd grown used to over the last few years while working nights to make ends meet.

Right now we were experiencing a lull in business, but in two hours the breakfast crowd would start pouring in, and there was a lot of prep work to be done.

Only myself and two other servers were on the floor right now, and I scanned my tables with a practiced eye, looking for empty plates or someone needing a refill. The giggling group of college girls by the door, obviously drunk, kept sending flirty glances over at one of my other tables, a quiet man who sat by himself in the back, his square jaw tense and dark gaze locked on the hospital across the street. His nice black suit was slightly wrinkled and his dark silver tie hung askew from his thick neck. Even though he wore his golden-brown hair back in one of those man-bun things I normally hated, on him it looked Viking-warrior hot.

I hadn't really paid that much attention to him earlier, too busy trying to divide checks among a group of eleven nurses, but now that I could take a breath, I found myself oddly fascinated by him, even though he wasn't the type of guy I was normally attracted to. I tended to go for...well, if I was being honest, I went for weak men. Nonthreatening. Guys who looked like they spent their spare time screwing around with video games instead of hitting the gym. The man sitting at my table was sooooo not that. He was raw, visceral, and even in his obviously high-quality suit managed to look rough—like the kind of guy who would play a villain in the movies.

But I couldn't look away.

Something about him was familiar, and I studied him closer.

A layer of light brown scruff covered his thick jaw and he had deep lines going across his heavy, prominent brow, as well as lighter ones bracketing his deep-set eyes. It almost gave him a caveman-like profile, but his high cheekbones and solid jaw balanced it off, giving him an intensely masculine vibe. He was staring out the window and it gave me a chance to go secret stalker on him, to indulge this odd, intense curiosity I had about him.

When I looked down to his large hands grasping the white ceramic coffee cup, I noticed what appeared to be faint dots of blood on his cuffs, and followed his line of sight to the hospital across the street.

Oh no.

I'd been admiring him when he was obviously worried about something, or someone. Shit, he must have brought a loved one into the ER, or was visiting someone at the hospital. Someone close to him or someone he knew was hurt or sick. That's why he appeared so closed off from everyone else in the room, as if he were living in his own personal bubble.

I knew what that felt like, to lose someone close to you. My younger sister had died of childhood leukemia a little over ten years ago, and I can still remember feeling separated from the rest of the world, like I was alone and no one could ever understand what I was going through. My parents totally cut themselves off from me emotionally, despite my rather desperate efforts to be the perfect daughter and make them love me. When I'd moved away to college, they'd pretty much stopped all contact with me other than an occasional Christmas or birthday card. I never went home to visit and they never invited me. Hell, I saw my cousins in Michigan, halfway across the country, more than I saw my own parents.

So yeah, I knew what it was like to be alone with your grief, and I knew it sucked.

With these thoughts in mind, I made my way across the faded tile floor armed with a fresh pot of coffee. I'd go over, offer him a refill, and see if he wanted to talk. Sometimes people did, sometimes people didn't, but I couldn't see a gloomy person without wanting to make them smile. I'm one of those people who're happiest when I'm making other people happy, and I feel their grief like my own. I realize this makes me vulnerable to the assholes of this world, that many would confuse my kindness for weakness, but I can't change who I am.

Pasting on a bright smile, I approached his table and he totally ignored me.

Okay, maybe this wasn't the best idea.

Up close, I could see the small web of fine lines around his eyes, the scars marring his skin, and my sense that he was dangerous was blaring warnings through my mind.

Yet that feeling of familiarity remained.

I had a job to do, so I forced my voice to be cheerful as I asked, "Can I offer you some coffee?"

His eyes, so dark brown they almost appeared black, flicked to mine and I nearly dropped the coffee pot when his gaze struck me like a physical blow. "Yes, please."

Instead of giving me his cup, he slid it forward with his large hand still wrapped around it.

I hesitated, and then, in an unusually graceless move, managed to pour steaming-hot coffee on his hand instead of in the cup.

"Shit," he hissed, and shook his hand out.

"I'm so sorry!"

Horrified, I jerked the pot up and back—scalding a small section of my *own* arm this time, which made me drop the insulated metal coffee pot with a sharp scream as intense pain lit up the nerves and agony sizzled along my skin.

Instantly tears filled my eyes as I checked my arm, the skin growing angry and pink as the burning seemed to increase with every passing second.

Before I could move, I found a big arm looped around my waist, hustling me back to the bathrooms as I cradled my arm and cried.

Thankfully there was no one in white-and-black tiled room with us, but I didn't really give any of that a thought. My only focus was on getting the pain to stop, and I was aided in that task when a calloused hand gently grasped my arm and turned on the cold water at one of the four sinks facing the mirrors, forcing me to hunch over the bleached-to-death white tile. As he helped me get comfortable, I became aware of how large he was, how he could almost perfectly rest his chin on the top of my head. He surrounded me, and as the burn began to die down, I turned my teary eyes to the mirror and found him watching me with a searching look I didn't understand.

"Hannah, are you all right?"

His voice was deep, raspy, and I almost shivered as he shifted behind me, widening his stance while he guided my arm beneath the flow of water.

"How did you know my name?"

"You introduced yourself when I first sat down."

"Oh, right."

"And you're wearing a nametag."

I glanced down at my chest to confirm something I already knew, and noticed his hand resting on the faded sink countertop, the skin an angry bright pink.

Without thinking, I turned on the faucet of the sink next to us then grabbed his lightly haired wrist and thrust his large hand beneath the water, while he still held my arm beneath the other mercifully cold stream. The skin on the back of his hand looked like it hurt and I cringed inside. I'd injured him, like really hurt him, and his first reaction was to take care of me. Guilt swamped me and I sucked in a shaky breath.

The rushing water almost drowned out my voice as I whispered, "I'm so sorry."

"Hey now," he rumbled, the vibrations of his voice pinging off my nerves in a seductive baritone. "Look at me."

He said that with such authority that I followed his command without thought. The serious set of his expression, the absolute dominance he gave off, washed over me in a soothing wave of heat. Next to my slender frame, he was positively beastly, a mature and grown man who knew who he was and what he wanted. Authoritative older men have always been a secret weakness of mine, and the man behind me embodied every one of my fantasies come to life. My nipples peaked and I was glad the ugly apron of my uniform hid them from his probing view.

Good Lord, what was wrong with me? I'd burned the shit out of a customer and all I could think about was how good he would feel on top of me.

Still holding my arm beneath the water, he pinned me to the spot with his dark stare. "Hannah, did you spill the coffee on purpose? Do it just to see me in pain?"

"What? No, of course not." Offended that he would think that, I tried to pull my arm away. "It was an accident."

"Then you have nothing to apologize for." He removed his hand from my grasp then gently examined my skin with a care that made something melt inside of me. "Come with me, I think you should see a doctor."

My shit insurance had a crazy-high co-pay, and unless I was dying, I avoided going to the ER at all costs. "That's okay. I'll just ice it and look up how to treat burns on the Internet."

Wow, when he frowned, he was scary.

Before he could say anything, Beth, the night manager, came into the bathroom then let out a little shriek at the sight of the guy with the burned hand.

"Jesus, you're a big one." Her gaze found mine and went to my arm. "Hannah, are you okay?"

"I'm fine," I lied. "I'm more worried about Mr..."

I looked at him, realizing I didn't know his name, and found his gaze already on me. "Leo."

Well, that fit. Bet with his hair down, he would kind of resemble a lion too. "I burned Mr. Leo's hand."

"Just Leo, Hannah, and I assure you, I'm fine. In fact, I'm more worried about your arm. You should see a doctor."

Beth approached and spoke up with a nervous flutter of her hand in my direction, "I agree, Hannah. Take the rest of the night off and go to the ER. I've burned myself before and it's no picnic."

Thinking of all the corners I'd have to cut in my budget to afford a trip to the hospital, I pasted on a smile and tried to pretend the nerves in my forearm weren't screaming from pain. "Really, I'm okay. I'll just go home and ice it."

Leo spoke up from behind me. "I'll take her."

Turning back to face him, I had to tilt my head up to meet his determined stare. "No thank you, I'm fine."

"That arm isn't fine."

"Neither is your hand."

He seemed bemused when I gave him my meanest

glare, the one that I used while babysitting.

Beth clucked from beside me. "Really, Hannah, you need to get this looked at."

Lowering my voice until it was barely a breath, I leaned down so I could whisper in her ear, "I can't afford the co-pay."

"I'll take care of it," Leo said from too close behind me.

Once again, I glared at him for getting up in my personal space, but it was like trying to intimidate a statue. "Thank you, but I'm sure I'll be fine. I'm the one who injured you, I can't possibly let you pay for my medical care."

"Stubborn little thing with a strong moral compass," he murmured, and that icy look in his eyes softened.

"What?"

"Hannah," oh, I liked the way he said my name, way too much, "I promise you, nothing will happen to you while you're with me."

I licked my lips, wincing as the skin of my arm felt like it was still burning, and internally cursed. "Thank you, but no."

"Actually, Hannah," Beth said with a hesitant smile. "The diner will pay for your medical care, and Mr…uh, Leo's as well."

"See, no reason not to let me take care of you."

"Uh—hello? Stranger danger?"

With a smirk, he pulled out his wallet and I couldn't help but wince at the sight of his hand, the skin an unnaturally bright pink color. "Here, Beth, this is my business card. If anything happens to Hannah, you can take it to the police."

While Beth read the card, I asked in a low voice, "Does your hand hurt?"

"Yes, but I've endured worse." A low sigh escaped his deep chest and the look he gave me was more than tinged with exasperation. "Hannah, stop martyring yourself and let me help you."

Before I could make any sense of that odd, but I was pretty sure offensive, statement, Beth gave me a nudge in the lower back. "Go ahead, Hannah, grab your stuff. I'm sure Mr. Brass will take care of you."

At the odd, tight tone in her voice, I turned to look at her and was confused by the way she was watching Leo with wide, almost fearful eyes. "Are you sure?"

She blinked a couple times, then glanced at me. "Yes. You need your arm looked at."

"Fine, take me to a doctor," I huffed then jerked my head at Leo. "Come on."

The left side of his mouth quirked and I almost got a smile, but I turned away before I could be sure. Being outside of the bathroom helped me get my bearings and I quickly made my way to the back of the restaurant, enduring a few moments of my coworkers all coming to see if I was okay before I could shuck my apron then grab my purse and lilac fake leather jacket. It was down in the sixties tonight and I automatically went to put it on, only remembering too late that my arm was injured.

I bit my tongue to keep from screaming as I eased the jacket off, sure I was going to be taking a layer of skin with it as I whimpered in discomfort.

Male cursing came from my left and I blinked through my tears to find Leo at my side, his irritation moving through the air in skin-prickling waves. "I see

I can't leave you alone for one moment."

I held my arm out, biting my trembling lower lip before I asked, "How bad is it? Did I lose much skin? Will I need plastic surgery?"

He surprised me by laughing softly, then placing a gentle kiss on the unharmed skin of my inner wrist. "No, I think you'll be okay."

I peeked and was almost disappointed to find my skin an angry pink color when it felt like it should be covered in blisters, and I lamely said, "It really, really hurts."

"Be brave for me, just a little longer, and I'll take care of you."

The deep rumble of his gentle tone made my belly flutter more than a little bit. "Okay."

He smiled, and I swear I gasped as he rumbled out, "Okay."

I was only able to function after he turned away and led me out of my work and into the night. With his hand on my lower back, he guided me to our adjacent parking lot where a sleek black sedan idled. I may not have born into wealth, but Kayla's family had serious money and I'd spent a lot of time at her house while we were growing up. Plus, I loved to read those gossip columns about the rich and famous doing stupid things, then dream about what it would be like to have that kind of money. Because of my love of celebrity dirt, I knew the car in front of us was a Rolls Royce, and I knew it probably cost over half a million dollars. One of the stars I read about in an entertainment blog had bought his girlfriend one to make up for cheating on her with his maid.

A man got out as we approached, dressed in a suit

similar to Leo's. He had light brown hair and his gray eyes that matched his suit studied me intently. His gaze went from Leo, to me, to the arm that I was clearly favoring, and he frowned.

"Mark," Leo said from behind me as we approached. "Call Dr. Gardener and let her know we're coming in. Hannah burned herself and refuses to go to a hospital."

Feeling like a scolded child, I frowned at him and resisted the urge to step on his big foot. "Hey, not all of us are rolling in a Rolls, bro. Some of us have to work for a living."

Mark gave me a shocked look while Leo stared at me like I was some kind of weird insect. "Rolling in a Rolls...*bro*?"

My arm had begun to throb, making me more snippy and irritable than usual. "Can we just get to wherever we're going? It's starting to really hurt."

Leo brushed away a tear that had managed to escape. "Of course."

He helped me into the car and I got situated in a way that the top of my forearm wouldn't touch anything. Leo got in next to me and it wasn't until we were moving that I had a chance to look around inside. Though it was dark, I could see through the tasteful and dim lighting to the back of Mark's head, above the cream and dark gold leather seat. I'd never been surrounded by such luxury, and I took my time studying it, wanting to memorize the details so I could tell my friends. They'd never believe it, and I wondered if Leo would think I was weird if I took a selfie in his car.

"Where are we going? The hospital's the other

way."

"My downtown office."

"Why are we going to your downtown office?"

"That's where the doctor is." He studied me in the passing light, and I tried to keep from squirming beneath his intense regard. "Do you believe in destiny?"

"Um—pardon me?"

"Never mind. If you'll excuse me for a moment, I have some messages I need to check."

Confused, tired, and hurting, I tried to relax and get as comfortable as I could without jostling my arm. This led to me sniffing back tears and shifting restlessly, which drew Leo's attention back to me. When I noticed him watching like a hunter assessing his wounded prey, I stilled and pretended to examine the buildings we passed in the business district of Phoenix. This kept my mind off the sting for approximately ten seconds, and I tried to not whine like a baby. If Leo could be typing a text message with his injured hand, the least I could do was suck it up just sitting here, so I stared out the window and tried to resist the urge to stare at him instead.

We were let off in front of one of the newer office buildings and I was tempted to throw my coat over my shoulders to hide my uniform, but just the freaking breeze felt like someone was briskly rubbing my arm and my hurt overtook any embarrassment.

Leo must have seen me flinch, because he ducked down to look me right in the eye. "Just a little bit farther and we'll take the pain away. You are doing so well, being so strong for me."

I blinked back tears then wiped under my eyes

with my good hand. "Crap, is my makeup all messed up?"

He cupped my face and I was instantly aware of a sense of calm and safety enveloping me. I'd never felt anything like it before, and I could barely breathe as some kind of energy flowed from his body into mine, leaving me trembling in his power. When he closed his eyes my knees went weak, and I closed mine, anticipating his kiss, hoping I didn't faint.

To my disappointment he didn't press his lips to mine. Instead he kissed my forehead, but if a forehead kiss could be erotic, this one was. The slow brush of his lips against my skin, the faint scruff of his stubble, his musky smell that all men had, even the faint scent of detergent from his shirt overwhelmed my senses.

Oxygen rushed into my lungs as he drew back, an almost wild look in his eyes that froze me in place.

A predator stared down at me with a possessiveness I found both frightening and intriguing. What would it be like to have a man like this in my life? Someone I could trust, someone who thought I was a treasure? A man like Leo would guard me with his life. Well, that is if he didn't accidentally play with me too rough and kill me first. I had no illusions that I was anywhere near this man's league and even if he did want me, he wouldn't want to keep me. No guy ever did.

I'm a clinger. Like being-threatened-with-a-restraining-order, girl-you-have-a-problem clinger. It's a failing of mine and I'm aware of my problem, but I can't stop myself. When you're starving for affection, and someone finally gives it to you, you'll always want more, leeching on to them until you drain them dry. Unfortunately for me, in my past relationships, that desperate need for attention scared guys off pretty quick. I was my own worst enemy when it came to men.

My injured arm brushed his and I hissed, jerking back.

Leo's firm lips thinned and the lines around his eyes deepened. "You distract me. Come on, I'm failing in my duties."

"What?"

He didn't answer me, merely leading me through enormous spinning glass doors and into the cool interior of the office building. The entryway was flanked by large white marble desks on either side, each manned by four intimidating security guards who looked nothing like any security guards we had on campus. Those men were older, often with a gut and lazy eyes as they drove modified golf carts around the campus of Arizona State. The four guys flanking us were fit, in their prime, and they all stared at me like I was something interesting.

It had to be because I was with Leo. I wasn't the kind of girl who attracted male attention of this caliber on my own. They were probably wondering what he was doing with a mousy little girl who smelled like French fries and coffee when he probably dated supermodels. I found the thought more depressing than I should and forced myself to pay attention to my surroundings, when all I wanted to do was snuggle into Leo's side and hold his hand despite my self-doubt.

How peculiar.

When we reached the elevators, I examined the

stone and polished-steel lobby, softened by an array of massive potted plants.

The doors to the elevator binged open and Leo followed me in. He tapped a code into the keypad then the buttons for the top four floors lit up. After selecting the twenty-first floor, Leo stepped back, ignoring both me and my curious looks. He didn't say a word as he escorted me down a long hallway to what appeared to be a cross between a room in a hospital and a high-end hotel suite. It was windowless, but somehow managed to be bright and cheery with sunflower paintings on the walls and an enormous flat-screen TV that played some crazy-high-definition picture of a tropical sunset. The whole place screamed money and I wondered what it would be like to do post-surgery recovery in a room like this, rather than a regular hospital. Bet their food didn't suck.

Turning, I found Leo studying me, his hands shoved into the pockets of his pants.

"Um—where are we?"

"This is one of two medical floors in this building. There's also a lab, an executive floor, and a surgery suite."

"Surgery? Why?"

"The corporation I work for has a vast number of holdings and investments, one of which is with a team of world-renowned plastic surgeons. There's also a dental surgeon, an optometrist, and a gym. My employers believe in taking care of their people. It's probably why the Cordova Group is one of the highest-rated corporations in Arizona for employee satisfaction."

"So…you work here?"

He closed the door behind him and studied me intently, making my nipples peak again beneath the cheap fabric of my work shirt.

Suddenly reminded of the fact that I smelled like greasy food, and probably looked like blotchy shit warmed over from my crying, I turned away from Leo on the pretense of exploring the room. I could feel his presence behind me, an intangible caress that drew my attention like nectar to a bee.

"I do."

"And what's your job?"

"Everything security related."

I snorted. "That's helpful."

"I'm one of the heads of security."

"Must be an important job if you can afford a Rolls."

He shrugged. "What about you, Miss Hannah with no last name? What is it you do?"

"It's Hannah Barnes. You mean what do I do aside from working at a diner?"

"Yes."

Taking a seat on the edge of the bed, I tilted my head and looked up at him, admiring the way the light brought out the strands of gold among the brown of his tied-back hair. With the scruff and muscles, he had a "Dangerous Viking Marauder in a thousand dollar suit" air about him.

For a moment, I entertained the fantasy that he was interested in me as a woman, instead of some girl he was making small talk with while we waited for the doctor.

"I'm going to ASU."

He nodded as if he expected me to say that. "Let me guess what you're studying...childhood education."

I blinked at him, totally thrown for a loop. "Oh my gosh, how did you know that?"

His grin was playful, and absolutely devastating to my panties. "Lucky guess."

A knock came from the door and it swung inward, revealing a very pretty woman around Leo's age, maybe a little older, in a lab coat. She had her dark hair pulled back into a bun and wore these really cool cat-eye glasses. Tattoos peeked out on her wrists from the edge of her jacket and heavy black liner highlighted her big green eyes.

The way she smiled at Leo was openly affectionate and I let out an inner sigh. Of course he had a girlfriend. He was a hot-as-ballz rich guy, even if he was a bit scary. And of course she'd be uber beautiful and cool in a way I could never hope to be.

"Hello," the woman said in a honeyed voice. "I'm Dr. Gardener. It's nice to meet you, Hannah. I hear you've been burned."

The flirty looks she kept giving Leo irritated me and I called myself a moron for reacting like a jealous shrew. Pulling myself together, I gestured to my arm, then Leo. "Hi, Dr. Gardner. Yeah, I accidentally spilled hot coffee on both of us. Check out Leo's hand first, I think his is worse than mine."

"Leo?" the woman asked with raised brows as she looked over at the man in question. "You mean Mr. Brass?"

Moving to my side, he placed a hand on my shoulder. "Hannah has permission to call me Leo.

Her needs come first. Take care of her, and I'll wait."

Confusion followed by hurt flashed through Dr. Gardener's eyes, but she forced a smile. "Of course. Well then, let's take a look at your burn."

Less than ten minutes later, my arm was covered with a blissfully numbing salve and lightly wrapped in a clean white bandage. I'd been given some painkillers and they must have been stronger than I thought, because I was having a hard time keeping my eyes open. My muscles were loose, relaxed, and when someone said my name, I could barely keep my eyes open.

"Hannah," the vaguely familiar man said again. "Lay back, sweetheart."

"Tired," I mumbled as I frowned with my eyes closed.

"You've had a long night. Go to sleep. I'll watch over you."

"M'kay."

In my dream, I was listening to two men talking in a Victorian house, their voices distant but compelling. Dressed like a 19th century lady in a green and black taffeta gown, I walked down the long corridors of the manor, following the baritone sounds of their conversation. Soon I came to an ornate, closed door and I paused. The men were on the other side and I could almost hear them, so I sank to my knees, the fabric of my dress rustling loudly around me, and pressed my ear to the keyhole.

The voices were still faint, going in and out, but I managed to hear them speak.

"She's young," a man said in a low voice with a

very faint Hispanic accent.

"Yes, she is."

"And very innocent."

"I'm aware."

"She reminds me of someone..."

"Audrey Hepburn."

"Yeah, that's it...those big brown eyes and pretty lips. I didn't know you were attracted to such elegant women. She's for sure not your usual porn star partner. Why Hannah? Of all the women in this world, all the women you've had, what is it about this one that makes her 'the one'?"

"Those women were toys, nothing more, nothing less. They never meant anything to me besides a body to play with."

The stranger let out a low whistle. "That's cold."

"It's the truth."

"But why this girl?"

"Because she's mine. She's my destiny."

"You really think that?"

"I know it, feel it in my balls and my gut."

"My mother approves of her, by the way."

The man with the smooth baritone voice snorted. "Of course she does. If Judith didn't care for Hannah, she'd already be on a plane to Germany with a one-way ticket—or worse."

"This's true."

"What has Judith said about her?"

"Aside from talking about the progress you were making with your experiment, she mentioned that at least you had the brains to pick a good woman. She's also worried that this life might prove to be too much for Hannah, that the experiment will fail and we'll have to...deal with the consequences."

"There will never, ever be any consequences to deal with. I'll take care of her every need, give her everything she could want, and I'll slit the throat of anyone stupid enough to even look at her wrong."

"Crazy fucker," the other man muttered before he was silent for a long moment. "Think it's gonna work?"

"Yes."

"Maybe I'll find myself someone young and sweet to train."

"Just be aware, the sword cuts both ways."

The other man laughed, and it wasn't a nice sound. "Fuck that shit. I'll never give any woman that kind of control over me. I wish you luck, my friend. She's going to wake up ravenous."

Dark satisfaction filled the slightly familiar voice as he said, "I know."

My dream shifted, twisted, and I drifted away from the voices.

Awareness hit me in stages, the first being the fact that dryness coated my mouth and tongue. The second was that I felt a little floaty, and the third was the gentle caress of a large male hand stroking my neck and collarbone. My injured arm still throbbed, but it was nowhere near my earlier pain. I lay back on something immensely comfortable, and the room was very, very quiet, other than my breathing and his.

"Hannah, wake up for me, baby girl," Leo said in a low, sinful voice. The hand moved from my arm to my face and his fingertips traced along my jaw.

"Ugh—my mouth tastes terrible."

My eyes were still closed as Leo helped me sit up against what I was assuming were pillows. A straw was brought to my lips and I eagerly sucked down some crisp ginger ale before he pulled the drink away. The cool liquid soothed my throat and my stomach gurgled as it hit.

"Enough, or you'll get sick."

Slowly opening my eyes, I was relieved to see the lights were dimmed so I wasn't blinded.

Then I looked at Leo and lost my breath.

He sat in a dark cinnamon leather chair next to the hospital bed I was lying in, his jacket off and his forearms showing, with their dusting of golden-brown hair and thick muscles. The scruff on his face had grown in even more, and his eyes were so dark beneath his heavy brow I could barely make out the difference between his pupil and iris. A slight flush stood out on his cheekbones as he gave me an intense stare that should have unnerved me, but aroused me instead. I liked how it seemed as if all his attention was focused on me, like I was something important, someone worth noticing.

"How are you feeling?"

"A little dizzy, but otherwise okay."

"Have you ever taken painkillers before?"

"Um...once when I broke my leg while playing soccer. And when I sprained my wrist."

The side of his mouth quirked up. "That's what I thought. The medicine was only supposed to relax you, but it put you to sleep instead."

"How long have I been out?"

"Five hours. I tried to wake you a few times, but you told me to go fuck myself gently with a chainsaw."

"Oh…oh jeez. I'm sorry. It's from the eighties movie *Heathers*."

The darkness of his eyes lightened to melted chocolate. "I know."

"You've seen *Heathers*?"

He shrugged. "I like to watch movies, especially the older ones."

"Me too."

"Well, that's one thing we have in common."

My sleepy mind wanted to be closer to him, so I rolled over onto my side…then frowned. "Why does my hip hurt?"

"You must have bumped it. At one point you tried to get up out of bed, and that's probably when you hit it."

On my back once again, I rubbed my hip with a frown, not liking that I couldn't remember. "That's it, nothing stronger than Tylenol for me."

He gave me a smile I could only describe as indulgent. "How's your arm?"

"Much better. How's your hand?"

The gold watch on his wrist gleamed as he held up his hand wrapped in an Ace bandage. "Fine."

I snorted and went to lean up, forgetting almost instantly that my arm was injured.

When I yelped, Leo stood and scooped his arm behind my back, supporting me without any effort. "What are you doing?"

Flushing, I cleared my throat and looked away.

"I have to use the ladies' room." I was hyperaware of how easily he lifted me out of the bed then carried me across the room. "I can walk, you know."

Setting me on my feet, he gave me that tender, lingering forehead kiss again, the one that made my toes curl and my chest fill with warmth. Then he smacked my butt with a little tap that had me laughing as I moved away. "Go."

I was tempted to turn around and stick my tongue out at him, but I managed to act like an adult. The bathroom was nice, but it was still obviously a hospital bathroom with its extra railings and handicap-accessible shower. A wrapped toothbrush and little thing of toothpaste sat next to the sink, and I gratefully gave my mouth a good scrub while examining myself in the mirror with a wince.

At some point, someone must have taken my ponytail out because my hair fell down my back in its usual boring, bone-straight way. The edge of my right sleeve was still splashed with coffee near my biceps and my eyes were red-rimmed from crying. With a sigh, I wished I had a hairbrush and a team of makeup artists to work some magic on me, but unfortunately the best I could do was pinch my cheeks to try to add some color to my pale face. My light brown eyes were bloodshot with dark circles beneath them and overall I resembled a zombie apocalypse survivor, but splattered with coffee instead of blood.

"Hannah, are you okay?"

"Yeah," I yelled back right away, afraid he'd come in and catch me mooning over myself. "Just washing up."

I cleaned my hands in like three seconds then dried them on one of the fluffy white towels hanging next to the sink before girding my loins and opening the door.

Leo stood on the other side of the room, talking with Dr. Gardener, who regarded me with a rather forced smile. "Feeling better, Hannah?"

"Yes, thank you. Am I okay to go home?"

"Of course," Dr. Gardener said as she typed something into her phone, avoiding my gaze. "If you don't need me for anything else, Mr. Brass, I have a patient that I need to attend to."

"You're free to go."

She cast him a brief look of longing as he strode towards me, then left.

While I've had a problem with jealousy before, I've never felt as intensely possessive of a man as I did Leo, and we weren't even dating. What in the world was wrong with me? Maybe I needed to go see a psychiatrist again before my anxiety started up. This fixating on a man I barely knew, who was so different from anyone I've ever been around, couldn't be healthy. All I could think of as he closed the distance between us was that he would be strong enough to hold me up while he fucked me against the nearest wall.

My breathing sped and when his wide chest filled my world, I found myself afraid of meeting his gaze, afraid of the desire he would see in my eyes.

"Leo, can you take me home please?"

I checked him out as surreptitiously as I could, wanting to run my fingers down the open collar of his shirt to the light brown hair of his chest. His pulse beat against the tanned skin of his neck, making me want to lick him there. My need for him was so strong, I had to press my thighs together in the hopes of easing the ache.

"Of course. Dr. Granger left some medicine and antibiotic cream to take home with you, along with a change of bandages. There shouldn't be any scarring."

"Thank you." I hesitantly reached out and gently touched the fingertips of his injured hand, telling my hormones to shut the hell up as guilt reared its ugly head again. "Leo, I'm so sorry I hurt you."

"Don't worry. I have a very, very high pain threshold."

"I don't."

"I know." He sounded amused as he took a step back, then gestured to my lilac jacket nicely hung over the back of a nearby chair. "You might want to answer your phone, it's been ringing a lot."

"Oh, crap, my roommates!" I stumbled over to my jacket and dug my phone out, groaning at the amount of messages and texts from Joy. The only one I had from Kayla was to tell me—not ask me, tell me—that I needed to run her library books back for her, like she couldn't do it herself.

No doubt she'd sleep all day tomorrow, the day her books were due, and continue to beg me to take them back while looking pitiful and laying on a guilt trip. Normally helping her didn't bother me…but right now, it irritated me that Kayla just got to coast through life, using her money and connections to do whatever the heck she wanted while I busted my butt to just get by.

Rather than answering all the individual texts, I called the house and Joy answered, "Hello?"

"Hey, it's me."

"Hannah! Are you okay? You never came home and I got worried so I called your work. They said you burned yourself and left with some guy."

Conscious of Leo watching me, I turned slightly and said in a low voice, "I'm fine. In fact, I'm on my way home. I spilled coffee on one of my customers and myself, burning us both. He was nice enough to take me to get medical treatment at a fancy private clinic."

"He did what?"

"I'll talk with you when I get home."

Something in my voice must have alerted Joy, because her tone changed as she asked, "Is he hot?"

"Oh yeah."

"Is he standing right there?"

"Yep."

"Do you want to lick his balls?"

"You suck."

She giggled, and I had a hard time keeping my blush under control. "Uh-uh, I bet *you're* the one who'll be doing the sucking. Tongue all up in his—"

"Anyways," I said loudly, "I'll be home in a bit."

"I'll make some cookies and hang out and wait for you."

"You don't have to. I know you have a study group this afternoon."

"No way. I was worried sick. I'm just glad you're okay and that you're having an adventure. You need an adventure, bad. Just be safe. I'd have to go on a path of vengeance if anything happened to you, and that means I'd have to start jogging or some shit."

Knowing Joy used humor as a defense, I softened my voice and tried to make my friend feel better. "I'm sorry, honey."

"Love you, cupcake."

"Love you too, pookie bookie wookie."

"Oh, and if you don't want to come home and want to boink his brains out instead, feel free."

"Thanks."

Laughing, I hung up the phone, only to find Leo watching me with a dark look that set me on edge — and aroused me. "Who was that?"

"Uh — Joy, my roommate."

"Do you love her?"

"Of course, she's been one of my best friends since high school."

The stiff line of his body, the anger that I glimpsed in his eyes, all melted away. "I see."

Grabbing my jacket, I stuffed my phone in the pocket. "I'm ready when you are."

A bright, beaming sun pouring through the floor-to-ceiling windows pierced my eyeballs with its rays as we stepped out of the elevator and into the foyer, people bustling about as the room echoed with various conversations. Everyone was dressed for business and I stuck out like a sore thumb, especially with the bright white bandage on my arm. Leo had his bandaged hand on my lower back and the heat of his palm pressing against me was distracting to say the least. Unknown feelings zipped along my nerves, and I wanted to reach out and grab a handful of his bubble butt. Really, having an ass that good must be illegal.

Realizing I was looking over my shoulder to stare at his butt in a totally obvious move, I turned and forced my guilty gaze straight ahead, hoping Leo didn't notice. If he did, he didn't say anything, instead escorting me to the curb in silence. I swore I could feel him next to me, electricity connecting our bodies with invisible waves so it felt like I was pressed to his side instead of walking by him.

Mark, the driver, was waiting for us and I could feel the eyes of curious people walking past, staring. They were probably wondering why a man like Leo was slumming around with a dork like me. My usual negative thoughts didn't have time to take root, my entire being distracted by the heat of Leo's body as he slid in next to me. I studied him in the full sunlight, taking in the deep shadows that his heavy bone structure gave his face, the crinkles around his eyes and his firm lips. While he'd never grace the cover of a magazine or star in a movie based on his looks alone—he wasn't pretty by any means—I found him to be the most delicious thing I'd ever laid eyes on.

The soundproofing inside the car was excellent, so I was able to hear the way his breath hitched when he looked over at me.

"Come home with me," he all but demanded, his tone confident and incredibly sexy.

"What?"

"Come home with me. Call your roommate and tell her you're spending the day with me."

"Why?"

"Because I want you to."

I started to laugh, but the intense expression on his face made me hesitate. "Seriously?"

"Absolutely."

"But—why?"

He leaned back in his seat, studying me before his

deep voice filled the car again. "Are you attracted to me, Hannah?"

Blushing hot enough to fry an egg on my face, I looked away. Did I tell him yes then feel like a moron when he says he's just trying to be friends with me and wants me over to play Scrabble? Did I tell him no and not only lie to him, but also possibly offend him? Or worse yet, hurt his feelings?

"Tell me."

The snap in his voice had me blurting out, "Yes."

"I find you very attractive as well." The corner of his mouth curled up in a smile and the emptiness in his eyes filled with warmth. "I also find you kind, smart, and funny. I'd like to get to know you better. Come home with me, spend time with me. You must be hungry, let me feed you."

I was hungry all right, hungry for his dick, and the mental image of him feeding it to me had my pussy squeezing tight with longing. My mind couldn't seem to stop thinking about what it would be like to touch him, to taste him. I'd like to get to know him by ripping off his clothes and fucking him in the backseat of his car. With each beat of my heart, heat rushed between my legs and I squeezed my thighs together.

"Are you sure?"

"I am absolutely positive."

"Okay. I'd enjoy having lunch with you, but after that I have to go home to get my stuff for class."

His smiled, and I couldn't help but smile back. "What class is it?"

"Art History, it's one of my favorites."

We talked about my classes while we drove farther

than I'd expected, the road lined with big palm trees swaying in the hot desert breeze. "Where are we going?"

"Paradise Valley. I have a home out there." He reached out and took my hand in his, sending a flurry of tingles running through me. "I think you'll like it."

My breath came out in a rush as he rubbed the back of my hand with his thumb. "I'm sure I will."

Chapter 5

We passed through two massive security gates before the Rolls climbed the drive to a magnificent Mediterranean-meets-desert-southwest style home that took my breath away.

Pressing my nose to the window in a no doubt undignified way, I breathed out, "Oh, Leo, I love it."

"Do you?"

I turned to face him as the car came to a stop. "I really do. It's magnificent."

The lines around his mouth deepened as he smiled and the leather of the seat creaked when he leaned forward. "I'm glad."

When Mark opened my door and helped me out, I tried not to gawk at the immaculate landscaping filled with desert flowers and mature trees. While there was only a small patch of grass, there were these gorgeous rock formations that the builder had included that gave the place a raw beauty. The mansion was situated high on a hillside, isolated from its neighbors, and I imagined that at night the view must be amazing.

Leo reclaimed my hand in his own, leading me through a pair of massive weathered wood and black wrought iron doors into the cool cream and burgundy two-story foyer of the house. Summer in Phoenix was no joke, and the blessed kiss of air conditioning made me sigh in delight.

I was too busy enjoying the feeling of the faint breeze on my skin to pay attention to his home, at least at first. By the time we moved through a formal sitting room and into what I can only describe as a luxurious, glass-enclosed patio filled with potted plants and invitingly deep couches and a daybed, my jaw was probably hanging all the way down to my chest. This place was remarkable; it was everything I'd ever wanted in a home, right down to my dream massage chair that cost like ten grand which I'd glimpsed during our walk to the patio.

"Hannah?" Leo asked me as we came to a stop before the vast windows that looked out over the valley below. "Are you all right?"

"What? Yes, of course. Sorry, it's just…your house is perfect. I mean—it's like you looked into my head, plucked out my dreams and made it real. I probably sound dumb, but this place is just amazing. I can't believe you live here. If this was my place, I'd never leave the house."

He smiled then raised my hand to his lips, the brush of his skin against mine making my nipples tighten. Sensuality filled the air around him and I was having a hard time remembering my name, let alone the reasons why climbing him and kissing him until I tasted blood suddenly was a bad idea. My skin prickled and my nipples were so hard, they stung as they rubbed against the cheap lace of my bra with every heavy breath.

Still holding my eyes, he lightly sucked my pointer finger into his mouth and I swear my pussy quivered at the feeling of his warm, wet tongue stroking me.

A hard surge of some emotion I could only

describe as aggressive desire tore through me as his teeth scraped along my skin while he watched my every reaction, fed from it. My heart began to pound and the need scraped against the surface of my body, begging to be let out, demanding a release. Every inch of me was primed for sex, my panties flooded as if I'd been teased for hours instead of barely touched. Not that any lover of mine had ever bothered to tease me for more than a few minutes, but I imagined hours of sensual torture would feel something like the hunger burning in me.

My lip lifted in a snarl as he began to lick my palm, the move so sensual it had an honest-to-God growl coming out of my throat.

I've never, ever growled in my life, and it startled me enough that I tried to move out of his hold, but Leo wasn't letting me go anywhere. "It's okay. I want you to let the dirty girl that lives inside of you out to play, Hannah. Take me, use me, do whatever you want, and I will fucking love every minute of it."

His words stunned me and I pressed my hands to my cheeks, trying to get a grip on my out-of-control body. My skin was so sensitive my clothing felt like an irritating abrasion, and I wanted to tear away anything separating my skin from his. Stimulus flooded my mind and I started to shake, the sexual feelings I was experiencing so abnormally intense, I began to freak out.

Damn but he smelled good, and he was so…virile. So alive and in his prime. He practically radiated good health and my lower stomach nearly cramped with the wave of desire crashing through me.

Fear battled with my desire and I gave Leo a

panicked look. "Something's wrong."

In an instant, he had me cradled in his arms as he carried me to the wide sage-green and mist-gray daybed against the far wall. Bright gold and different shades of green pillows surround three sides of the daybed, making it the perfect place to relax in a nest of comfort. He removed my shirt with slightly trembling hands and I basked in his open adoration as he helped me sit up so he could take off my bra as well. The moment my nipples were exposed to the air, they crinkled and I hissed, lightly rubbing my palms against them.

"Leo," I nearly whined, "they hurt."

"Let me make them better."

Sliding his big hand over my back, he bent and ever so gently began to lick my stiff nipple, my back arching instantly at the sensation of his warm mouth taking away the sting, soothing the hurt. Thank God he was being so careful with me, because even the lightest scrape of his teeth against the tender bud had me clenching my jaw. Then he switched to my other breast, repeating the soft licks until my hips were instinctively rising up, offering my body to him.

He caressed my back as I rubbed against him and purred, shameless in my pleasure in a way I'd never experienced, tingles of an almost burning intensity readying me for him. He pulled away from my breasts and I whimpered. My nipples still hurt, and I ground them against his chest in an effort to seek relief, moaning when the ache only increased.

"Touch me," I begged.

"I will, baby. I'll allow you to order me around, use me as you wish, but only for today…and maybe as a special treat in the future. While I can play at being the submissive and enjoy it, it's not who I am."

"Who are you?"

He smirked and I squeezed my thighs together tight as he said, "When we're fucking, or I'm in the mood, I'm your dominant, your Daddy."

Shit, not only did he have my dream car and home, he was the wicked lover from my dirtiest fantasies. "If you're my Daddy, who am I?"

"You're my princess, my baby girl, my everything."

His large hand began to inch up my side, closer to my meager breast, and I lost my mind to his touch. I swore every tingling inch of my skin buzzed like I was being tickled with an electric wand, the inner walls of my pussy contracting rhythmically to squeeze on a cock that wasn't there.

Why was I empty and hurting? I had a beautiful, dangerous, virile male animal right here who said I could use him as I wished. My breath hitched and he stared at me with arrogance as I visually devoured him.

Biting my lip, I sat up in his lap and pushed him back onto the bed, assuming the dominant position over him. While I realized it was like a house cat pouncing on a lion, I still felt a heady dose of power that he was allowing me to do this to him, that he was fighting his nature for me. My sensitive sex pulsed as I ground along his erection, appreciating anew how fucking thick he was.

Grasping my breasts, I leaned up and tossed my head back as I tweaked my nipples and cried out at the firestorm of amazing sensations consuming me, making me wild.

A hard shudder went through Leo and my need increased. I looked down and found him watching me as if I was the most essential thing in the world, like I was glorious. His attention was almost as good as the feeling of his body between my legs, and I fell forward, rubbing myself against him like a cat in heat. His luscious mouth tempted me and I closed the distance between us, eager for a taste of his lips.

The moment my tongue stroked his, the restraint he held on to so carefully snapped and he grasped my hips, taking over and rubbing me against his cock.

Allowing him to take control of my movements, I followed his lead without effort, his commands becoming my instincts. Unlike my previous boyfriends, I didn't have to try to direct him, or pretend I was enjoying his fumbling, hesitant touch. No, Leo knew exactly what he was doing with a woman's body and I reveled in his experience. My orgasm began to build and I had to place my hands on his chest to balance myself as his movements became more violent. His ridged length stroked over my pussy, pressing hard against my swollen labia and even more swollen clit.

No doubt my hips would have bruise marks from his fingers but the pain only spurred me on and threw me into my orgasm. The muscles of my lower stomach bunched, tightened, and my pussy clenched so hard it hurt. The whole world seemed to freeze, then I exploded while Leo groaned beneath me, his head tossing side to side as his back arched violently. He would have thrown me from his body with the strength of his thrusts if he hadn't been holding me so tight.

I couldn't wait to feel him pounding into me.

Panting, I slumped over his big body, bliss softening me until I was a useless puddle. His heart beat hard and steady beneath my ear while I lifted and lowered with his heaving breaths. The scent of him washed over me and I utterly lost myself in him.

The first thought that came back to my shattered mind was that I was pretty sure I'd just made him come in his pants like he did to me. Amazing. Best orgasm of my *life*, and he was fully clothed.

The craving for him hadn't abated, that aching and empty feeling still twisted in my gut, and I rolled off to the side then sat up on my knees. "Can I still touch you however I want?"

Eyes glittering, he nodded with a wide smile.

"Take off your jacket and shirt."

I sat back on my haunches while he sat up and did as I asked, revealing a thickly muscled body covered in scars.

The sight of so many injuries still couldn't detract from the magnificent torso he'd just revealed for my pleasure. Using one hand, I pushed him down onto his back and began to explore him, caressing every inch of skin available to me, shivering with sparks of pleasure as I enjoyed the hard curves of his muscles and crisp sensation of his body hair. It was a shade darker than his golden-brown hair and covered his chest before narrowing down his abs to his pants.

His pants with a wet spot.

A rather filthy impulse filled me and I found myself unbuckling his pants with a big grin, my mouth practically watering at the thought of licking him clean.

A quick glance at Leo's face showed me he was all for whatever I had in mind.

"Up," I said softly as I pulled first his black suit pants down to his knees, then his white boxer briefs.

At the sight of his steadily hardening dick, wet with his climax, I let out a little quivery sigh of appreciation. He had a beautiful dick, thick and not too long, with a flared crown that would stretch me just right. Veins pulsed along the length and I wondered if I'd be able to feel them when he stretched me open.

With a moan, I leaned down and began to lick at the head of his pretty dusky-rose cock, savoring his taste as he gathered my hair into his fist then lifted it so he could watch as I continued to give him a tongue bath, excited little whimpers leaving me when his taste exploded on my tongue. It was exactly what I was craving, exactly what I wanted, and I soon found myself sucking at him eagerly, probing the slit in the head of his cock for more. Grasping his heavy balls, I squeezed them gently as I sucked harder, making him give me more of his essence.

With a low growl, he pulled me off his now rock-solid erection, the skin a deep brownish-red from both my mouth and the blood rushing to his dick. The solid flesh jerked as I strained against his hand, my tongue snaking out to graze the head. An almost pained noise left him but he continued to withhold his visibly throbbing erection from me, despite my protests.

"Give me your cock," I snarled as I pulled against his grip, the pain coming from my scalp turning into a wonderful burst of pleasure. "You said I could have whatever I want, and I want you to feed me more cum."

"Filthy little girl." Despite the fierceness of his grip on my hair, his voice was gentle. "Wouldn't you rather have all this dick shoved inside of you?"

"Fuck yes," I breathed. "Now."

Laughing, Leo released my hair and I flipped onto my back. "Now?"

"Right now." I spread my legs wide, making room for him between them.

"Hold still."

The need to move had my muscles twitching, but when he pulled out a knife from an ankle sheath I hadn't noticed, I froze. A tremor of real fear went through me as I took in how dark his eyes, his entire person, became when he had a blade in his hand.

After freeing himself from his pants, he leaned down and I fought the need to flee, a harsh sweat breaking out all over my body. I don't know how I knew; I was just sure, from the top of my head to the souls of my feet, that Leo was capable of great violence, and that he enjoyed it.

Instead of ending my life, he grasped the crotch of my pants. "Do not move, Hannah."

"I won't."

"Good girl. Now hold still for your Daddy so he can take care of you."

Oh fuck, that word brought instant naughty pleasure that had my sex pulsing with need. It was as if the word was a trigger, a button I could push for a burst of erotic sensation. Daddy…he was my Daddy. He'd love me and take care of me because that's what

Daddies did — they took care of their baby girls.

I didn't realize I was saying those words aloud until Leo repeated them. "That's right, sweetheart. Daddies love and take care of their baby girls. Now lean up on your elbows and watch me split this tight little pussy open with my dick."

He lowered the knife and I was unable to respond as he carefully cut right through the crotch of both my pants and panties, leaving my pussy hanging out in an obscene manner. That weird mixture of fear and passion obliterated my mind as he lowered the tip of the knife to my sex. I was panting as though I'd just run a marathon while he ever so carefully stroked the deadly tip over my clit, delicately rubbing the flat of it on the tender skin of the hood covering my nub. One wrong move and he'd cut me, badly, but I couldn't look away while he continued to pet me with the blade.

Just when I thought I might pass out from the tension, he lifted the tip of the knife to his lips and licked it with a guttural moan.

"Leo," I pleaded as I spread my legs even wider, arching my hips up as I whimpered for him.

With a growl, he turned and threw the knife, hitting the wall with perfect accuracy.

Before I could react, he was between my legs, rubbing the bulbous head of his cock against my extremely wet pussy.

"Do you want this?" he asked with an evil purr.

Closing my eyes, I grasped my breasts and squeezed, my body one big pulse of need. "Yes!"

"How badly?"

"So bad!"

"Do you want your Daddy to fuck his princess?"

"Please!"

"Then open up and take Daddy's cock."

By this point, I was mindless, and I wrapped my arms around his neck, clinging to him as he slowly began to slide into me, stretching me, making my sex burn. I hissed then stiffened, but Leo pushed on, ignoring my resistance and taking what he wanted. Each inch did what he'd said, split me wide open, and I had to fight back a small surge of fright at the pain. The burn increased until he was seated inside of me, and I swear to God his dick felt as thick as a soda can, my tender inner walls burning with the stretch. I was afraid to move, but at the same time I liked the hurt, liked the overwhelming sensation of Leo pinning me to the bed as he took and took from my oversensitive body.

I could feel everything, every vein in his erection, every hair on his body as he rubbed against me. We were locked together, entwined, from his legs pressing against mine to our foreheads resting together. His breath was my breath, his heartbeat my heartbeat. We were so incredibly connected that my throat burned with unshed tears as, for the first time in what seemed like forever, I wasn't alone. Leo filled not only my body, but the empty, needy place inside of me that craved affection.

Never, in all my dating, had I ever been with a man who'd even begun to repair the damage my sister's death and parents' shunning had caused in my soul. But this massive, terrifying, and crushingly intense man somehow soothed the jagged edges inside of me, and for the first time in forever I felt like I belonged to someone who actually cared about me.

His thumbs stroked my cheeks as he slowly moved in and out of me, his lips parted and his eyes grew heavy with pleasure. Wonderful feelings surrounded me when I stared up at him, proud that I was giving him such obvious enjoyment. The hard lines of his face softened and even his eyes grew lighter, whisky instead of darkness.

I couldn't stop touching him, couldn't stop myself from digging my nails into his back, gripping the hard muscles of his body as he moved over me. Dipping his head down, he sucked one of my dark raspberry-colored nipples into his mouth, leaving it wet and glistening as he propped himself above me and began to thrust harder. I wrapped my hands in his hair, holding his head still so I could stare into his eyes, my newfound favorite addiction.

My heart thundered as I met him stroke for stroke, gasps and moans pouring from me with abandon while I encouraged him to give me more, give me everything. He listened and was soon fucking me so hard, all I could do was take it, endure the punishing thrust of his hips, and savor the painful drag of his thick cock. My clit throbbed and every time he came down, he leaned forward the slightest bit to give that greedy part of my body a good rub with his pelvis. God, he fucked like a porn star, and my toes curled so hard they began to cramp. My body grew tighter, even my jaw clenching as my release built and built.

Leo must have sensed it, because he reared back and threw my legs over his shoulders before leaning forward again, bending me almost in half and fucking the hell out of me.

He hit some magical place inside that sent starbursts of white-hot bliss rocketing through my mind, everything going dark as my orgasm ripped through me. Guttural noises came from deep in my chest while Leo easily pinned me to the bed and ground his body against mine, his roar loud enough to shake the windows as he reached his climax. The feeling of his cum filling me was so profoundly satisfying that I clung to him as my pussy milked him for every drop.

Our bodies shivered and shuddered against each other as Leo nuzzled his face into my hair, occasional soft grunts coming from him, usually followed by a full-body tremor.

With a sigh, Leo rolled us, his dick still inside of me as he spread me over him. My arm was hurting a little bit from our activities and I managed to pant out, "How's your hand?"

"What hand?" Leo mumbled. "All I feel is heaven around my dick. You have the strongest pussy I've ever felt squeeze my cock."

I laughed, which made my inner muscles contract, and we both moaned while I gave a little wiggle, a weak pulse of desire fluttering through me. "Kegels. Joy's mom is an OB nurse and she pounded into our head that Kegel exercises help women have easier births. You get to enjoy the result of four years of exercising."

The deep, rumbling laughter that poured out of him surprised me, and I couldn't help grinning down at Leo as I lay perched on his chest, my long hair flowing around us.

"I'll have to meet that woman someday and let her

know how much I appreciate the result of her efforts."

He grew harder inside of me and I gave another experimental wiggle, yelping when he smacked my ass.

"Stop that. You need a break. I don't want to fuck you raw right out of the gate."

"That's a charming way to put it. Comparing a woman to a horse that you rode is a sure way to win her favor."

The tips of his fingers ran over my bottom as he let out a satisfied sigh. "I'll just have to find other ways to win you over. Are you still hungry?"

"Hmm?" My mind was centered on the way he was caressing my stinging ass and reawakening my desires. "Let's stay here and have sex instead."

He rolled us again so I was on my back and he stared down at me with what I could only describe as a sweet smile. "Afraid you'll have to do without my cock for a little bit. Coming so hard my balls just about blew off, twice, will do that to a man. But I'll never leave you hungry."

"I don't—"

My words became a garbled moan as he spread my thighs with his broad shoulders then buried his face in my pussy, his long hair tickling over my skin.

Embarrassment and arousal had me twisting beneath him. "Wait! You came inside of me."

Giving my pussy a big, slurping lick, Leo growled out, "I know. You taste like me, and I fucking love it. Could eat this plump little pussy all day. I just might do that; fill you up over and over only to clean you out again. Now open up, baby girl, and feed your

Daddy."

"Shit," I whispered weakly, then did as he ordered.

His hair caressed me with his suckling movements, partially obscuring his face while he ate me with an obvious enjoyment that destroyed any resistance I might have had. My world dissolved into nothing but his velvety licking, his probing tongue, and his biting teeth. The skin on my inner thighs stung from where he'd taken a particularly deep bite into my flesh, the throbbing pain merely blending into the rush of hormones scoring through me. My already overwhelmed body struggled to keep up with the demands of both my libido and Leo, each of which seemed determined to drive me right out of my damn mind.

My head rolled helplessly back and forth on the now destroyed daybed, sweat coating me while I gripped Leo's thick, heavy hair in my fists and fucked his face with snapping rolls of my hips.

He pulled away and I worried that I was hurting him, but when he looked up at me, his gaze was positively feral. "Harder. Make me feel."

Those words blended into the drugging high of touching him as I leaned up and gripped the back of his thickly muscled neck with my nails.

"More, Hannah. Give me everything."

The slick pleasure of his tongue rubbing against my clit sent chills radiating through me, and I ran my nails lightly up to his scalp, raking them through his hair before fisting it. To my delight, the harder I pulled, the harder he sucked, and in moments I was shattering for him, his strong hands pinning me to the bed while I writhed and shook, probably looking like

I was being electrocuted. The world went dark and I lay still…so very still and peaceful.

Mmmmm, this was nice.

Then someone smacked my ass, hard, and said, "Breathe."

I sucked in a gasping breath of air, then another. Opening my eyes wasn't going to happen, but at least I'd surfaced enough from the blissful darkness to keep myself alive. After a few shuddery breaths, I managed to calm myself enough to stop panting.

Leo pulled me into his arms, curving himself around me, pressing my slight body to his muscled bulk. We must look like a grizzly hugging a ragdoll; I was certainly as limp as one. Floppy. The thought roused a sleepy giggle from me.

"Are you okay, baby girl?"

"Very." I snuggled into him, completely relaxed.

"You did so good, I'm proud of you. I thought I knew what it would be like to have you, but I had no idea. You make me feel more…I don't have the words for it, you just make me feel more than I've ever experienced with a woman." He kissed my sweaty temple. "Never letting you go. You're mine now, all of you, every bit—mine."

I drifted off to sleep in Leo's arms, and did it with a smile.

"Hannah," a man's voice said in a low rumble. "You need to wake up and eat, sweetheart."

I reached out and grabbed a pillow, pulling it over my face as I turned away. "No, sleeping."

Muffled laughter came through the pillow, then someone ran their hand over my ass—my bare ass—

before giving it a good slap.

Whipping the pillow off my head, I sat straight up and snarled, "What the fuck?"

Leo, casually dressed and crouching next to me, took one look at me and burst out laughing, rocking back on his heels while I glared at him.

I don't wake up from naps happy.

"What?" I scowled as I rubbed my bleary eyes.

He shook his head, still smiling. "You look well fucked."

I reached up to touch my hair, wincing when I found it a big rat's nest. "Oh no."

"Don't worry, we'll get you straightened out, but you need to eat first."

My stomach rumbled when he stood and moved enough that I could see he had a tray full of food on the bleached wood table next to the daybed. As soon as I saw what looked like roast beef sandwiches on fresh-made bread, saliva filled my mouth and my stomach roared like a jet engine. I was absolutely starving, and I loved roast beef sandwiches. Reaching out eagerly, I snatched one up then sat back on the bed, pulling a big teal and orange embroidered pillow onto my lap for modesty's sake with one hand while I crammed the sandwich into my mouth with the other.

My pants had been split all the way from the front to the back and were useless, and when Leo had stripped my shirt and bra earlier, he hadn't been gentle about it. I did indeed look well fucked, and I felt like I'd been rode hard and put away wet. My arm was starting to hurt again and I gave it a quick look, relieved to see the bandage had stayed in place during all our romping.

Wolfing down a big bite of the sandwich, savoring the spice of the horseradish, I narrowed my eyes at what looked like the setting sun outside the big windows then mumbled, "What time is it?"

"A little after seven."

"What?" I almost choked on my food and Leo quickly handed me a big glass of iced water with a straw. After gulping down a few swallows, I managed to say, "I have to go. I have to work…shit, I missed class. Fuck—fuck fuck fuck! I know it's a summer class and the professor is slack, but I never miss class. I can't afford to have my grades slip at all."

"Relax. I already called your work and spoke with Beth, letting her know you'd be out for the next week and that you had a doctor's note, which I had Dr. Gardener fax to her. I also contacted your roommate Joy, who said she'd let your professor know what happened, and emailed her a copy of the doctor's note to forward if needed. As soon as you're done, she wants you to text her so she knows you're all right."

I gaped at him. "You did what? Wait…how did you know Joy's number?"

A smile twitched his lips, but something dark and watchful moved through his eyes. "You really don't remember me at all? Not even a little bit?"

I stared at him, trying to find some point in my memory where I would have met him. "Uh—no."

"Two weeks ago I drove you home from Obsession after you had a bit too much to drink."

Blinking at him, I tried to comprehend what he was saying. "*You're* the hot guy who brought me home?"

"The hot guy?"

Not wanting to tell him how Joy had been going on and on about his fuckability, while Kayla said he looked like a Neanderthal, I shook my head. "I can't believe I don't remember you."

He smiled. "Don't worry. Joy explained that you're not much of a drinker."

"Why didn't you tell me earlier?"

Shrugging, he picked up a sandwich then sat down next to me on the bed, having changed at some point into a pair of dark jeans and a chocolate brown t-shirt. "When you obviously didn't remember me, I didn't want you to know I'd purposely showed up to your work, hoping you'd go out on a date with me. I'd hoped to talk to you and maybe that would jog your memory."

"And instead I burned you." Looking down at his hand, I frowned when I saw he had the bandage off, the skin a little pink but not as bad as it had been.

"A small price to pay for the pleasure of your company."

He looked like he really meant what he was saying, and I ate while gazing out the windows, the lights of Phoenix starting to gleam like bits of gold scattered against the darkening mountains. I wondered why he was being so nice to me and as my hunger and thirst faded, weariness tugged at me again, despite the nap I'd just taken. After setting aside my almost empty glass of water, I allowed Leo to pull me over as he scooted back, setting me between his legs with my back to his front.

At first I thought he was playing with my hair, but when the bristles of a brush dragged over my scalp, I shivered.

He was brushing my hair.

Slow, gentle, spine-tingling strokes.

I adored having my hair brushed.

My little sister had been fascinated by my hair. She'd inherited my mom's light brown, wavy hair while I'd come out with my dad's bone-straight, silky black locks. I was lucky that my hair was naturally shiny, and I didn't have to do anything other than wash and condition it with the occasional trim, even if it wouldn't hold a curl to save its life. My sister used to brush my hair, then braid it with bright ribbons as though I was her favorite doll.

Since then, the only people who had brushed my hair had been either my friends or my hair stylist. But I'd never felt this sense of sensual satisfaction and relaxation with any of them. No, when Leo brushed my hair, it was like he was stroking my entire body, the tingles cascading down my nerves from my sensitive scalp.

I was as mellow as the sunset and Leo was quiet behind me while he brushed my hair into a shiny curtain, then ran his fingers through it, slowly, over and over again with obvious pleasure while I was practically purring with happiness.

Slouched back into his solid body, I felt like some kind of decadent queen lounging on her favorite warrior while her court watched her take her pleasure.

A quiver went through my tender folds and I shifted minutely, a shiver running down my spine as something sparked through my blood, some catalyst that drew my attention from the twilight sky to Leo.

I turned around and studied him in the now dim lighting, my gaze flicking to his knife still embedded in the wall. Any normal, sane woman would have been running for the hills after his little clothes-cutting stunt—hell, she'd have been gone at the first "Daddy"—but I was twisted enough to find it hot. His brows were so heavy they almost totally shadowed his eyes, but those deep mahogany orbs somehow glittered in the meager lighting.

On my knees, I leaned closer as he sprawled out before me on the daybed. He radiated power, control, and my whole being ached with need for him. Heat prickled through my veins, spreading from my heart and into my body in a heady rush. My breathing sped up and I took my time examining the predator watching me with such interest.

For some reason, my attention focused on his hand slung over the back of the bed, the sight of him slowly rubbing his fingertips together strangely arousing.

Why did I find everything he did so exciting? It was like he was an incubus and his magical cock cast a spell over me. This wasn't me, I wasn't someone to just fall into a random, sexy-as-fuck guy's bed and attempt to fuck him to death. Or at least I tried not to be. With Leo, I never stood a chance. We'd been about as intimate as a man and woman could be, and we obviously fit like lock and key on a sexual level, but I didn't know anything about this man that had me tied up in knots.

Giving myself a mental slap, I forced my hormones into a box and said some things I should have said a long time ago, and would have if I hadn't been blindsided by his super-thick shaft.

God, he stretched me so much...it felt amazing.

My gaze wanted to take a look at his jeans to see if the monster in his pants was still asleep, but I managed only to sneak a quick peek before refocusing my attention on his face. "We need to talk."

His eyebrows rose. "It's never good when a woman says that."

Rolling my eyes, I gestured to the room. "Can we have some lights in here? And do you have a bathroom somewhere in this place?"

"Go out the way we came in, first door to your right."

The sudden, pressing needs of my bladder had me leaping out of the bed, only to yelp and grab a suede pillow to cover myself with.

Grinning, Leo tried to pull the pillow away from me. "Since I'm the one responsible for cutting and tearing your clothes off your gorgeous body, I felt it was only fair I replace them. There's a box on the table across the room, go get it."

"You—" He jerked the pillow from me, leaving me naked in this very-exposed-to-the-outside room. "Give me that back!"

"No." I tried to ignore the fact that his scolding, stern voice was hot. "You're beautiful and I love watching you, now put your hands down and stop trying to hide yourself from me. I'm a selfish man and I take great pleasure in looking at you, so you will indulge me. Jesus, your body is insane. Get dressed. You're far too distracting when you're naked to talk about anything other than my prick going down your throat."

I flushed, caught between embarrassment, anger, and glowing happiness. "Fine, but only because I'm not parading naked around your house."

"We'll see."

The amused, sexy smile he gave me as he stretched out had my hands reaching for him before I could stop myself.

Unable to resist the lure, I stroked my hands down his sides, bumping over shifting muscle and hard ribs before reaching the indent of his waist. He had trim hips and I can personally attest that his furry V and hard abs were like visual candy. Even now, clad in a brown t-shirt that fit him perfectly, I could see the divide between his large pectoral muscles, the broad sweep of his solid shoulder.

Tingles raced through me when I looked up into his face again, finding him studying me closely, as always. I must be getting used to it, because all his staring did was make me feel happy and bouncy inside.

"Do you like what you see?"

"Yes."

"So do I." He gave my butt a smack with an unrepentant grin. "Go. I have some calls I need to make while you freshen up. There's a full shower in there, but try not to get your arm wet. I'll change the dressing after you get out. Oh—and I'm clean, by the way, since we didn't use protection."

"Crap! Uh, yeah. I'm clean and on the birth control shot, so no worries about a baby."

"I'm not worried about that."

"What?"

"You keep standing there naked and I'm going to

have to fuck you again."

Flushing, I grabbed the box and strove to keep my walk slow and sedate, as if I didn't have a care in the world, when internally I was wondering if he thought my knees and elbows were knobby and how my ass managed to be both nonexistent and jiggly.

Moving in almost a daze, I went into the cool and welcoming silver and hunter green bathroom, marveling for a moment at the iridescent glass tiles that lined the shower stall. Like the rest of the house, it was perfectly in line with my tastes and I couldn't help but giggle, the sound bouncing off the high walls and ceiling. I wonder if having the exact same taste as his interior decorator counted as fate bringing us together.

While I washed myself, not the easiest thing to do with one hand, I wondered how the hell I got here. Right now I should be trying to get some sleep or getting a bit of studying in before work, not admiring the massive showerhead that was like standing beneath my own personal rainstorm. Water trickled down my face, dripped off my chin and seemed to wash away all the cares and worries I usually carried around with me like shackles. I felt remarkably free, unburdened and content to just exist in the perfect moment, instead of worrying about the past or future.

Once I got out, I took my hair down from the sloppy bun I'd put it in, surprised when it fell down my back like silk, then I remembered how Leo had brushed it and that giddy tingle went through me again. Who does that? I've never had a guy…well…groom me before. And he bought me clothes. I'd have been lucky if my last serious boyfriend bought me a Happy Meal.

Curious about what was in the box, I set it on the creamy stone counter and lifted the lid, a small gasp of surprise escaping me at the lovely dress inside.

The gorgeous maroon Emilio Pucci dress with its low, square neckline, wasn't something I'd ever buy on my own, but oh my goodness how I instantly loved the elegant cut and the rich red wine color of the fabric. It was stunning, figure-hugging to the waist and decorated with a large eyelet lace pattern on the skirt that flared out from my hips. It was also sleeveless, so it would be perfect for a hot day.

There were matching maroon ballet slippers with bits of sparkling navy glitter at the toes that added a nice pop. No bra—thank God—just pale rose silk panties. I was barely a B cup, and I could only guess that sex distracted Leo from really noting my size…even if he did spend a good deal of time touching and kissing my small mounds. In the bedroom, I've never had any complaints about my breasts, but when your best friend has large, gravity defying, and amazingly perfect double D tits, while you've got mosquito bites, it doesn't take long for cleavage envy to settle in.

Slipping the dress on, I slid my feet into the comfortable flats then did a little turn in the mirror, smiling as the skirt flared out slightly. It was sexy and short, showing a good amount of leg, but at the same time it was classy and innocent despite the deep red color.

Not that I felt the least bit innocent about the things I'd done to Leo, the things I wanted to do. I hadn't taken the time to really appreciate his ass. Seriously, it was a work of art, and I'd only groped it a bit. No doubt this was just an afternoon fling for Leo. He was rich, hot, and so intensely sexual, any women couldn't help but get a quiver in her belly when he looked at her.

Jealousy hit me hard and fast as I cursed myself for getting too attached too quick. In typical stage-five-clinger fashion, I was already picturing myself living here with Leo, waking up with him in this perfect house and just watching him sleep. Some people may find my nocturnal habits unnerving, but when I love someone, I felt so…*good* when I look at them. It lights me up inside, fills the void just a little bit. One boyfriend had caught me doing it and instead of him finding it romantic, my staring totally creeped him out.

My stomach cramped as I thought about Leo's reaction when he found out how needy I was.

Just like all the others, he'd run the other way, maybe even quicker than most.

After all, he was…astonishing, and I was me. Even playing dress up in these designer clothes, pretending I belonged in this massive home, I was still the lonely, nerdy girl I've always been. I should distance myself from him now, get ready for the inevitable rejection and play it off as no big deal when I get the "we should just be friends" speech. Or worse yet, when a guy started inching away and muttering, "Well, it's been fun. Later."

I hope Leo at least gives me a ride home.

That thought was a bit melodramatic even for me, and I gave myself a brisk mental kick, then straightened my shoulders and stood taller. No, I wasn't going to have a pity party in his lovely bathroom, with the most perfectly thick towels I had ever used, and a cool glass sculpture on the counter that I really wanted to touch. I was going to go out there, smile, thank him for a lovely time, and ask if he could call me a cab even though I couldn't afford it. That way he'd be off the hook and it would sound like I was the one making the decisions.

Pain pierced through my chest at the thought of saying goodbye and I blinked back tears, trying to get a grip on my crazy emotions.

Not giving myself time to get worked up — well, any more than I already was — I headed back to the patio room where I'd been fucked until I lost my mind. Hoping my hard nipples weren't visible through the dress, I said, "Leo, thank you so much for…"

He wasn't here.

The daybed was fixed and the remains of our meal gone, leaving the room looking like it hadn't been the sight of much debauchery.

"Leo?"

I waited a minute, hoping he would come in, but when he didn't, I looked around for my jacket and purse, wondering where they went, if I should wait for him, or if I should try to find my stuff and go.

God has given me many, many gifts. Patience is not among them, so I wandered through the big house, pausing now and again to silently admire the lush rooms. I felt like I was on the set of one of those rich and famous reality shows.

His huge pool even had a sunken seating section in the middle of it, complete with a fire pit and mood lighting.

How neat was that?

Thankfully it didn't take me long to find Leo in the kitchen, speaking on his phone in Spanish. I'd picked up a phrase or two growing up, but he was obviously fluent. His eyes tracked me the moment I entered and I gave him a little wave. He didn't wave back, but he did continue to watch me as I spotted my purse and jacket laid out on the big kitchen table. I dug through my bag until I found my phone, sighing when I saw the battery was at ten percent.

While Leo continued to talk, I responded to my messages then checked my school email for any assignment updates.

"Sorry about that," Leo said from right next to me.

I gave a little startled gasp, then shook my head. "Jeez, for someone so big, you're really quiet."

He shrugged, then gave me an appreciative look. "You're absolutely stunning."

"Thank you — I mean, thank you for the dress and everything else. You really didn't have to. I would have been okay with something from Target."

"Allow me to spoil you. It makes me happy."

"Spoiling women makes you happy?"

He shook his head. "No, spoiling *you* makes me happy."

"Why?"

"Because you deserve it."

"Oh." My phone chimed with a text from Kayla, telling me she needed me to stop by the dry cleaners for her, then to go to the drugstore for her.

I love my friend, I really do, but sometimes I feel like she thinks I'm her servant.

Frowning, I typed back a reply that I was busy and got a pleading message back, begging me to do it for her.

Kayla doesn't like to be told no. She likes it even less when being told no resulted in her having to do something she didn't want to do, which was everything. Seriously, the girl was twenty-one years old and she'd gone grocery shopping for herself, by herself, once. It was always "Hannah, can you" and "Hannah, while you're out", and stupid me, I always put up with it, afraid I'd make her mad and lose her friendship. Normally I'd cave, but there was no way in hell I was leaving Leo's side to run errands for Kayla.

I sent her a brief "no" back and got a bunch of frowny faces in return.

Great, I'd be getting the cold shoulder from her when I got home.

"When do you have class next?"

"Um—Monday."

His rough, calloused hands cupped my face and I set my phone on the table before I dropped it. "Stay with me."

"What?"

Leaning forward, he brushed his tempting lips over mine, causing a wave of heat to unfurl inside of me. "Stay with me. For the weekend."

"Seriously?" I meant for my statement to come out as incredulous, but instead it sounded hopeful.

Even though I fought it, my ultra needy side loved the idea of never leaving the man who made me feel so amazing. It was like being drugged around him, my entire being tingling at his touch, my nipples hardening with anticipation. I knew how well he could fuck me, how good it felt to have him inside of me, and like a kid who'd just had her first bite of ice cream, I wanted more.

"Yes. There is no one I'd rather spend time with than you."

Remembering all of Joy's speeches about not thinking every man I dated was the love of my life, and not grasping on to every guy who gives me any attention, I tried to pull away, but one of Leo's hands slid into the back of my hair and fisted it.

My voice came out breathy as I said, "I don't want to be an imposition."

His grip eased into a caress, and my eyes went half-lidded with pleasure as he began to run his fingers through my hair, slow and steady in a soothing rhythm. "Do you want to stay with me? Honestly."

The seductive, yet demanding tone of his voice flipped some submissive switch inside of me. "Honestly, yes."

"Then stay."

"It's not that easy. Kayla has dry cleaning," I said lamely, scrambling for an excuse.

On some level, I knew this was all happening too fast, that something was off, but the strength of Leo's personality overwhelmed me. "What does your roommate's dry cleaning have to do with us?"

"I...well...nothing?"

"That's right, nothing. I like you, Hannah, and I don't like many people in this world. I'd like to spend more time with you. You may not have enough experience to recognize it, but what we have between us…it's special, and I'd like to explore it further with you."

My inner teenage romantic just swooned, but I managed to rally my defenses and not melt into a dreamy-eyed puddle at his feet. "I like you too, but I hardly know you."

"All the more reason to stay the weekend with me. We'll get to spend time together, just us. For all I know, you could be annoying as shit, one of those girls who won't eat any bread and considers bacon a caloric sin. Or the kind of woman has more shoes than brain cells. Quick, which can you name faster, five presidents or five up-and-coming New York designers?"

Laughing, I pushed lightly at his chest. "Washington, Adams, Jefferson, Madison, and James Monroe."

The lines around his mouth creased and his eyes sparkled with laughter. "In chronological order, nice."

"Well, I did think about teaching junior high American History at one point, but then I did some student teaching at a middle school with my roommate, Joy, and we decided there is no way in hell either of us could deal with all those kids going through puberty at once. It was terrible. The girls were bitchy and the boys were trying to hump against anything that stood still long enough to grind on."

He burst out into laughter then pulled me into his arms, nuzzling his face against me, his slight scruff abrading the sensitive skin of my neck. "Stay with me."

The demanding growl of his voice sent my

hormones into a tailspin, but I managed to keep my mind out of my pants, and his, for a minute. "Okay, but I'm not committing to the whole weekend. We'll do this one day at a time. And I do need to run home and get my stuff."

"No," he said quickly then looped a possessive arm around my waist and pulled me close.

"No?"

"I have supplies on the way for you. Anything you need, I'll get for you. Our time together is precious and I don't want to waste it dealing with trivial shit."

"Supplies?" I glanced at the green numbers on the clock above the stove. "At eight at night?"

"Trust me," he purred, then leaned down so he could lick the side of my neck. "All I want to do is take care of you. You may not believe me now, but someday you'll understand just how much your life is about to change for the better."

I wanted to have faith in him, very much, but I'd been so foolish with my heart in the past I had a hard time believing this too-good-to-be-true man, in his too-good-to-be-true house, with his amazing dick and filthy mouth, wasn't some kind of illusion.

No, my entire being was burning with desire, so hyperaware that even my most vivid of dreams could never match this intensity. Everything felt like…more. More colorful, more intense, and unbelievably filled with sensations. I came to life in Leo's presence, and I wanted to savor this rush for as long as I could.

And I needed another taste of him.

Or should I say, I needed him to take another taste of me.

As I stared at his mouth, my clit began to gently pulse and I leaned forward, unusually bold with my desires. "Are you still mine to command?"

He glanced down at the gold watch on his thick wrist. "For another four hours or so."

A quiver of excitement tightened my internal muscles and I was shaking with anticipation and nerves as I gave in to my desires and said, "Then I want you down on your knees, eating my pussy, now."

Chapter 6

The width of his chest and shoulders seemed to swell, to grow wider, to thicken somehow as he loomed over me. His dick had certainly hardened again, the form of it pressing against his dark jeans, making me short of breath with desire. Maybe I should have skipped foreplay and gone right for the main course.

"Anything you want, baby girl." He licked his lips and everything inside of me buzzed with anticipation. "But at midnight, you're mine."

Sucking in a quick breath, I didn't even have time to steady myself before he sank to the floor before me, still impossibly big and dangerous. He licked down the valley between my breasts, exposed by the dress, his tongue incredibly soft and wet. My nipples were tingling and my body grew slick with want. Unable to resist, I gathered his hair into my hands and gently pulled on it, his soft and light kisses over the swell of my breast relaxing me further. While the wild and rough sex I'd experienced with him was wonderful, there was something to be said for the almost worshipful way he was touching me. Every once in a while, he'd pull back and just look at me like he couldn't really believe I was here.

I lost sight of him after he winked then threw the skirt of my dress over his head. Reaching back, I braced myself on the black slate countertop and widened my stance at his urging. I didn't know what to do with myself while he kissed my panty-covered mound, didn't know where to look or how to focus on anything other than Leo. He was a hurricane and I was the sparrow in the storm, singing my heart out but totally eclipsed by his roaring presence. Yet his hands were incredibly tender as they peeled my panties down, and the delicate swipe of his tongue parting my slit had me offering myself to him.

His pleased murmur made me smile and I closed my eyes, reveling in the feeling of his tongue tracing between the folds of my inner and outer lips, clenching internally when he bit one swollen labia hard enough to sting. Right away he sucked that tender flesh into his mouth and soothed the pain, turning it into pleasure as he slowly inserted first one, then two fingers inside of me, stroking me with slow, easy, devastating pumps that tightened my sex and made me gasp.

"That's it, baby girl," Leo said from beneath my dress, "rub that sweet cunt on my mouth."

I almost lost my balance but he braced me with one of his hands behind my ass while he continued to finger fuck me with the other. My clit twitched against his lips as the way he said "baby girl" rolled through my mind, turning me on by its taboo nature. The thrill of doing the forbidden, of being dirty, had always been my secret vice. Well, maybe not so secret. My eBook collection was full of stepbrothers, forbidden office affairs, and taboo couples like priests and nuns. So being Daddy's baby girl fell right into what turned me on.

In a mindless state of arousal now, I moaned and

did as he asked, my hips moving against his lips while he stuck his tongue out and let me rub my clit against it. "Thank you, Daddy, it feels so good."

He growled against my pussy and the vibration had me going up on my toes. With ruthless efficiency, he sucked on my clit and I realized he'd been playing with me, stretching this out, because he could make me come in less than ten seconds if he put his mind to it. Tremors shook my legs and he guided me down to the floor so I was on my back, Leo eating my orgasm the whole damn time.

If I hadn't been coming my brains out on his greedy tongue, I would have been impressed by his coordinated movements. As it was, all I could do was tell him over and over again in a weak voice how good he was, how hard I came, and how much I loved his tongue, his cock, his fingers, and just about every other body part of his that brought me pleasure.

When he finally raised his head from beneath my skirt, I was puzzled by the fact that he didn't look at me. No, he stared over my head with an arrogant smirk as he stood while helping me to my wobbly feet. I was dizzy for a moment, swaying before he steadied me, his gaze still trained behind my back.

When I turned around to try to figure out what he was looking at, I screamed and darted behind him, humiliation filling me as three men dressed in black suits stared back at me.

Awesome, three strangers had just watched me climax, then babble about how wonderful Leo's thick fingers were, how much I loved them stuffed inside of me.

They were all Hispanic, with lovely dark skin and

thick black hair that they both spiked on top. They stared back at me with impassive expressions, as if finding Leo eating out a girl in his kitchen was the norm. Leo growled next to me and suddenly of the guys looked over my shoulder, obviously pretending I didn't exist.

The third man who continued to watch me, despite Leo's territorial growl, was a very handsome, but intimidating dark-haired man in his early thirties, with skin the warm tone of lightly creamed coffee. Like Leo, he had longer hair than was currently in fashion, but his was slicked back and tied in a low ponytail that somehow managed to look sexy instead of sleazy. He was wearing a nice suit and grinning hard enough that a dimple appeared in his tanned cheek. There was something about him, maybe the hint of a tattoo that I saw peeking up around the collar of his white dress shirt, that reminded me of the boxers I would see through the window of the gym near my apartment, muscled but compact, all power and speed instead of brute strength like the two behemoths behind him.

To complete my humiliation, Leo sucked the fingers he'd had inside of me into his mouth, licking them clean with obvious relish before growling out, "What do you want?"

The dimpled man cleared his throat. "I brought the items you requested. When Judith told me what you needed, I had to come see for myself the only woman allowed to call you by your first name."

"What?" I stared up at Leo. "What's he talking about?"

"Get out," Leo growled, ice coating his gaze and

making my belly cramp with a rush of fear. "Now."

Holding up his hands, the cocky man stared back at Leo, the smile falling from his face as if it had never been there, leaving behind a really scary guy. His hazel-green eyes were dead, cold—kind of like Leo's right now. But something about him let me know he was afraid of the man holding me to his side. I hate to admit it, but I liked that people were afraid of Leo, and that I was safe with him in a way they never could be. I'm not sure how I knew this, I just did, as well as I knew Leo was getting more and more pissed with each passing second. Being hyperaware of others' emotional states means I can sense someone's growing anger when normal people still can't detect it.

The strangers facing us were close to the edge of violence and I needed to diffuse the situation. The rising tension scared me enough that I managed to shrug off my embarrassment and force a smile. While they'd heard plenty, they didn't get to see more than my skirt moving around as Leo practically licked me into a coma of pleasure.

I could pretend nothing was wrong and be an adult about the situation. "Hi, my name's Hannah Barnes, nice to meet you."

Chapter 7

Leo

There are a few men in this world I consider true friends. Ramón was one of them. Lucky for him, because the appreciative look he was giving Hannah would have gotten him killed otherwise. And only after a good deal of pain and torture, but I couldn't blame him.

Hannah was a striking young woman who radiated life and innocence in a way that made me want to shelter her, protect her fragile beauty. She was an irresistible temptation to men such as me and Ramón. Especially when she was so pretty after she came. A high blush colored her cheeks, and her breath still panted out a little bit fast. The dress set off her elegant body beautifully, and she somehow managed to exude class in what was no doubt an uncomfortable situation for her. But I knew what a dirty girl she was beneath the thin veneer of civilization.

Plus, the room reeked of the musk from her dripping cunt. These men could taste it with their every breath, and I knew her slit was as delicious as it smelled. The guard standing to Ramón's right took a slow, deep breath in through his mouth and I tried to keep from growling.

Some may think that by allowing Ramón and his men hear and watch her climax, I was sharing them with her, but it couldn't be further from the truth. That sexual act was my public stamp on her with these men, a branding that could not be mistaken for anything else. I know Judith, and I know she'll be tempted to see if Ramón can sway Hannah's affections for me. He can be very charming when he wants to be, but I don't think Judith counted on how much he'd changed over the past year.

Gone was the playboy known for breaking women's hearts right and left, and in his place stood a cold man who looked at most females with contempt.

I couldn't imagine the kind of woman it was going to take to break through his defenses, and wondered if he already had a girl in mind.

That is, if this worked.

I could feel Hannah getting ready to bolt, but Ramón still had a way with women, because the warm smile he gave her made Hannah hesitate. "It's nice to meet you. Forgive the interruption, but I have some pressing business with Leo that can't wait."

Fuck business. I didn't want to let her go, craved her touch, but Ramón wouldn't have come here without a good reason. I'd hoped to have at least a few days with her, uninterrupted, so I could imprint myself on her the way she'd imprinted herself on me. I was her slave, plain and simple, would do anything for her, and I worried about her learning just how obsessed I was with her. Even now I could scarcely believe I was touching her, that she curved herself into my side, trusted me to support her light weight.

Sure enough, Hannah tried to pull away. "Of course. I can just get my things—"

"No," I said, maybe a bit too harshly. "Please, this

won't take long. Stay."

Her soft caramel-brown eyes looked up at me and I could easily read her lingering embarrassment. The vulnerability in her gaze, how she seemed honestly worried that I didn't want her here, all tugged at the pit of my stomach, making me feel unfamiliar but pleasant things. Her pink, swollen lips pulled into a delicious pout, only increasing her air of sultry innocence.

"Are you sure? I don't want to be an imposition."

"It won't take long," Ramón said in a gentle, almost coaxing purr that raised my hackles. "Please, don't leave on our account. I know Leo would be pissed if I scared you away, so spare me the ass-kicking, if you would."

Hannah's chiming giggle drew everyone's attention as she smiled at Ramón, then up at me, her dark eyes flashing with sweet humor. "Well, I wouldn't want that on my conscience."

The playful light in her doe-eyed gaze drew me in and I spiraled out of the cold darkness that was my normal state of mind, straining for the warmth of her affection. She softened me, made me weak, and I could not be weak in front of anyone but her. Conscious of the way we were being watched, I took her hand in my own and inwardly groaned at her shy smile. The way she tilted her head just so, the lace of her dark lashes framing her eyes, had my cock jerking.

"Come on, you can hang out in the media room while I do business."

"Media room? Fancy schmancy."

I could see Ramón watching us with fascination as

she teased me. Normally I treated the women I fucked like toys, because that is what they were and that was their kink. It was a mutually beneficial relationship in which we both got off without having to deal with any bullshit. The women I kept were certainly never allowed to speak to me like an equal, and always called me Mr. Brass, but Hannah could not only say my first name, hell, she could call me anything she wanted. Every time she breathed out "Daddy" in her husky-sweet whisper, she wrapped me tighter around her little finger.

My hand drifted down to the small implant in her hip that had begun to slowly distribute a low dose of D128 into her bloodstream, keeping her arousal simmering close to the surface. Not enough to have her trying to mount every man within reach, but enough to draw her out past the painful rules of her personal demons. I've found that once a woman reaches a certain level of arousal, once I get her in the right headspace, the world disappears and I'm the center of her entire universe. Except with Hannah, she was the center of mine.

Stepping closer to her, I noted the way her hard nipples pressed against the fabric of her dress, rounded like gumdrops. They would be tender and soft at first beneath my lips, but after a few nips and tugs, they'd crinkle nicely and jut upwards. Long nipples like hers would look lovely in a pair of nice, tight clamps.

I wouldn't be surprised if she masturbated while I was gone. She'd eventually be weaned down to a lower dose of D128, then off all the way once her mind was fully conditioned to crave me. In theory, her body would desire only me after a few days, but I wanted all the time I could to seduce her into loving me. I was going to spend a lifetime fucking this woman, planting my seed in her, and watching her raise our children with the kindness and tenderness I worry that I'm incapable of. In choosing Hannah as my wife, I was guaranteeing my future offspring a childhood as good as mine was, but with enough money to be able to give my family the best of everything.

But first I had to deal with Ramón's bullshit.

Grasping her small hand in my own, I led her away from the men watching her with open interest and deeper into what would soon be our home. Like the sun room, the media room was big and built exactly to Hannah's taste. I'd scoured her social media for postings about things she liked, and had given them to my interior designer, who translated Hannah's contemporary, yet comfortable, dreams into reality. It was amazing what you could learn about someone now just from looking at the information they willingly shared with the world. The insights had allowed me to build her fantasy home, a glittering trap designed to make her want to live here, to stay with me. I wanted to enmesh her in my life so tightly she couldn't escape, wouldn't want to.

I would never give her up, and the fact that I had potentially brainwashed her into being loyal to me didn't bother me in the least.

She gave a squeal of delight then pointed at an enormous black suede beanbag that was as big as a sofa. "Oh my God! I've wanted one of those forever."

Laughing, she tore herself from my side and ran

across the room, kicking off her shoes before launching herself into the beanbag, her giggles sparking over my skin as she snuggled into the plush, dark surface.

"You approve?"

She squirmed around, giving me a glimpse of her pink pussy, which made my cock ache to slip between her still wet folds. I was addicted to her cunt, couldn't wait to sink my tongue into it again as she fed me her orgasms. Or slide into that tight heat and just stay there, biting her nipples and tickling her so her sex would clench and release around my dick. I'd show her how I could make her climax without moving my cock at all, just bring her to a pulsing orgasm over and over again until she wrung the come out of me.

"I totally approve."

Grabbing the remote from the table, I turned on the wall-sized television, smiling as she gasped.

"Whoa."

"Watch whatever you want. There's a refrigerator beneath the counter, help yourself to anything you find; my maid stocks it so I have no idea what's in there. I won't be long."

"Wait!" She struggled to get out of the chair that seemed to have her sucked her in. "Help me."

I grasped her slender hand and hauled her out, surprised when she laced her arms around my neck and pulled me down for a kiss. Every damn time she willingly touched me, I felt like I scored a major victory in battle and I reveled in both my satisfaction and her little moans of arousal. The way she sucked my tongue into her mouth had my cock pressing against my pants hard enough that I had to readjust myself before my dick bent in half.

Grasping her hand, I rubbed it over the bulge, trying to soothe the ache. "Feel what you do to me?"

"Mmmm, sure we don't have time for a quickie?"

"Perfect," I whispered against her mouth, tempted beyond reason. "I won't be long, I promise."

"Fine." She pouted, then smacked my hand away with a laugh as I grabbed her ass. "Go so you can come back."

A playful impulse, something I almost never had, made me pick her up and toss her gently back into the beanbag just to hear her laughter. After not giving a shit about anyone but myself for so long, it felt odd to care so much about another human being. But she was exceptional in every way.

Already regretting my decision to talk with Ramón, I strode through my house then into my dimly lit tan and burgundy office before slamming the heavy door behind me. "What's going on?"

"I thought you might be interested to know that my mother had the dose of D128 Hannah's getting upped."

I froze, only my deeply ingrained loyalty to the cartel keeping me from hunting Judith down and wringing her neck.

She'd argued that I wasn't giving Hannah enough, that I needed more in order for her to be in the right headspace, but a stronger dose meant danger for Hannah. The more D128 that was in a woman's system, the more they smelled like they were fertile to men, even if they were on birth control to prevent ovulation, like the shot Hannah was on. It was an odd side effect, but in test after test, we'd found these women instantly became more desirable to the straight males around them. Gay women didn't seem to pick up on it as much, but for men, it triggered the need to find that fertile female and breed her.

Maybe Judith hadn't upped the dose by a lot. Maybe she'd used restraint. Maybe she'd pick the innocence of a young girl, a stranger, over her children's future happiness.

Yeah, right.

"How bad is it? When could you smell her?"

"We were a room or two away." He frowned. "She's an adorable little thing, but not my type. You know I like my women extra curvy, and Hannah has the body of a ballerina. That said, up close, after you finished making her speak in tongues, the smell of her pussy still made me want her. Bad…like enough to consider whether I could lure her away from you. Just like my mother wanted, and I protested against. I told her to back off and let you do your work, but you know she's going to try to meddle. Not just because of the experiment, but because she honestly thinks Hannah would be a good mother—which in Judith's mind, means a good addition to the family. I'll hold her off as long as I can, see if she'll allow me to observe Hannah for now, and buy you some time before she starts pushing for results."

Our jaws tightened in unison and it took a great deal of restraint to keep from trashing my office. Hannah might want to see it, and I'd rather not explain why the bookcases were torn from the walls. I don't think she'd buy the excuse of a localized earthquake.

"Someday, Ramón, she's going to go too far and

someone is going to kill her."

"I told her that ten years ago, and yet here she still lives and breathes, energetic enough to still fuck with our lives."

"Do you think I can remove the implant without messing Hannah up?"

Steepling his fingers, he stared off into the distance while shaking his head. "No, no—you need to leave it. Mom's already proven how far she'll go to make sure this experiment is a success. You'd be better off working *with* her, rather than against her. That doesn't mean I won't tell her that her move was complete bullshit, but I wouldn't mess with it. The dose won't harm Hannah, but it does make her smell good enough that she'll be fending off more attention than usual."

"Which means I'll be killing stupid-ass college boys when she goes to class."

A ghost of a smile hovered over Ramón's lips. "There is that. How is it going?"

He tried to keep the desperation out of his voice, but I heard it. "It's too soon to tell, but I will say this—she is completely into my particular brand of sex."

Arching a brow, Ramón almost smiled again. "Really? I thought she'd be a lights-off, missionary girl. You gotta admit, she lives a very…safe life. Not the kind of woman to seek out excitement or be comfortable with a Daddy."

While I'd been watching Hannah, I'd requested that everyone else back off and leave her alone. Judith wanted men watching her, claiming she would be safer with more protection, and I'd compromised by having Judith's men watch Hannah from an apartment across the street from hers. That was close enough to keep her safe, but not close enough to invade her privacy. Yeah, I was a stalker, but that didn't mean I wanted anyone else coveting the treasure that was my baby girl.

"Once again, this just proves you don't know shit about women. Hannah had a fascination with Dominance and submission long before I came into the picture. Her porn of choice is usually rough, and she enjoys being taken care of...probably why she gets along so well with Joy."

At the mention of Hannah's busty blonde roommate, Ramón's gaze flared, but he didn't say anything.

"The hypnosis I did on her never would have worked if the desire wasn't already there. I can't make her be something she's not, but I can program her body to respond positively to Daddy play, and other things. So don't expect to just grab a random woman off the street and tell her you're going to be her Master and she's going to be your sub."

Ramón merely raised a brow and regarded me with a blank look, like I didn't know all about his taste for bratty submissives. "My dad wants to have Hannah over for dinner next weekend."

Shit, I knew this was coming. They all had so much riding on my success, but I needed more time to get her used to me, to the idea of us, before I sprang the Cordova cartel on her. "She's not ready."

"Is it working? Your plan? Is it making her fall in love with you?"

The leather chair beneath me creaked as I leaned

back in it and held my bored expression firmly in place, when I really wanted to throttle him for making me repeat what I've told him over and over again. "For the last time, neither D128 nor the truth serum cannot be used to make someone love you. It can only addict her body to mine and allow her to push past the boundaries of what society thinks is right and wrong. Any affection, any love she feels for me, has to be earned."

"I know that," he smirked. "I just like to get you riled up."

Staring at him, I wondered how upset Hannah would be if I came back to her with bloody knuckles. "Don't you have somewhere to be?"

Ramón grimaced and looked down at his nails. "No. Since I've given up pussy until the perfect pussy comes along, I've found I have a lot of free time on my hands. It's given me a chance to reevaluate things…and one of the problems I have with my mother's brilliant idea to ensure loyalty is that it could take away a woman's free will. I absolutely do not want that. Am I clear?"

"If—*if*—this works, it may not work with every woman. Hannah happens to be one of those people that's very susceptible to suggestion, others are more resistant. And you won't be able to claim the woman you choose, not until you've done enough reconnaissance on her to know, truly know, her likes and dislikes, who she is as a person, what she needs to be happy. If I don't style the suggestions exactly right, her brain will reject them, no matter how many drugs we pump into her."

Giving me a frown, Ramón adjusted himself.

"Fuck, I think my dick'll fall off by then."

I couldn't help rubbing Hannah in his face, remembering all the times he teased me for my obsession with her, for giving up any woman until I could have Hannah coming beneath me.

"It will be worth it in the end—and you'll know you have the right woman if you're not being led by your dick."

"Yeah, I suppose you're right. Look, just come to dinner in a few weeks. I promise I'll make sure Hannah has fun, and everyone will behave. They're genuinely curious about her, not just because of what she represents for the future of the cartel, but because they want to get to know the woman that won your heart. In their own fucked-up way, my parents want to see you happy."

A heavy sigh escaped me as I gave in to the inevitable. "Can you promise me Judith will behave?"

Rubbing the back of his neck, he gave me a wry grin. "Miracles can happen."

I sighed again and stretched my arms high above my head as my upper back cracked. "Next week is still too soon. Tell your father I'll see him in two, maybe three weeks. Give him the excuse that Hannah has finals and I want to wait until they're over before I start to show her our world. She's worked hard at school, and I'm not going to fuck that up for her."

"You really care about her, don't you?"

"I do, very, very much. Judith needs to understand that, and back off. This isn't a science experiment, this is my life, and if I'm made to feel like I'm living in a lab, I won't like it."

Nodding, Ramón's gaze shifted to the bookshelves

around me. "Never pictured a house like this for you, but I like it. Feels more like a home than your place in the city. Hannah like it?"

"She does."

"I'm going to apologize in advance if I'm weird around her. After watching the living room camera at her apartment so much, I feel like I know those girls."

Tensing, an unexpected jealousy burned through me. "I didn't know you were keeping such a close eye on them."

"Easy, *mi amigo*. It wasn't your woman I've been watching."

I hoped he meant Joy, but decided to fuck with him a little. "Please tell me it isn't Kayla."

"That cokehead cunt? No, not her."

"Ahhh, Joy then. She's very beautiful, very loving, and a good friend to Hannah."

A hint of red tinted his cheeks and I swore he was blushing. "Indeed. And kind, smart, funny—and feisty."

"But also very independent."

"She is, but much like Hannah used to, Joy picks weak men who need to be fixed in some way. I believe her maternal instincts are stronger than she wishes to admit, that taking care of people, nurturing them, is what makes her happy. And I know she wants children of her own."

"How so?"

"I've seen her looking at baby sites and browsing baby names. She looks very wistful while she does it. Her sister has recently had a daughter out in Oregon and Joy misses her terribly." His fond look dimmed. "I keep waiting to find something wrong with her, but she's so freakishly...*good.*"

"You like her."

"No, but I want to. I can't give myself permission to feel anything for her other than friendship until I know for sure she won't betray me, that she wants a strong family-centered life as much as I do. That she'll not only indulge my desire to have her be my submissive, but will find immense pleasure while wearing my collar. I'm a good Master, I know how to please my subs, and I can't imagine a life where I have to hide my desires from a wife who isn't into the same things I am." A scowl twisted his full lips. "I'll end up like my uncle Ed, married to a bitch who won't spread her legs without the lights being off and fuckin' church music playing."

I couldn't help but laugh because what he said wasn't a lie. "True, but I don't think you'd have to worry about that with Joy."

"No, I wouldn't. She's like a sexual nuclear bomb waiting to be set off. The lovers she brings home don't satisfy her. She always ends up masturbating after they leave, and it's a crying shame, because she comes like a porn star. All quivering tits and aching moans." Some of the Ramón I used to know surfaced from beneath his grief, a flash of the prankster who loved to make people smile. "You should see her nipples, *mi amigo*, the areolas are big and dark, like half-dollar-sized chocolate drops."

I cleared my throat and leaned forward. "As far as I know, I don't have any cameras in Joy's room."

Ramón grinned with more mischief than I'd seen in his eyes in a long time. "No, but I do."

For one brief moment his entire demeanor softened

in a way I hadn't seen before, and I knew Ramón liked Joy more than he was willing to admit to even himself.

Interesting. I'd thought for sure he would have gone for a more passive woman; even I could see that taming Joy would be a challenge and a half. This would change my plans a little bit, I couldn't use Joy to blackmail Hannah in the future if I needed to, but I knew it would be much easier to keep Hannah in my life if Joy happened to be married to one of my friends. I wasn't sure if Joy's sassy nature would bend to Ramón's iron will, but if Ramón had been watching her, then he knew what he was getting himself into.

Or at least he thought he did.

"I met her before," he blurted out in an uncharacteristic display of nerves. "Six months ago. Total coincidence. I mean, I didn't even recognize her at first. She was pissed. At home, she's always happy and smiling, plus I was used to looking at her from the angle of the cameras in the corners of the rooms. She looks different in real life. Shorter."

"You still haven't told me how the hell you met Joy."

"Remember when my cousin Jonas was being a dumbass and partying at college instead of studying, pissing away his chances of a good future?"

I nodded without comment. Of course I did, I was the one Judith and her sister Doris had sent to scare the fuck out of Jonas and rough him up a little, letting him know his mother and aunt did not appreciate him screwing up his chances of becoming a lawyer or doctor. He'd been spending most of his time with a particular girl, so I used her as leverage against him as well, and he'd quickly become a straight-A student.

"Well, we were only tipped off about his fucking up by his tutor. She drove all the way from Tempe to Sedona to visit my Aunt Doris, so she could inform her that if Jonas didn't show up for his next tutoring session for the class he was failing, she was going to report him to her counselor. Evidently, she only got paid if he showed up, and she was tired of his empty promises. She yelled all of this at *me*, of course, because I was the one unlucky enough to happen to have been visiting, and opened the door for her." A faint smile curved his lips. "We didn't exactly hit it off, but Aunt Doris thought watching a little sexy-as-hell blonde *chica* mouth off to me was hilarious, right up until the point in Joy's rant about Jonas failing his classes."

"I bet. Why didn't you tell me earlier that you knew her?"

"Because I *don't* know her. I only saw her that once, and right after I had to head down to San Salvador to meet with our distributors and make some heads roll."

He meant that, literally — Ramón enjoyed beheading his enemies — and I smirked. "I could see how that might distract you."

"Yeah." He rubbed his hands over his face. "But I thought about her...Joy. A lot. She became the star of my wet dreams, but I never did anything about it. After dealing with the human filth who thought they could steal from the Cordova cartel, I felt like a bastard for even considering tainting her with our messed-up reality."

I shrugged. "Hannah's better off with me than without. It's a cold, dark world out there that loves to try to snuff out bright lights like my girl."

He nodded, understanding all too well what I was telling him. "Then I wish you luck. I'll let my father know and stall him as long as possible, but you'll have to bring her over sooner than later. Will she be weaned off the D128 in a couple weeks?"

"It might be closer to a month before it's entirely gone."

"Closer to a month, got it. Last thing I want is Hannah trying to ride your dick at the dinner table."

"Remind your mother that it's her fault she can't meet Hannah earlier because she decided to up the dose behind my back."

"You say that like she'll care."

"Good point." Eager to get back to my woman, I stood and Ramón followed suit. "On that note, it's time for you to get the fuck out."

"You sure you don't want me to stay and have a drink? Maybe play a game of cards with you and Hannah?"

"Out."

I didn't bother to see him to the front door, instead going the opposite direction and all but running to the media room.

Chapter 8

My throbbing shaft was already rock hard and I had to take a moment to grip myself and calm the fuck down. I'd hurt her if I went after her like an eager bull, damage her small body. The only pain I wanted to cause her was intentional, not accidental, and never anything that she didn't enjoy.

When I walked into the room, I found her still in the beanbag chair, with her legs spread wide, her head thrown back, and her breath coming in harsh pants.

Jesus fucking Christ.

The scent of her pheromone-heavy arousal drenched the air, a biological byproduct of the D128. As her desire increased, so did her body's need to mate, and like any healthy female animal, she gave off subtle signals to the male of her species that she badly needed cock inside of her. Any man within a hundred feet of Hannah would be unable to stop his instinctive response, and I sucked in a deeper breath, the savage urge to breed her making me crazy with lust. Her fingers were so pale and slender as they plunged into her deep reddish-pink, swollen folds. Arousal glistened between her legs and even from here, the sound of her slick pussy teased me.

I fisted my cock, squeezing it hard as a spurt of precum tingled up from my tight balls.

A quick glance at the time showed I had one more

hour until I could take charge, so that meant I couldn't indulge in my first impulse to fuck her.

This was still her show, and I needed to push her into taking what she wanted because when I took over, when Daddy really came home to play with his princess, there would be no mercy.

"Baby girl."

To my surprise, she began to orgasm, her hips snapping as her hand worked busily beneath the short maroon skirt of her dress.

"Oh, Daddy," she moaned, and I just about filled my pants with cum, again.

I stood frozen while her body twitched and undulated, her face tightening as if in pain, then relaxing into the sweetest smile I've ever seen.

Once she was breathing somewhat regularly again, I said, "Hannah, you have less than an hour left of being in charge. If you have any fantasies you want to explore, you need to fulfill them now."

Lazily, she opened her eyes, one hand still stroking, the fabric of her dress moving with her panting breaths. "Get naked."

I did as she asked with a smile, loving the way she visually devoured me, her hand moving faster, her lips parting as she stared at me like I was a god. Clad only in my white boxer briefs, I strode over and stood before her, confident in both my body and my cock. When she struggled to sit up in the beanbag, I once again hauled her out, smiling when she jumped up so her legs were wrapped around my hips. The rounded curves of her ass filled my hands as I supported her, watching her react to me. Reaching between us, she arranged my dick so it stuck straight up past the waistband, the sensitive head of my shaft rubbing against her smooth belly.

"I want to try something," she whispered as she looked down at my chest, her voice hesitant even as her pussy ground against my cock.

"Anything."

"Take me to a bathtub, please."

Curious, I did as she asked, carrying her the length of the house to the master bedroom. She was too busy sucking on my neck, and getting herself off, to notice the enormous four-poster bed, or the delicate white furniture, or even the framed original prints of an artist she adores. It was a built and decorated just for my girl, and I hoped she enjoyed it, but right now I needed to be inside of her with a fever that set fire to my blood, making me fight to keep from just finding any hard surface to fuck her against, now.

Christ, her pussy smelled incredible. Distilled sex. I needed to lick that sweet cunt clean at some point, after I dirtied her up.

Hannah let out a little huff of warm air against my bare chest when I set her down in the master bathroom. Orange, red, and gold-shot solid marble slabs made up the walls of the big rectangular room, the smoked glass skylights above slices of darkness against the cream stucco ceiling and dark exposed wood beams. The recessed lighting brought out the glass mosaic floor that looked like a carpet of fall leaves, and the bathtub was big enough for five people, though I never intend on having anyone but myself and Hannah in it.

There were four faucets to fill up the tub quickly and I turned them all on, the rush of water filling the air around us with quiet thunder.

Turning, I took a moment to admire her delicate beauty before I rubbed my hands over her shoulders, the skin so incredibly soft. "May I undress you?"

"Please."

She basked in my attention as I carefully stripped her down, pausing to kiss the indent of her hipbone, to tease her ribs with light flicks of my tongue.

When I reached her navel, she pushed me back then crossed her arms, hiding her elongated, raspberry-pink nipples from my eager view. "In the tub."

Counting down the minutes until her time in control was over, I sank into the warm water with a sigh. Baths weren't something I normally did, I didn't have the time or the patience for them, but with Hannah in my life now, I'd be indulging in all kinds of new things simply so I could experience them with her. She'd always wanted to go skiing, and I already had a chalet in Aspen reserved for two weeks in December, where I planned on taking her for Christmas. I know she normally went home with either Kayla or Joy for the holidays because her parents were self-centered pieces of shit, but this year she'd have me, and everything would be different.

The burn on my hand stung slightly as it hit the hot water, but I ignored it in favor of the arousing sight before me. The only thing I could focus on as I leaned back against the padded ledge of the tub was the gentle grace of Hannah's body as she climbed in with me, sliding down between my legs until her front was hidden by the water and her head just above the surface. The look she gave me was shy and hesitant, but her small hand gripping my cock beneath the water wasn't.

"I can do whatever I want?"

"Anything."

"I can touch you, uh…anywhere? Like, even in places good girls aren't supposed to want to touch? Naughty places?" Her exaggerated sweet pout was positively sinful as she sat before me, wreathed in fragrant steam.

It took me a moment to puzzle out her meaning, but her hand on my cock drifted down, skimming over, then under my balls to stroke over my perineum. When she pressed her finger against my rear entrance, unknowingly teasing me, I had to grit my teeth and force back a grunt. The expression on her face got me off as much as her touch, a heady blend of surprise, nervousness, arousal, and the beginnings of a wicked smile. My baby was feeling powerful, and I loved watching her realize she really could do anything she wanted.

Like play with my ass.

I've had women do all kinds of things with my ass before, nothing is off the table when it came to fucking, and I enjoyed it, but the thought of Hannah doing something she obviously found so taboo made my balls draw up tight. The shy, hesitant manner in which she asked me, combined with her big doe eyes, screamed innocence, and I wanted to both rip it out of her and protect it with my last breath.

In response to her question, I spread my legs farther, inviting her to explore as she wished.

"Anywhere."

"Will you like it?"

"I like anything you do to me, sweetheart."

She blushed and returned her hand to my cock, where she traced the veins with her fingertips. "I don't really know what I'm doing. Can you teach me?"

Fuck yeah, I could teach her. I planned on training her to know just how I liked it, how to service me perfectly, and how to take the most enjoyment from every delicious torment I rained down on her. The mere thought of having her dress up like a naughty school girl while I taught her various lessons had my voice coming out in a low growl. "Do you know what a prostate is, Hannah?"

Her head ducked down with her cheeks bright red as she tried to hide from me, her hand tense and not moving on my erection. "Kinda, but not really."

"There's a spot inside my ass that, if you stroke it, will make me seep precum uncontrollably. It feels intensely good, like a G-spot orgasm for women. Have you had one of those?"

"I don't think so?"

Amused, I shook my head, then smoothed her hair back. "You'd know."

"Teach me, tell me what to do."

"I'll show you how, but in exchange, I get to do the same to you."

"Uh—I don't have a prostate."

"No, but you do have a sweet little asshole that I want inside of."

I couldn't hold back a laugh as she shifted away from me. "No way, your dick is too thick, I can barely fit you in my pussy."

"We'll see. You have ten minutes left until it's my

turn to play, Hannah. Use them wisely. And, if you're going to play with my ass, we'll need lube."

"Well, since I brought you into the tub to get you clean first, I thought I might…ummm…" Her cheeks flushed an even deeper pink and she was so sexy, yet adorable, I fell even deeper under her spell. "Well, I thought that since you're clean, I might lube you up with my mouth."

Fuck…just…fuck. The mental image of Hannah putting her little pink tongue up my ass just about had my dick leaking again. I'd teach her how to drive me crazy and return the favor. Soon. I just had to play her game a little longer and behave myself.

In an effort to get ahold of myself before I pounced on her, I nodded. "That would work, but for deep penetration, you really want a good, high-quality lube if you want your partner to enjoy it."

"Of course I want you to enjoy it. You would, wouldn't you?"

"I told you, baby girl, anyway you touch me is just right. You're perfect."

"Really?"

God, she was so fragile, so afraid to believe in herself. "Yes, really. Now, tick-tock, baby girl, your time is running out."

Giving herself a little shake, which I found cute as hell, her shoulders went up and she focused on me, the tears that had momentarily threatened never managing to fall. "Okay, lube."

The serious, intense expression pursing her lips had me biting back the urge to laugh. "In the bedroom, top drawer of the bureau next to the window."

"Right. Come on."

She dragged me out of the water then toweled me off with record speed, pausing only to lick some water from my nipple. The suction of her pretty little mouth drove me crazy and I needed to fuck her, but I had eight minutes until I took over. Eight minutes to try to hold back my orgasm as she explored my body. It would be a miracle if I didn't spray all over her face and firm little tits.

The sexy lilt to her voice undid me as she whispered, "On your back, please."

I did as she asked, my muscles beginning to coil with anticipation of taking over, of fucking her the way I really wanted. She'd be lucky if she could walk without wincing tomorrow and I knew I had to reign back my inner beast with Hannah, but being around her brought that savage part of my personality to the surface, a part of me that usually only took control when it was time to kill. The colors of the world sharpened, my senses expanded, and as Hannah squirted a generous amount of lube on her fingers from the new bottle, I relaxed as much as I could.

"Play with the outer muscles first," I instructed. "Tease me, build up anticipation. If I had my way, I'd just fuck you until you were raw and not spend a minute outside your silky-smooth cunt, but both of our orgasms will be so much better if we draw them out a little, have some fun with edging."

"Edging?"

"Riding the edge of orgasm, making me almost climax then pulling back before I can bust a nut."

"That doesn't sound very fun."

"Oh, baby girl, pain and tension can bring you so

much pleasure. I'm gonna fuck you hard, play with you harder, and I promise you that at some point tonight, when you finally come all over my cock, you'll be crying, overwhelmed, and shaken—but not broken. I never want to break you, only protect you, to make you mine. My perfect, sweet, dirty girl."

She let out a shaky breath and I studied her closely, reading her yearning and fear, an erotic combination that called to me. Fuck, she was made for me. I don't give a shit what anyone said; this woman had been put on this earth to service my cock.

The seconds ticked by in my head and I had to hold back a smile as she sat there, wasting her time while staring at me. Someday, when I gave her the treat of being in control again, she'd know me well enough to take advantage of every moment.

I couldn't wait to start training her.

"Get on your hands and knees," she murmured. "Please."

That sweet "please" at the end killed me, and I quickly moved to do as she asked, enjoying the way her breathing sped when I was on my hands and knees. Her hand that didn't have lube on it stroked over my ass and I arched into her touch, loving the feel of her. The responding sound of pleasure that she made had me hoping my triggers had worked, that my pleasure was calling forth a responding surge of desire from her body.

When she leaned forward and began to caress my balls, while gently biting my butt, I wasn't sure if I was going to last long enough to hold true to my promise and not spurt all over the sheets as she literally bit the cum right out of me. Fuck, this was

Hannah, *my* Hannah, purring as she began to lick the crack of my ass while continuing to inspect my balls, weighing them in her small hand and stroking me until sweat beaded on my brow.

Shit, no torture in the world compared to the sensation of her hair brushing over my legs, her hand now fisting my cock and pulling it like she was milking me. My rough grunts seemed to echo off the walls like the growls of a beast, and those grunts became snarls as she stroked her finger against the puckered entrance to my body, then pressed in, just enough to breech the ring of muscles and send an electrical jolt of pure erotic bliss through me. While Hannah might claim to have no idea what to do with a man's ass, I knew she'd watched a great deal of porn involving women playing with a man's prostate, milking him, and she worked me like a pro. That slender finger sliding in and out, stretching the tight muscle, rubbing against my prostate and making erotic fire burn through me.

So fucking good, too damn good…I was gonna come.

Luckily I only had ten seconds left before I could flip the tables on my charming little temptress.

"Hannah?"

She blinked rapidly, her dreamy gaze coming back into focus.

"Times up." Her yelp lit me up inside as I tackled her, flipping her over onto her stomach before grabbing her hands and holding them behind her back. "Daddy's home, and he's ready to play with his hot little slut. And you are hot for me, aren't you? Is your cunt wet for your Daddy?"

Her gasp made my balls draw up tight and I sat back on her upper thighs, my cock jutting over the creamy curve of her round ass. "Oh my God."

Displeased, I gave her ass a smack that echoed in the room with a loud crack. Instantly the skin turned a cherry red and my cock jerked, a drip of my arousal dangling from the tip before landing on her wiggling buttocks. Ignoring her whimpers, I rubbed the slick liquid into her skin, enjoying the burn of where I'd hit her.

"I asked you a question. Are. You. Wet. For. Me."

"Yes, yes!" Her struggles grew weaker as her ass pushed up, brushing against my shaft. "Please, please, I need you inside of me. I feel so empty. Fill me up, take me over, make me yours, please. I need you. Your baby girl's pussy hurts so bad, she needs her Daddy."

Another crack of my hand, this time to her other cheek as chills raced through me. Her shoulders rose up but I kept my grip on her delicate wrists, grinning as matching handprints rose up on her pale rear. The muscles along her spine tensed as she gave a sharp scream, the animal inside of me loving the sound of her discomfort.

Now, *now* we would see if the hypnosis worked, if she'd been primed for my brand of fucking.

Painful.

Chapter 9

Hannah

Red-hot sparks of stinging discomfort shot from my burning butt and somehow straight to my clit, leaving me a confused and desperately horny mess. My muscles went slack and it was only the strength of Leo's hands holding my arms behind my back that kept me upright, my overly sensitive nipples barely touching the sheets. I struggled against him, but it was like a puppy taking on a lion, not gonna happen. All I could do was submit, give in, and hope he didn't hurt me too badly.

I knew without a doubt that I was in for some kind of pain, that he was a sadist, but instead of being turned off, I was desperately wet and needy.

He could do anything he wanted to me and I'd beg for more as long as he filled this horrible emptiness inside of me.

The potential for violence hung in the air like a thick, seductive smoke that you knew was bad for you, but inhaled anyways. His effect on both my body and mind were certainly drug-like, heady bursts of emotions and sensations that I'd never experienced before, never even imagined. I'd thought my past lovers were decent, for the most part, in bed. They were attentive, made sure I was taken care of-ish, considerate, and they all made love to me in such a tentative way, I never felt anything near the satisfaction Leo's hard brand of fucking gave me.

Whatever Leo and I were doing, it didn't involve love. Lust, obsession, and danger? Yes, but not love. Or at least not a kind of love I'd never experienced before.

Even as his hold on my wrists turned painful, the strain on my arms a burn, his voice washed over me like a cooling breeze as he murmured with a bass hum to his voice, "You are so beautifully made, so fragile. It drives me crazy, this need to own you. And you belong to me, don't you, Hannah? I can do anything I want with you, can't I? I could hurt you and you'd beg for more."

Fear cleared my head as menace seemed to ooze from him. I knew if I was facing Leo right now, his eyes would be that dead-flat black that scared me. Something lurked inside of him, a sense of wrongness that should have sent me running, but I was helplessly drawn to him, like a ship going down a whirlpool. He sucked me under, into his spiraling darkness, and I was afraid of becoming so lost in him I forgot myself.

My skin prickled and I shivered, suddenly chilled.

Then the warmth of his hand spanking my bottom cut through the fear, drowning it beneath toe-curling, blistering sensations. The throb of my clit increased and I tilted my hips the best I could, begging for more. Something to keep me grounded; the white-hot light of hurt to cut through Leo's darkness. It was both my punishment and my comfort, and I craved more of it. Being around him unlocked some previously hidden part of myself that reveled in his violence, in his need to hurt me, to make me feel alive.

But was it really hurting me if I consented? If I got pleasure from it as well? Because I'll tell you what, I'd never been this aroused in my life. Every moment I was with Leo, I want to jump his bones and devour him.

Two spanks this time, one on either cheek, the stinging sending a rush of adrenaline through me. "Answer me."

Desperately, I tried to remember what he'd said and blurted out, "Yes, Daddy, I'm yours. Do whatever you want with me."

"Good girl," he purred, then lifted himself off my thighs.

I turned, wanting to see how red my cheeks were, but instead I was treated to the sight of a naked, glistening Leo gazing at my ass with what I could only describe as fierce worship. My muscles turned to jelly when he lowered his mouth to my right buttock, licking the stinging flesh then blowing on it. I whimpered, my gaze growing fuzzy as my attention focused only on what he was doing to me. Each lick was so tender, so calming, that I found myself floating in a lovely haze, a no doubt silly smile curving my lips.

"I like being your good girl," I mumbled, my hips rising, inviting him to lick elsewhere.

"Why?"

I shrugged, just a small twitch of my shoulders while he kissed my left buttock. "Because...because it's what I want to be. Do I make you happy?"

"Do you make me happy?"

I stilled at his odd tone, fearing the inevitable rejection when his realization of what a loser I really was came sooner than I'd anticipated.

"I had no idea emotions like the ones you make me feel even existed. There are no words for the pleasure I derive from being around you. Simply looking at you makes me happy. You are so very special to me, Hannah. More than you can imagine."

My smile became full-blown and I let out a soft sigh, that floaty sensation coming back, this time caused by his words rather than his actions. Safe, I was so safe and cared for when I was with him, spoiled with attention. He made me feel special, amazing in a way I'd only dreamed of. Was this what love felt like? This endless ocean of affection mixed with the craving for his dick that never seemed to go away? If so, I can see why love makes people crazy.

"Thank you, Daddy."

"So sweet," he murmured before taking a bite out of the sensitive skin of my inner thigh, hard enough to jerk a gasp of pain from me as he released my wrists. "And so wet."

Reaching back, I stroked my hand through his golden-brown hair, darker in this shadowy light than in the full sun. "Only for you."

He rewarded me with a smile that sent a burst of delight through me, then rewarded me even more when he shoved a pillow beneath my hips, and pressed me down to the bed with one big hand firmly between my shoulder blades.

The tip of his cock pushed into me and I let out a long, rough moan of pure enjoyment, the sensation of the bulbous head of his dick stretching my inner walls completely divine as I clawed at the sheets. The rough hair of his body scraped along my skin when he lay almost fully on top of me, giving me this wonderful sense of safety and satisfaction. I felt so close to him in this moment, while he slowly rocked his hips, the gentle glide of his erection stretching me, awakening all the nerves in my pussy with his thick girth. When Leo fucked me, I felt it from the top of my tingling head all the way down to my curling toes.

He did this twist thing with his hips that had me seeing stars. "Oh, Daddy, you feel so good!"

"My little girl likes that? Likes it when her Daddy fucks her?"

"Yes, so much."

"I like it too; in fact, I love it. Having you under me like this, your cunt gripping at my cock, the heat from your red ass pressed against me…fucking perfect. Everything about you, Hannah, every inch of you, was made for me. And look at how beautifully you respond, how you took that pain for me. Spanking you, the way you responded to my touch, had me ready to come all over your ass. You turn me on that much."

His voice had taken on a rough, growling tone by the end as he increased his pace, still pressing me into the mattress with his weight, driving me down farther with every hard thrust. Little gasps of air escaped me as he pounded my overstrung body, the first of what would be four orgasms catching me by surprise. Like a machine—no, like an animal—he fucked me, never letting me move, trapping me as he had his way with me. I was nothing more than his little sex toy, and I loved it.

Then he began to bite me, hard nips that drew corresponding yelps from me, each mark of his teeth matched by the thrust and grind of his hips, turning me into his pain slut.

I'd never had a man fuck me with his whole body before, and I couldn't help smiling wide as I reveled in being his.

I moaned, arched, and reared my hips back as I cried out, "Daddy, please, come inside me."

He shuddered, something I could clearly feel as we were pressed so tightly together. After my third orgasm, we flipped, and now I was on my back, looking up at the man staring down at me with something that resembled reverence. He never looked away, always studying me, always watching my every breath as if I was absolutely fascinating. It made me feel powerful, feminine, and desired.

Overwhelmed, I drew his lips down to mine and exchanged the softest of kisses, which in turn triggered his climax.

Raw, powerful, menacing, the lines of his face deepened as he reared back and his mouth fell open with a low groan.

I stared, fascinated by every twitch of his muscles, the scars along his body that told a tale of violence, along with his glorious hair. Unable to help myself, I leaned up and plunged my hands into his long strands, fisting it while he growled. Inside of me, his cock twitched hard enough that it sent more waves of pleasure through me, causing my core to contract, and he gasped. I swear, in that moment, I felt like we were connected on some visceral, cosmic level. My breath came out in sobbing gasps as the pleasure went on and on.

"That's it, baby, drain me fucking dry. Pull

harder."

I did as he asked, my pussy quivering when he shot yet another burst of hot cum inside of me, bathing me and triggering a slow, rolling orgasm that milked him further and had me incoherent, once again babbling out how much I worshiped him.

By the time I returned to earth from my trip to nirvana, Leo had managed to roll off of me, his arms thrown over his head in a relaxed pose, a small and soft smile curving his firm lips as his chest heaved.

When our eyes met, I couldn't help but smile, then giggle. "Wow."

He just turned his head back to the ceiling, closing his eyes with a smile. "You're going to kill me, but what a way to go. Is my dick intact? I'm pretty sure I blew it off inside of you when your tight little cunt gripped me like a squeezing fist."

Laughing, I stroked my hand down his sweaty stomach, the fur of his happy trail leading me to his still semi-hard cock. "Did you take Viagra or something?"

Grinning, and keeping his eyes closed, he stretched out, all rolling muscles and mouthwatering strength, utter contentment radiating from him. "You *are* my Viagra."

"Thanks…I think."

"You're welcome. While I don't give a fuck about falling asleep right now, all sweaty and sticky, I know you like to go to bed clean. Let's shower, then I'll feed you, eat you, and put you to bed."

Groaning, I rubbed my face. "Yes please, I'm exhausted."

"Come on, baby girl, let your Daddy take care of

you."

He turned his head to look at me and I gave him the only answer I could. "Okay, Daddy."

The next morning, I awoke to find another set of brand-new clothing for me as well as all the cosmetics and girly stuff I needed for the day. This time the outfit he chose for me was a silky red shirt that hung artfully off of one shoulder, and a pair of skin-tight, dark jeans that had enough stretch to fit comfortably like yoga pants. He'd also included a pair of tasteful gold hoop earrings and a gold necklace made of a waterfall of tiny gold circles linked together, along with a pair of cute black ankle boots.

The whole outfit was somehow familiar, and as I stared at myself in the mirror, I couldn't help but admire how the jeans gave my butt a nice rounded shape. Without a doubt, I felt expensive, and though I'm sure there are those who would argue I don't need costly clothes to feel good about myself, it certainly didn't hurt. I left my hair loose and smiled as I tossed my shiny locks over my shoulder, not a tangle to be found, thanks to Leo's fascination with running his hands through it. Just the memory made my eyelids grow heavy, and a hot flush burned my cheeks.

I found Leo in the kitchen, eating a pile of pancakes while he stared down at his tablet, a cup of what I'm assuming was coffee throwing steam in the early morning light. He was dressed casually in khaki shorts and a worn-looking pale blue t-shirt that brought out his tan, along with his gold watch circling his thick wrist. This morning his hair was down, and I really wanted to grasp a handful of his wavy gold and brown mane.

He looked up as I approached, his dark eyes flashing with warmth as he smiled. "Good morning, beautiful."

Butterflies took flight in my belly, spreading out to all my limbs in a dance of happiness. Feeling as if I was floating on a cloud, I basked in his attention and open affection. I ducked my head then gave him a small wave, probably flushed pink with pleasure from chest to ears.

No matter how close we'd been physically, we were essentially strangers, and that bothered me because it reminded me that in reality, we were moving too fast, and I'd promised myself I wouldn't get instantly, possessively attached. But this…this feeling, this experience between us, was different. Leo was different. He was hardened, jaded, and world weary in a way that had marked him. It was like life had ground away all the softness from him, leaving only solid rock behind.

But when he looked at me, all that stiffness relaxed, and I knew deep in my gut this was a man who allowed very few people to see this side of him.

"Morning, Leo."

"Love the breathy way you say my name, sweetheart. Especially first thing in the morning. There's food under the silver domed trays. Help yourself. My housekeeper made it earlier for us."

I piled the lovely blue and gray plate I found waiting for me on the counter with food, grabbing a double portion of the scrambled eggs that had some kind of fragrant salsa in them, along with a couple sausage links.

I joined Leo at the big table, sitting next to him where a glass of orange juice and a cup of coffee were waiting for me. In the center of the table sat a curved lavender glass vase full of peach and yellow roses, along with white lilacs, one of my favorite flower combinations. When I looked from the flowers to Leo, he gave me a slow quirk of his lips, his gaze smoldering. Distracted by all that sexiness being aimed my way, I forgot how vigorous some of our activities had been last night and I let out a hiss as my sore bottom met the hard chair.

The heat vanished from Leo's gaze, replaced by deep concern. "Are you okay?"

The way he seemed ready to leap up from his seat had me smiling ruefully. "Yes, I'm okay. My butts a little sore, but in a good way…um, no pun intended."

He didn't smile. "Maybe you should see a doct—"

I held up my hand, noticing a few bruises around my wrist that probably came from when he was holding me down and I was coming my brains out. "If you're suggesting that I go see a doctor because I've been well fucked, you're insane."

The worry vanished from his eyes, replaced by a pleased, almost smug expression as he leaned back in his chair, the thin cotton of his shirt stretching nicely across his wide chest. "Good point."

Eager to get off the subject, I returned my interest to my meal as I asked, "So, you have a cook?"

"Yes. I'm afraid to confess I don't have much of a domestic streak. My chef comes in three times a week and cooks, but also leaves meals for my housekeeper to prepare for me on the days he's not here."

"I'm guessing a yard crew as well? This place is immaculate, and I can't imagine you being the kind of guy to pull weeds in his spare time."

His dark eyes watched me closely, his lips curving into an easy smile that didn't match his gaze. "You're right. I have much better things to do than pull weeds. In what little free time I've had to spend here, I've mostly enjoyed the pool and sauna."

"Sauna? Wow, nice." The delicious bitterness of coffee helped clear my thoughts a bit. "You live here alone?"

His brows arched and he abandoned the relaxed pose he'd been in, leaning forward on the table, exuding menace. "Do you think I'd bring you here if I lived with someone else? That I'm in the habit of sneaking around with women?"

Realizing I offended him, I tried to do damage control. "No, no. I'm just saying, it's a big house. You need to get a dog or something."

The anger left him as if it had never been there and I resisted the urge to blow out a relieved breath. "You're right, I do need a dog. In fact, I was considering going to the pound at some point to find a puppy."

I tried to compose myself, but I couldn't help my happy little squeal. "Really?"

His lips twitched and his eyes crinkled as he took in my glee. "Yes, really. This place is too big for me alone, but I've been too busy working these past few years to give a dog enough attention."

I sighed, my enthusiasm waning as I thought of all the reasons I couldn't have a dog. "I know how that is. I've wanted a dog for like, forever, but it wouldn't be fair to get one and then keep him in a cage. Then there's the fact that I live in an apartment that doesn't allow pets, and Kayla doesn't like animals…so yeah…no dog for me."

"Did you have a pet growing up?"

I had. Before my sister had gotten sick, we had a sweet golden retriever. Then the endless rounds of hospital stays began and we couldn't care for our dog, so my parents gave her away to one of their friends. I'd been devastated, but when I'd protested, my mother had berated me for being selfish.

"When I was younger. What about you?"

The lazy, unhurried way he sipped his coffee as he stared at me made me fidget in my chair, like he knew there was more I was holding back. "A dog was a luxury my mom couldn't afford when I was growing up. She was a single mother with a high-school diploma who worked two jobs to support us."

"Wow, that sucks."

"It did, but in a lot of ways I had it better than most kids. She loved me with every ounce of her considerable heart, and I had a good life despite the circumstances. Our house was always the best looking, even if she used decorations she got at the Dollar Store. While I'm a right selfish bastard, she was one of the most giving, always helping others." His broad chest lifted with a sigh as he examined me. "She would have liked you."

"Really?"

A small, sad smile quirked the corner of his mouth. "Yes, Hannah, she would have adored you."

Warmth flowed through my veins, sweet as honey and sunshine. I didn't know what to say and looked away, pretending to be super interested in the remains of my eggs. If I was Kayla, I'd have some kind of urbane and witty remark; if I was Joy, I'd know how to take a compliment. But I was neither of them, instead I was incredibly needy and Leo's nice words were my addiction, my pleasurable fix. A tingle started in my nipples and headed south, past my clenching lower stomach to my sensitive sex.

"Hannah." Leo's voice was thick with desire. "Come here."

I took a quick sip of my juice before complying and coming to stand between his spread legs. "Yes?"

"Your nipples are hard."

"Um...you have good air conditioning."

His broad hands grasped my back then pulled me closer so he could nuzzle my breasts, need and want coiling inside of me as his lips brushed my pulse. "You have the sweetest tits. Show them to me."

Normally I'm a lights-off kind of girl, but once again my desire for Leo overrode any feelings of doubt. He worshiped my body and by the bulge of his erection against his pants, I knew I turned him on. It was a heady feeling to look down and watch his big, golden-maned head rub against my slight chest, the way his eyes closed as if he was absorbing the feel of me. I was certainly enjoying the feel of *him*. The soft folds between my legs were drenched already with my arousal, and he'd barely touched me.

I think I was turning into a nymphomaniac.

Eager for more, I quickly removed my shirt and tossed it haphazardly onto the counter, my skin so sensitive, the rasp of his lips over the curve of my breast was almost too much. As if he sensed my mood, his touch turned gentle, his big hands cradling my body while his firm lips pressed butterfly-light kisses across my collarbone. My insides burst into flames when he finally lowered his mouth to the tip of my breast, his name breaking free from my lips with the first light suck. The gold of my necklace glinted in the strong sunlight spilling through the windows and warming my skin, highlighting how pale I was compared to his bronzed splendor.

I clutched his head to me, his hair thick and soft between my fingers, the fresh and clean scent of his shampoo released into the air with each stroke of my hand. Holding him close to me like this while he suckled on my breast was divine, but I wanted more. It was as though we'd never even had sex, like I'd been deprived and horny for years rather than hours. I brushed my leg against his erection, delighting in his low growl while his sharp teeth nipped me in a way that made my chest hitch.

"My baby girl need to be fucked?" he asked before blowing on my damp nipple.

Every beat of my heart increased my desire until I was once again wanton for him, the need to feel him inside of me overriding everything else. "Yes, please."

"Get naked."

After stumbling a bit while hauling off my boots, more eager than seductive, I was once again naked before him in short order, my hands literally trembling with the need to touch him.

"Pull my shorts down and take my cock out, then ride me."

I eyed the armless sides of his chair, trying to figure out how much leverage I would get. "Are you sure?"

He bit my nipple, hard, and I let out a sharp scream. "Shit!"

"Don't back talk unless you want to be punished."

Oh, that pissed me off, but at the same time, I was unable to argue that being bossed around lit a fuse inside of me that couldn't be denied. With a little bit of a pout, I leaned down between his legs, helping him get his shorts over the rounded curve of his muscled ass before pulling the material down to his feet where he kicked them off. Naked from the waist down, there was something very obscene about him lounging there, idly stroking his swollen cock, the darkened head shiny with precum. My mouth watered at the sight but as I was reaching for him, he made a tsking sound.

"I didn't say touch, I said ride."

Flushing, I placed my hands on his strong, rock-like shoulders in order to straddle him, then steadied myself as he rubbed the flared crest of his cock around my wet entrance, awakening the nerves that ached for him. Slowly sinking down onto his body, I met his gaze and found him smiling at me, his wide shoulders flexing as he arched his hips, changing the angle of my descent. I was too busy absorbing the divine feeling of him stretching my tender inner muscles to smile back.

"So beautiful," he said in that sex-rough voice of his that I loved. "Use my cock to make yourself come, sweetheart. Get Daddy wet."

Since I wasn't able to get much leverage, I could only rise up an inch or two before lowering myself back down and grinding. Shit, that felt amazing. I canted my hips, my breath coming in short bursts as I gripped Leo's shoulders and circled my clit into his pelvis.

Leo continued to watch me, then stretched his arms out and put them behind his head, leaning back slightly and giving me a little more room to move. His lips were parted, swollen and damp as he devoured me with his gaze, the intense regard giving me a sense of power and pride.

Bouncing on his dick now, I chased my orgasm, pulling my nipples and pinching them tight.

"Harder," Leo commanded. "Make your pretty tits hurt."

My pussy convulsed and he gave me a savage smile.

Everything felt so damn good, and I ground down, my hips snapping as my breathing became choppy. "Yes, Daddy."

Little darts of white-hot pain shot from my nipples to my clit as I pinched them hard enough to make me hiss with pleasure.

"Come on, baby, work me, make me fill you up."

My hair stuck to my sweaty skin as I reached up and sank my nails into the back of his neck, holding on while I lost myself in him. My orgasm was strong and fierce, but also immensely relaxing. When I was having sex with Leo, the tension inside of me built up so much it actually hurt. Then my climax would hit and the easing of those tight muscles was just another facet to my overwhelming pleasure.

He hugged me tight while he emptied himself inside me, an almost desperate sound escaping him as he buried his face in the side of my neck and bit down. My body clenched from the pain of his bite and a delicious trill of shivers raced through me. Then he began to kiss and lick the sore area, soothing me with his gentle touch. It was so odd how he could hurt me, and enjoy it, then moments later touch me with such veneration.

"Morning," I breathed as he lifted me slowly off of him, semen running down my inner thigh.

Grinning at me, Leo brushed my hair back. "Best morning I've had in a long time."

"Me too."

"Come on, let's get you cleaned up. We have someplace to be."

"Where?"

"It's a surprise for my baby girl." He took my hand and led me back towards his bedroom.

"A surprise?" I loved surprises. "Really?"

He gave my hand a squeeze. "Really. Now, no more questions or I won't eat you clean in the shower."

It should be impossible, but his words sent a hard tingle between my legs. "Yes, Daddy."

Chapter 10

Leo

Hannah laced her fingers through mine as we got a couple's massage at the Cordova Country Club's spa. The treatments we were receiving were top of the line; Judith demanded it since the country club was owned by the cartel, as were the attached restaurants, stores, and the two golf courses. The pools were world famous and they had weddings booked for the next three years with people eager to take advantage of our five-star service.

One of the few bits of green interrupting the desert landscape, the eighteen-hole courses cost a fortune in upkeep—the emerald-green grass wasn't exactly native to the desert—but the overpriced membership more than made up for it. It cost close to four hundred and fifty thousand dollars a year just in membership dues, and things like the spa were extra. But the elite who joined this club were beyond wealthy in ways most people couldn't imagine. Entertainers, bankers, entrepreneurs and trust-fund babies, drug lords and despots, the club members were used to the best and had no qualms about paying a high price for it.

Judith had grown up in obscene wealth in El Salvador, the only child of a mayor and a drug lord. She was used to the best things in life and knew how to cater to the privileged, which kept the club coffers full and allowed us to launder a great deal of money without detection. It was also Judith's social standing that kept the place packed. I've never met anyone as good at coldly manipulating others as she was, and I'd learned a great deal about how people think from watching Judith influence them.

Next to me, Hannah let out a soft sigh and I smiled into the clean, fresh-smelling white sheet covering the massage table.

The older and still beautiful Hispanic woman working on my back hit a knot of muscles and I had to force myself to try to relax, to shut my mind down. Typically, I was thinking of at least three things at once, my brain always busy. The only time my overactive mind gave me a break and went quiet was when I was focused on Hannah. While I might be conditioning her body and mind to accept only me as a lover, *my* body and mind were already hers.

The workers at the country club, familiar with me, had openly stared as I laughed and smiled at Hannah while giving her a tour of the place. I must be more of a scary bastard than I thought, because a few looked worried for Hannah's safety as she strolled with me, holding my hand with complete trust. Not that I could blame them; the image we'd presented in the floor-to-ceiling mirrors lining the foyer of the place had been an interesting one. She was so beautiful and ethereal, like a fairy princess, while I hovered over her like an overprotective beast.

I hadn't anticipated how tense being out in public with Hannah would make me, but even here, in a business owned and protected by my cartel, I kept scanning the area for an attack. It was only due to the fact that I had known Esmerelda and Florence for years that I even allowed them to touch my girl. That, and Hannah's blissful sighs, which echoed in the vaulted ceiling of the room like erotic music.

She was facing me, with her midnight-black hair pulled back into a braid that trailed off the side of the white leather table like a thick rope. Her full lips were curved up at the ends and her fingers were limp in mine, only the occasional slow stroke of her thumb over my hand giving me any indication she was even awake. I let my gaze take in the elegant slope of her shoulders, the smooth flow of her skin. Unlike me, she wasn't covered in scars—but she *was* covered in bruises that sent a tingle down my spine and into my balls.

Lying on her stomach, Hannah was completely nude and coated in an almond-scented oil that made her pale skin glow and highlighted my marks on her. Deep purple circles from my teeth scattered all over her shoulders and back, while her buttocks still had a pink tinge to them and her hips were lightly bruised from my grip, my fingerprints plainly obvious. I know I should feel regret for those no doubt sore spots, but instead I only had a sense of pride.

And if my programming had worked, Hannah would derive pleasure from each bruise that I touched.

As Florence smoothed her hands over Hannah's buttocks, my girl's hips gave a little twitch, the slightest catch in her breathing and the way her nostrils flared all alerting me to her reaction.

Her big cinnamon-brown eyes were on me now,

the pupils wide as she gave me clear "fuck me" signals. I wondered if it was me or the drugs and hypnosis she was responding to, then decided I didn't care as long as she *was* responding. I watched with avid interest as she looked right at me then bit her lip in a coy little maneuver that made it uncomfortable to lie on my stomach due to my hard-on.

In Spanish, I ordered Florence to massage Hannah's butt a little harder and she did without complaint, knowing better than to challenge me on anything.

A soft, low groan escaped Hannah and she flushed, closing her eyes with a whimper. When she opened them again, she smiled when she found me watching her. "You have no idea how good this feels. Thank you, Leo."

I ignored the way both Florence and Esmerelda froze when Hannah said my name, and smiled at my girl. "You're welcome, baby girl. I figured it was the least I could do, considering I'm responsible for your current…tender state."

Blushing again, Hannah smirked. "This is true."

Her eyes grew heavy lidded as she slowly perused my equally nude body then licked her lips. "What are we doing after this?"

"I'm having you for lunch."

She giggled, then whispered, "I'm starving. When can we eat?"

Loving the ravenous gleam in her eyes, I shifted my hips on the table, my erection now actively pissed off at being pressed up against the unyielding table instead of Hanna's giving body. "Ladies, we're done for now. Thank you."

Both older women made a quick exit, no doubt running off to gossip about my obvious shows of affection with Hannah. There were rumors that I was a sexual deviant incapable of having a relationship, that I was incapable of love, and as fucked-up as it was, some women were all the more attracted to me because of my emotional detachment. Usually I could avoid women who wanted more than sex, but every once in a while, one of my partners would think she'd be the one to change me. That I'd take one dip in her magic pussy and fall in love. Stupid bitches. There was only one woman for me, and it would always be my Hannah.

Right now, she was trying to slide off the side of the table without flashing me, something I found highly amusing. The sight of my teeth marks high on her inner thigh had me remembering the taste of her and I was eager to lap up her sweet cream again.

"Hannah," I said in a low, commanding voice. "Up against the wall, legs spread, ass sticking out. Now."

"Are...are you going to hurt me?"

The trembling anticipation in her voice had my dick jumping.

Holding her unsure gaze, I nodded slowly. "Yes, I'm going to hurt you, sweetheart."

The sleepy, relaxed look left her face and her body stilled, the soft bumps of her raspberry pink nipples stiffening before my eyes. She bit her lower lip, glancing at the wall, then back to me with a lovely tremor now shaking her hands, her pussy nice and wet. Sick fuck that I am, her being scared only made my dick harder. With visible hesitation, she placed her hands on the wall, the black rope of her braid hanging down her back. When she spread her legs and arched her back as I'd instructed, the muscles of my thighs tensed, the need to rut and thrust into all that soft, wet heat tearing at my self-control.

I was up and off the table before she'd fully settled into position, my eager hands stroking over her oil-slicked skin.

"Good girl," I praised her, noting the way she relaxed beneath my touch. "Did it hurt when Florence touched your bruises?"

The tension returned to her body while I skimmed my palms over the slight curve of her rounded buttocks. "I—yes and no."

I moved behind her and rubbed my dick along the oiled crease of her ass, pressing against the little puckered hole of her anus and enjoying the way she instinctively tightened up. "Explain."

"It felt...good, but still hurt. I can't explain it."

"Hmmm, interesting."

Pressing the tip of my cock against her resisting asshole again, I enjoyed the tremor that ran through her. Leaning forward, I picked a particularly harsh bite mark I'd left on her shoulder and slowly, softly, stroked my tongue against it. Little goosebumps formed on her skin and I smiled as she whispered my name in a breathy voice. I picked a particularly deep bite mark on her shoulder and gently ran my teeth over it.

Her reaction was swift, a harsh cry that had her pressing back against my cock, teasing the tip by letting me in just the slightest bit. As much as I wanted to pound her ass, she wasn't ready for me. Instead, I tormented her with the threat of my cock breeching her virgin ass, licking at her bruise like it was her clit and loving her pleasured moans.

"That feels so good, better than it should. Why does your mouth feel so good?"

"It's your reward," I breathed against the shell of her ear, feeding just a little more of the head of my shaft into her clenching ass. "For taking the pain, for being my good girl."

"Daddy…" She tried to push back more. "Please, I want you to fuck me."

Giving her a warning nip, I withdrew completely before I gave in to her dirty begging. "When we get home, I have an anal hook I'm going to use on you, then I'm going to fuck you while your ass is stuffed full of cold steel. Won't take you long to warm it, though. When you're horny, your pussy gets so fucking hot."

I positioned my dick with one hand while purposely putting my thumb on a rather large welt. She let out a low wail as I slid into her, massaging the bruise like it was her clit. Instead of pleading for me to stop, she came all over my dick before I was all the way inside of her.

Gripping her hips, I fought the convulsions of her sex, the way her inner muscles tried to hold me still, to grip me deep while Hannah screamed through her orgasm. I gathered her braid into my fist, holding it with one hand while I slapped her ass with my other, ruthlessly taking what I wanted from her while luxuriating in her multiple climaxes. Power, raw and pure, flowed into me as she surrendered, giving me everything. Time seemed to slow and each thrust grew more intense, each stroke of her inner softness making my balls tighten. Our rough breaths echoed in the room, along with the wet smack of my hips plunging against her.

"Leo," she gasped in a shattered voice, "I'm going to pass out."

"Go ahead, I'll just hold you tight and keep fucking you."

"Oh God."

I let go of her braid and wrapped my hand around her throat, supporting her and cutting off her air the slightest bit. "I want you to come so hard you faint with my cock still inside of you. I want to fuck your limp body, knowing that I made you feel so good you couldn't handle it. We're going to train you to take more pleasure, but if it's too much, go ahead and let go. This body is mine, and I'll fuck you if you're awake or not."

"Shit, yes, take me, use me. I love it so much." Her head lolled against my hand as she ground her ass into me.

Gritting my teeth, I changed the angle of my hips and fucked her in short, hard strokes, determined to spill my seed deep inside of her.

Her neck felt so delicate as I increased my pressure, the temptation to have her body totally at my mercy testing my self-control.

She grunted then stiffened, her torso convulsing in my arms to the point I had to ride her down to the floor and pin her beneath my weight, removing my hand so she could breathe while I tore her apart.

Weak, almost confused sounds came from her as she continued to orgasm, her eyes rolling back in her head as she groaned, then passed out.

Fucking like a mad man, I reared back on my haunches and picked up her unresisting hips, satisfying myself with her lax form, loving how her pussy clenched around me even as she drifted deep in something beyond subspace, some special place only I could send her.

I couldn't fight the burn anymore and gave in to the need for release, a bright white light filling my vision as sheer relief thundered through my blood while I emptied myself into her.

All the strength left me, but I managed to roll off of her then pull Hannah against me, the soft rush of her breath against the sweat-dampened skin of my neck the best thing I'd ever felt.

The rest of the day continued in the same glorious fashion. After Hannah woke up, we bathed then dressed and ate at one of the restaurants at the golf course, where Hannah wolfed down a steak and baked potato like she hadn't eaten in months. With her already high metabolism, I'd have to make sure I fed her enough to deal with the calorie loss that came from frequent, hard fucking.

Later that night, after tying Hannah up and ruling her body until she broke with pleasure, I pulled her limp form into my arms and smiled, snuggling her against me and falling into the best sleep I've ever had in moments.

Chapter 11

Hannah

As I clambered off the back of Leo's royal blue Ducati street bike, I was uncomfortably aware of all the stares I was getting. It could be because of the motorcycle — it was super awesome and sleek in a way that you just knew it cost bank — or it could be the sight of Leo in padded black leather with his hair tied back and a nice five o'clock shadow. But I was pretty sure it was because I'd almost fallen on my ass trying to get off the back of his bike with my new, heavy backpack filled with gifts from Leo.

Dressed in a black leather riding outfit that matched his, and I mean totally matched, right down to the smallest detail like the royal blue stitching, I shifted on my new biker boots and tried to ignore the fact my outfit was skin tight.

Okay, so maybe our outfits weren't exactly the same. While his safety gear looked like pants and a jacket, masculine and kind of beat up, mine fit me like a cat suit and made me uncomfortably aware I was nude beneath it. Before we'd left his house so he could get me back in time for class, Leo had kept me nude and spoiled, indulged and petted like some pampered princess. It had been utterly divine. While I was with him, my oversexed body hadn't felt that sore, but after the bike ride, every muscle was protesting the rough treatment.

I'd been ridden hard — really, really hard — and I was so not used to the intensity of Leo's lovemaking. While I was already missing him like crazy, my overworked inner core was whimpering with relief. Still, I wish I'd thought to grab a shirt of his to bring with me so I could smell him while we were apart. A pang of longing went through my chest and I really wanted to skip class and stay with Leo, but I managed to fight off my clinger tendencies.

The rumble of Leo's engine was loud and I felt suddenly shy as I handed him my helmet, sure my hair was a crazy mess despite the braid he'd put it in. "Thanks for giving me a ride home."

He grinned just the slightest bit and shook his head, the smoky riding glasses he wore hiding him in an odd way from me. I felt like I could read his emotions much easier when I could see his eyes. Then again, we hadn't been out in public much. Maybe he was aware of the people who'd stopped to watch us like we were important. In a messed-up way, even though it made me self-conscious, I liked the attention and I was more than aware of curious, and sometimes envious, eyes on us.

Leo leaned forward and I met him halfway, my breath already hitching with anticipation as I lifted my free hand to cup his jaw, committing to memory the feeling of his skin beneath mine, the taste and smell of Leo as he sucked on my lower, then upper lip, his touch unbearably sweet.

Sometimes he did this, was so careful with me, and every reverent caress was magnified by his gentleness. By the time he pulled back from what had been in reality a rather short kiss by our standards, I was already flushed and breathing hard. The side of his firm, kiss-swollen lips quirked up and I just about died on the spot of an overload of hormones. He was just so…masculine. His presence made me feel female, sensual, powerful. Standing a little taller, I adjusted the pack on my back and stopped hunching forward, a bad habit I'd developed as a kid when I didn't want to draw attention to myself.

Which was all the time.

But in Leo's presence, I felt like a goddess.

"I'll miss you."

The words just kind of slipped out like my brain-to-mouth filter was malfunctioning, but before I could play it off, Leo smiled wide and I swore I heard a couple women behind me sigh. "I'll miss you too, baby girl. What time are you done with your study group tonight?"

I tried to remember when I'd mentioned my study group, but couldn't. It must have been one of those hazy times when, sexually exhausted and satisfied, I'd just babbled about anything and everything with Leo. He was a great listener and seemed to really enjoy my random thoughts about the best kind of peanut butter, or how quickly the oceans were going to rise in the next century, or what kind of rose smelled the best. Odd conversations with no rhyme or reason, but immensely satisfying. I connected with him better than I ever had anyone before, and the feeling of belonging I got from lying in his arms, being stroked and coddled while we watched a movie, was completely addicting.

And our conversations were interesting. He knew

lots about the world, things I'd never considered, ways of looking at events that seemed totally foreign to me. It's like if we both looked at one of those ink blot pictures, I'd see a puppy and he'd see a gun. Well, maybe not that bad, but I couldn't easily dismiss how much he seemed to know about the criminal elements of the world.

I vaguely remembered complaining about last semester's expensive books that I'd been forced to buy for my courses, only to never use half of them. We'd gone on to discuss how the textbook industry was a scam, and Leo had some amazing insights into how a scheme like that worked. Without a doubt, I was now sure our corrupt government could be bought out by anyone, including the textbook industry.

Shaken out of my memories by an engine revving behind Leo in the big circular drive leading to my apartment building, I nodded, the fumes from the exhaust of the bike strong in the desert heat, tainting my every breath. "It was canceled, too many people had other things going on, and for once I don't have to rush off to work. They gave me two weeks off to heal. I haven't had this much free time in forever. Seriously. Last vacation I took was to my aunt's funeral in Michigan three years ago, if you can even call that a vacation."

His lips tightened and he shook his head. "That's no way to live your life. You've never had a chance to go anywhere, see anything, or experience new things because you've been working yourself to the bone. We're going to change that. From now on, you get to enjoy life, Hannah, not watch it pass by."

All I could do was nod quickly, hoping my chin wasn't quivering as badly as it wanted to. Stupid emotions, they always overwhelmed me. Older kids at my school used to love how quickly they could make me cry, no matter how much I fought to retain my tattered pride.

Cars drove past us in the drive, and on the wide stairs leading to my apartment stood three girls I knew from the floor below us, not so secretly snapped pictures of us on their cell phones while Leo caressed my cheek with his leather-clad hand. "I know you'll positively pine away without me, but I'll see you at eight."

Laughing, I shook my head and let go of the past before it could drag me down. "Make it nine. I need a little bit to hang out with my roommates."

For a moment his lips thinned then turned down, but his angry expression was gone before I could really be sure if I'd even seen his frown. "Nine it is."

Feeling like I'd somehow offended him by not seeing him at eight, I tried to hand him the helmet. "Thanks again, Leo. I had an amazing time."

He gently pushed the helmet back at me. "Keep it, it's yours. And I had an amazing time as well. Now get in your fucking apartment before I rip that tight suit off your ridiculously hot body, bend you over my bike, and fuck you in front of your neighbors. Show them who you belong to."

Thankfully he said the last part low enough that I was probably the only one who'd heard him — well, me and the girl from down the hall, who was now staring at us with her mouth hanging open a couple paces away and her tanned cheeks darkened with a hard blush.

"Hannah," Leo growled, "eyes on me."

Without thought, I did as he commanded, already responding to his orders like I'd been born to do it. I'd be more concerned about my sudden passivity if it didn't feel so good to let him take charge. Handsome, successful, and so charismatic, he was a man who obviously had his life together and knew who he was and what he was doing. I was more like a lump of half-formed clay, waiting for someone to finish me off, to help me find the shape I was meant to be.

"Good girl," he said in that same low, growly voice. "Entirely too tempting. I'll see you at nine. Text me when you get back to your apartment so I know you're safe."

His concern over my safety made me all glowy inside. "Okay, goodbye, Leo."

"Don't say goodbye."

"What?"

"Say, 'I'll see you soon'. Say it, Hannah."

"I'll see you soon."

"Before you know it."

With that, he smiled and put his helmet back on, leaving me with a wet crotch and cursing the fact I wasn't wearing panties.

During an uncomfortable walk through the small foyer of my building, I smiled at the people openly staring at me, faces I've seen a hundred times who never gave me a second look. Now, dressed like some rich street racer's girlfriend out of an action flick, I had their attention. One guy who was cute even tried to hit on me, but I found him completely lacking, and for the first time in my life, didn't feel desperate for more of a man's attention.

There was only one man I wanted thinking about me, lusting after me, and it wasn't the sad excuse for manhood from unit 5A, who regularly left his laundry moldering away in the communal washers on the main floor.

By the time I made it to my apartment, I had about twenty minutes to get ready before I had to leave for class. I needed to get in, get dressed, and get my shit together.

This plan was thwarted by Joy and Kayla both being in the kitchen, arguing about who needed to do the dishes. Joy wore jeans and one of her blazers, probably on her way to her job as a tutor for rich and spoiled kids. Joy's blonde hair was up in an artful bun, and her tanned cheeks were dark red, her body language promising violence as she yelled that she did not have time to clean up Kayla's shit, and that we were going to get fruit flies.

I wasn't surprised in the least to see that the sink was full of Kayla's crap, and I knew there was no way Joy was going to clean up after her.

No, that fun job was reserved for me, because even though I didn't like it, I let Kayla guilt me into doing it, unable to handle it when she'd basically shun me for not doing what she wanted.

Except, for the first time in what felt like forever, I wasn't guilt-ridden for being mad that Kayla couldn't clean up after herself for one damn day.

"Just clean up your shit," Joy yelled, her cheeks flushed with anger. "You're disgusting! There's a moldy bowl of oatmeal in there that has dried to concrete. How long has it been since you picked up after yourself?"

"I don't have time—"

"You don't have time? Are you kidding me? Hannah and I both work full time and go to school; what the hell do you do? Attend your *one* class? Bullshit. You party until six a.m., drag your ass in here and sleep all day, then get up long enough to destroy everything Hannah spent all day cleaning before going out with your new fucktard dealer friends and getting wasted."

Kayla squinted her eyes and dramatically threw her dish into the sink, milk and cereal splashing everywhere, including the wall, and one lone piece of brightly colored cereal slid down the window. "Fuck you!"

Before Joy could respond, I said in a low, super-pissed voice as I set my helmet down on the small foyer table, "I am *not* cleaning that up."

"Hannah?" Kayla blinked once, twice, then cocked her head to the side like a confused dog.

"Holy shit," Joy squeaked before setting her bowl on the counter and coming to look at me. "What the hell is this?"

"This," I couldn't help but grin, proud to be the one showing off for once, "is Leo's version of 'something to wear when you're on my bike'."

Kayla suddenly appeared in my line of sight, her gaze locked on my ears. "Are those real?"

I self-consciously touched my ears, where a pair of lovely diamond and gold-filigree hoop earrings sparkled. "Um—yeah."

An ugly frown distorted Kayla's normally pretty face. "He gave you diamonds? This guy fucks you for a few days and gives you *diamonds*?"

Joy turned on Kayla, pissed, but I spoke first as anger sparked through me. "He sure did. He not only gave me diamonds, he also gave me a designer wardrobe, more jewelry — oh, and his super-thick cock. And let me tell you, he is absolutely amazing in bed. Fucks me like a grown man who knows what he wants, and he eats pussy like a starving person. Anything else you want to know?"

For a long, long moment, both Kayla and Joy stared at me before Joy lost it, laughing so hard she was cackling as she held on to the counter. "Ohhhh, burn."

"Fuck you," Kayla hissed at Joy then flounced off to her room, her black bob bouncing with her pissed-off gait.

Still snorting with laughter, Joy waved her hand in the direction Kayla had stomped off. "Ignore her. Stupid bitch just got home from partying with some rough, and I do mean rough-looking guys. I don't know what's up with her, but her taste in men has gone right down the shitter."

Loud music poured from Kayla's room, like a teenager throwing a tantrum, and Joy and I exchanged a look then sighed.

Glancing at the mess Kayla made, I shook my head. "I really am *not* cleaning that up."

Her light green eyes slowly examined me from head to toe, then back up again. "So, you finally got some dick?"

Laughing, I gave her a one-armed hug. "Yes. Now, let me get changed and I'll give you the scoop before I go to class."

"Wait, you have to tell me something!"

Trying to distract her, I switched to a topic I know always riled her up. "Don't you have some delinquent to go tutor for your internship?"

Sure enough, the tips of her ears turned red with anger. "They're not delinquents, they're high school kids. Well, some of them are delinquents, but that's beside the point. It's great experience for me and I feel like I'm really making a difference. It's sure as hell more satisfying than tutoring spoiled rotten little shits here at ASU. I swear, if I get one more trust-fund baby failing out of basic math because no one has ever made them accountable for themselves, I'm going to flip out. Drives me up a damn wall."

She followed me to my room, both of us ignoring Kayla's door when we passed it. After slamming my door shut, Joy flopped onto my messy bed. One of the trashy gossip magazines I liked to read slid off the bed, falling open to a picture of a shirtless football player with a really tight bubble butt selling deodorant. The guy in the ad had an ass almost as good as Leo's.

Damn, I never did get to play with it as much as I wanted. I'd just gotten to the good part when my time was up. He was right, if he gave me the gift of being in control again, I wouldn't waste it, because Leo took charge in a way that left me no room for thoughts, only actions.

"Earth to Hannah, I asked you a question."

Realizing I was staring at the magazine on the floor instead of opening the full backpack to see what kind of goodies Leo had put in there for me like an eager little kid on Christmas morning, I smiled. "Sorry. I'm still processing the last few days."

"You mean thinking about fucking him. Tell me! I want details about how you got that dreamy look in your eyes."

I glanced at the time, then startled, panic filling me. "Shit! I'm going to be late. Can you unpack that for me while I shower, please?"

After I washed up in record time, I peeked out the door to make sure my room was empty before I came out. The bruises on my torso and buttocks disturbed even *me* a little bit, and I knew how much fun I'd had getting them. Joy would freak out.

Luckily the room was empty, my friend probably had to head out to work, but then I saw a long white box and a note from the pad of purple paper I kept next to my bed.

Hannah,

Oh my God, you little freak! The man bought you a personalized, diamond-encrusted butt plug! Girl...I can't even. PLEASE go show it to Kayla so she can shit herself with envy. No pun intended.

Joy

PS: Bitch, we are so talking when you get home!
PSS: Does Leo have a brother?

I stared at the box, aghast, and sure enough, when I opened it, what I think of as a starter-size gold butt plug gleamed merrily away on a bed of red velvet. It really was pretty, and it was indeed personalized. There was a lovely H on the end of the plug done in diamonds. I stared at it, imagined being Joy and seeing it, stared some more, then began to laugh until I had tears streaming down my face.

Because it was a summer class, the lecture was winding down at six instead of seven and I was losing my mind with the need to see Leo.

I craved him, pure and simple. I craved his touch, his taste, his laughter, and most especially, the way he looked when he smiled at me. The memory of him holding me close as we cuddled, the scent of his skin when I buried my nose into the crook of his neck, all of it tormented me with little waves of desire that were growing annoyingly intense.

Ahead of me, my fading hippy professor droned on about economics in Bulgaria and I tried to pay attention, but my mind kept wandering to Leo.

What was he doing? Where was he? Was he thinking of me as much as I was thinking about him?

"Hannah," a familiar guy's voice whispered from behind me.

"What?" I replied softly without looking back.

"I was wondering what you're doing this weekend, if you wanted to hang out or something."

For a moment I just stared at my professor, thrown for a loop by that question. I took a quick glimpse over my shoulder to be sure that, yes indeed, popular and cute Tommy Pierce had just kind of, sort of asked me on a date. Had I fallen asleep in class and was dreaming this? Right now I should be freaking out inside, Tommy was hot as hell in an All-American-Boy kind of way, and he was nice to boot, but I felt...nothing. A scary blankness where there should be emotion.

"Hannah?"

I realized I'd been silent for a good deal of time as I tried to figure out why my emotions felt so dimmed.

"Yeah sorry, um…I'm kind of seeing someone."

"Oh." He sounded truly disappointed, then cleared his throat. "No worries. If you're ever free, look me up. My cell phone number is on our group sheet."

"I will."

I spent the remainder of class in a vague daze, barely remembering my walk from the lecture hall to my apartment building. When I reached the front door, I ran into one of my neighbors, an artsy dude who lived one floor above my apartment. We occasionally had to call them to turn their TV down, but they were nice guys and hot in a very emo way. I think they might have played in a band or something.

Roger, a tall and light-skinned black man with long navy-blue dreads, held the door open for me as he smiled. "Hey, Hannah. How are you?"

"Good, I just got done with class. How are you?"

We entered the ancient elevator together, the wood paneling peeling near the fluorescent lights of the ceiling. "Doin' good. My band has a big show tonight down at the Cycle, you should bring your roommates and come. I'll get you backstage passes."

He winked and I had to laugh, because the Cycle's backstage consisted of the kitchen prep area. "Tempting, but I'm afraid I'll have to pass. I already have plans tonight."

"That's too bad," he murmured in a way that should have been sexy, but barely made me tingle.

We came to my floor and I gave him an awkward wave. "Bye, Roger."

"I'll see you soon, Hannah."

By the time I made it down the long hallway that smelled faintly like bleach and curry, I was more confused than ever. Did I look different today? Were any of my bruises showing?

Then again, I was pimped out in another amazing outfit that Leo had put together for me, along with a note requesting that I wear it today, which I loved. Normally I wouldn't have been drawn to the bright teal-blue shorts, but they went perfectly with the sleeveless taupe silk blouse and accompanying Native American jewelry. You can't grow up in Arizona without learning a thing or two about turquoise, and I knew the cuffs I was wearing, which hid my bruised wrists, and the cute floral turquoise earrings were worth a lot.

Being so dressed up made me feel...well, pretty. Special. While some women may think it made me a gold digger, I really enjoyed it when Leo spoiled me, when he put thought into what he got me so they weren't just expensive trinkets he was throwing my way to keep me occupied.

Like the butt plug. That heavy piece of gold and jewels haunted me, made me squirm as I thought about what it would feel like inside of me. Leo hadn't said anything about using it in his brief note, so I'd hidden it in my stack of jeans in the closet. Shit, I wondered if I should maybe get a safety deposit box for something intended to go up my ass.

Or his.

I felt a warm tingle when I thought about putting anything in Leo's spectacularly rounded ass, but that arousal died a quick death when I walked into the empty kitchen of my apartment.

The plates were still in the sink, and the cereal splashed on the wall had dried to a crust, but for once

I ignored it. I'd promised myself I wouldn't clean up after Kayla, that she had to do it herself, even if it did smell. Instead I brewed some mint and lemon tea, something my grandmother used to make for me when I was stressed out.

Just the fresh smell filling the small room soothed me and some of the tension left my chest. I hated fighting, hated disagreements, and dreaded the eventual confrontation I'd have with Kayla about taking care of her shit. She'd cry, pout, whine, and try to manipulate me, but I had to stand up for myself. I was tired of defending her actions to Joy, tired of pretending Kayla didn't know she was being a bitch. Once upon a time, when we were young, Kayla had been the kind of girl that would stand up for me in front of the entire school, who'd been a good friend and someone I considered family. But she'd changed, we both had, and I didn't think I could be friends with the person Kayla was now.

I had to come to peace with the fact that the girl I once knew had grown up into a woman I didn't particularly like.

By the time I had my cup of tea and was sitting on the couch, I felt marginally better, though sitting had hurt my well-spanked ass more than a bit by the end of class. It was odd, when I was around Leo, I didn't notice any of the pain he'd inflicted on me, but now that I was alone, those sore spots hurt. Part of me felt as though I should be worried about the level of violence Leo exhibited in the bedroom, but I somehow knew he wouldn't hurt me. And I'd never told him to stop. No, I'd welcomed his violation, blossomed beneath his harsh touch into a phoenix reborn.

Maybe that's what guys sensed about me today, that I'd been well and truly fucked.

The front door rattled and a moment later, Joy came barreling in, tossing her blazer off to reveal the peach-colored blouse she wore beneath while she simultaneously kicking off her sensible heels. I had just enough time to put my teacup down on the table before she launched herself at me, pinning me beneath her, the smell of her strawberries and peaches body mist surrounding me.

Grinning down at me, she gave an evil cackle. "Now you can't escape! Tell me everything!"

"Get off of me and I will. Your giant boobs are squishing me."

"I'll smother you with them if you don't give me all the dirty details."

"Oh, girl, you have no idea how dirty things got."

While I didn't give her *all* the details, what I did share made the smile slowly slip from her cupid's bow lips. "So now you're into hardcore BDSM?"

"No, it's not like that — well, in some ways it is, but Leo isn't about being my Master..." I licked my lips, hesitating before whispering, "He likes for me to call him Daddy."

"What?" Joy gaped at me, her mint green eyes wide. "Hannah, that's disgusting!"

"No! Not like that." I smacked her arm. "Not like weirdo pedophile incest stuff. More like...this is so hard to put into words...he takes care of me. Makes me feel safe. Tells me how special and beautiful I am. And when I say he takes care of me, I mean he takes care of me, in all ways. I've never felt so...cherished by someone before. I know I've said this before, but I feel like we were meant to be together, like we complement each other really well."

"When are you seeing him next?"

"In an hour."

"An hour. So you spent the entire weekend with the guy, haven't been home long enough to even make a sandwich, and then you're taking off with him again?"

"When you say it that way, it sounds bad. Am I being a clinger? You promised you would tell me if I am."

"Did he ask you out or did you ask him out?"

"He asked me."

"And have you two done anything other than have sex? Go out in public at all? Meet any of his friends?"

"Yes, we did things other than have sex, yes we went out in public, and yes I met one of his friends.

Technically we also ate and slept, we went out in public but had sex there as well, and I don't know if meeting some of Leo's friends in his kitchen while coming my brains out and speaking in tongues was something Joy would approve of, but she didn't need to know any of that.

Rubbing my face, I groaned. "I really like this guy! He's different, seriously."

With a laugh, Joy shook her head, but worry etched a line between her brows. "Where have I heard that before?"

I cringed when I recalled how many times I'd told my friend the particular guy I was dating at the time was "different". How this guy understood me, how we were a great couple, and all the other foolish things I'd deluded myself into believing. I'd stalk his social media and study up on everything he liked, so when we talked, he'd be dazzled by my knowledge of the things he loved, even if it was only a surface knowledge.

And Joy, patient and understanding Joy, was always there to dry my tears when the inevitable happened and my heart got broken — or at least bruised. And her curvy form was so squishy, she gave incredible hugs that just wrapped you up in softness and love.

Too bad we weren't lesbians; she'd make a great girlfriend.

With a melodramatic sigh, I flopped back into the well-broken in couch. "But I really want to see him, and he made me promise I'd come over tonight."

"He made you promise?"

"Yes," I snarked, "he wants to see me and made me promise."

"Hmmm, maybe he's an even bigger stalker than you are, Hannah."

I flipped her the bird. "Eat shit, Dolly Parton."

"Whatever...but if he really asked you first," she ignored my irritated glare, "then I suppose it's okay."

"Thank you, Mother."

"It's just weird, this need-to-spend-time-with-you thing he has going on."

Trying to keep the hurt out of my voice, I fiddled with my hair. "Yeah, because why the hell would any guy actually like me and want to be with me?"

Wincing and scrunching up her nose, Joy held her hands up. "Okay, that came out really bad."

"It did."

Somewhere above us, someone flushed their toilet and our cheap ceiling did little to muffle the rush of water while Joy pondered. "Don't get me wrong, you are a stone-cold fox and I've been telling you that for years, but he seemed so sophisticated and…um, worldly when he was here."

"Joy, just spit it out."

"Don't get mad, his body is smoking and that hair is something else, but isn't he a little…mature for you?"

I frowned. "What do you mean?"

"It's just that, when he brought you home from the club that night, I couldn't help but notice how different he was from us, how out of place he looked in our shithole. That gold watch of his was a custom job and it probably cost as much as a year's tuition. I'm guessing from your new outfit that he likes to buy you things, expensive things. What kind of guy does that for a girl he barely knows? Does he want to be your sugar daddy or something?"

"No, he's not my sugar daddy. I know it sounds crazy, but he really likes taking care of me. We went to some luxe golf club and got a couples' massage," I hoped she didn't notice the way my cheeks were heating, "then had lunch and went for a walk through their gardens. He held my hand and talked to me, told me about growing up poor and how he loved being able to take care of his mom before she died."

"Wow, he talked to you about his mom dying? That's big."

"I know."

"Did you talk about your sister?"

"I did, and I cried a little, but not my usual

breakdown. And he held me while I cried, didn't say anything, just held me."

I thought of his response when I'd sent him a picture of me in my new outfit, his praise and admiration, the way he made me feel so beautiful, so good.

Joy glowered at me.

"What?"

"You keep spacing out and getting this silly smile on your face like you're high." She gnawed on her lower lip while staring at me hard enough to make me squirm. "This is worse than I thought. You really like him."

"I *told* you I like him."

"He sounds pretty intense, Hannah. I'm not sure if you need that type of guy in your life."

"What type of guy?"

"The type I'm not sure you're ready for."

Joy was a fixer. She liked to find broken people and attempt to fix them, which worked out pretty much never. I was her favorite project, a childhood friend she'd seen shatter before her eyes. Her almost maternal need to take care of me probably wasn't healthy, but it made both of us happy in a completely dysfunctional, codependent way.

I knew this because she'd announced that revelation our freshman year after her first day of Psych 101. Yep, one psych class and she was an expert on the workings of the human mind. When I'd tried to argue with her about it, she'd simply waved my objections away and said our codependency was healthy, that it was my relationship with Kayla and the mental scars that my parents left behind that were the toxic issues in my life.

"You've always looked out for me, and I probably wouldn't even be here if it wasn't for you taking care of me, but you need to let go a little bit. I'm an adult, and I promise you, what I have with Leo is special and it is mutual. I'd appreciate it if you respected my decision, as crazy as Leo liking me may seem to you."

The look on her face would have been funny if I didn't see the hurt in her wide eyes. "I just don't want to see you destroyed again. It's painful, Hannah, to watch you emotionally harm yourself over and over again. It's like watching you cut yourself and not being able to stop you from slicing into your skin."

My stomach clenched at that brutal imagery—and I had a sudden revelation of my own.

Shit, why hadn't I thought of it before?

Joy's cousin had killed herself when we were kids, and Joy had taken it hard. I remember having long discussions with her about death, me trying to deal with losing my sister and Joy trying to deal with losing a cousin who'd been more like a sister than her own. At twelve, these had been hard conversations, and it had been a dark time in both our lives, but we'd gotten each other through it.

It had been Joy who'd been there for me when Tiffany had finally died after spending months in a coma. It had been a hard, bitter process, made all the more difficult by my parents' inability to face reality. At twelve, I felt more like an adult than they did as the doctors argued that they were merely prolonging Tiffany's suffering by claiming they had faith she'd wake up cured. When their faith had failed them and they went insane with grief, it was me who'd ended up talking to the funeral parlor on the phone when they'd called, needing details for the ceremony. Thankfully, Joy's mom took over and dealt with the arrangements after I asked her what I should dress Tiffany in for the funeral.

My heart briefly ached, the remembered pain of attending my little sister's funeral, of watching her go into the earth, still had the strength to wound me all these years later. Then again, I guess you never really got over that kind of loss, and it would pop up when you least expected it. A song would remind you of them, or a joke they'd find funny, and you'd think about them like they were alive for just a moment, just a taste of what life used to be like when they were there to light your world.

Then you'd remember they were gone and your heart would die all over again.

"Look, I swear to you, Leo is a good guy. I got to know him this weekend and I really like him. Please, just give him a chance. It's not like we're getting married or anything, we're…" I couldn't think of how to put my complicated feelings into words. "We're building something good."

Once again, that familiar protective look came into her eyes, but without the fire. "I don't know if a weekend fuck-fest really counts as getting to know him, but I'll give him the benefit of the doubt. After all, he could have easily taken advantage of you at the club, or just tossed your ass into a cab, but instead he personally drove you home then carried you to bed. And the look he gave you as he left after bringing you home…my panties combusted just from being in the same room as you two. I figured he'd come back, I just didn't expect you to disappear for three days when he did and return dripping in diamonds. Then again, you are a sweet young thing. Bet he hasn't had pussy as tight as yours in years."

Not liking the thought of Leo being with any woman, I chucked a throw pillow at Joy's head. "Shut up!"

Wiggling her fair eyebrows in an obscene manner, she giggled. "Mmm, yeah, nice, fresh college girl snatch. Bet he ate it like a fat kid left alone with a hot batch of his favorite cookies."

"Knock it off, weirdo, I have to get ready for Leo."

"I bet you do. He's gonna be all, 'Oh, Hannah, I'm so glad you trimmed your beaver for me.'"

"That is a horrible impression of the male voice; you sound like a drag queen with a sinus infection."

Picking up the pillow, Joy stood and said again in an artificially deep voice, "Oh, Hannah, it's so goooodd, your pussy is so tight I could hook a hose up to it and use it as a vacuum."

"Shut up!" I scream-laughed. "You are so deranged."

Joy smacked around her imaginary dick before humping the pillow.

"Your pussy is so tight, you must use a needle as a dildo," Joy fake moaned as she tried to keep from laughing.

"Stop, you're going to make me pee my pants!"

"Oh baby, take that big, beefy blood sausage of lust in your tight, wet hotdog bun."

"That's just disgusting."

When she began thrusting into the pillow, I couldn't help but fall back into the sofa, laughing.

"What is wrong with you? Seriously, knock it off, you crazy hooker."

"Now tell me, you naughty little slut bucket. Who. Is. Your. Dad. E?" Wiggling her hips like Elvis on steroids, she yelled, "Who owns that tight pussy? Take that big ol' porn star Daddy dick. Oh baby!"

A knock came from the door and I managed to lurch up from the couch, Joy still too intent on fucking our throw pillow into submission with exaggerated manly groans and excessive of use of the word "cunt" to even hear that someone was here.

When I peeked through the eyehole, I felt a heady rush of tingles from the pit of my belly explode into my bloodstream. Happiness filled me at the sight of Leo standing on the other side wearing a dark gray t-shirt that lovingly hugged his muscular frame, his hair pulled back in a tight man-bun.

Hell yes he was older, and hell yes he was out of my league, but if he seemed as into me as I was him, then I was just going to thank fate and accept her gift instead of questioning everything to death. Damn, it was kind of refreshing to let all that useless fretting go. Liberating even.

Hearing Joy still yelling in the living room—once she got on a roll with something that amused her it took her a while to wind down—an evil impulse came over me and I quietly opened the door.

Leo's thick, light brown eyebrows rose up as I whispered, "Shhhh, follow me."

He did as I asked and I was practically choking on my laughter as we snuck up on Joy, who was now either pretending to have a screaming orgasm, or having a seizure while grinding against the pillow like a stripper on payday.

I waited for a pause in her theatrics, right after she moaned out about how good it felt to fill my pink taco up with her man mayonnaise, then cleared my throat. "Excuse me, Joy, this is Leo. I believe you've met before?"

She froze, completely, then I swear the only part of her body that moved was her wide eyes as they rolled to look at us. "Uhhhhh…"

Leo merely smirked while he looped an arm around my waist, drawing me closer. "Nice to see you again, Joy. Hannah thinks very highly of you."

Rolling over, she flipped her wayward curly blonde hair out of her face as she awkwardly clambered to her feet. "Uh, hi. This…this wasn't…"

Laughing, I leaned into Leo and hugged him tight then looked up at him, giving Joy a chance to pull herself together. "You're early."

"I was in the neighborhood and hoping you'd be home."

"What were you doing in the student ghetto?"

"Hoping you'd be home."

To my delight, he cupped the side of my face and slowly brought his firm lips down to mine, the merest brush of his skin tightening my internal muscles as my pussy began to grow more sensitive. My mouth parted on a gasp and he swept in with delicate and controlled strokes of his warm tongue that devastated me. A small, sexy-as-hell groan escaped him when he buried his head against my neck then took in a deep inhalation against my skin, the warmth of his gusting breath feeling like silk against me.

"I missed you," he murmured.

Smiling, I held on to his broad shoulders as he brushed his lips over my banging pulse, my eyes closed to better absorb the feel of him. "I missed you too."

Joy cleared her throat. "Can I offer you anything to drink, Leo?"

He stiffened then moved the slightest bit away from me, a serious look coming over his face as he gently said, "It's Mr. Brass. Only Hannah gets to call me Leo."

"Are you serious?"

"Completely."

She blinked a couple times and I could see she was equal parts scared and irritated. "Okay, Mr. Brass, would you like something to drink?"

"I'm afraid I'll have to decline. Hannah and I have plans." He grasped my hand in his own then raised it to his lips. "If she has no objections, I'll be keeping her until her finals on Wednesday."

"I'll need to study," I said in a breathy voice more suited for the bedroom than my living room.

He ran his knuckles down my cheeks and I noticed fresh cuts on the back of them. Grabbing his hands, I examined them and they also appeared swollen. Concerned, I looked up to find him watching me with that stupid void expression of his that I hated. His mental walls went up and I couldn't get a read on him at all. It was like I'd been receiving his signal loud and clear, only to find nothing but static where he'd once been.

"What happened to your hands?" I raised one to my mouth and kissed his poor knuckles.

"Hard workout," he muttered. "Got carried away

while I was fighting."

I could just picture him in some kind of silky shorts, prowling around a boxing ring, but I didn't like the way he was so casual about his body suffering abuse. "Well, try to be more careful in the future. Seeing you hurt, it bugs me."

The connection between us blazed to life as his dark gaze lightened, turned to milk chocolate and filled me with happiness as warmth and happiness encompassed me. "That's sweet, baby, but don't worry, I'm fine. Grab your stuff, especially what you need to study. I'll help you."

"You'll help me study?" All kinds of debauched images came to mind and I pressed my legs together to ease the sudden ache.

Chuckling, Leo gave my ass a little smack. "Yes, now go get your things. Don't bother with clothes. I have plenty for you at the house."

"Leo, you didn't have to do that."

"I know, but I want to. There's a difference." He smacked my ass again, "Go."

Laughing, I rubbed it while giving him a mock glare. "Fine, fine, fine."

I got my stuff as quickly as I could, using the nice backpack Leo had given me, and by the time I made it back to the living room, Joy and Leo were laughing together like old friends.

For a moment I stood back and watched them, an unwelcome jealousy pinging through me when Leo smiled at Joy. I wondered if he liked a woman built like a porn star, because Joy's rack was magnificent, the kind of breasts men devoted entire websites to, and her rear-end was equally well rounded, despite her small waist. Insecurity reared its ugly head and I almost went back to my room, but I noticed something that kept me frozen in place.

While Leo was giving her a charming smile, he was playing a part. The man joking with my friend wasn't the Leo I knew, wasn't the affectionate and open person I was used to. I mean he was, but there was something that alerted me, made me look closer at his face. It was in his eyes, in the crinkles around them. When he smiled at me they deepened, but when he smiled at Joy they remained almost smooth. His eyes weren't smiling.

Yes, it was crazy I noticed things like that, but when you'd been raised for most of your life by emotionally unavailable adults, you tend to look where you could for any indication of life. If it wasn't for my mother's occasional random flash of anger, I would sometimes wonder if she wasn't a robot. Leo caught me watching him and my suspicions were reaffirmed when his gaze filled with life and warmth. The change to me was profound, but Joy was oblivious as she nattered on about some class she'd taken with me in high school.

Something in my expression must have alerted him to my unbalanced emotional state because Leo quickly crossed the room and took my backpack, looping it over his shoulder and carrying it for me like a gentleman. Then he held out his hand, as though he knew I needed to connect with him, and I slipped his fingers between my own, instant relief filling me.

My mood lightened and when I turned to look at Joy, my smile was genuine. "I'm off. Text me if you need me."

She looked between me and Leo, then back at me again, and a grinned. "Bye, it was nice seeing you again, Mr. Brass."

"And you. By the way, since you were asking earlier—*I'm* Hannah's Daddy."

With that, we left a stuttering Joy, and I burst out laughing as Leo closed the door behind me. "Oh man, you got her good. How much did you hear?"

"Enough." He smirked at me, but it wasn't a nice smile. "I take it you told her about our kink?"

Suddenly realizing he might not have been cool with me talking about it, I quickly stuttered out, "I'm sorry, I didn't mean—"

Sighing, he pulled me into a hug and kissed me into silence before guiding us into the elevator. "Hannah, it's okay. I was just teasing you. While I hope you'd use discretion, I'm not embarrassed about anything that has to do with you or us. I could give a fuck what other people think, truly, so if you need to talk to your girlfriends, have at it. Just remember, I'm trusting you with this part of myself, and I hope that you wouldn't talk about our private life to any random person."

My shoulders drooped and I felt like crap. "I really am sorry."

"I know." We exited the elevator and I barely noticed the people entering staring at us. "Just in the future, keep in mind that I'm a wealthy businessman and people have tried, and will try, to blackmail me with all kinds of bullshit. It's the price I pay for being successful in a cut-throat business. There are many, many people that would love to tear me apart, so you have to be careful where you talk and who you talk to, and not just for me, but for yourself as well."

"I understand, really, I do." Guilt still dogged me as I thought about how upset I'd be if I found out he was telling his buddies all about how I was his baby girl. "I'll be more discreet."

"That's all I can ask."

Chapter 12

I was silent as I approached the Rolls waiting for us at the curb, still unused to people filming me with their cell phones as Mark gave me a nod then opened the door for us, his gray suit once again matching his eyes. The world was a different place now and my being with Leo meant I was going to have to get used to the lack of privacy. For someone with introverted tendencies like myself, it was uncomfortable, but my attention-loving side reveled in their open stares and envy.

Out of the corner of my eye, I saw a familiar face grimacing at me.

"Hannah," Kayla yelled out from the edge of the growing crowd.

I turned, my mouth tightening when I saw her decked out in a cute little pink dress that showed off her trim and fit figure, but was more suited to a party than walking to class. Her black, bobbed hair was perfectly styled and her makeup flawless. That, combined with her gleaming white smile and beauty queen good looks, usually made me feel inferior, lucky to be around her.

But not today. She still dressed, and acted, like we were in high school, and it was getting old. I know I'd been fortunate she was my friend in school, that a mean girl had taken me under her wing, but now I wondered when I'd grown up and she hadn't.

She looked like she was on her way to a club, not class like she should be. Her calculating gaze took in the Rolls, then Leo, and I could practically hear her speculating about his bank account. When she fluttered her lashes at Leo, I had the sudden urge to punch her in the face.

A warm breeze scented with a hint of desperately needed rain stirred the air and thunder rumbled off in the distance.

Struggling to keep from acting like a crazy bitch, I forced myself to say, "Hey, Kayla. I'm about to leave, what's up?"

She pouted at me. "You promised you'd watch Kiki for me tonight."

Kiki was Kayla's aunt's pain-in-the-ass Pomeranian that destroyed anything in its reach, and that we—meaning me—had to watch at least once a week. Normally I'd stay home and watch the dog, mainly because I didn't want it demolishing any more of my stuff. If Kayla was home, she'd put him in his crate, then our neighbors would complain when Kiki started up his incessant howling until someone let him out. Once again, usually me.

"No, I didn't. I told you I wouldn't be able to watch the dog because I have to study for finals."

"But you don't look like you're studying." Kayla sniffed as she took in the Rolls again, an ugly gleam entering her gaze.

"Hannah has plans," Leo said in a firm, no-bullshit voice. "Excuse us."

"Excuse *me*," Kayla snapped, the bitch that lived beneath her candy-coated exterior surfacing. "I wasn't talking to you. I was talking to *my* roommate, so butt out."

I was pissed, seriously pissed, as I growled, "Do not take that tone of voice with him."

"Really, Hannah? You're going to take his side?"

Tears filled her eyes and I wanted to apologize in order to keep her from crying, but I wasn't going to let her manipulate me.

"I'm not taking anyone's side. You asked me to watch Kiki, I said no because I obviously have plans, and now we're going. I'll see you on Wednesday. Bye!"

With that, I entered the car, leaving a stunned Kayla standing on the curb. Before Leo closed the door, she started to yell, but he slammed it shut, cutting her off as Mark quickly drove away. The silence rang in my ears and my heart thundered as I realized what I'd done. I'd stood up to Kayla. I'd rocked the boat and the world hadn't ended. Adrenaline began to wane from my system and the shaking set in, so much so that my teeth chattered.

Leo hauled me onto his lap, his erection pressing against me, distracting me from my freak out. "Breathe with me, baby girl. I've got you. Hold on tight and breathe."

I did as ordered, wrapping my arms around him as best I could while he cradled me close. "I can't believe I told her no."

He pressed his lips to my hair, his hands already stroking me in a soothing rhythm. "I can't believe she expected you to drop everything to watch a pain-in-the-ass dog."

I sighed and shook my head, hoping I wasn't messing up his nice suit. "The dog wouldn't be that bad, but its owners think of it as an accessory, like a purse, and put it away when they don't want it."

"I stand corrected. Sounds like the owners are pieces of shit."

"They really are. But her parents are worse," I whispered, as if afraid they'd somehow overhear me. "They were so mean to Kayla growing up."

"Were Kayla's parents mean to you as well?"

"Yeah, but in a different way. They always held me up as the shining example of a perfect daughter in order to make Kayla feel bad about herself. I hated that and would try to make them stop, but they'd only act even worse, so after a while I just stopped going over there. I know it hurt Kayla, a lot, and I always felt guilty about that."

"Jesus, your life has been filled with fucked-up people. Is Joy the only semi-sane friend you have in your life?"

"I guess she is; her and her family. They're a little odd, but in a good…normal way. Other than her cousin committing suicide, Joy's family lives a peaceful and happy life. I liked that, like the open love they have for each other. It always felt welcoming in their house, filled with life and people. I want that someday. I want to have a big house filled with family and friends, everyone happy to be there because they know our house is a good place, a safe place, and they're always welcome in our home."

"*Our* house?"

Realizing I'd let one of the daydreams I'd had during class slip through, this one about living in Leo's awesome house and having a big family together, I blushed. "Sorry, slip of the tongue."

To my surprise, he smiled. "I'll give you a slip of the tongue, but later. We have to stop by my office first. I unfortunately have unfinished business that I have to attend to before I can take care of you. But once that's done with, I'm yours until you have to go back to class."

"Really?" I sat up in his lap and smiled into his eyes. "Are you sure you can do that?"

"I may have to deal with a few things from time to time, but you're my priority, Hannah."

Sure I was glowing like an idiot, I gave Leo a quick kiss on his smooth cheek, pausing a moment to rub my lips over his skin. A bright spark of arousal sent a throb through my body and my nipples tightened so fast it almost hurt. The urge to taste him filled me, and I brushed a few long stray hairs off the side of his neck before licking him right above his collar, along his pulse. I could faintly taste his cologne, but it was mostly male sweat and musk. Delicious.

I took another lick, savoring his taste along my tongue, delighting in the way his body flexed against me. A muttered oath escaped him and he grasped my hips hard as he set me back in my seat with a firm grip and a teasing grin.

"Behave, little girl, because my control around you is seriously strained." He grabbed my hand and ran it over his hard length. "Feel that? Feel how much I want you?"

"Yes, Daddy," I whispered while looking into his eyes.

A throat cleared from the front seat, reminding me that we weren't alone. "We're here."

Still holding my gaze, Leo said, "Thank you. We'll

be right out. Go inside and tell them I'll be there soon."

Realizing that he had important things to attend to, and that I was being selfish by getting him all hot and bothered, I looked away. "I'm sorry."

"What could you possibly be sorry for?"

"Well, I'm the reason you're late for your meeting."

"You have no reason to feel bad about anything Hannah, understood?"

With a sigh, I blinked up at him and nodded. "Understood. Do you want me to wait out here?"

"No, darling, I want you as close to me as possible." He placed a soft, so sinfully soft and luscious kiss against my mouth, my bones melting like butter in the sun. "Come on."

He led me out of the car and I blinked as I saw where we were, the parking lot of a local animal rescue. I always dropped off my old clothing here to be used for bedding for the animals inside, and I'd dreamed of being able to take one of them home with me. I whirled around to stare at Leo, who watched me with an amused smile.

"This isn't your office."

"No, it's not."

"But why are we here?"

"Surprise."

Stunned, I actually stumbled back a step. "What?"

"Pick any dog you want...but I have a few rules. He or she must be housebroken, they must be good with children, and they must also be good with cats. My housekeeper's cat had kittens a couple weeks ago and I promised I'd take one off her hands."

I think I might have had a heart attack right there

beneath the dim, starry desert sky. "You're getting a dog...and a kitten?"

"I am."

I clutched my hands to my chest like some ditzy heroine out of a bodice ripper, my heart pounding as a huge smile stretched my face. "Really?"

"Really. I've been considering it for a while now. My neighbors had a cat and he was pretty cool. Kept to himself, and made you feel like he was doing you a favor if he let you pet him." The distant look on Leo's face in the harsh streetlights seemed especially poignant. "Some psycho fuck killed him, stabbed him and left him for dead in the alley behind our place."

I closed the distance between us, tears burning my nose as I grabbed his hand. "That's horrible, I'm so sorry it happened. Did they ever find out who did it?"

"Yes."

"Were they arrested?"

"No. I took care of it personally."

I opened my mouth to ask him what he meant, but caught myself at the last second. Some intuition told me I wouldn't like his answer...and I stood at a precipice. Did I really want to know the dark truth about him yet? Did I really want to know just how far his sadistic streak went? Or did I just want to let it go, to dismiss my paranoia and enjoy rescuing a dog from a life of loneliness and heartache?

So I turned a mental blind eye to my half-formed, disturbing thoughts and smiled. "Okay."

"Ready to go pick out a dog?"

"Absolutely."

We were the only people in the shelter, and I had a feeling Leo had made a rather large contribution to keep them open past normal hours. The staff was all smiles, giving us a tour of their facilities and explaining what they did. By the time we reached the kennels, I was afraid the middle-aged redhead taking us on the tour would offer to give Leo a blowjob next. The top two buttons of her shirt were undone, revealing a rather generous amount of tanned cleavage. She was nice enough, I'd seen her before since she ran the clothing drives for the shelter, but I was feeling distinctly hostile to her as she kept throwing Leo fuck-me vibes.

For his part, Leo ignored her, focusing all his attention on me and playing the part of the perfect gentleman, opening doors and escorting me from room to room with his hand on the small of my back.

I became very conscious of that hand, my skin warming beneath the weight of his broad palm, his fingers curving just slightly over the top of my butt. It was a proprietary gesture, and I couldn't help but walk a little taller next to him, proud to be his. I liked old fashioned manners; I liked how Leo treated me like a lady in public and a depraved whore in the bedroom. Yes, some feminists might stain their knickers at the knowledge that I enjoyed the virgin/whore dynamic, but fuck them. I liked what I liked and I didn't need their condemnation, or blessing, for how I lived my life.

"Well, here we are," Mindy purred as she gestured to the clean and spacious kennels. "We've got a full house. If you tell me what you're looking for, I can help narrow it down for you."

Leo repeated his requests, then nodded his head in my direction. "Hannah will have the ultimate say in which dog we pick for our home."

He winked at me as he said the "our home" part, and I know I flushed pink because the tips of my ears felt like they were burning in the hot sun. The look Mindy gave me was part disbelief, part jealousy, and part embarrassment. The childish urge to stick my tongue out at her filled me, but I managed to not act like a bratty teenager and instead focused on the small spaces holding the dogs on either side.

"I'd like a dog between the ages of six months and two years. One that's had a good family, and has had training. No small dogs, please, but also no giants. I don't care about breed as long as they're healthy."

"Of course," Mindy said in a voice that was less breathy and seductive than it had been for Leo, but her small smile was genuine. "I have a couple dogs down here that might suit you."

Mark joined us as we began our search—he knew a lot about dogs—and they were very patient with me as I took my time meeting all the animals. In the end, I kept returning to the cage of a sad-eyed, two-year-old, gold-and-tan-colored pit bull. She'd been with a military family who were now stationed in a country that didn't allow her breed, so they had to give her up. That had been five months ago, and no one had shown any interest in her because of the bullshit reputation of the pit bull breed being killers. Plus, she wasn't perky like most of the other dogs. She didn't jump and prance, barking for our attention or anything like that. She merely watched me with pale blue eyes that were filled with loneliness as her tail gave a hesitant wag, as if she was afraid to hope.

"This one," I said with certainty. "This is our dog."

"Let's see if she wants to go home with us," Leo said, and pulled me into his side before kissing the top of my head. "Can we pet her?"

"Of course, she's a real love hound."

When Mindy opened the door to the room, the dog suddenly came to life, her butt wiggling so fast she could barely walk as she barreled into me. I sank down to my knees and held her, giving her a good rub down while she sat then covered me in kisses. Leo crouched down behind me, enveloping me in his arms and steadying me while we scratched the pretty dog's belly and ears, telling her what a good girl she was while she went into ecstasy over all the attention. Mark gave her a few scratches as well, a rare smile breaking out on his face as he told me I'd made a good choice, and pointed out her doggy body language that showed us she was over the moon with happiness at getting attention.

Mindy grew more animated as we talked about the pale gold and brown pit bull, whose name was Honey, and Mindy learned I was familiar with the shelter. Turns out the dog had been raised with a cat, and was very friendly towards them, especially kittens, so Mindy thought introducing Honey to her new friend in a few weeks, after she'd had a chance to settle in, would be a great idea. Tonight, they'd prep the dog for going home with us, give her a bath, microchip her, and give some of the other volunteers a chance to say goodbye to a shelter favorite before we came back and picked her up tomorrow.

I gave Honey a long, big hug and promised her we'd see her tomorrow to take her to her new home, where she'd have the best life, because I knew without a doubt Leo would make sure Honey was always happy.

I was practically vibrating with excitement as we left the shelter, bouncing on my toes as I walked.

A shriek escaped me when Leo swept me into his arms then began to kiss me senseless, his hand winding in my hair and holding me captive as he ravaged my lips. I was glad the business district we were in was almost deserted this time of night, because our kiss was more than borderline indecent. He gripped my ass with both hands and I returned the favor, making out with him like a horny teenager in front of God and everyone. By the time we separated, I was breathing heavy, but still grinning so wide my cheeks hurt.

"This is the best surprise ever."

"I'm glad," he murmured, his eyes incredibly tender as he studied me. "You have no idea how good it feels to know you're happy, to know I've made you this way. Your smile is more precious to me than anything."

"Leo," I whispered then went in for another kiss, but he dodged my attempt with a chuckle.

"Come on, let's get you home so I can take care of you properly."

I flushed, then recalled how uncomfortable I'd been all day. Of course, right now, none of the residual soreness or body aches were there, but I wasn't used to rough loving and needed to take it slow. That didn't mean I wouldn't take him any way I could get him, but I trusted Leo not to hurt me, and part of that trust meant I had to be truthful with him about my body.

"Can we go...careful tonight?"

He helped me into the car and I was glad to see the divider was up between us and Mark. "What do you mean, careful?"

I sighed as he tapped the divider twice before we pulled away from the curb. I buckled up then turned in the lush and totally comfy seat to face Leo. Some of his hair had escaped his rubber band and I tucked it behind his ear, unable to stop myself from basically petting him. He seemed to find my touch fascinating and soon his eyes became heavy-lidded with pleasure as he relaxed.

"I liked everything we did, a lot, but my body isn't used to such...vigorous activities, and I was very sore today in class. It was uncomfortable and made it hard to concentrate."

His jaw clenched and I found myself nervously licking my lips as he stared at me like I'd done something wrong. "You were hurting today?"

"Well, yeah." I tried to laugh it off. "It's okay, nothing I couldn't handle. Just forget I said anything."

"Forget you said anything," he rumbled. "You want me to forget the fact that I harmed you beyond what you can take?"

"You didn't harm me! I'm just sore." I glanced at the partition between us and Mark then lowered my voice. "Really, I liked everything you did to me, and while you were doing it, I swear it was the best thing ever. Just today—well, I've never had that much sex in such a short period of time. My previous boyfriends were more of the one-shot-wonder variety than marathon-sex types."

His nostril's flared and my nervousness increased.

"I don't want to hear about your previous lovers, lacking or not. Do you wish to hear about women I've had sex with? Should I tell you how they serviced me, how they compare to you in bed?"

Pain lanced through my heart and I gave him a wounded look. "No."

"Well, I don't want to hear about men you fucked either."

His comment about comparing me was mean and cutting, something I didn't deserve, but I don't like fighting so I remained silent, curled against the door of the car. Leo didn't try to talk to me and by the time we pulled up to his house, I was desperate to get out of the tension-filled space. Before Mark could get to my side, I flung my door open and darted out, anxiety filling me as I tried to decide if I should even stay.

Leo got out of the other side and looked at me over the roof of the car. "What's wrong?"

"I don't have to be here. I mean, I can go home if you'd like."

His jaw dropped slightly. "Why would I want you to go?"

Mark discreetly walked away, leaving me alone with Leo in the semi-darkness of the artfully illuminated driveway. "You're mad at me, so you probably don't want me around."

The purpose and strength in his stride distracted me as he came around the side of the Rolls, his mouth tight and annoyed. "Why in the world would you think that?"

I hated how small and scared I sounded when I said, "You were upset with me."

He took my hands in his own and hunched down a bit so he could look me in the eye, his gaze searching my face. "Is that how it was with your family? When they were mad, they didn't want to see you?"

Uncomfortable, I tried to pull away, but Leo held me fast. "Kind of. I really don't want to talk about it, please."

"Fine, but listen to me. We may get mad at each other, we may fight and yell, rage and scream, but no matter what, you need to know that I don't want you to go anywhere. Ever."

"Ever?" I tried to make a joke of it, even though I not so secretly found the thought thrilling. "Isn't that a little permanent?"

He only smiled then bent to give me a brief but warm kiss. "It is."

I didn't know how to respond to him, so I slung my backpack over my shoulder. "What time is it?"

"Close to eleven."

I muffled a yawn, suddenly tired. "Yikes, I didn't realize it was so late."

"Come on, sweetheart, you've had a long day."

"Try a long couple days." I cuddled into his side as he put his arm around my waist and walked me into the house, the cool air conditioning feeling nice against my skin.

"True."

When we made it up to the bedroom, I found a very pretty, silky cornflower-blue nightgown with spaghetti straps lying across the bed.

"Is this for me?"

Leo glanced over his shoulder at me as he took off his gold watch and set it on the elegant silvery white dresser made of raw, bleached wood. "I don't think it's *my* size."

Rolling my eyes at him, I picked up the soft fabric, running it through my fingers and thinking of how expensive it felt, then thinking about Joy's "sugar daddy" comments. "It's lovely, but Leo, you don't have to buy me such expensive things."

He finished unbuttoning his shirt in silence, then took my hand in his and led me back to the bed before sitting on the edge. After pulling me between his legs, he took the nightgown from my hands, his long and skilled fingers stroking my skin as he did. I watched him as he carefully put the silky piece of fabric down, then looked back up at me, his gaze unexpectedly sad.

The need to soothe him had me cupping his cheeks, stroking his neck, and basically petting him. Thankfully Leo seemed to bask in my attention, and my skin tingled when he ran one of his hands up the back of my thigh, to just below the base of my ass.

"Do you want to know what one of the happiest moments in my life was?"

Thrown by his unexpected question, I nodded.

"I told you how we were poor growing up, right?" I nodded, looping my arms around Leo's neck as he scooped me up onto his lap, cradling me close like a security blanket as he talked. "Well, I started working as soon as I could, doing anything and everything around my neighborhood to make a buck. My hard work paid off and when I was seventeen, I was able to move my mom out of the ghetto and buy us a house."

"At seventeen?"

"Yep."

"Doing what?"

"I worked my way up through the Cordova Group. First as a currier of sorts, then an assistant, and finally becoming part of their security team."

"What about school?"

"I'm a drop-out, baby girl. Left after my freshman year and never looked back."

I stared at him, thrown by the idea that someone so rich, so successful, never even completed high school. My parents may have pretty much sucked in the nurturing department, but they made sure I went to school and got good grades. It was probably so I could be self-sufficient after they cut me out of their lives when I graduated high school, but I'd still been raised to believe that if you didn't go to college, your life would be shit. And only stupid people dropped out of high school, the kind who would spend the rest of their lives asking if you'd like to large-size that meal, or became petty criminals.

But Leo...he'd beaten unbelievable odds to get where he was today, and I couldn't help but feel that warmth inside of me increase tenfold as I gazed up at him with admiration. "You're incredible."

He seemed surprised, then he caressed my cheek, sending pleasurable sensations washing through my body in a powerful wave. "Why? 'Cause I gave my mom a fucking heart attack when I dropped out?"

"I'm sure you did, but to see you come so far, to have overcome so many obstacles—it's a little intimidating."

"You're intimidating," he said with complete sincerity. "You have no idea how you affect me, how much power you have over me, and what I'd be willing to do to keep you."

Instead of scaring me, his intense words thrilled me and I smiled. "You say the sweetest things."

The rich sound of his laughter soared through me, lifting my spirits and sending little bubbles of delight through me. "I've never heard that before. Now where was I?"

"You, being the overachieving super genius that you are, bought your mom a house at the same age I was babysitting to save up for concert tickets."

He kissed my nose, then continued, "I wanted it to be a surprise, so I took her for a drive one Sunday. She loved to do that, go for long car rides on nice days and see the world. My mom had this shitty little camera, but she took thousands of pictures with that thing. So she was busy snapping away, singing along to the radio, when I pulled up to our new place. It was in an older neighborhood in Tucson on the south side, and it was only a three-bedroom ranch with a nice yard, but when I took her up to the front door and handed her the keys…"

There was a hitch in his voice, in his body, in his entire being, as if he'd been dealt a deep blow. I didn't say anything, or even move, sensing that he was fighting himself, battling the tears that wanted to fall. Whenever I thought of my sister, all these years later, when she's been dead longer than she'd been alive, my nose still burned and my throat wanted to close. So I got what Leo was going through and I gave him as much space as I could to get himself together.

A few moments passed then Leo cleared his throat and adjusted his hold on me, loosening it a bit so he could look at me while he spoke. "You should have heard her shriek, Hannah. It was so loud, a couple of the new neighbors came out, no doubt wondering who the crazy woman doing a touch-down dance in the front yard of an empty house was, and if they should call the police. I was laughing so hard I nearly pissed myself as she celebrated, but when she finally calmed down, she began to cry. Not bad tears, you know, happy ones. She told me how proud of me she was, how much she loved me, and I felt about a hundred feet tall." His grew deeper, rougher, and I stared into his eyes as he bared his soul to me. "That's the way I feel when I'm able to give you something nice, something you've always wanted but thought you'd never have. It makes me feel a hundred feet tall."

Unlike Leo, I couldn't fight off the tears spilling down my cheeks. "I…Leo, that's…thank you. Thank you for sharing that part of your past with me, and thank you for all the beautiful things you've given me and all the wonderful things you've done. No one has ever spoiled me like this, ever, and it's an amazing feeling to know that someone cares. Not that buying me stuff equals affection, I like to think I'm not that shallow, but I've never had nice things, so I appreciate it. I guess what I'm trying to say is, I appreciate you, Leo."

Before I knew it, I was on my back on the bed, his face buried against my neck as his firm lips kissed the spot behind my ear and chills raced down my spine. The bed was so, so soft beneath me but Leo's kisses were even softer, ghosting over my skin as he slowly began to undress me. I swore every time he touched me it was the best feeling ever, but tonight his caress was different. The passion was still there, but it burned deeper, hotter.

Lifting his head, his long hair spilling over his shoulders, he whispered, "Hannah, the way I feel for you is beyond explanation, but I want you to know that I'd do anything for you, baby. You're so very special to me."

"Leo," I sighed as he lifted my shirt enough to access my bra, pulling down the cups to reveal my hard nipples.

The gentle press of his lips to those pebbled tips sent a hard beat of fierce desire echoing through my body, the need growing inside of me like a snowball turning into an avalanche.

"These are the prettiest tits I've ever seen," he growled before gently lapping at a sore nub, a direct contrast to his almost pissed-off tone. "Are these mine?"

"Yes," I sighed in languid delight as he began to stroke my body while he licked, each pass of his hands magic along my skin.

Silky, thick hair brushed over my chest as he kissed over my heart. "And this?"

Deep in his sensual spell, I spilled the truth without thought. "Yes, especially that."

"Most beautiful part of you," he murmured as he rubbed his cheek over my chest. "This belongs to me now, forever. You gave it to me and I'm keeping it, Hannah."

A ripple of pleasure whipped through my body and I worried I'd read more into his statement than he meant, but his eyes—oh his beautiful, chocolate-brown eyes—shone with a bright emotion that had the breath catching in my throat.

Sitting back on his haunches, he drew me up so I sat, my face level with his chest. The soft scrape of his calloused hand over mine as he pressed my palm to the light brown fur covering his chest had my whole body tingling. His steady, strong heart thumped beneath my fingers, and I absorbed the sensation of the vital life and energy pouring off of this healthy male animal before me.

"This heart, fucked-up though it is, belongs to you."

I sniffed back tears as I slid my hand up from his chest then around his neck, going to my knees before him so I could be closer to him. "I'll take good care of it, I promise."

He made a pained noise, then wrapped his arms around me and buried his face against my neck. "Let me take care of you."

"Please."

The warmth of his lips on my skin deepened my hunger for him, especially as he laid me back and began to descend down my body, stripping it as he went, until he had my very wet pussy bare to his gaze.

"So pretty," he said in a soft, distracted voice as he trailed his fingertip through my folds, grazing my clit and making my hips twitch. "And so responsive. I bet you don't even know how responsive you are."

I was going to ask him what he meant, but he reclined between my legs, forcing them open wider to accommodate his broad shoulders. Looking down the length of my body, I tried to burn the image of him there, from his dark eyes staring into mine from the harsh plains of his face, to the way his muscles flexed against his skin. I was so pale against him, a creature of darkness who'd never seen the sun, and Leo radiated a sensual warmth that curled through me like a hot breeze off the desert.

Instead of going straight for the good stuff like I expected, Leo pressed my left thigh open until my knee rested against the sheets, fully exposing me. He bent down and began to kiss a circle around a particularly harsh bite mark he'd left on my inner thigh. When his big hand grasped my calf to hold me still, I marveled at the total concentration on his face as he got closer and closer to the heated bruise, the same mouth that had injured me so violently now the epitome of gentleness.

"I'm going to show you how responsive you are, baby girl. Bet you didn't know I could make my bite mark feel like this."

My breath left in a harsh rush as he began to tongue the injury, lick it like a lion tending his mate. The soft, velvety rasp of his tongue on my inner thigh went straight to my clit, and I tried to lift my hips, but he held me in place. Each slow, sensual lick had my back arching, my head rolling to the side because of how damn good his mouth felt on me. The tension inside me rose while I whimpered and groaned, pleading with Leo to take me.

But he didn't.

Instead, he brushed his thumb once over my clit while still licking my inner thigh, bringing me to an almost instant orgasm.

The first contraction hit and my eyelids closed of their own accord, my body trying to process this burst of release that blindsided me. While still in the middle of coming, I suddenly felt Leo's hot, wet mouth sucking at me, his tongue probing my sheath and driving me right out of my damn mind. I screamed with pleasure, my voice breaking when he took my clit into his mouth and rubbed it in slow circles with his tongue. Hypersensitive by this point, I tried to push him away, to fight him off, but he was having none of it.

He reached beneath my thighs, his hands gripping my ass to keep me captive, pressing on the tender flesh of my bottom. Bursts of stronger pain mixed with the pleasure, breaking my mind down to the point I could do nothing but processes the intense sensations he was ripping from me. The firm hold of his hands on my body, combined with his deep, primal grunts of pleasure, had my legs quivering in his grip. With his thumb, he lightly stroked the big bruised bite mark on my inner thigh, adding yet another source of unexpected pleasure.

Like the soreness from his hard grip on my tender butt, I found only decadent satisfaction in him playing with his bite mark, my toes curling as another orgasm rippled through me, rendering me limp. When he lifted his head, I took a fistful of his hair and dragged his unresisting body up mine until I could kiss him. Our hands worked between us and I had his hot length free of his pants in no time. With a little wiggle of my hips, my aching core was rubbing against the impossibly hard crown of his shaft, the thick flesh pushing into me while Leo groaned.

"Fuck, so good," he whispered as he slid his hands up from my butt to my back, holding me tight as he rocked into me.

The lazy flex and roll of his hips was exactly what I needed, stroking the thick heat of his dick in and out of my clutching pussy, each slide of his flesh inside of mine better than the last. I clung to him, rubbing my face against the crinkly hair on his chest, then I licked at his skin and tasted the salt of his body, felt the tremors go through him with my every touch. If I was insanely responsive to Leo, he was equally responsive to me, groaning loudly as I gently scored my nails up his back with a smile. This—this perfect moment in time between us was absolute bliss.

His thrusts became stronger, deeper, the broad head of his cock bumping my cervix in a way that stung. He must have heard my hiss because he adjusted his hips, the rounded edge of his flared crown finding my G-spot and working it until my legs shook so hard, I had to lower them from his hips to wrap around his legs. Pushing himself up so he could look down on me, Leo, torso rippling, did this move that had me thrusting up to meet him, wanting more, needing everything he had to give me. I was so empty before I met him, so alone, and now he'd filled me to overflowing in every way possible.

Sweat made his back slippery as I clung to him, encouraging him to take me, telling him how good he felt deep inside of me.

When he finally found his release, he did it while crying out my name, and as I cradled his shaking body against mine, I had to fight back tears as I realized how much I truly, deeply loved him.

The next morning, an excited barking woke me and

I opened my bleary eyes, staring at an empty bed where Leo had been earlier. Sliding my hand beneath the sheets, I took in the lingering heat from his body still trapped there. The thought of how nice it had been to sleep in his arms last night warmed my belly, but the barking started up again and I bolted upright with a smile.

Honey.

After leaping out of bed, I rushed through washing up, finding another outfit from Leo placed across the settee situated against the far side of the room beneath a window. Today it was a super cute Alexander McQueen black romper that appeared to be a tiny flower-covered dress that hit high on my thigh, but was actually a pair of flowy shorts. It fit me perfectly, and as I adjusted the crisscross straps in the back, once again with no bra, I wondered how Leo knew my style so perfectly. A pair of comfortable black sandals completed the outfit and I pulled my hair up into a high ponytail, foregoing any makeup in favor of getting to Honey as quickly as possible.

I hustled through the house, following the sound of male voices and her occasional bark to the kitchen. Leo leaned against the slate counter with one hand scratching behind Honey's ecstatic ear, the other holding a cup of coffee. He looked good this morning, his hair down and loose in messy, damp waves, his face freshly shaved and just perfect for kissing.

As soon as I entered, Honey went alert, gave me a big doggy smile, then bolted across the room to me with a skittering of claws against stone floors. I braced myself, thinking she was going to jump so she could slobber on me, but instead she came to a halt before me and sat as pretty as you please. Bemused, I crouched down and loved on her, giggling when she licked all over my chin with excited little whines.

"I'm happy to see you too," I said with a laugh as her tail wagged a thousand miles an hour. "Thanks for not knocking me over."

"She was trained by her owners to sit when she wants attention, so she didn't accidentally knock their kids down," Mark said from near the sink, his grin wide and friendly, happier than I'd ever seen on his normally dour face. Today he was dressed much like Leo, in a pair of jean shorts and a t-shirt, though his was black instead of Leo's gray.

Not having seen him earlier, I turned my head so I could smile at him, still cuddling with Honey, who was a total love hound. "Hi, Mark. Thanks for bringing her home."

His smile brightened as he looked at the dog, who'd now flopped on her back and was in the throes of ecstasy while I rubbed her smooth belly. "She's a great dog. Smart, sweet, and will be easy to train. Honey is a perfect name for her, because she loves just about everyone she meets."

"Mark," Leo added with clear pride for his friend in his voice, "used to train dogs for the Detroit Police Department."

Taking in my man's relaxed demeanor and friendly smile, I mused that someone was in a good mood today. Then what he said sank in, and I turned to Mark with no doubt wide eyes. "Really?"

Mark nodded. "Yep. Leo asked me to train Honey, if that's all right with you."

"What are you talking about? Honey is Leo's dog,

you don't need my permission."

"Wrong," Leo said after he gave me a quick kiss. "She's our dog."

I flushed, wondering what Mark thought of our hyper-speed relationship, then whispered to Leo, "Really, she's your dog, you don't need my permission for anything."

"Really," Leo whispered back, "she's *our* dog, and I want you to be okay with Mark training her."

"Of course I'm okay with it."

Mark leaned against the counter and watched us pet Honey. "I'm going to introduce her to the other guards."

"Other guards?" I glanced over at Leo. "How many guards do you need?"

He exchanged a glance with Mark, who appeared unhappy, before returning his attention to me. "I'm a wealthy man, Hannah, and there are people who'd love to take what I have away from me. The grounds are constantly patrolled by at least four guards. You may see them occasionally, but they've been ordered to give us privacy so you probably won't interact with them much. There are two guest houses, Mark's and the one the guards use. Mark's home is the adobe-style ranch we passed on the way in. I had it built after I bought the land so I could always have him nearby. He's not only my bodyguard, he's my assistant, and we do a lot of work for the Cordova Group together."

I tried to remember the house, but was distracted when Mark crouched down next to me, rubbing Honey's neck as he said, "The nice thing about always having someone here is that Honey will never be alone. She'll have plenty of people to spend time with, which a dog like her needs. Folks think pit bulls are some kind of man killers, but they're actually very people friendly and they pine away for human contact if left alone for too long. I don't think I'll ever be able to teach her to attack a person on command, it's not in her nature, but I'll be able to teach her how to alert you to danger."

"Danger? What kind of danger?"

Leo quickly said, "There are snakes on the property, and the occasional coyote. I own ten acres and most of it is kept as wilderness."

"And scorpions." I made a face as I shivered. "I *hate* those things. One stung me once when I was a kid and my foot swelled up so bad I couldn't wear shoes for a week."

Mark chuckled. "Well, I supposed I could train her to sniff out scorpions as well, but I'm pretty sure Leo has this place sealed up tighter than Fort Knox. I doubt even a scorpion would be stupid enough to show its face here."

Honey rolled to her feet and began to sniff around the kitchen, her tail wagging so hard her butt swayed back and forth with a big old doggy grin. "She looks happy."

Pulling me into his arms, Leo rested his chin on top of my head. "She is, and you can play with her later, after you study."

I groaned, practically flopping in his arms in protest as I whined, "I don't wannnaaaaa."

Both men laughed as Leo supported my overly dramatic limp form. "I told you that your education is important to me, Hannah, and I don't want our relationship to have a negative impact on your grades."

"You're no fun," I grumbled.

His hot breath, lightly scented with coffee, whispered over my ear, "Oh, I'm lots of fun, baby girl, you just have to earn it."

Mark cleared his throat. "I'm going to take Honey for a walk around the property."

"Thanks, Mark," Leo replied as I gave Honey love before watching her leave with the other man.

"It's nice of you to share Honey with him like this, he needs it," Leo commented as he made his way over to the coffee. "Want some?"

"Yes, please." I took a seat at the kitchen table, tucking my feet beneath me as I watched Leo fix me a cup, putting just the right amount of cream and sugar in it. "What do you mean he needs it?"

Leo paused, the muscles in his forearm tensing. "It's not my story to tell, but Mark's wife was murdered a few years back. Happened while he was working and, as I'm sure you can imagine, he's had a hard time dealing with it. Gave up dog training, she was a trainer as well and it brought back too many bad memories, so Honey's the first dog he's let into his life in a long time."

I hugged myself, my heart hurting for the older man. "Oh my God, that's terrible. Poor Mark."

Making a shushing sound, Leo held my chin and tilted my face up to meet his eyes. "I won't let anything happen to you."

I was thrown for a loop by his statement, then remembered that his mother had been murdered. Part of me wanted to argue that bad things happened all the time, that he wasn't God, but I had a feeling that wasn't the right way to approach this. We all have mental minefields, triggers that, when tripped, unleash a host of unwelcome emotions and memories, and I didn't want to hurt Leo, I wanted to heal him. Truly, from the bottom of my heart, I believe love can heal just about everything, and I wanted Leo to know he had that from me.

"Of course you won't." I kissed his cheek, then nuzzled against his neck. "I trust you."

A timer went off, but he gave me a quick and hard kiss before going to the oven. "Hope you're hungry. The chef made waffles and sausages this morning."

I certainly was hungry, and we had a nice breakfast together, the time passing easily between us, and I found myself more relaxed with Leo than I'd ever been with a man. I wasn't worrying about how to impress him, how to make myself so attractive to him he'd never leave me. No, Leo made me feel secure for the first time, and those hateful feelings of self-doubt and inadequacy simply didn't exist when we were together. I couldn't explain it, and didn't want to overanalyze it like I did everything in my life; I simply wanted to enjoy the peace he brought to my world.

After breakfast, I camped out in his massive gold, red, and gray living room with its cool u-shaped suede couch and amazing pale wood table inlaid with a Native American designs done in semi-precious stones. I'd seen something similar once in a book, or online somewhere, and spent a good deal of time examining the bright and intricate surface. Onyx gleamed next to mother-of-pearl, brilliant lapis lazuli next to turquoise, the lines perfect and the faceted deep garnet flowers in the center of the design sparkling with flares of deep wine-red fire.

It was a struggle to force my mind onto studying for my Abnormal Psych exam, but I managed to get a few good hours in while Leo dealt with work of his own.

When he returned, I was daydreaming, staring out the window at the big infinity pool that seemed to spill directly into the red and brown desert valley below, the clear water sparkling in the bright sunlight.

"You don't look like you're studying very hard," Leo said from the doorway with a teasing scold in his voice.

Abandoning my tablet, I flopped back onto the couch then dramatically threw an arm over my eyes. "I'm studied out."

"Did you take your practice test yet?"

I frowned. "Noooooo, but I'll be okay. I've got this."

"Hannah." His tsking sound came from right beside me, and when I lifted my arm and turned my head, I found him sitting on the sturdy table, watching me with an amused gleam in his dark eyes. "My responsibilities as your man extend beyond the bedroom. I want you to succeed at everything you try, and I want you to have everything you've worked so hard to earn. I'm here to build you up, not tear you down."

"Leo, that's very sweet, but I'm twenty-one years old and I've been taking care of myself for a long time. I know what I'm doing."

He must not have liked my snotty tone, because his lips firmed and his body seemed to swell somehow, grow bigger. The perverse part of me liked it when he got intimidating and authoritative like this. It made me so incredibly hot when he showed his dominance.

"Well then, you won't mind a test, will you? And since you're so sure that you know the material, I'm sure you wouldn't mind if we made a little game out of it."

"Game?"

He nodded and I nervously licked my lips at the rather sinister smile now creasing his cheeks. "I may have dropped out of high school, but even I know learning is more fun when it's a game."

"This is true. What kind of game is it?"

He leaned in then smoothed a few stray baby hairs off my forehead. "I'd rather show you than tell you."

Oh, he knew just how to tempt me, and if I was being honest with myself, I was all for whatever he had planned, knowing I'd soon be out of my mind and boneless with bliss.

"Yes, Daddy."

He clucked his tongue. "That's yes, professor. Come with me."

"Yes, professor."

He arched a brow when I went to reach for his hand. "Tell me, Ms. Barnes, are you in the habit of trying to hold hands with your instructors?"

I tilted my head, then smiled. "No, professor. I'm sorry."

"Keep your hands to yourself. You've taken up my precious free time by being here to give you the test you missed. Do not irritate me further."

Tingles raced through me as I let myself sink further into the fantasy that Leo was my professor. Trust me when I say none of my teachers had ever, ever looked as hot as Leo, but I let myself fall into the realm of make believe, watching his ass and wanting to grope it. The mental image of him walking slowly in front of a large class, his silky black dress slacks molding to the bubbled curve of his butt, had me practically panting with desire by the time we arrived at his office.

There, in the middle of his massive stainless steel and wood desk, sat an odd contraption that seemed vaguely familiar. It was black and looked like a really big mailbox shape covered in black leather. There was something flesh-toned and rubbery on top, a strip of latex-looking material that had hundreds of tiny nubs on it. Frowning, I went to walk closer to it, but Leo cleared his throat.

"We'll get to that in a minute, Ms. Barnes. Sit."

I sat, my mouth dry as I stared up at him. The soft gray leather chair I perched on was big enough to fit two people, and I wondered if Leo planned on fucking me on it. If the fire in his gaze was any indication, he was just as turned on as I was, if not more. His cock pressed against the softness of his jeans, a little sigh leaving me as I remembered the pure ecstasy of having Leo inside of me…hard…so very, very hard.

"Ms. Barnes," Leo snapped. "If you'd pay more attention to my lecture than my dick, you'd have much better grades in my class. Don't think I haven't noticed the way you can't keep your eyes off of me, how you stare at me with such hunger. I can't touch your throbbing cunt without losing my job, and you your scholarship, but there is no fucking way I'm letting you leave my class without your punishment for being such a cock tease."

The rush of arousal through me was so intense it was momentarily painful, drawing a little squeak from me.

Taboo, the teacher and the student, so dirty and hot.

Getting into it, I gasped and leaned back, putting my hand to my chest. "How dare you! I'll report you to the dean for sexual harassment."

He smirked. "I have video of you playing with your pussy during class. Honestly, Hannah, did you think you could sit in the shadows and I wouldn't see up your short skirts as you spread your legs and watched me?"

I'd let him do just about anything to me at this point, he had me so turned on. "I'm here to take a test, aren't I? Or did you just come here to yell at me because you have blue balls?"

His lips twitched, but the darkness in his gaze gave me pause. When I fought back, when I got bitchy with him, my insolence challenged him in some fundamental way he couldn't allow. The way he slowly bit his lip, then released it in a drag of flesh had my nipples stabbing against my shirt with a painful rasp. Shit, that need was building in me again, the one that scared me with its unnatural intensity. No normal woman could keep up with Leo's sexual demands, but I not only matched him in his sensual insatiability, I was even greedier than he was.

With this in mind, I uncrossed my legs, the wide

leg of the romper almost revealing my panties. The position did expose the bite mark on my inner thigh, which was an even deeper purple and green today. Holding his gaze, I slowly ran my fingertips over the mark, the hitch in his breath filling me with a sense of power. His cock jerked against his shorts and my sex clenched in response.

"Hands behind your back, Ms. Barnes. You obviously have no self-control."

Around Leo, I absolutely didn't, and I allowed him to position my arms behind my back so my hands were holding the opposite elbow. It wasn't a super comfortable position, but I liked how it held me in place, made me even more helpless for my Daddy. He produced a length of soft black rope, which he wound around me while I was still completely dressed in the cute floral romper. It made the rope play all the more obscene as he crisscrossed the black cloth over my chest, then began to lightly bind my breasts. It wasn't tight, there was no pain, but it did give me the sensation of being held somehow.

Embraced.

While I reveled in the feeling of being tied up, Leo retrieved the strange object from his desk and sat it on the floor before me. As I examined it, that sense of familiarity came again, and when he plugged in the controls, then plugged the object into the wall, it clicked.

Holy shit, that was a Sybian—basically a high-end sex toy that I could never afford, but had seen in pornos and coveted. A woman straddled it like she was riding a horse, with the soft silicone parts pressed up against her sex. When the device turned on, those parts vibrated like a Formula One race car engine and they gave pretty much every woman that I'd ever seen a series of epic orgasms.

A full-body shiver went through me as Leo pulled my hair to the side, licking my neck before giving my earlobe a gentle bite. "Do you know what that is?"

"Oh yeah."

He fisted his hand in my hair and tugged hard enough to sting. "Is that how you talk to your professor?"

"No, Sir," I gasped, my clit pulsing in anticipation.

With his hand still clenched in my hair, he guided me over to the Sybian. "What is this?"

"A Sybian, Sir."

"What does it do?"

"Hopefully blow my mind?"

My hips thrust into the air as pain radiated from my scalp when his harsh grip tightened to truly uncomfortable levels. "Impertinent girl. It's time for your test. If you score higher than a B, the grade you need in order to keep your scholarship, you get to orgasm."

"What if I get lower than a B?"

"You get to find out just how painful orgasm denial can be. I'm not a nice man, Ms. Barnes, and I don't appreciate you wasting my time by not applying yourself. Now sit down and get comfortable."

With a squirm to my hips, I did as he said, the thin fabric of my romper and tiny scrap of panties I wore making it feel like I was bare against the device.

He strode over to his desk then turned on his computer, his gaze focused on the screen, not me. I didn't like that, didn't like that his attention was diverted, and some of my arousal died, replaced by unease. Even though I knew it was nonsense, the insecure part of me wondered if I'd displeased his somehow, if he'd be cold and cruel to me. When he glanced briefly over at me, I stared at him, hoping the adoring man I knew would return, but he only smiled cruelly, worrying me further.

"Question One: Give me examples of maladaptive behavior."

His expression was stony, bored even, but nothing could hide the dark lust in his eyes. I was distracted by him, drawn into his powerful presence like a moth to a flame, and I flexed against my bondage, the need returning. Then he turned the Sybian on and I nearly fell off of it.

"Ms. Barnes," he snapped. "I asked you a question."

"Depression," I blurted out, "alcohol and drugs."

"Very good."

His praise felt almost as nice as the machine vibrating against my clit and pussy, the tingles of an impending orgasm already building inside of me. "Thank you, professor."

The flare of his nostrils and clenching of his teeth let me know how much he liked this little game and I tilted my hips forward, only to whine in disappointment when he turned it down to barely a hum.

"Next question: Why are people who commit crimes considered free from psychological disorders?"

I struggled to recall what my study group and I

had discussed about this subject, but the power of the machine was creeping up again, rendering me dumb.

"Ms Barnes, I'm waiting."

I panted, wanting to grind myself into the vibrator but knowing Leo wouldn't like me making myself come without his permission. "Because criminals know what they're doing is wrong, are fully aware they're breaking the law, they have no delusions about right and wrong. They know they're criminals."

I slumped and groaned, my head rolling back as the vibrations increased even more, to the point where I was jerking with each powerful pulse.

"Good girl, so smart," he said in a low, dark voice, and I hovered on the edge of orgasm. "Come for me."

Tilting my hips forward, I pressed my clit fully to the wonderfully pulsating device between my legs, the rope biting into my shoulders as I arched, the orgasm rocking through me. As I panted, the vibrations mellowed, but even that was too much and I tried to stand — only to find Leo's big hands on my shoulders, pressing me back down, forcing me to take more. I made little pleading noises, but didn't fight him as he ran his fingers soothingly through my hair, letting my face rest against his thigh.

When I'd recovered enough to sit on my own, he returned to his desk as I shifted uncomfortably, my arousal soaking my underwear until it felt like it wasn't even there. My poor clit was beyond sensitive, but I still craved more, craved Leo's approval and soft touch. Resting my head against him while I coasted down from my climax had been one of the best moments of my life, and I was eager for more, to bask in the sometimes painful light of his attentions.

"Now: What is the main factor that decides if a behavior is socially acceptable or not?"

The hum started again and I sat back, which only ended up pressing my anus against the vibrator, sending entirely new sensations through me that had me squeaking out a startled, "Oh!"

"Is something wrong, Ms. Barnes?"

"No—no professor." My words came out in a moan, but I was proud I managed to speak at all. "It's umm, people have their own beliefs and…and…oh God."

My whole body was one big ball of need as I spread my legs wider, then cried out in dismay when the vibrations stopped.

"Wrong." The harsh tone of his voice brought my attention to him and his disappointed frown devastated me.

"I'm sorry, Sir."

"Don't think your tears and big sad eyes will gain you any sympathy. They make me hard, Ms. Barnes, my dick is like granite, and it pisses me off that I'm not inside of you. Makes me want to punish you."

I bit my tongue as a tear rolled down my face. "Yes, Sir."

"What are the signs of Ghost Sickness?"

Wanting to please him so badly, I composed myself enough to answer in a watery voice, "Because of a suppression of anger, people become panicked and depressed."

"And what do you think, Hannah. Is this true?"

"I think it's mostly true. You can't paint everyone with the same brush, people's minds are so different and they react to things differently, but I'd say in general, hoarding your anger does have a negative impact on both your psychological and physical health." Thoughts of how often I'd repressed my own anger came to mind. "You know how they say you can be worried sick? Well, I know you can also be angry sick, like so mad your stomach cramps but you can't let it out, have to swallow it down like bitter poison. Know what I mean?"

He'd stood from the desk while I was talking, making his way over to the now silent Sybian before lifting me off of it and carrying me over to the couch. "No, I don't know what you mean. If I'm angry, I don't bother to hide it."

With my arms still bound, he had me straddle his lap, his thick and rock-hard cock replacing the Sybian—warm flesh instead of plastic. He felt infinitely better than the toy and I rubbed against him as much as I could, relying on his hands spanning my back to keep me steady. I swear his cock pulsed against me and I wished my hands were free so I could touch his face, trace his lips and rub my fingertips over the thick fringe of his eyelashes beneath his heavy brow.

"I don't like people being mad at me."

"That's the difference between you and me, I don't give a fuck. I'm a selfish bastard, while you have a heart so big, it could love the whole world. But you need to protect your heart, keep it safe for me, and that means even if someone gets mad at you, I want you to stand up for yourself."

The rope around my arms loosened and I let out a hiss as I shook my wrists out, pins and needles filling me. "I do stand up for myself."

The look he gave me clearly said he was calling me on my bullshit and I frowned. "What? I do."

Running his hands through his hair, Leo glared at me and I glared right back. "Your roommate, Kayla...how often do you do things for her, like getting her dry cleaning and watching her aunt's dog?"

Even though I knew it was totally wrong, I automatically defended Kayla without thought, just like I always did. "It's not that bad, I mean, I obviously like dogs."

I didn't, however, like to clean up after dogs that were over five years old and still pissed and shit everywhere.

"How many times have you shown up at one of Kayla's classes to take notes for her because she was too hungover to get out of bed?"

"I was already on campus, all I did was sit in her class and record it on my laptop for her."

And take notes, and forge her signature in the giant lecture hall, but I wasn't going to tell Leo that.

When I tried to push away from him, he snarled, "How many times has she ditched you to leave with some random guy at a club? When I took you home with me, Hannah, Kayla didn't give one fucking shit about if you were safe or not. She was too busy doing coke in the bathroom to care, then too busy fucking some guy in his car in the parking lot and doing more coke before going home with him. Your friend is a drug addict who is going to eventually hit rock bottom, and she's going to try to drag you down with her so your body can cushion the fall."

"No she wouldn't, and she doesn't do hard drugs."

"Really, Hannah?" He scoffed at me, making me feel like a fool even as I grew more irrationally angry. "You don't think that spoiled bitch wants to waste her life away being either drunk or high and avoiding all her responsibilities? Pull your head out of your ass, Hannah, before she sucks the life out of you."

I shoved myself out of his lap so violently that I almost got away, but he gripped me tight and I had no choice but to stay in his embrace. "Let me go!"

"So you can run and hide from the truth? No."

"Fuck you," I shouted. "Let me the fuck go, now, Leo! I'm not kidding. Let. Me. Go!"

He abruptly released me and I stumbled away from him, my chest heaving as I pointed my finger at him. "You have no idea who I am, who Kayla is, and what we've been through. You have no right to judge me or her when you don't know either of us. So she has some problems, we all do, that doesn't mean I should just abandon her like her parents did."

Tension filled the air between us as Leo stood then stalked across the room to me, close enough that his wide chest bumped my accusing finger. "Why are you defending someone who is such a shitty friend to you? Someone who uses you, someone who treats you like a doormat, and you let her."

"She loves me!"

"She loves herself more. Are you really so desperate for acceptance that you can't see that?"

Pissed, so pissed I was seeing red, I swung out to hit him, but he gripped my wrist before I could make contact.

"Fuck you!"

Quicker than I could blink, he had me wrapped up

in some kind of crazy submission hold and taken down to the ground, his weight pinning me as I writhed and raged, calling him all kinds of names. Adrenaline pounded through me, turning me into a spitting-mad mess as I took out my rage on Leo, venom spewing from deep inside my soul.

I'd never, ever lost my cool like this but it felt good to let loose some of the pressure I'd pushed down deep inside of me. I liked to pretend that I'm normal, that I'm just like everyone else, but I'm not. My emotional shields are as fragile as glass, and it doesn't take much to shatter them, which is why I avoided confrontation. My mother had freaked out like this, became inconsolable as she gave her wrath free reign, and the thought of being like her terrified me.

"Don't let me," I sobbed to Leo.

With his weight still pinning me to the floor in complete submission, he shifted the slightest bit so I could breathe easier. "Don't let you what?"

"Don't let me become my mother. I don't want to hurt people like she does."

"You're worried about that? Hannah, you are nothing like your mother."

"You don't know her." My throat tried to close up and I shivered. "Her words can cut you like a scalpel, peel your skin from your muscles and flay you alive."

A low growl rumbled through his chest. "Anyone that would do that to their own child doesn't deserve to live."

"It's not her fault—"

"If you say it's not her fault because your sister died of cancer, I'm going to have to strangle you," Leo cut in as his hands tightened on my bruised wrists, sending jagged shards of pleasure-pain spinning through me. "Your mother was an adult who decided she didn't give a fuck anymore about anyone or anything but herself. That was her *choice*, not something that was thrust upon her. People die every day and their loved ones manage to go on, manage to honor their memories without eviscerating an obviously sensitive kid on a daily basis."

I almost said it wasn't that bad, but bit my tongue, because it was.

Rolling off of me, he stood up, then leaned down and lifted me off the floor, his body barely straining. "You deserve so much better, and I'm going to make sure that from now on, you get it."

Chapter 13

Four weeks later, I stood next to Leo in my lime-green, crocheted Valentino sundress, nervously playing with the delicate gold bangles stacked up my left wrist. I had matching gold bangles on my right wrist as well, hiding the bruises on my pale skin that never really seemed to go away. Probably because I'd beg, cry, and pout to get Leo to tie me up and hurt me into an orgasm coma when they did. I liked knowing they were there, liked knowing proof of his obsession with me was visible on my skin, a branding.

My nipples tightened and I threatened my body with no sex if it didn't behave. This was an important night and I didn't want to screw it up by acting like a horny bimbo. I'd spent hours going through the massive closet Leo had filled for me with designer duds at his place, finally resorting to begging him to help me pick out what to wear because I had too many choices. He'd happily agreed to. I think Leo had a not-so-secret fetish for dressing me, but he had great taste so I was happy for his help.

While I'd hung out with Leo's friends — we had them over for various dinners — the elder Cordovas were the closest thing Leo had to parents, and they wanted to meet me.

So basically, Leo was introducing me to his mom and dad for the first time.

Yikes.

The urge to check my hair was strong, but I knew Joy had sprayed the hell out of it after she'd put it up into a high ponytail, secured with a decorative gold band. We'd had an unusually rainy few days and the humidity didn't give my hair any extra body, just made it look lanky and greasy. So up it went, and I hoped no one noticed the fading bite mark on my shoulder. Joy had commented on it, but we'd doctored it up with makeup while she told me to tell Leo to take it easy on me. If she'd seen my hidden bruises, she would have no doubt freaked.

The creak of the large, weathered oak front door opening drew me out of my thoughts and I clutched Leo's hand in mine, hoping he didn't notice how sweaty my palm was.

To my relief, a familiar face appeared and I smiled at Ramón. He'd been over a couple times after the kitchen incident and had been nothing but nice, going so far as bringing me a bottle of wine from his family's vineyards in El Salvador after we'd talked about it one day. Leo had been grumpy over that, but I ignored him.

I'd learned he got grumpy a lot when it came to men paying me what he thought of as too much attention, even his friends. While I thought it was sweet that he got jealous, I wanted him to know he had no reason to be, so I made sure I touched him in ways that left no doubt we were together and I was his, whenever he felt insecure. Not that I'd given Leo a hand job at the club after some random guy had hit on me, but I did give Leo little touches and maybe a kiss, soothing the savage beast as well as letting everyone know who I willingly belonged to.

And what a magnificent beast he was.

Ramón dipped his head at me, the loose fall of his coal-black hair sliding forward to partially obscure his deeply tanned face. "Leo, Hannah, so good to see you. Please, come in."

We entered the front doors of the monstrous home perched on the side of Camelback Mountain, the grand Spanish-style foyer, with its gleaming white marble floors with bright sage-green and red tile work around the edges, took my breath away. One wall was covered with an enormous storm-pattern Navajo rug that must have cost a fortune, and the other held a really cool stainless steel and mirrored glass mosaic. This place was big enough to be a hotel, and I marveled at all the corridors branching off the large main foyer.

Leo had explained that Judith and Jose, Ramón's parents, had built this place large enough that each of their sons had their own wing of the home. Though all their sons had moved out, Judith and Jose hoped that someday this place would be large enough to house all the grandchildren they hoped to have for holidays and parties. It sounded like something I would do if I had the means, and knowing that helped me to relax somewhat.

I gave Ramón a brief hug, breathing in the citrusy cologne clinging to his silky black dress shirt, while Leo snarled behind me.

Used to it, we both ignored him.

"It's good to see you. I love this house, it's amazing. Like something you'd see in a movie."

He winked at me then held out his arm, the darkness of his dress shirt complimenting his bronzed skin and charming white smile.

Before I could move, Leo was between us, looping a possessive arm around my waist. "Where is everyone?"

"In the kitchen." His hazel-brown eyes moved between me and Leo, an amused glint lighting their normally chilly depths. "Come on."

My anxiety returned as we traveled through the massive, but empty house. It was odd to see so many beautiful, interesting rooms completely devoid of people. Even a little eerie, like we were walking through the empty set of some movie, just waiting for the cast and crew to bring it to life.

Any unease I'd felt disappeared when I walked into one of the biggest kitchen/dining areas I'd ever seen. The pocket doors across the room were opened to a fabulous garden and patio enclosure, making it feel like we were outside. Glazed bricks made up the floor and the dark wood cabinets created a U-shape with a massive slab of bronze, blue, and white marble in the center. A tall, comfortably rounded, silver-haired woman with cinnamon brown skin stood next to another lady dressed in what appeared to be a maid's uniform. Their voices were lowered as they spoke in Spanish and pointed to whatever was cooking on the stove in various copper pots and pans, which smelled amazing.

Ramón cleared his throat then said, "Hey, Mom, this is the girl that's stolen Leo's heart. Hannah. Pretty, isn't she? Hannah, this is my mother, Judith."

I smacked his biceps, but Ramón remained unrepentant as I blushed while Leo grinned down at me.

The elegant woman with the kind smile and silvery hair was dressed in a sharp teal blouse and black slacks that complimented her coloring perfectly. She crossed the room towards me with her hand held out, a big sapphire ring sparkling like the deep ocean on her right ring finger, a dazzling marquise-shaped massive diamond on her left. She had plump cheeks and a motherly smile, but I wasn't fooled in the least. According to Leo, Judith was the power behind the throne of the company he worked for, and shouldn't be underestimated. But she was also Ramón's mother, and the look she gave him was one hundred percent exasperated parent.

"Hannah," she said as she gave me a brief hug, the scent of her chic perfume momentarily enveloping me. "Welcome to our home. Can I get you anything to drink? Some wine perhaps?"

"Yes, please."

"It's such a pleasant evening, I thought it would be nice to eat outside tonight."

Leo kissed Judith on the cheek, and I didn't miss the way her smile softened. "Good to see you again, Judith."

"I've barely seen you at all these past few weeks." She took a bottle of wine from a wine refrigerator beneath one of the cabinets after giving Leo a fond but scolding look.

Leo smiled at me and I couldn't help but smile back, the affection and pride in his gaze fizzing through me like champagne bubbles. "I've been a bit preoccupied."

"Ahh, young love," she said as she led us out the open doorway and to an elegant black wrought iron outdoor seating area. The dining table was surrounded on two sides by mature palm trees before opening to a luxurious grass lawn that flowed down the side of the mountain. "I remember when I first met Jose, we were inseparable."

"How did you meet?"

The surface of the large table was made out of what looked like polished granite, and I took a moment to admire all the effort Judith had put into making everything look nice. During my time with Leo, I'd learned about all the crap involved with throwing a dinner party, and I had to hand it to Judith, she had quite a spread going on. A black Native American style vase filled with fresh orange and purple flowers stood in the middle of the table and it complemented the colors of the cushions covering the chairs perfectly. Gas lights flickered around us and dozens of tea lights in crystal votive holders threw a golden light over our faces. To my delight, tortilla chips were laid out in big black stone bowls, surrounded by smaller matching bowls filled with what I assumed was salsa.

My stomach faintly growled. I'd been too nervous to eat earlier and now I was starving. Thankfully Leo didn't hear it, or he'd have been at my side with a cheeseburger in an instant. I couldn't help but smile as warmth filled me over the thought of how much Leo enjoyed taking care of me, and how much I enjoyed his endless attention.

Leo held out Judith's chair, then mine right next to hers, before taking a seat himself on my other side. Right away he held my hand in his, and I relaxed, enjoying the splendor of a warm desert night in a fabulous setting.

While Leo poured the wine, and I chowed down on chips, Judith told me how her family had immigrated from a beautiful coastal city in El Salvador when she was in her early teens, and how she had trouble fitting in with her upper-class peers in America. One boy had been giving her a particularly tough time about her heavy accent when Jose had overheard then beat the bully to a pulp. From that point on, they'd been inseparable, and many years and three children later, they were still deeply in love.

By the time she finished her charming tale, I'd sucked down a glass of wine and was feeling rather mellow, yet giggly. We were waiting on her husband and other sons, who were on their way back from a business meeting, and passed the time chatting and laughing. Leo looked on fondly while I answered her questions about myself, flattered by Judith's genuine interest. As we talked, he leaned in his chair so he could put his arm around my back, his hand softly rubbing my shoulder, the warmth of his palm welcome in the cooling night air.

"Sorry we're so late, Mom," a husky male voice said from behind me.

I turned in my chair to find Ramón with men I assumed were his father and two brothers. All four men were cut from the same cloth, tall, dark and handsome, but there were slight differences between them. The man I thought was Jose had shaved his head bald, his salt-and-pepper eyebrows standing out on his tanned face. Next to him were two men in their early thirties I was sure were Diego and Fernando.

Both Leo and Ramón had mentioned them before, so I knew they were twins, but they sure as hell didn't look like it.

The guy on the right had hair so long he wore it in a braid down his back, giving him a vaguely Native American look. His copper skin glowed with good health and he filled out his khaki shorts and white t-shirt nicely. The man next to him was lean to the point of being unhealthy, a scraggly black beard matching his scraggly hair. His clothes were clean, but something about him just seemed…wrong. Maybe it was his overly bright eyes, or his jerky motions, but his presence set me on edge.

He completely ignored me and instead took a drink from a flask he pulled from his pocket, smacking Diego's hands away when he tried to take it from him.

Frowning, Jose cleared his throat. "Fernando, not now."

Fernando finally looked at me, and when he did, it was with such contempt that my entire body broke out in a cold sweat. "Why, afraid I'll scare off the *pendejita*?"

Leo started to stand, but Ramón was there. He whispered something in Leo's ear that took some of the fire out of his eyes, but boy was my man pissed. I'd never seen him this mad, and it was a terrifying sight.

My heart raced as anxiety took hold, and I wondered how I should handle the moment. Fernando was obviously sick, probably an alcoholic, and I could see how utterly mortified his family was by his behavior. And he was so thin, I hadn't really noticed how bad it was until his virile and healthy father and brothers stood right next to him.

"That's enough," Jose growled out, deep red burning on his cheeks as he glanced over at me with an apologetic look.

"What the fuck does it matter? He can just do his voodoo shit again and turn her back into his good little puppet." For a brief moment, sympathy crowded out the empty anger in Fernando's glazed, bloodshot eyes. "Why the fuck would you want to taint something so good with our filth? What the fuck is wrong with you people? When will innocents stop dying for our sins? People...*demons* like us don't deserve her."

"Fernando, *controlate*!" Judith said in such a loud, pissed-off voice, I couldn't help but swing around to look at her.

A loud crash came from behind me and I jumped, but Judith and Leo were already out of their chairs, blocking me. I tried to see around them, to figure out what the commotion was, but I couldn't see beyond Leo's broad form from my seat, all I could hear were angry male voices speaking in a mixture of English and Spanish.

Fernando was now yelling—no, screaming something in Spanish that was so rage-filled, it made me instinctively cower into a ball.

Judith said something in Spanish in a loud voice and Fernando's crazed shout got closer, switching to English as he said, "Like I give a fuck about meeting his mindless little sheep, like having some braying woman at my side is going to make everything better! She's nothing more than a puppet, a little whore puppet. Fuck this—leave me alone and let me rot in peace!"

Leo snarled and practically leapt forward, landing on Fernando with a roar as he put him in a headlock. Ramón and Jose struggled to both break them up and drag them into the house. To my surprise, Jose was unexpectedly strong for being in his sixties, and he was the one who managed to rip Leo off Fernando as I lost sight of them.

I went to follow him, but Judith put her hand on my shoulder and easily held me in place. "No, this isn't for your eyes."

The sound of fighting soon filled the night and I trembled, imagining Leo being beat up.

Unable to stand it, I tried to get up again. "Let me go! He might get hurt! I have to help him!"

The sounds of brawling grew distant, like the combatants were moving deeper into the house, and Judith looked at me with an arched brow. "What do you think you can do to help him? Unless you have some martial arts training I'm unaware of?"

"I could have knocked someone in the head with a vase or something."

"You mean you could have knocked my husband or sons out?"

Flushing, I looked away, pretending to study the flowers in the middle of the table. "If necessary."

I might have been more convincing in my tough act if my voice hadn't cracked.

"Well, I'm sure we're both glad that won't be necessary tonight."

I took another gulp of wine, draining the glass. "Why are they fighting? And why was Fernando saying all those mean things? What's wrong with him?"

When Judith sat, it was without any grace; she looked weary and beaten as she toyed with the edge of the table. "A little over a year ago, Fernando lost his wife and son in a terrible accident."

I sucked in a breath, my hand going to my mouth. "Oh—oh no. That's horrible."

"It is. He's had a very hard time dealing with the loss, and I'm afraid he's turned to alcohol to try to drown his pain. Earlier today he was sober, and I thought he was having a good day, but evidently I was mistaken. Please don't take to heart anything he says. He's just…not himself these days."

My heart hurt for her and I reached out, placing my hand on hers and giving it a gentle squeeze. "Don't worry about me, I'm fine. What he's dealing with, what you're all dealing with, isn't easy. I was too young when I lost my sister to even consider using alcohol as a Band-aid, but I don't judge Fernando. I'm so sorry for your loss."

"Thank you." She gave me an odd look. "Leo didn't tell you about it?"

"No. He probably didn't feel like it was his place to share your business."

"Yes," she said in a tight voice. "He's very good about not sharing our secrets. Goodness knows there are those who would use anything they could against us, including Fernando's grief. He's having enough issues dealing with the situation alone; I can't imagine what it would do to him to have the gossip columns hounding him about being an alcoholic. We've managed to keep it out of the papers so far, and they've kept their distance out of respect for his mourning, but his fans won't stay away for long."

"His fans?"

The side of her mouth, the lipstick now wearing off unevenly, quirked up. "Yes, my Fernando was—no, *is* a very successful race car driver, among other things."

"Wow."

"He always loved going fast, even when he was a boy and riding his bicycle downhill at full speed. Jason, my...my grandson, was the same way. They went skiing together in Aspen every year, scaring me half to death as Fernando zoomed down the smaller hills with Jason, but oh how he loved spending time with his father."

I swallowed back tears, the hollow feeling in my chest growing as my mind began to build an image of what Jason must have looked like, been like. There was nothing I could really say to make things better so I just kept quiet, being there for her while she fought to compose herself. My mind went to Leo and I hoped that he was okay, and that he hadn't hurt Fernando too much. Or vice versa, though I don't think Fernando could outbox a fly in his current state of inebriation.

"We're not normally like this, you know." Judith sighed and gestured to the table and our surroundings before subtly wiping at the few tears that had managed to escape. "Please don't let our drama scare you off."

Laughing, I smoothed my dress. "Don't worry; my mother could give all of you a run for your money when it comes to drama. I'm used to it."

"That surprises me."

"Why?"

"With as calm as you are, as peaceful, I would have thought your mother would be the same."

I shrugged. "I'm not usually this relaxed, I normally have a lot more anxiety, but Leo…he…he makes me a better person. I know I'm not supposed to say that, because the only people that can make us better are ourselves, but honestly, since I've met him, I've been in a better place emotionally than I've ever been before. He makes me feel solid, feel like I have someone at my back, someone who cares about me. I can't tell you what a positive difference he's made in my life."

She tapped her red nail against the base of her wine glass, the shadows from the candles deepening the lines of her face. "And you've only known him a month?"

Inwardly, I groaned. Joy, during the few brief nights I'd stayed in our apartment rather than at Leo's place, had said the same thing in the same careful, but doubtful tone of voice. "Yes, but I feel like we've known each other longer."

"I'm sure." Her red-rimmed eyes crinkled in the corners as she smiled.

"I know it sounds lame, but it's true. Leo's an amazing man and any woman would be thrilled to have him in her life. He takes such good care of me. I'm not just talking about the pretty things he likes to dress me in, he pays attention to everything I say and do. If I happen to mention there's a Chinese place I've been meaning to try, we're there the next night. When I told him about what a nerd I was in Junior High and how no one had ever asked me to a school dance, we went to Obsession that night and he had the DJ play a bunch of songs that were popular that year. You'd never know it, but that man can dance. Honestly, I feel bad because I can't give him the same things in return."

Judith was smiling fully at me now, the tracks of tears still running through the makeup on her cheeks, but the slope was gone from her shoulders. "Oh, I think you give him more than you know. Ramón has told me that he's seen Leo laugh, on multiple occasions, without someone having to die first."

I gave a little giggle, wondering what she was talking about with the "having to die first" part, but ignoring it. "He's funny! He really is, but his sense of humor is very subtle and dry. If you don't pay attention, you miss it. I love it when he laughs. He's got all that lion-like hair and with his deep voice, it comes out like a rumble of thunder. You feel his laughter in your bones."

"I've never heard him laugh that loud," Judith mused, "even before his mother passed. No, I think you do much more for Leo than you could possibly imagine."

"I don't understand how you could think that."

"It's not my place to tell, but rather, knowledge that will come to you when the time is right."

Slumping back into my chair, I crossed my arms, a chill racing over my skin. With very little personal padding, I got cold quick. Already my hands would be turning red, and eventually end up purple. It was part of the awesome perks of being super pale.

Wood creaked as Judith stood, then drank a big

gulp of wine right from the bottle, her wrinkled throat working before she let out a rough breath. The veneer of civilization fell away a bit, exposing a woman who was just as dangerous and intense as her sons, adopted and otherwise. Leo had warned me she was a power unto herself, but she'd kept that charisma dimmed around me, until now.

The very air between us changed as she slammed the bottle back on the table, her expression holding some sympathy in it. "What I *can* tell you is, things won't be easy when dealing with men like Leo…and women like myself. We think differently than most people. Our brains operate in a different way, not enough to label us as mentally deficient, or a danger, but enough that the way we see parts of the world, and how we react to them, are a bit off."

Almost too scared to ask the question, I breathed out, "Is…is Leo sick?"

"No, no, nothing like that. He was just born with a savage soul, the kind that could belong to a killer. Probably would have ended up in jail if he hadn't met up with my company at the tender age of fifteen. God bless his mother, but he was driving her crazy, and she asked me if I could find some kind of job for him on our construction site one summer in Tucson. Leo, as I'm sure you know, is a well-built man and able to take direction. He was a dream to work with and I wondered why his mother had been so hesitant about his ability to handle the job."

A bird called off in the distance, the sounds of the awakening nightlife filling the cool air as Judith continued, "I already knew Leo's mother, our sons had been friends for a few years by this point, and she made me promise, mother to mother, back when he was young and adorable, that I'd take care of him if anything happened to her. I just didn't think she expected it to happen so quickly, or violently, and that Leo would think he'd failed her or could have prevented her murder if he really paid attention. It marked him, to be sure, and I wondered if he would ever find the woman who fit all his edges and curves just right, the one who would not only join him, but heal him. Leo needs the balance of a good woman in his life, all my boys do, but he's the one who not only needs it the most, but is ready to bring the right woman into his heart permanently."

I really, really wanted to ask her if he was ready for it with *me*, if she'd had this conversation with another woman, what he'd said about me, what he hadn't said about me, and anything else relevant. I had no interest in what he did at work, it was all Top Secret security stuff I wasn't allowed to know about, but his personal life drew my obsessive attention.

I'd already torn through his house from top to bottom when he wasn't home one day, inspecting it, looking for some sign that would lead me to believe Leo was anything other than what he appeared to be, the perfect man. Instead, all I'd found was an almost brand-new home that showed pretty much no signs of being lived in, other than when Honey and I romped through the place. If we didn't dirty it up, the maid would have no job, so we did our best to leave stuff lying around and mess the house up. I did most of the destruction, while Honey napped near my feet.

It was an odd thing to do, but I'd heard Leo talking about firing the housekeeper's assistant, and I felt bad that she didn't have work because I cleaned up after myself. The first time I left dirty dishes in the sink, I stressed all night about it, but when I woke up, the place was as clean as I would have made it and the housekeeper had left me a tray with freshly brewed coffee and a creamy orange-frosted muffin.

I took the hint and began to drop clothes on the floor and not rinse out my glasses, but cleaning up after myself was an ingrained action that was hard to break. I told Leo what I was doing so he wouldn't think I was weird, but he merely laughed and said if he'd known I liked her, all I would have had to do is tell him, instead of making our bedroom a pigsty.

Threading my fingers together over the green crochet of my dress, I smoothed the skirt, trying to cover some more skin on my chilly legs.

"Cold, dear?"

"It is getting brisk."

"You must be starving, let's go inside and see what the chef has cooking."

I followed her back inside, the soothing silk of cool air blowing over my skin in a tingling rush. "Do you think they'd mind if we ate?"

"Of course not. I bet food burns right through you. I had a cousin like you, she'd eat six meals a day and still be hungry. You have a high…what's the word…metabolism—correct?"

"Fortunately, yes. I can eat pretty much whatever I want without getting unhealthy. Thankfully Leo is there to try to make sure I'm eating better than I was. He cooks for me all the time."

"He cooks for you?"

"Well, kind of. He tells the chef what to make for

me. His cook and I also go over every week's menu and we have a lot of fun doing it. Luckily the chef's really cool, and we come up with some unusual but good food pairings. Whenever we get super creative, Leo has the chef make a 'just in case' steak and potatoes so Leo has something to eat while I try more exotic fair that isn't always good. Though the ginger-infused pear soaked in apple schnapps was pretty yummy. We filled it with light chocolate and salted caramel so when you bit in, the combination of flavors was transcendent. I've been playing around with ideas for a more kid friendly version."

"It sounds like you've been busy."

"I have. Because of my burn, I wasn't able to go back to work for a bit. In fact, I won't return until next week, got some kind of extension. They're paying me while I'm out, and I don't have school, so for the first time in my adult life, I get to do whatever I want and it is amazing!" I let out a happy sigh before returning my gaze to an amused Judith. "And then there's Leo."

"I worry that Leo is too attached to you, that you might be feeling a bit smothered."

"If I'm being honest, I like it when he smothers me with attention. I'm...well, I'm kind of needy. For someone like me, Leo's overwhelming attentiveness is exactly what I want. He fills me up, Judith, and I've been empty and sad for so long."

"Have you been depressed as well, Hannah?"

The alcohol combined with Judith's kindness loosened my tongue. "Pretty much my whole life, but I deal with it. Occasionally I go on meds when it gets really bad, but as I've gotten older, I've learned to cope. That's not to say depression didn't totally mess with my life when I was in its clutches after my sister's death, but I had a great support system, outside of my parents, who held me together."

"What about lately?"

"I'm good. Really good."

"Amazing what true love will do to the wounded heart, how much strength can be gained from a genuine bond between two people. Do you really feel that bond with Leo?"

I darted a glance around, as if he was lurking nearby. "I do, but he doesn't know."

Judith adjusted her sapphire ring before shaking her head. "I'm pretty sure he does. I knew the second I saw you together. It shone from you like golden light, beamed from your smile, and the way you looked at Leo set even my old and jaded heart beating faster. If he's blind to that, he's a fool, and my son is no fool."

"Do you, you know, do you think he feels the same for me?"

"Well, he's never brought a woman to meet us, and according to gossip, any woman that he doesn't consider a close friend or family has to call him Mr. Brass, I should think so. There's also the fact that he had you calling him Leo from the get-go which shows me how absolutely sure Leo was that you were the one, the woman that was meant to be his."

"Really?" I tried to keep my cool, but it was hard. "Wait, that's crazy. Rational adult minds don't work like that; love at first sight is a myth."

"Or is it something so many people covet that when they don't get it, they try to make the gift a curse, or pretend it isn't real at all? I don't know what you believe in, but I know in the time Leo has met you, he's become a changed man, for the better. You give him the only thing he's ever wanted, the love and devotion of a good woman."

A little flutter of butterflies went through my belly and I really hoped she was right. He never failed to tell me how much he cared about me, how special I was to him, but he hadn't used the "L" word yet and I didn't want to be the first one to say it. All too often I'd told a guy I loved him, sure he was the one, only to get the dreaded "thank you" in return. If Leo responded with "thank you" instead of "I love you", I might just slip into a depression so deep I'd never escape.

So instead, I was desperately in love with a man who I was too afraid to tell.

How pathetic.

"Hannah," Leo said from behind me.

When I turned around, the smile on my lips faded at the sight of a bruise rising along his jaw. "Leo? Are you okay?"

"Yeah, I'm fine. Look, I need to spend a little more time with Fernando. Are you okay having dinner alone with Judith or should I have Mark take you home? I don't think I'll be much longer, I just want to make sure Fernando is…settled before I leave."

The thought of poor Fernando, trapped in his grief, made my heart hurt with empathy for the man and his terrible loss. "No, no, you're fine. I can do whatever is easiest."

"Are you sure?" He glanced over at Judith, who appeared to be busy on her phone. "You don't have to stay if you don't want."

"Really, Leo, it's fine. Judith is lovely and I'm starving, so if you don't mind, I'll stay here and have dinner with her."

Some of the shadows melted from his eyes as he scanned my face. "Thank you. I'll make it up to you."

"Nothing to make up. Now go, hang out with Fernando and I'll just have to suffer through some no doubt delicious meal without you."

My little bit of teasing worked and the gentle kiss he gave me had a reverent feel to it. "Thank you."

He said something in Spanish to Judith that I didn't understand, then gave me another kiss before leaving.

As soon as he was out of sight, the phone began to ring in my purse, an emergency beep alerting me that whoever was calling had something important to tell me.

After muttering an "excuse me" to Judith, I dug the phone out, hoping that it wasn't Kayla calling with some bullshit emergency instead of a true problem. This past month had been trying with her because I'd finally found a backbone—and she didn't like it. I'd never realized how much Kayla treated me like her maid until I stopped cleaning up after her, or an errand girl after I stopped running around and doing all her shit. I wasn't home enough to really be bothered by her inability to pick up after herself, but Joy was just about ready to slit her throat.

I walked a few paces away to stand by the dark window before answering it. "Hello?"

"Hannah, you need to come home," Joy said in a tense voice.

"What's going on? Are you all right?"

"Honest to God, if you don't come home right now, I'm going to call the police on Kayla."

"What?"

"Hannah, please, I need you to help me sit that stupid bitch down and listen to reason. Please. We got an eviction notice today!"

"Are you kidding me? How? We pay our rent every month!"

"No, we give our money to *Kayla*, who supposedly pays the rent. The notice from the landlord says we're three months behind! I don't know what to do! I mean, I have enough to cover it in the bank, but then I won't have any money for school in the fall. All of our names are on the lease, this could majorly screw with our credit."

Worry filled me and I looked around the room, hoping to spot Leo. "I'll be home as soon as I can."

"Okay. I'm so sorry to ruin your night like this, I know you were meeting Mr. Brass's surrogate parents tonight, but this is an emergency. Please apologize to him for me."

"Don't worry, I'll be there."

I hung up then chewed on the edge of my phone, my mind pinging between the missing rent, what was going on with Kayla, and finding Leo.

"Hannah," Judith said from right next to me. "Is everything all right?"

"I—no, no it isn't, and I need to get back home to deal with some issues."

"Is someone hurt?"

Not yet, but when I found Kayla, I was going to strangle her.

"No, just roommate drama, nothing life-threatening but I really need to be there for a sit-down with them. Can you give me the address here, please, so I can call a cab?"

"Don't be silly, I'll have one of my drivers take you back. But I think it might be a good idea if you waited for Leo to return."

"I don't want to rush him, but I really do need to get home and have a meeting with my roommates."

"I understand. Just wait here and let me call my driver."

"Are you sure? I can catch a cab."

"Really, it's no problem at all."

Taking out her own phone, Judith began to text as I sent Kayla a text as well, asking her where she was. I didn't want to let her know about the eviction notice, she'd just avoid us so she didn't have to face the music, but I was baffled as to why she hadn't paid the rent. She had a trust fund that deposited ten thousand dollars a month straight to her bank account, in addition to whatever money her parents sent her. There is no reason she couldn't send the landlord a check for less than a grand.

It wasn't until I was in the back of a luxurious Bentley on my way back to my apartment that I sent Leo a text, letting him know what was going on. When I didn't get a response, I leaned back in my seat, really wishing he was here with me. Everything was easier when Leo was around, probably because he took care of everything, but I missed more than just his need to care for me.

I missed *him*. His laugh, his kiss, the way he always watched me with what I imagined was love.

Chapter 14

By the time we pulled up to the apartment, I was feeling decidedly mopey and pissed. Mopey because Leo hadn't returned my text—he was probably still busy with Fernando, so that was fine—and pissed because Kayla hadn't returned my text or call either. She'd posted some pictures of herself at some party a few hours ago, taking a selfie with some chick I recognized from the movies.

Great, we were getting evicted and Kayla was off partying with movie stars.

I thanked the driver as he let me out, absently noting the people staring at me again. When I looked up at the building, I found a few people looking out their windows at me and nervously smoothed my hair behind my ear. I'd become something of a sensation in my apartment building and Joy liked to cackle about the rumors that I was some overseas movie star in hiding, a model, or a princess. Kayla, on the other hand, hated the attention I was taking away from her; she was used to being the object of envy, and went out of her way to try to upstage me.

I hadn't seen it at first, but after she changed into a beaded gold evening gown that would have fit right in at the Oscars before Leo was due to pick me up, then answered the door with her most flirtatious giggle, I caught on. While Kayla claimed that Leo was ugly and not her type, she sure went all out to try to get his attention when he came over. We're talking everything from making sure his favorite beer was always available, to touching him if she was able to get near enough to sneak a grope or 'fall' around him.

Not that I had anything to worry about. While Leo was polite to Kayla's face, and very good at acting like she didn't exist, I noticed the mask he wore around everyone slipping just a little bit and revealing his loathing for her when she was around. He didn't just dislike Kayla, he despised her. Once, when Kayla had tripped going down the stairs of our apartment to the sidewalk, she'd tripped, for real, and for a moment I was positive Leo was just going to stand there and watch her fall down the hard steps to the equally hard concrete below, with a smile. The look in his eyes was actually scary at times, like he was thinking of different ways of killing her during the brief times they interacted. Because of this, I tried to avoid her as much as possible, but she was always around if she heard Leo was coming to pick me up. Stupid bitch was either oblivious, or so fucked in the head she really couldn't see that Leo thought she was scum.

Joy said that Kayla had always done that with my boyfriends, that her self-esteem was such shit that she couldn't stand the thought of someone wanting me more than her. At first I'd defended her, but the more I thought about it, the more I realized Joy was right. Kayla had flirted with my boyfriends right in front of me, but I'd always made excuses for her, that she was just being friendly and the like.

A sinking feeling hit my stomach and I wondered if she'd ever slept with any of them.

As I passed our neighbors place I sighed as the loud heavy metal they liked pounded through the thin walls and I wondered how long I'd have to listen to 'Bang Your Head' before someone complained about the noise. To be honest, I barely even noticed it anymore after living here for two years. The first thing I'd noticed about Leo's house was how absolutely quiet it was. Here, in the beehive of my apartment building, there was constant noise and in a way I liked it.

The first thing I noticed about our front door was the bright yellow notice of unpaid rent from our landlord taped to it and embarrassment tightened my muscles, along with irritation. Joy and I busted our asses to make sure our bills were paid on time, that we were never late in order to build up good credit, and Kayla couldn't be fucking bothered. My hand shook slightly as I opened my door, and shame filled me as I wondered how many of our neighbors had seen the notice.

After letting myself in and tossing my purse on the kitchen table, still holding the moldy remains of Kayla's cereal and oatmeal bowls, I found Joy marching down the hallway from the direction of our bedrooms. She was still in her work clothes, a cute beige and black suit that flattered her curvy frame, and her wild curls had been tamed into a bun. Clenched in her hand was another bright yellow piece of paper that matched the one on the door and she waved it in the air.

"We have three days to either pay the rent or the landlord will start the eviction process."

I took the paper from her, scanning over it and

reading the notes about how many notices we'd been sent, including a registered letter, all of which Joy and I knew nothing about.

"Are you fucking kidding me?" I hissed.

"I told you that bitch was getting into some shady shit."

My heart broke a little bit as I realized my longtime friendship was finally, and irrevocably, dead. "Joy, I'm so sorry."

"This isn't your fault. Jesus, don't take the blame for this."

"But both you and Leo tried to tell me that Kayla was trouble, and I didn't believe you, didn't want to believe you-even though I knew you were right." My nose burned as worry and guilt twisted through me. "I'm so sorry, Joy, I'll find a way to fix this."

Joy grabbed me by my shoulders, and to my surprise, shook me. "Listen to me, woman, this isn't your fault. What you need to do is help me get ahold of Kayla and find out what the fuck is going on. While that bitch isn't on my favorites list at the moment, I *am* worried about her."

"Me too." I made my way into the living room before collapsing onto the battered couch, looking around the space that had been my home for three years. "Fuck. What are we going to do?"

Joy kicked off her heels then sat next to me, tucking her legs beneath her. "We'll figure something out. Worse comes too worst, we can stay with my parents until we can find a new place. And I can't imagine Leo will let you be homeless, so there is that."

"Leo has plenty of room, I'm sure he wouldn't mind you staying."

Before Joy could respond, the front door banged open and a bleary-eyed Kayla wearing the same sparkling green dress I'd seen in her selfie from earlier tonight, stumbled in, laughing with her arms draped around some not-hot older guy and two of his friends.

I shrank back into the couch as I got a better look at them when they came deeper into the apartment, the scary vibes the guys gave off made the hair on my arms stand up in a harsh prickle of instinctive fear. Joy must have felt the same way because she pressed up against my side, exchanging a worried glance with me.

I gazed at the kitchen table across the room where I'd left my purse with my phone in it.

They were all laughing, loud, like wasted loud, and that laughter died off when they spotted us.

Kayla hung off the older man, her eyes overly bright as she seemed to struggle to focus on us before smiling. "Girls! I didn't think you'd be home. This is Manny, Ray, and Doug. Guys, these are my girls I told you about!"

"Kayla," Joy said in a tight voice. "Can we speak with you, alone, please?"

Snorting with laughter, Kayla mocked Joy, "No, you can't speak to me alone. You're always such a party pooper. Come on, live a little!"

We didn't say anything and I studied the men with Kayla. The older guy, Manny, was busy groping my friend's ass, but the two burly guys behind him, probably in their thirties, stared at Joy and myself like we were two pieces of meat on display in a butcher's case. The one on the left, Ray, had dark brown hair that brushed his ears and mean little eyes. The one on the right, Doug, had light brown hair cut short and a cold gaze that made me even more uncomfortable.

"What, cat got yer tongue," Manny said with a wide, super-white smile. "Don't be shy. Any friend of Kayla's is a friend of mine. You girls party?"

I shook my head mutely while Joy said, "No, no thank you."

"No thank you," Doug said with a not-so-nice smile. "What, you one of those straight-edge girls? You don't like to have fun?"

"What about you?" Ray asked while taking a step closer to me, the gold necklaces draped around his thick neck glinting in the lamp light. "You look like the kind of girl that wants to have fun."

Kayla, oblivious to the drama, giggled as Manny tapped out a line of what I was assuming was cocaine onto the back of his hand before holding it up for Kayla to sniff off.

She took a big snort, closed her eyes and sighed, then shouted, "Party!"

I felt like I was going to puke, and that feeling heightened when Manny squinted his eyes and looked at me. "Who're you?"

"Nobody," I whispered.

"Hey!" Kayla squawked as Manny abruptly pushed her towards Doug, who caught her with a leering grin.

Approaching the couch, Manny's nostril's flared as he stood before us and smiled wide enough that I could see one of his molars had been replaced with a gold tooth. "Pretty little thing, aren't you? Normally I like my girls blonde, but I think I got a taste for something exotic tonight. You be nice to me, I be nice to you, right?"

Joy clenched my hand harder and scooted down the couch, away from Manny, pulling me with her. "Wish we could, but we have to run, you guys have fun. We have to get going. Meeting up with our boyfriends. They're waiting right now."

Kayla snorted. "Oh please, you don't have a boyfriend. Just stay and hang out, stop being such a bitch. I swear you're so fucking uptight."

I gritted my teeth when Manny sat down next to me, throwing a meaty arm around my shoulders and pulling me to him, the musky scent of his BO grossing me out. "Nah, I think you girls are gonna stay right here with us."

For the first time, Kayla looked slightly alarmed as she stared at Manny trying to draw me closer to his side while I resisted. Jealousy, along with worry, flared in her gaze, not that I gave a fuck at this moment. With her creepy ass…whatever he was leaning into me, I was fresh out of fucks to give for her emotional state. The stink of his heavily applied cologne hit me and I wanted to push him off, but I had a feeling if I slapped him, he'd be the kind of man to beat a woman to a bloody pulp. While he was thick around the belly, he was also big, and I didn't doubt he could break me with one hit.

The pungent odor of some kind of heavy alcohol and cigarettes washed over my face as he leaned closer, the smell of him invading my senses. "You ever try coke?"

Trying to inch away from him, unsuccessfully, I shook my head and battled back tears. "No. Please, I have a boyfriend."

He laughed, gold tooth gleaming, and it wasn't nice. "That's fine, I don't need a girlfriend—I got a wife. I just wanna fuck you."

"Her boyfriend," Joy piped up, her voice breaking. "He's not the kind of guy you want to mess around with."

The men all laughed while Kayla had a vaguely uneasy look on her face, like she knew something was wrong but was too wasted to figure out what. "He's an asshole. Makes me call him Mr. Brass instead of Leo. Why does *she* get to call him Leo and I don't? I'm prettier!"

Manny jerked back as if he'd been hit, his whole demeanor changing from scary to terrifying. "You're Leo Brass's woman?"

I opened my mouth to say yes, but nothing would come out. My vocal chords had literally frozen and I made an unpleasant choking sound. Manny narrowed his eyes, then slapped me. "What the fuck is wrong with you, bitch? Are you or are you not Leo Brass's woman?"

I couldn't say yes, couldn't make myself say the word, and I had no idea why.

Desperate to avoid another slap, I nodded as hard as I could.

That wasn't good enough, because I got another smack by his big hand, this time to my other cheek, leaving me with a throbbing face and what would probably be bruises. "I asked you a fucking question, bitch, use your fucking words or I swear to God you're going to regret it."

"Yes," Joy blurted out, "she's dating Leo Brass. Big

guy, long blond hair, scary. Rides around in a Rolls. Please—don't hurt her. They've only been together for a few weeks. She hasn't done anything."

Loud music continued to pound through the wall from our neighbor's place and I prayed someone still managed to hear me.

"Cunt, no one asked you your opinion." Ray fisted his hand into Joy's curls and held her as he slapped her once, then twice, snarling when she cried out. "Shut the fuck up. I don't wanna hear none of your bullshit."

Moving sparingly fast, Kayla tried to put herself between me and Manny. "Leave her alone."

I let out a sharp scream, my vocal chords finally unfreezing, as Doug grabbed Kayla by the back of the neck and slung her across the room so hard she hit the wall with an ugly thump.

"Get these bitches out of here," Doug snarled. "Take 'em to one of the bedrooms and tie 'em up."

Ray grabbed Joy by the hair, then Kayla, shaking them hard when they tried to fight him. "Bitch, you better shut the fuck up and behave or I'll fuck you with my knife, cut you up good from the inside out."

"No," I gasped. "Please, don't hurt them! Just do what he says."

Doug turned to me and I held my breath at the violence, the hate in his gaze. No one had ever looked at me like this and I despaired as I realized these guys were bad, like truly bad, and I was in great danger.

My brain went into panicked-rabbit mode and it took a great deal of effort to comprehend Doug's words as he looked me in the eye and said, "That motherfucker you let in your snatch killed my brother. Tortured him to death over slicing some stupid whores. Must'a taken Leo days to do it, and that sick fuck loved every minute of it. Bet he jacked off while he was cutting Kamron up. Been waiting a long time for a chance at revenge, and you, doll, are going to suffer."

"I don't—"

Doug hauled me up then he hit me in the stomach, so hard it knocked my air out in a painful blow. "Bitch, you brought this shit on yourself. You think you can fuck the Cordova cartel's torture master and not face the consequences? You spread your legs for a fucking monster."

The blow to my heart was greater than the agony of my body. "What? I—"

Before I could finish my statement, Doug hit me so hard my vision splintered into bright white fragments as I slammed into the wall from the power of his blow. Blood filled my mouth as I raised a shaking hand to my face, sobbing when I touched my deeply split lip.

Doug's nostril's flared and his eyes were opened so wide I could see the white all the way around. Screams filled the air before they became muffled and black dots danced around the edges of my vision. I have no idea how men fought all the time, because one good hit and I was down for the count.

"Shut those bitches up!" Doug roared down the hall, and I curled into myself.

Torture master, torture master—the words kept repeating over and over in my head in tandem with the racing beat of my heart.

With a tsking sound, Manny laid a hand on Doug's

shoulder. "Hold on, hold on. We need to do this smart. Doug, lemme get my phone out so I can record this. Don't kill her, don't hurt her too bad 'cause we need her mobile, but fuck her up enough to get his attention."

"No, please, no!"

I tried to fight him off, but he was too big, too strong. Jerking me up by my hair, Doug smiled as he laid a harsh slap over my already throbbing face, pain roaring through me. I would have screamed but he sent a fist to my ribs next, hitting hard enough that I couldn't even draw a breath. Fear paralyzed me, but did nothing to ease the pain as he hit and punched me, calling me vile names, spitting on me and ripping at my clothes. I managed to rally when he started to take my pants off, but he merely choked me until I almost passed out then continued.

Drawing in any kind of deep breath hurt and I stopped trying, hoping that I could go unconscious, make the pain stop, not be aware of the violation that was going to happen next.

They were all circled around me now, spitting on me, calling me names, saying horrible things about Leo. My insides shriveled as they discussed who'd get to fuck me first and in what hole, in the most humiliating terms possible.

All I could do was moan in abject pain, the discomfort so great it robbed me of the ability to do anything but exist in the moment. Blood coated my mouth to the point where it was all I could taste, dripping down from my probably broken nose over my already blood-soaked chin. My fingers throbbed from where Manny had stomped on them, and I prayed Joy and Kayla were all right.

At least with the men distracted breaking me, they were momentarily safe.

Holding me up by the hair, Ray wrenched my head back and stared down at me. "Her jaw may be too fucked-up for a proper blow job. I'll have to fuck her ass instead."

"You hear that, Leo," Doug mocked as he stared into the camera of his phone, taking a fucking selfie with my battered body. "Ray's gonna tear that little asshole up real good, then we're gonna take her someplace quiet and give all the boys a chance to help us fuck her to death. She's gonna die covered in our sperm like the whore she is. After that, we'll let the dogs have her and we'll film it all, make millions off your whore."

Nausea bubbled in my stomach and I began to retch. Ray dropped me like I'd caught fire, and if I wasn't so busy trying to keep my internal organs from rupturing as I threw up, his aversion to vomit would have been funny.

My abdominals cramped as I continued to heave, my retches loud enough that I missed the initial crash of the door to my apartment being knocked down. I forced my sore neck to turn and had to squint to try to see what was going on. My blood roared in my head, dark spots dancing on the edges of my vision as I finally made out who had arrived.

While it wasn't Leo, it was Mark, along with a man I didn't recognize, and both men were armed and furious.

With his lips pulled back from his teeth, Mark shot Ray in both legs with his silencer-equipped gun, the man's cry of pain satisfying a dark part of me that craved his suffering.

"Secure them," Mark snapped to the man behind him before he rushed over to my side and knelt down. "Oh, Hannah, sweetheart, where do you hurt?"

I couldn't speak, could only groan as I collapsed, trying not to do it in my puke. Mark made little crooning noises as he gently ran his hands over my body, inspecting my injuries. When he touched my hand, I cried out, and his voice shook as he soothed me. He told me it was going to be okay, that everything was all right, but nothing was okay and it probably never would be.

Somehow the man I loved, I worshiped, was responsible for me being beat to a pulp.

"Leo wants an update," some guy said from nearby.

"Tell him I think two of her fingers are sprained, maybe broken, as well as her wrist. Her nose is okay, it looks like they were more intent on inflicting pain than actual damage. She might have some internal damage but her face is too fucked-up for her to talk. You check out the other two girls?"

"Yeah, they were tied up and knocked out. The blonde will probably need stitches for a nasty gash she has on her temple. Hannah's in the worst shape." Footsteps came near us and the stranger made a low, unhappy sound. "Shit, Leo's going to lose his mind."

"He is, but tell him to hold himself together, Hannah needs him. I'm taking her to the clinic right now."

"Mrs. Cordova said to bring Hannah to the

compound if she's well enough to travel. She has her private physician waiting and can get him any diagnostic equipment he needs."

Mark cursed and I continued to cry, hurting too much for any type of conversation. "Hang in there, Hannah, we'll take care of you."

Chapter 15

I had no idea how much time had passed, the world was a haze of pain that I finally escaped by fainting, but what must have been many hours later, I woke up in a very nicely furnished orange and cinnamon-brown room that seemed blurry. I blinked, and that simple action sent a wave of pain through me. Swollen...my whole face felt tight and swollen. Next to me, a monitor beeped, and when I raised my right arm to touch my cheek, I winced at the poke of the IV in my hand.

"Hannah?"

Leo's familiar voice instantly soothed me and I croaked out, "What happened?"

"Here, drink this."

I groaned as he supported me, lifting me enough that I could grasp the straw between my swollen and throbbing lips. The water hurt my throat, but the pain was dulled to a manageable level. As the cool liquid hit my belly, my thoughts cleared a little bit.

"Joy, Kayla...are they okay?"

An angry growl escaped him and I looked up at Leo sitting in an orange suede chair he'd pulled up next to the bed. "They're fine."

"Who were those men?" I tried to clear my groggy thoughts. "Why did they do that to me? It was you...they hurt me because of you."

The guilt and pain on his face confirmed it and my

heart broke.

The door to my room opened, admitting Judith and her husband Jose. Wearing a conservative amber-silk dress, Judith's eyes were red as she took me in with tight lips. I watched her, strangely impassive as she stood next to my bed, like I was watching a memory rather than participating in the present. Jose joined her, dressed in a sharp navy suit, and his face was filled with a sympathy that didn't reach his eyes. He was wary of me, and he had a right to be. I wasn't feeling very stable at the moment.

"Hannah," Judith said gently. "How are you?"

"Get him away from me," I said in a whispery, trembling voice as a harsh sweat broke out over my skin in a stinging rush.

"Pardon me?"

I held her gaze, letting her see as much as I could through my battered features that I fucking meant it. "Get Leo out of here, now."

"Hannah," Leo said in an agonized voice, but I couldn't even look at him.

My throat hurt, bad, as I shouted, "Get your *torture master* the fuck out of here!"

"Hannah," Leo tried again, touching my arm, and I lost my fucking mind.

"Get out!" I screamed into his face. "I hate you! You lied to me about everything. Looking at you makes me sick! Get out!"

I struggled to sit upright, crying out when my right arm, which I just noticed was bandaged at the wrist, sent a bolt of pain through me so sharp, it cut through my hysteria.

Leo lifted me and I went wild, screaming and

hitting at him even though it hurt. My IV tore out of my hand and my blood spurted across the pretty burnt orange and cream bedspread. Cursing, Leo attempted to press the sheets to my hand, but I writhed against him, not able to stand his touch. How dare he act like he cared?

"What the fuck?" a man said in a loud shout. "What is going on?"

I screamed, a high-pitched sound that came from the center of my shattered heart. "Get him off of me!"

Abruptly I was released and I collapsed back into the bed, sobs racking me as I closed my eyes. Strong hands held me down, but they weren't Leo's—I knew his touch—so I didn't fight. A feminine hand smoothed my hair from my sweat-soaked brow.

"Look what you did to her," a man rasped from somewhere to my left. "Look what you and your fucked-up protégé did to her."

"Fernando—"

"No—fucking look at her! She's nothing but a kid and you let him have her, let him brainwash her. You screwed with her head so good she couldn't even say that she knew him. It makes me sick!"

Judith shouted at him in Spanish, but I could truly give a fuck. My fragile mind and heart had been struck a severe blow, one so harsh I didn't think I could recover from it. There was the sound of a scuffle as a new IV was placed into the vein at the crook of my elbow.

A few seconds later, cool relief flowed through my bloodstream and my sobs tapered off as blissful numbness washed through me. I knew people were still talking around me, and that I should pay attention, but I just couldn't make myself care anymore, about anything.

Two days later I stared at Judith, then the long, clear tube in her hand, and then back to Judith.

"You will either willingly eat, or I will personally force-feed you. And trust me when I say you will not like it."

Holding her eyes, I shook my head and folded my arms.

It was tough to look intimidating when propped up in bed on pillows, healing, but still unbearably weak.

Across my gilded prison/recovery room, Leo twitched, but I pretended I didn't see him. I was very, very good at that, at pretending he didn't exist. Since they were keeping me prisoner here and not letting me leave because I "knew too much", Leo had been a constant shadow that was slowly driving me crazy. After I realized no amount of pleading or empty threats would get them to release me, I decided to go on a hunger strike. Not one of my brighter ideas, but I hurt so much—both physically and mentally—and I wanted Leo to suffer like I did.

Just the thought of him sent a cramp of pain through my heart, or maybe it was only my empty stomach cramping. I managed to hold myself together and not give in to my hunger. I'd missed two breakfasts, two lunches, and now almost two dinners. They were probably giving me something through my IV, but I knew I'd already lost weight I could hardly afford to lose. But they couldn't make me eat and that was one small victory in my shattered world.

I'd be proud of myself if I wasn't starving, but my body was the last thing I had any kind of control over, they'd stripped away the rest, and I needed some form of rebellion.

"Please, Hannah," Leo said in a low, strained voice from nearby. "Please, you have to eat."

I swore I could feel him, maybe a pace or two away, his hands twitching with the need to touch me. Last time he'd dared to lay a hand on me yesterday, I'd gone a little crazy, reinjuring myself and getting knocked out again in the process. I've found the Cordovas are quite fond of putting people who annoy them to sleep. Sometimes forever.

"Leo, out," Judith said in a tight voice.

"Don't—"

She stared at him, and even I shrank back against the bed I was in. "Are you telling me what to do in my own house?"

I held my breath, waiting for Judith to beat Leo to death with the tube or some other irrational shit. Isn't that what a cartel lord would do? And as outlandish as the thought was of this sweet old lady cutting people's eyes out and feeding them to the fishes, Judith was indeed a cartel lord. Not like the drug lords you see on TV, no, the Cordova Group was run like a corporation, and this woman was the CEO. That's not to say her husband, Jose, was a sweet old man by any stretch of the imagination, but when Judith spoke, *everyone* listened.

I'd picked that up as I'd pretended to sleep, then eavesdropped on whoever was in the room with me talk. They never left me alone; the one time they had, I'd tried to smash a window to escape, which had only resulted in me collapsing in pain from my injured ribs.

It was Judith who'd found me gasping on the floor as I writhed in agony, who'd sighed and had her bodyguard pick me up and take me back to bed, while she lectured me on being a stupid child determined to cripple myself.

"I won't allow anyone to hurt her, even you."

She replied in Spanish, and whatever she said made Leo eventually leave the room, my stupid heart mourning the loss of his presence even as my mind celebrated a hollow victory.

"Now then," Judith returned her gaze to me as I eyed her bodyguard watching us impassively, waiting for her to order him to jam the tube down my throat. "I've had quite enough of this. While I understand your anger, you are damaging your body, and that is just stupid. Starving yourself to death to spite Leo is just plain cruel."

That had me staring at her, and my voice, rusty with disuse, croaked out, "Are you kidding me? *I'm* cruel?"

I didn't miss the small gleam of triumph flash across her lined face that she'd made me talk. "Very. The only thing Leo ever tried to do was make you happy."

I gawked at her, incredulous. "Judith, he tortures people to death for a living."

She waved her hand at me, the stunning ruby ring on her right hand flashing with inner fire. "So do I. What's your point?"

She sat at the end of the bed, a chill radiating from her that made me want to pull the covers over my head and hide.

"That's kind of an important thing to share with someone."

"He would have, eventually."

"And let's not forget the fact that he has enemies that will try to torture *me* to death the moment they learn of my existence."

My voice broke at the end of the sentence but I managed to swallow past the lump in my throat.

Clasping her hands together in her lap, Judith's lips twitched a couple times before she said, "That was my fault; you never should have been unprotected. I was so worried about Fernando that I forgot I'd pulled my security detail off your building. Leo didn't have anyone watching the apartment—"

I held up a shaky hand, irritated at how quickly my strength was waning. "Wait, you had people watching my apartment?"

"Of course we did. While you may think the worst of us, I do try as hard as I can to protect my boys, my people. The moment Leo fell in love with you, you belonged to me, and I protect what is mine."

That statement was disturbing on many levels. "I belong to myself."

"You do, but your heart is infinite, so even if you gave an enormous part of it to Leo, you'll never lose yourself."

Confused, irritated, and not liking this "benevolent/violent wise old woman" thing Judith had going on, I tried to rally my cause. "I'm not eating."

Shaking her head, she stood and moved to my bedside table, picking up the chocolate milkshake that

Leo had brought me earlier.

"If you drink half of this, I will allow you to see Joy."

That had me paying attention and I sat up, slowly because it hurt, but all the way. "Seriously?"

I hadn't been allowed to see either Joy or Kayla, probably because I was too busy acting like a mad woman.

"Yes, but on one condition. As far as Joy knows, those men were corporate rivals of the Cordova Group who Leo helped put out of business. It is best if she continues to believe this. It will allow her to live as normal a life as possible."

In other words, shut my fucking mouth about the Cordova cartel or my friend would pay.

"Understood."

"Good. Now drink."

I did as she commanded, slowly at first because my stomach cramped as the cold, thick liquid hit it, then faster when my brain registered the fact I was once again helping to keep my body alive and released the hunger hounds in my stomach.

I'd finished well over half of it by the time I handed the glass back to Judith before turning my head to burp.

"Good. Now, you'll learn that I'm a woman of my word, but all trust is built a step at a time. Are you ready to see Joy?"

"Now?"

"Yes." Her lips twitched and I swore she had a fond look in her eyes. "She's been rather…insistent about seeing you."

A quick phone call later and the door to my room

flung open, a wide-eyed Joy coming to a halt as she got a good look at me. Her blonde curls trembled as she visually inspected me, her hands nervously clutched in the denim dress she wore that fit her curvy frame perfectly. As I looked closer, I noticed her entire outfit had a new and expensive look to it. I'll say one thing about the Cordova cartel, they knew how to dress a girl.

"Oh my God, Hannah," she breathed, her eyes welling with tears. "Are you okay?"

Used to the pitying looks — my face was a swollen and bruised mess — I nodded. "I am."

"You look terrible," she said in a half sob, and to my surprise, Judith came to her side and gave her a one-armed squeeze.

"But she's okay. Just like I told you she would be, *mija*."

Not liking Judith being so nice to Joy, afraid the crazy old bitch would get attached to my sweet friend, I held out my hand, trying not to wince as Joy joined me on the bed, jostling me with her movements.

"What about you? Are you all right?"

"I am. Mr. and Mrs. Cordova, I mean Jose and Judith, have been great." She absently touched a large Band-aid on her temple I hadn't noticed before because it had been covered by her blonde curls. "I only had a mild-concussion and a few stitches, but Hannah, you look...I'm so sorry I told them about Leo."

"What?"

"I mentioned him. I brought your relationship up because I was hoping it would scare them off." Her eyes welled with tears. "And when they asked you if you were dating Leo, and you wouldn't say that you were...I thought you were too scared to talk or something so I told them. I didn't...I didn't know they'd react like that. I swear, honey, I was trying to protect you."

I thought back to that terrible night, remembering how I literally couldn't speak. "I don't know what was wrong with me. I tried to say yes but I couldn't, it was like someone was choking me. You didn't do anything wrong, I was trying to say yes. And please, please don't blame yourself, okay? I may not look amazing right now, but I'm going to be all right."

Joy took my uninjured hand in her own. "We're so, so lucky Mark came to pick you up."

I frowned, looking over at Judith watching us with a carefully pleasant expression. It reminded me of the fake mask Leo wore around people. A pang went through my chest as I wondered if he wore one around me as well, if the intimacy I thought we'd had was all an illusion.

"Yes, very lucky."

My stomach gurgled and Joy laughed. "How are you feeling?"

"Better. Um...how's Kayla?"

Closing her eyes, Joy let out a low breath. "That stupid bitch is in some expensive rehab out in California. That stuff she was snorting? That wasn't coke, it was heroin."

"What?"

"I know, heroin!" Joy shook her head, her curls bouncing as she clenched her jaw. "I talked with her for a little bit before she left, tried to find out what the fuck was going on with her. Basically, she's a helpless mess. She failed out of all her classes last semester because of her partying, which only led to more partying."

"No way."

"Yes way. She fell in with a bad group of people with expensive tastes, spoiled trust-fund babies like her, but with much bigger funds. She tried to keep up with their jet-set lifestyle but couldn't. All her credit cards are maxed, and she can't touch her other trust funds until she's twenty-five. But did that bitch want to deal with reality? No. Since she couldn't afford her own shit anymore, she hooked up with Manny and basically whored herself out for drugs."

"Shit," I whispered. "How did I not see this?"

Joy shrugged. "It's only gotten really bad since you started seeing Leo these past few weeks. Kayla's always been jealous of you, and to see you so obviously happy, with a great and successful guy who worshiped the ground you walked on, you really made her feel like the loser she is."

I wanted to laugh, because if Kayla knew what kind of man Leo really was, she'd consider herself lucky to be alone.

With a sigh, Joy patted my hand. "Please thank Leo again for letting me stay at his place, and thank Mark for putting up with me."

"What are you talking about?"

"Since our place is trashed, Mark offered me one of the spare bedrooms at his house."

"Oh, uh, right. So you're staying with Mark?"

"Yep, he's a very nice guy, quiet, but nice. Cute, but no romance vibe happening between us at all. It's more like living with my older brother."

"And there's enough room for you? You don't feel crowded?"

"No way, his place is freaking sweet! It even has a pool, and Honey is awesome."

My lower lip trembled as I thought about the loving dog that I had to somehow rescue from Leo…so I could do what? Live with her on the street while I'm homeless? A tear escaped and I brushed it away with a shaky hand.

"Why are you crying?" Joy asked as she rubbed my arm, unintentionally hitting bruises the long sleeves of my nightgown hid.

"I just…I'm tired and my pain meds are wearing off."

"Shoot, why didn't you tell me?"

Joy went to stand but I gripped her arm. "No, please, stay."

"You need to sleep and heal, so you can come home and show me around your new crazy house. Leo took me on a short tour when I arrived, and I gotta say, no wonder you were never home. Our place must have seemed like a third world country shit hole to you after spending time in Leo's mansion. Hell, now I'm mad I never made time to take you up on your invitation to have dinner there. Oh, and your chef says hi, and he's been working on some new recipes in anticipation of you coming home. And the housekeeper says hi as well. They all really like you, Hannah, and send their love."

"That's—that's very nice of them."

"And girl, that fire pit Leo has in the middle of his freaking pool! You have to talk him into letting us have a party there so my parents can meet him. I told them all about Leo and how he's taking such good care of you. My mom thought it was soooo romantic!"

She obviously thought things were still peachy between Leo and me, and I didn't dare tell her otherwise. "Yeah, romantic."

Trying to cheer me up, she stood and straightened her denim dress. "And just think. Once the doctor gives you the okay to travel and come home, we'll be able to hang out. Kind of. I mean I still have work, and we'll both have school, but think about the fun we'll have together! We can make sangrias and hang out in that fab pool."

"Sounds great, honey."

She gave me a careful kiss on my forehead, one of the few unbruised places on my face, then left in a flurry of curls and smiles. "Okay, I need to go pick up the books Leo ordered for you."

"Books?"

"Yeah, class starts next week."

"But I can't go to class."

Joy stared at me. "Didn't he tell you? In order to make sure you graduate on time, Leo arranged it so you can take the classes online until you can physically make it back."

"But—how did he do that?"

Joy grinned, her dimples popping. "I don't know if you noticed, but I'm pretty sure Leo can do just about anything he puts his mind to. He's kinda scary, but he loves you beyond reason so he'd move heaven and hell to make you happy."

I lay back into my pillows, closing my eyes and struggling to control my breathing as her words hit me like a blow to the chest.

"Hannah?" Judith asked in a soft voice. "Are you all right."

"Yeah, just a little dizzy."

The sweet scent of Joy's strawberry-and-peach body mist filled my senses as she gave me a gentle hug. "Miss you, babe. Sleep tight and heal up so you can come home."

"I will. Love you."

Giving my good hand a squeeze, she said softly, "Love you too."

She left and I still didn't open my eyes.

The room seemed so silent, so empty without her bright presence in it.

"She thinks I'm going to live with Leo."

"*Are* you going to live with him?"

"Not willingly."

"Because he's a killer."

"Among other things, yes."

"You do know he only tortures the guilty, right?"

I opened my eyes and managed to sit up a little bit. "What are you talking about?"

"Take those men that hurt you, for example. When Leo killed them, he did the world a favor by ridding it of absolute scum."

The chocolate shake in my stomach lurched and I had to swallow a few times before I could say, "He killed them?"

"Yes. And he made them pay for hurting you, just like he's made hundreds of child molesters, rapists, murderers, and psychopaths pay. He dispenses justice in a way the broken courts of this land never will, a justice that no matter how brutal, could never exceed the brutality of the crimes these bastards had committed. That same justice was brought down on the men who beat you so badly, men that would have gleefully raped you to death, and recorded it for a snuff-porn website they help run."

A cold sweat broke out over me as I remembered the blows of their fists, the men's foul words about tearing me open and passing me around, giving me to their dogs to fuck. "Okay, it does make me feel a little better to know they're dead."

"It should. Those men will never harm you again, and Leo made an example of them, showing the world what would happen if anyone were to ever hurt you. He loves you."

"No he doesn't, it's all a lie."

"He does, and all the denial in the world won't change that. You need to realize how very lucky you are to have a good man like Leo, how very blessed you are to be with a man who thinks the world is lit by your smile. I know this is a lot for you to take in, that you've lived a very sheltered life, but you need to let go of your fear and anger, it's blinding you to the truth. Forgive him, Hannah. Give him a chance to explain, please. He'd do anything, anything at all to make you happy, and I know you love him. That kind of feeling doesn't just go away."

I couldn't argue with that so instead I said, "I'm getting a headache."

She looked like she wanted to say more, but instead nodded. "I'll have the chef prepare a light dinner for you when you wake."

"Thank you."

In the quiet of the room, my heartache

overwhelmed me and I cried, wishing Leo was here with me. Even if I ignored him, his presences soothed me, held me together in some intangible way. I did love him, so much, and I wondered if what Judith said was possible, if I could forgive him, if I could accept him for who he was. Was I brave enough to be the wife of a cartel member? Was I out of my damn mind for even considering it?

The truth, both bitter and sweet, was that I adored Leo, loved him enough that maybe someday I could find it in me to forgive him, to live the beautiful life he'd tried to build for me.

Fuck, I wish he was here right now to hold me, to make everything better again, because I was so lost and didn't know what to do.

Those thoughts swirled around in my head, drawing me into a restless sleep.

I have no idea how long I was out, but someone shaking my shoulder woke me up.

The first thing I became aware of was the stench of alcohol, and when I opened my eyes, I found Fernando standing next to my bed, clearly agitated and shifting from foot to foot.

"What are you doing?" I asked in a thick voice.

While Diego and Ramón had come to visit me, Fernando had made himself scarce.

"I only have a few minutes before the cameras to your room cycle back, so you need to listen to me."

My mind shook off the remains of sleep and I sat up, smoothing my hair back from my face as I did. "What is it?"

"You've been brainwashed by both Leo and my

mother to love him."

"What?"

"Your feelings? They aren't real. Leo made you love him. I'm sorry. I should have told you sooner." He glanced over at the door, distressed and swaying. "I didn't know if it worked until I heard you yesterday, when you were with Joy."

"How—"

"Cameras, they have cameras everywhere. Even in your apartment. Now shut up and listen, time is running out. I knew his brainwashing had worked on you when you couldn't tell his enemy his name. When you couldn't speak? When the words wouldn't come? That was their brainwashing trigger kicking in to make sure you didn't betray Leo."

I thought I was going to be sick. "No, that's not true, that's science-fiction stuff. Brainwashing isn't real."

His humorless laugh made the hair on my arms rise up. "Oh, it's real. Those emotions you feel? They're hypnotic triggers left by Leo after he drugged you and warped your mind."

"No, no I do love him. That can't be faked. I *do*." My voice had a desperate pitch to it as everything started to fall into horrible place, making sense in a devastating fashion.

I had no idea what love was. Time and time again, I'd fool myself into thinking this was it, the forever guy, and every time I'd been let down. But being brainwashed into thinking I loved someone? I couldn't even process the idea.

"You know how hot you get for him? He forced that as well with a drug we call D128—an honest-to-god aphrodisiac that can make a woman desperate to fuck. Leo used it on you to make sure you gave him what he wanted."

"But why? Why would they do that to me?"

"Because Leo wants to keep you, make you his wife, but women can't be trusted." His head hung and his whole body sagged like his strings had been cut. "I'm sorry, I promised myself no more innocents would get hurt, that I'd make it up to Jason…but look at you."

"I don't understand what you're saying."

"Everything they told you about my wife and son was a fucking lie! The evil bitch that was my wife had my son kidnapped and held for ransom, she was greedy and stupid, believing the cartel she gave my son to wouldn't harm him. Instead — instead they killed him, and then my mother killed her. Mom and Leo devised a way to make sure no woman would ever betray us again, would ever sacrifice her child like my dead wife did. So they picked you, a perfectly innocent little girl that Leo fixated on for whatever reason. You're their experiment in loyalty, and you passed the test."

"Jesus."

His wristwatch beeped and he darted to the door. "If I were you, I'd keep this conversation between us. The cameras will be back on you soon, so you might want to pretend to sleep."

With that, he left me staring at the tangle of blankets, my already shattered world splintering into nothing.

Chapter 16

Leo

In total despair, I stared at Hannah and willed her to acknowledge my existence. For well over a week it had been going on like this, I'd talk to Hannah, try to get her to listen to reason, and she'd pretend I wasn't even here. And she was good at it.

Nothing I said seemed to penetrate the wall she'd built around herself. It was like she'd never even loved me. Everyone told me to give her time, to let her adjust, but something was wrong. If she was mad at me, I could talk with her, get her to at least give me one brief taste of her light before she hid it away again, but nothing I said made a difference. She didn't care that the men I'd tortured to death on her behalf had brutalized dozens of girls in the past. She didn't care when Diego explained how the Cordova cartel actually helped protect people and gave them good lives. And most of all, she didn't care that I was dying without her.

She'd wake up, eat, then stare out the window like a robot until her silence drove me mad, making me flee the one thing I craved most.

The only time she became animated was when she was doing schoolwork, and even then she'd only do it if I wasn't around, so I had to force myself to stay away.

Once again the terrible pressure of her silence

forced all the air from my lungs, leaving me desperate for a breath only she could provide.

Honestly, I'd thought by now she'd have forgiven me.

Instead, she got worse every day.

After telling her how Mark had trained Honey to open the door to the fridge using a towel, and grab him a beer, I went to touch her, and like always, she flinched away before I could make contact.

That, that flinch, was the only thing that gave me any hope at all.

If my touch still had the power to hurt, it also had the power to heal, but Judith had warned me not to push things with Hannah, and for now I was listening to her advice.

Fuck it all if I knew how to fix this breech between us.

Hannah was miserable, sad down to her core, and so hurt it made me bleed on the inside for her.

My phone vibrated and I saw a text from Fernando, asking me to meet him in the game room.

Delaying as long as I could, hoping she'd at least look at me, I finally gave up, drinking in her beautiful profile, still as a statue, like a starving man. "I have to go, Hannah."

Her long, dark hair gleamed as she cracked her neck, then went back to ignoring me, the brief glimpse of life slowly seeping away like grains of sand running through my fingers until I was left with only her shell.

With a heavy heart, I left her alone again, knowing as soon as I was gone she'd relax, then stretch out and go about her day, trapped inside of a cage I never intended her to be in.

I ignored everyone as I stalked through the halls of the Cortez manor, the urge to bring Hannah home with me tugging at my mind. I needed her in our bed, in our house, where she'd remember everything we had together, how good we were. Leaving her here was getting harder and harder, no matter how much Judith said Hannah needed space to heal.

I think Judith felt guilty about what happened between Hannah and myself, and her role in it, so she was treating Hannah with kid gloves.

I passed through the large, arched entryway to the game room, basically a massive finished basement that held shit like pool tables, poker tables, video games, and just about every grown-up toy known to man.

Fernando sprawled out on the far side of the room, a beer dangling from one hand, a joint burning in the other.

He'd managed to gain back some of the weight he'd lost, but he still looked ill and his diet of mainly alcohol wasn't helping. The pale red shirt hung off his broad shoulders and the hollows of his cheeks were still deep enough to give his face a hauntingly gaunt look. When his reddened eyes met mine, I inwardly sighed.

He was wasted.

"Gotta tell you something, bro." Fernando took a hit of the joint, then put it out and set the almost full beer on the table.

Okay, maybe not wasted. His voice and hands were steady, and his clothes were clean. To my surprise, I noticed he'd trimmed up his beard and that his teeth were brushed. The air of sadness still clung to him, but not the stench of depression.

"What is it?"

"First, let me say you have every right to be pissed. What I did was out of line, no matter how good my intentions."

A sinking feeling dropped my stomach to my feet. "What did you do?"

"Last week, I told Hannah you brainwashed her into loving you, and that her feelings for you weren't real."

He had just enough time to register the mistake of sitting too close to me before I was on him, my hands wrapped around his neck, determined to choke the life out of him.

Unfortunately, Fernando, when he was sober, was a ruthless fighter who was more than my match because of his freakish flexibility. With a grunt, he broke my hold then kicked me back, his foot to my gut almost knocking the wind out of me.

So pissed I couldn't even breathe without growling, I launched myself at him again and we rolled around the room, breaking shit, throwing shit, and having a no-holds-barred brawl.

My nose was bleeding freely by the time someone heard the chaos and broke us up.

Fernando's formerly clean shirt was splattered with blood, and I was pretty sure his once pretty nose was also broken, thanks to a table leg to the face.

Furious, I tried to shake off the men holding me back, but we must have been fighting for a long time because my body was already filled with the post-adrenaline-rush shakes.

"What in the hell is going on in here?" Jose roared.

Fernando and I snarled at each other, right up to the point when Jose smacked first me, then Fernando, in the back of the head.

"That fucking bastard betrayed me!" I roared at Fernando.

"I was trying to do the right thing, you fuck! I didn't know you actually loved her!"

Jose stepped between us with a Taser. "Either you two start making sense, or I'm going to electrocute both of you until you do."

Knowing this wasn't an idle threat—Jose had used this method in the past to break up his hot-headed sons—I managed to spit out, "He told Hannah I didn't love her, and that I only brainwashed her into thinking she loved *me*."

Jose's face dropped, his wrinkles more pronounced as he turned on his eldest. "You didn't."

The fire left Fernando's eyes and he sagged against the men holding him. "I fucked up, *Papi*. I thought it was all bullshit, that they were fucking this innocent girl over. She almost died because your brainwashing was strong enough to keep her from saying your name, Leo, because it would have put you in danger. She literally couldn't speak because of your mind-fuck! That is some seriously messed-up shit."

Guilt hit me in an uncomfortable rush. "I didn't intend for that to happen."

"But it did." He shrugged off the guards. "Only I was wrong about one thing. You *do* love her, and it's real. She loves you as well. I know you keep saying you didn't brainwash her to love you—"

"I didn't," I growled yet again, wondering when in

the hell anyone was going to believe me.

"I know, I know. Fuck, I'm messed up, Leo. My brain isn't thinking right and…I need to go away for a while. Just get away from all of this and try to figure out what I'm going to do with my life besides waste it wishing I was dead."

Jose clasped his son's shoulder, his hammered-gold wedding band gleaming against his wrinkled brown skin. "Anything you need, we're here for you."

"I know, Dad, but I have to do this on my own. Don't worry. I'm over the whole killing myself bullshit. Obviously I still have stuff to do here on earth before God lets me see Jason again, so I need to figure out what it is and get to it."

Jose looked like he wanted to argue, but nodded instead. "I understand. Have you told your mother?"

"Do you see her trying to chloroform me?"

Everyone in the room laughed while Jose gave his son a wry grin. "This is true."

They hugged, Fernando smearing blood on his father's clothes, before he hugged me as well, our fight forgotten as I held him tight.

"Thank you for telling me."

He released me then nodded. "You want my advice?"

"No."

"Well, you're going to get it anyways. Stop fucking listening to my mother. She may think she knows what she's talking about, but she has no clue how your relationship with Hannah works, only you do. While distance may be what my mom needs in order to forgive someone, I don't think Hannah's like that.

You'll need to convince her that you love her, and allowing her to lock herself away in her mind isn't gonna get her to pay attention."

He said the words I'd been already thinking, and I nodded. "Maybe I've given her too much space."

"I don't blame you, the whole situation is royally screwed up, and I didn't make it any easier. But if you have a chance with Hannah, any chance at all, you need to make your move, and quick."

Chapter 17

Hannah

I sat in a comfortable floral, padded chair, completely ignoring Leo as I stared at the desert landscape outside. There were little bubbling sprinklers where I could watch the desert animals and insects come out of hiding for a drink. Though they didn't usually appear if Leo was around, like they had some sense a predator was close even if they couldn't see us through the one-way glass.

I hadn't spoken to him since the day I'd found out everything I felt for Leo was a drug-induced lie. Right now, Leo was droning on about something but his voice had just become a lulling cadence, a background hum that blended in with the hollow ache in my chest. I'd found that if I tried hard enough, I could let my mind drift in a kind of meditative state, unaware as possible of the world around me.

Still, no matter how hard I tried, thoughts of him slipped through, and they hurt.

I'd never been anything more than an experiment to Leo, some stupid little girl he could fuck and make her call him Daddy. A distant part of my mind argued that even before I met Leo, I liked the taboo power-exchange relationships, but I didn't pay it any attention. I'd become very good at drifting, at not thinking about anything.

"You have to eat more, Hannah, please."

Tuning out again, I tried to feel hungry, but I could still barely keep any food down. I wasn't sick, or pregnant—thank god—just broken. Not being able to trust my own emotions, wondering if I was some programmed yet self-aware robot, was terrible, and I wished I didn't have to feel anything at all anymore.

Any hope I'd had of ever leading a normal life was gone. Judith had informed me of that. I could never leave the world of the Cordova cartel now, I knew too much, but she was giving me a chance to heal before I made any decisions about my future. As if I had a choice. All I could hope was they allowed me to return to school for real at some point, to finish up my degree.

The thought of my hard work, my sacrifices, pissed away over the wrong man infuriated me, but I kept every emotion locked up tight inside. I knew Leo was deeply hurt by my silence, and I liked hurting him, liked sharing my pain. Misery loves company, and I was a big hole of darkness, drawing everyone around me into my despair.

When Joy visited me, I tried to put on a happy face, but knew I wasn't succeeding. She was worried that I was more hurt than I was letting on, that something was wrong, but I'd kept my silence about my real problems. Who the fuck would even believe me if I told them I'd been drugged and hypnotized into loving Leo?

Something Leo said caught my attention, like a shiny lure thrown into the deep abyss of my mind. I followed that thought, trying to make my mind remember what he'd been saying. My body language must have alerted him, because Leo lowered his face into my line of sight.

Usually I could look past him, focus on the scar above his brow, or the fine hints of a blond so light it was almost pure silver coming in at his temples, and just drift. But today his gaze captured mine, the old compelling force back in them instead of the guilt and sorrow I'd grown used to. I didn't like that he wasn't suffering like I was and swallowed hard to keep from saying anything. Mules had nothing on me when it came to being stubborn. Once a man broke my heart, I never let him back in, ever, and Leo was going to learn that the hard way.

"Thought that would get your attention," he all but purred. "You do a very good job of pretending I don't exist, but your body still belongs to me."

Another swallow, this time out of nervousness as he continued to stare at me.

When I said nothing, he simply held my gaze, then leaned back in his chair, my head unwillingly turning to follow him. He was too satisfied with himself, too sure, and it left me unsettled. Knowing he had my attention, he allowed himself a slow smile that screamed trouble.

"I realize I've been handling this the wrong way. You won't listen to my explanations of why I did what I did, and I'm done feeling guilty over it. You're right, I am a monster, and I will do whatever it takes to bring you back into my life. I wanted you to do it willingly, but I'll take responsibility and help urge you along. Enough with the pity party."

"Pity party?" My voice came out thick and scratchy from disuse, breaking as I said in a louder voice, "Pity party? I find out the guy I'm in a relationship with is a cartel-affiliated fucking sociopath and you accuse me of having a pity party? You are completely fucked in the head."

"I am." He shrugged and gave me a grin that was almost boyish, in a disturbing way. "A prime example of that is how I feel about you."

Holding up my hand, I rose from my chair and backed away. "Don't. Don't you dare say you care about me. I'll puke if you do."

He rolled his eyes—rolled his damn eyes at me—like I was the one behaving in an insane manner. "I never realized you could be so dramatic. Nice to know I bring out that passion in you. Now get back over here and sit down. We need to discuss this like adults."

Something huge, nasty, and ugly rose from deep inside of me, from the place festering with fear over what had happened, the constant tension I was in. I hated this, hated being afraid, hated being alone. Whatever he'd done to my mind had twisted me so I missed him with every breath and dreamed of him constantly. Every time I woke up, I missed him more, and loathed myself for it.

The smirk he gave me was the last straw, and I picked up a pretty decorative vase that probably cost a shit-ton of money and chucked it at him as hard as I could.

He ducked, lucky asshole, and it shattered behind him like a bomb going off.

In a rage, I threw the table the vase had been on against the wall, the shatter of the delicate wooden legs snapping only feeding my wrath.

I'd just reached for the mirror above the dresser

when strong arms grasped me tight.

Seething, I kicked back, trying to injure Leo—only it wasn't Leo I was kicking, it was Jose.

Abruptly realizing my error, I almost hit the floor before he tightened his grip and hauled me up. Fear ricocheted through me as I saw that Judith had come into the room as well. She looked first at the shattered vase, then the table, and finally slowly to Leo before she slowly turned those dark eyes on me.

I had the oddest urge to apologize as she unleashed the disappointed look all mothers had used to cower their children from the dawn of time. Yes, she was the wife of a cartel lord, whose nuts I'd just tried to kick, but she'd been nothing but nice to me. Maybe it was Stockholm syndrome or good manners, but I felt ashamed that I'd broken her stuff.

Leo stepped forward. "Judith, I hope you'll agree that we need to do things my way."

She sighed, her gaze going once more to the splintered remains of the vase. "I had prayed she would see reason, but you're right, she does love being the martyr."

I trembled as the anger crept back, fighting the urge to tell Judith to go fuck herself. "You said when I was healed I leave. Well, I'm healed, and I want to go anywhere he isn't."

Judith eyed me with an exasperated huff, as if I were a toddler throwing a tantrum. "Good luck."

They left and I glared at Leo. "I'm not going anywhere with you."

"Oh, yes you are." He smiled that not-nice smile that still sent a tingle through my deprived lady parts. "You're coming home with me, and I'm going to fuck some sense into you."

"If you touch me it will be rape."

"I won't touch you until you beg me."

"When hell freezes over."

"I don't think that will be an issue. In fact, I know it won't."

One thing I knew about Leo was he'd go to any lengths to get what he wanted, including me. "What did you do?"

"I'm just helping your body win the fight against your mind."

"What did you do?"

Closing the distance between us, he backed me up to the wall then caged me in with his arms. "Whatever is necessary to keep you. I told you I would never let you go, Hannah, and I meant it. I watched you for a year, planned for you, created the perfect home for you and did everything I could to ensure that you would be happy with me."

I wanted to say that included brainwashing me, but Fernando had risked his life to share that information, and I really didn't want to be responsible for his death. "You lied to me."

"I did, but not about what mattered. I wanted to give you a chance to see the man I really am before you found out about my profession."

"Your profession," I spat, "is to torture people."

His eyes flashed with anger, but he nodded, his body close enough now that the warmth of his frame washed over me. "It is, and I'm very good at it."

Disgusted, I ducked beneath his arm and backed away. "Leave me alone."

"I'm afraid that isn't an option. I'm addicted to

you, Hannah. I have to have you in my life. Without you, the word is a very dark place, and I refuse to let you go."

"It's not your choice," I cried out. "I don't want you!"

"You do. Honestly you do. I swear to you, baby girl, I'll make this right."

"You can't."

This time when he backed me against the wall, then he held me there with his muscled forearm over my chest. A sharp prick came from my thigh and I gasped at the sudden burning sensation. It was gone before I could move away and I stared up at Leo with hatred.

"What did you just give me?"

"Something to make this easier for you."

"You bastard! I hate you."

He cradled me so tenderly in his arms as my legs gave out. "I know you do. Trust me, I know.

Chapter 18

Hot, slightly stinky breath steamed up my face with humidity as something panted on me. I jerked back, but it was too late, and someone began to enthusiastically lick me. Christ, the side of my face was instantly slimy, and I sleepily tried to shove the warm, furry mass off me.

My mind kicked in enough to identify the creature as a dog, a very friendly one, and I woke up with a giggle and a smile, forgetting for a moment what had happened as Honey greeted me like she did most mornings.

Since I'd spent five out of every seven days over at Leo's, I was used to my face being Honey's first destination when she finished with her morning business. While she sometimes slept with Leo and me, she was mostly with Mark. This was partly because I didn't want her getting distressed when Leo and I got…feral in the bedroom, and partly because Mark was lonely and Honey made it better.

No doubt he was downstairs now in the kitchen, whipping up breakfast for all of us. Not only was he in charge of security for Leo's estate, he could also make frittatas so light and airy, yet so cheesy and bacony good, that you'd swear you'd died and gone to heaven. Both Honey and I were spoiled by his frittatas and my stomach rumbled at the thought. Maybe if I was lucky, he'd also make applesauce sausage, which sounded nasty but was just plain delicious.

Burying my face in Honey's neck, I let out a shuddering sigh as reality crept in, despite my best attempts to keep it out. It was the scent of Leo's cologne on the sheets that invaded my senses, sent a little pulse of desire through me. I almost reached across the bed, hoping he was still next to me, when I remembered what had happened in a violent rush. The sound of sorrow I made worried Honey and she nudged me, whimpering softly until I stroked her head and reassured her.

As she looked up at me with her big blue eyes, I whispered to her, "I'm not mad at you, it's your insane master that I'm pissed off at. When I leave, I'll take you with me and we'll start over in like…well, I'm not sure where, but it'll just be me and you, babe."

Mark's voice came from the doorway of the bedroom. "That's so very Thelma and Louise of you, but I'm afraid I must point out the obvious flaw in your plans."

Feeling calmer here than I had at the Cordova house, I tugged the blankets over my lap, hiding myself despite the fact I wore shorts and a loose t-shirt. "And what would that be?"

"Leo will never let you go. You can run to the ends of the earth and he'll find you."

"Because he's crazy and obsessed with me?"

"Because he loves you."

Glaring at him, I tried to choke back my anger as Honey picked up my mood and growled. "No, he doesn't. You don't lie to the people you love. All his bullshit about being able to be himself around me was just another way to manipulate me."

"Oh grow up, Hannah. So you found out he's a criminal, big fucking deal. He treats you like gold, bends over backwards to make you happy, and all you do is take."

"What? I don't take!"

"Oh yes, you do. I like you, but you're the neediest woman I've ever met. It would take a man like Leo to put up with you. *I* sure as fuck wouldn't."

My mouth went dry and Honey growled again, but Mark ordered her out and she did as he told her, leaving me clenching my sheets. "I'm not needy."

Denial isn't only a river in Egypt, said the chorus girl to the bishop.

"Please. Most women would feel smothered by Leo's level of attention, but you flourished beneath it. I bet before you met Leo, you were a different person, timid and scared of life, dating losers because you felt that was all you deserved. And that fucking bitch roommate of yours, she's lucky I didn't kill her instead of sending her home to Mommy and Daddy with a note to get control of their offspring."

The night came back to me with a rush, Mark's face filling my memory as the relief I'd felt when he'd saved me had me drawing in a shuddering breath. "I never thanked you for saving me."

The stiff line of his shoulders softened. "We should have been there sooner, but Leo hadn't realized you'd left the Cordova house, and the cameras covering your place weren't being watched because nobody knew you were home. He was busy dealing with Fernando, having an intervention and trying to get him into some serious therapy. I don't know if Judith told you, but they're as close as brothers."

I should be used to my overactive sense of guilt by now, should be able to harden my heart against it, but once again my empathy overwhelmed me and I asked in a low voice, "Is he going to be okay? Fernando?"

Mark sighed then ran both hands through his hair. "I don't know. Getting over the death of your family…never really happens, you know? He'll always be broken in some way."

Goddamn it, now I was feeling sorry for Mark and the loss of his family, but I didn't want to say anything. He'd made it abundantly clear he didn't want to talk about his wife, ever, and even though my natural inclination was to try and comfort him, I managed to keep myself in check. Sometimes the best thing you could do for someone was leave them the hell alone and let them deal with their grief in private.

Speaking of privacy, I was suddenly reminded of how mine had been violated on pretty much every level by Leo, and the man standing before me.

My stomach curdled as I recalled Judith gently explaining to me how Leo had been watching me for a year, taking his time to learn who I was and falling in love with me. Everyone was so damn eager to tell me how much he adored me, but it was too little too late. Maybe if he'd trusted me enough to be truthful from the beginning, I could forgive him. That is, if it wasn't for the fact he'd brainwashed me. Hell, I'd forgiven him for being a sociopath and dispensing brutal justice, I could justify the killings he'd participated in because of the videos Judith had shown me. The people he'd killed really had been terrible, the scum of the earth in every way, and they deserved to die.

I, however, did not deserve to be made into some crazy man's plaything.

Taking away someone's free will, forcing me to love him, the thought that my emotions could be so easily manipulated, made me feel ill.

"You know," Mark said as he pushed in a cart from the hallway, the amber in his light brown hair gleaming in the sunlight streaming into the bedroom, "he's been a right fucking bastard this last week. If I didn't love him like a brother, I would have put a bullet in him myself."

"I wish you had," I said with a growl.

"Awww, you don't mean that."

"I so do." Lifting the lid on the tray, he revealed both frittatas and muffins, making my stomach howl like a beast. "No thanks, I'm not hungry."

"Come on, you're going to turn down food made for you by the man who saved your life?"

Glaring at him, I snatched one of the frittatas up and pretended I wasn't having a mouth orgasm as I took a bit before saying through a mouthful of food, "Thank you."

He calmly poured me a glass of juice. "You're welcome, drink up. You look like shit."

"Yeah, well, these last few weeks have been rough." I snorted before taking a long drink of the tart juice.

"True." We ate in silence for a little bit before Mark asked, "Did you ever remember where you first met Leo?"

"Yeah, at the diner."

"Oh no, you met way before that. Around ten-ish years ago."

I frowned, thinking back to the year when my sister had lingered, then died. "When?"

"At the hospital. You were there, in the waiting room, the night his mom was murdered in a drive-by shooting meant to kill Leo. You sat and talked with him while he waited to hear that she'd died."

I gasped, a vague memory surfacing.

Holy shit, I remembered him.

Leo had looked different then. A lot leaner, almost gangly, with a spiky haircut and pierced eyebrow, with his shoulder tattoo fresh and black against his smaller biceps. I'd probably talked to hundreds of people in that waiting room, begging for someone to acknowledge I existed…but I remembered *him*.

"No fucking way."

"Yes fucking way. Imagine his surprise when, one night, on a night when he needed you so badly, you appeared out of nowhere, in a diner of all places."

Despite myself, I wanted Mark to continue. "Why didn't he say anything?"

"I think he wanted you to remember on your own. And did you ever figure out what a huge coincidence it was that Leo has your exact taste in home decor?"

"What are you talking about?" I looked around the bedroom then back to Mark.

"I'd say you're oblivious, but you have over five hundred 'bedroom inspiration' pictures on Pinterest so I'm not surprised you forgot about the image that inspired this room."

"Wait—you've looked at my Pinterest boards?"

"Not me, but Leo has. He's studied every one of

those boards, trying to build you the perfect house, fill it with the perfect stuff, and do everything he could to make you happy. And don't you dare say shit about him invading your social media privacy; you put all that crap up there for people to look at. Trust me, no guy who isn't in love with you is going to give one ripe fart about your favorite kind of sandal. And he sure as hell wouldn't make sure you have it in your size and favorite color, all because he spends time trying to figure out ways to make you happy. Those are the actions of a man who loves you."

Frowning, I looked down at my plate to my poor muffin, which I'd picked away at until it was a pile of crumbs. "Whatever, it's all a big lie anyways. None of this is real."

"*Man*, you are a downer. Leo was right, you need to get laid."

Pissed, I flicked a large piece of muffin at him, irritated when he easily batted it away. "That's the last thing I need."

"Me thinks the lady doth protest too much."

"You're irritating." Not liking the easy way he'd charmed me into relaxation, I snapped, "Do you help Leo when he tortures people?"

"When necessary."

That killed my appetite, and I had to wash down the food stuck in my throat with a big drink. "What's wrong with you?"

He shrugged. "Anyone that I torture deserves it."

"So you get to be judge, jury, and executioner? Who made *you* God?"

Instead of getting mad at me, his looked amused,

like I was some cute puppy yapping at him. "You sure like to judge people and situations quickly, don't you? So sure you know everything, so certain your view of the world is right. Makes it easy to comfort yourself with bullshit lies, to pretend you had no idea Leo isn't like most men. But you'll never admit that—because then you'd have to admit you aren't like most women."

Stung, I moved over to the windows, my arms crossed as I rubbed my elbows. "You're talking out your ass."

"Defensive," he said in a teasing tone that irritated me beyond measure. "You're so quick to call Leo out, but how about your little stalking habits? How many times have you been threatened with a restraining order? Gone a little too far in your efforts to make sure the loser you were with was happy?"

Ashamed, I turned away. "It's not the same thing as being a serial killer."

"No, it isn't, but you're stupid if you don't realize how perfect you and Leo are together. Unconventional, but you will never be as happy with anyone else as you are with him. I'm not going to lecture you, you're a big girl, but I will leave you with this. If the situations were reversed, if you were pursuing Leo, what *wouldn't* you have done to keep him? All he's ever tried to do is make you happy, Hannah, because you are literally the only person on earth he's given his full heart to."

"He lied," I whispered, the urge to tell Mark to shove it up his ass because I knew Leo brainwashed me battering at my self-control.

"Yeah, he did. He's human, we make mistakes.

You need to ask yourself if you want to turn into someone like your parents, holding irrational grudges against the people who love them the most."

I flinched, his words hitting me as hard as a punch to the kidney, and twice as painful. "Get out."

The cart rattled, then the door shut, leaving me staring out at the cloudy horizon, framed by soft curtains in a warm ivory tone. I wondered if it was going to rain and wished once again I had my phone. At Judith's, I hadn't been allowed to make any calls, and since I wasn't talking to anyone it made asking for a phone difficult.

Gnawing at my bottom lip, I wondered if my silence was childish, if I'd reverted to the negative habits that I'd grown up with.

Joy would know; I needed to talk to her. She was my touchstone.

A fat plop of rain pinged off the bedroom window, matching the tear trailing down my cheek.

With a start, I remembered that we kept a phone in here. I darted over to it, trying to remember Joy's number. Oh the irony of cell phones; without mine, I had no idea how to contact anyone.

When I picked it up and got a dial tone, I hesitated, tempted for a moment to call 9-1-1. But what would I say? Don't arrest him, just get me out of here? That according to everyone, Leo only tortured people who deserved it? The Cordova cartel would lawyer up and lie to protect him, but at the same time I couldn't do that to him, couldn't betray him like that.

For a moment, I wondered if that was just the hypnosis bullshit Leo had done to me talking, but quickly dismissed that thought. I've always been loyal, sometimes blindly and painfully so, and I just wasn't the kind of person that would turn on someone like that. Not only would it harm Leo, it would also endanger the entire Cordova family. Yes, they were drug-dealing bad people, but they had good hearts—in their own messed up ways. Maybe I was making excuses, but I couldn't help feeling compassion for them, especially Fernando. He'd paid the ultimate price for their criminal lifestyle, and he deeply regretted it.

With a press of my thumb, I hung up the phone, not wanting to talk to anyone right now as I tried to figure out the conflicted, tangled knot of my feelings.

Restless, I went to the door, not surprised in the least to find myself locked in. Thankfully there was a TV that dropped down from the ceiling and I flopped back into the bed, scanning through the channels as I flip-flopped between relaxation, and guilt that I was feeling relaxed. The desert storm pounded the house now, vibrating the windows and drawing my gaze to watch the tempest. Once again the scent of Leo's cologne comforted me and I grabbed his pillow, telling myself I was just trying to get comfy, not surround myself in his scent.

In the days since I'd taken that beating because of my association with Leo, I'd had a lot of time to think about my situation and my options. The harsh reality was, I really had none. It was either live a life based on lies with Leo, or start somewhere new, without the support of my girls.

Or at least the support of Joy.

Shit, who am I kidding? I'm part of the world of the Cordova cartel now, any ignorance that I might have had at one time no longer shielding me from the criminals. Because of Leo and Judith's scheming, I'd drawn the attention of predators, and they wouldn't hesitate to make their move once I was away from the protection of the cartel. I knew it, and more importantly, Leo knew it as well.

Once again it felt as if he'd taken my choices away from me, forcing me to live the life he believed I should have. And the thing was, life with Leo wasn't bad — in fact, it was good. So good I knew it had to all be a lie, and I hated the fact that I felt like I was deeply in love with someone who'd betray me like this.

With a heavy heart, I watched some show about small houses and tried to cut through the complicated tangle of my thoughts.

Warm lips brushed over my shoulder and a heavy, naked, and slightly furry hard body slid up against my back, cocooning me in his warmth and pressing me into the softness of the bed.

He'd shaved recently, and the brush of his smooth skin against mine was a luxuriant decadence that was as sweet as candy.

Then came the warm rasp of his tongue as he licked down the valley of my spine, pausing to kiss me here and there.

He'd reached my now wiggling hips by the time my brain caught up with reality, when it dawned on me that he was kissing my faded bruises.

I tried to roll away, but he easily pinned me beneath his weight before jerking away the pillows from under my face so I could breathe.

"Get the hell off of me!"

"No." He rocked his hips against my ass, the globes of my cheeks hugging his thick cock.

Hard…he was so hard against me.

I needed him.

No, fuck that, it was only the drugs talking.

"Leo, this is not going to happen."

"Oh yes, it is."

He flipped me over and before I could protest, wrapped something around my wrist. I moved to pull it off, but he grabbed my other hand and secured a familiar black bondage restraint around that wrist as well.

I tried to tell myself the full-body shiver racing through me was one of disgust, not anticipation, as I realized he'd pulled out our under-the-bed restraint system. I'd spent many, many hours in pleasurable bondage with these restraints and tried to pretend it was an automatic conditioned reaction or drugs, not true desire, that had my pussy wet.

"Don't you dare even think about it."

Ignoring me, he grabbed my ankle and dodged my violent kicks, pinning me to the bed tighter than usual.

Good call on his part because I was once again raging mad. "You let me go right now!"

He merely shook his head and smiled, his thick erection standing out from his body as he crawled over me to suck, then bite at my nipple.

Oh that felt so good, damn him, and my body lit up with fireworks.

Kissing his way between the valley of my breasts, he then worshiped my other small mound, drawing choking noises from me as I forced back the moans.

Not that it mattered, he knew my body well enough to read my arousal. My musk hung heavy in the air, blending with his and triggering nothing but happy memories. It was impossible to have him touching me like this and maintain my sanity. Even as I tried to tell myself over and over again this was all an illusion, fake, the result of drugs and trickery, it felt so, so good in a way that was *very* real.

"I'm not turned on," I blurted as his gentle kisses moved down my body before he rubbed his cheek against my belly. "It's the drugs."

"There are no drugs," he said with a soft chuckle. "Well, other than the sedative."

I thought back to how horny I'd been earlier and frowned at him. "Yes there was."

He lifted his head to look at me with a slight grin. "I think I'd know if I drugged you."

The sight of his broad shoulders between my opened thighs was erotic and my clit swelled further, to my embarrassment. "No, no, no. This isn't real."

"It absolutely is. The sooner you realize that, the sooner we can move on."

"Move on? Are you insane! You broke my heart!"

"I know, and I told you I would. I also promised I'd help you put it back together, and I will."

The tip of his rough finger skimmed my wet folds and I tried to keep my voice venomous as I hissed, "What, you're going to fuck me better?"

"Something like that."

"That won't happen, because I hate you!"

"You keep telling yourself that, baby girl. Let me know how it works out for you."

"Fuck you."

That curse would have been a lot more effective if my hips weren't chasing his light touch. Back and forth, back and forth, then a little rub around the outside of my clit, tugging the hood back a little to reveal my swollen nub.

I must be drugged, had to be, because my arousal was off the charts and way beyond what I'd ever felt with another man. I held my breath, straining when he spread my vaginal lips open like he usually did before he was about to feast on me. There was the barest whisper of heat over my folds and I gripped my hands hard enough that little darts of pain raced through me.

Then he pulled back, leaving me aching and open, ready to beg him but too stubborn to let a word past my clenched lips.

"Now that I have your attention," he purred, "let's talk about Fernando's late-night visit to your room."

I froze beneath him, then twitched when he pinched my clit. "I don't know what you're talking about."

In one smooth move, he was above me again, a shift of his hips rubbing his cock over my spread pussy, the ridge around his thick head hitting me just right. "Don't lie to me, I don't like it."

"And…I…don't like…"

My words trailed off as, with each pass of his hips, the tip of his erection pressed against my entrance, just enough to make me throb with need.

"Stop lying. Fernando confessed it to me, his newfound sense of guilt and morality working in my favor for once."

"Please, don't hurt him."

Leo actually rolled his eyes at me, snapping me out of my growing panic. "I'm not going to hurt him. I know you think I'm some psychopath, but I'm not. I'm closer to a sociopath, but I don't fit that profile either. I can form bonds, friendships, and love, but only with certain people. Fernando is one of those people, so I would never hurt him."

Tears pooled in my eyes as the feeling of betrayal swept through me once more. "You brainwashed me."

"I absolutely did."

"When?"

"The night we met at Obsession. I brought you home and hypnotized you before I returned you to your apartment."

"And drugged me."

His tip pressed against me and he slid just the barest bit in, enough to stretch but not satisfy. "I did."

"You made me love you!"

"I didn't."

"Don't lie to me! Fernando said you did."

"Fernando was talking out his ass. He has no idea what I said to you or how I influenced your thoughts, he only knows what he's speculated, because I haven't told anyone all of what went on, not even Judith."

"He wasn't there?"

"No one was there."

"But he made it sound like he was."

"I don't know if you've noticed, but Fernando is fighting some demons right now. Going on and off his meds, along with heavy drinking and depression, has fucked with his mind. He only thinks he knows what I said, based on what Judith wanted, but he has no idea. But one thing I've told him — I've told *everyone*, over and over again — is that I cannot make you love me."

"Another lie."

"Why? Because you *do* love me?"

"Of course I do, with everything I have," I shouted into his face, "but it's not real!"

With one growling thrust, he was in me, stretching me painfully, while all I could do was scream out in surprise as he pushed his way in. "It's as real as my cock."

My neck arched to the side and my shoulders hurt as I strained against my bonds, at once wanting to get closer and farther away. "I don't want this."

"Now who's lying?"

Me. I was a big fat dirty liar with a big fat cock stuffed inside of her.

My inner walls squeezed down on him as I twitched and moaned, overwhelmed by sensation.

"Hannah, look at the TV."

I ignored him, intent on moving my hips as much as I was able to so I could orgasm and start the blissful descent into subspace, where I would finally find some much-needed peace.

He leaned up and slapped my breast, the sting only adding to my pleasure.

Then he pulled out so, once again, only the tip of his dick was inside of me.

"More," I snarled up at him.

"Not until you turn your head."

When I did, all the fight drained out of me —

because on the TV was a still image of me, in my little black dress, smiling up at Leo in an unfamiliar room.

A shudder ran through me, but this time it wasn't desire, and I tightened painfully as he slid back fully inside of me.

Leo brushed my hair back from my face, but I didn't take my gaze from the screen. "I taped this for you, so someday you could watch it and understand how far I went to make you happy from the start, how much you mean to me."

"Please," I whispered, "I don't want to watch."

"Then you'll listen."

I was tempted to close my eyes and hum, but when Leo pressed play, I stared with horrified fascination as my image on the screen confessed my deepest and darkest desires to him. Not just my adoration of the taboo, but my intimate dreams of a family and the love I so deeply desired.

The urge to cry became too great as Leo then put me into some kind of fucked-up trance and began what I was sure was the brainwashing portion of the night.

Everything up to that point hadn't been so bad. I wasn't sure how I felt about him encouraging me to enjoy pain with sex, but I was about to watch him take away my free will, and I loathed him for it.

On the video, Leo was telling me that I couldn't betray him, that I would never endanger myself or my children, that I would be loyal to him and how I would never reveal him to his enemies.

"You bastard!"

I tried to buck him off, but he put his hand over my mouth then simply growled, "Watch."

I did—and my outrage began to fizzle as the Leo on the screen continued to instruct me.

Not to fall in love with him, like I was so sure he had, but to…well, to heal myself.

He told me to let go of the past, to release the pain my parents had instilled in me, and to love myself. Leo didn't order me to be his sex slave, he told me that I was worth loving, that I was amazing, and that I needed to stand up for myself and demand the respect I deserved. He told me to recognize that I was a strong woman, a beautiful woman, a treasure.

Over and over he repeated those positive messages, his whole body tense while he stared down at me as if he could force me to believe that I was an amazing woman worthy of love.

Instead of turning me into a robot, Leo had attempted to heal my damaged psyche.

The video ended, frozen on an image of him tenderly kissing my forehead.

"Do you understand, now, what I did?"

His hand was still over my mouth, so I nodded as tears spilled down my cheeks.

The rip of the Velcro was loud as he freed my wrists from the restraints. "Then you know that I never wanted to enslave you, never wanted your forced affection. I wanted to heal you, wanted to be able to do the impossible and erase the damage your asshole parents did, and this was the best way to do that."

I tried to speak, then narrowed my eyes at him until he lifted his hand to remove my restraints. "You were going to show this to me?"

"Yes, someday." He did this rolling thing with hips

that had me squirming beneath him, the width of his cock stretching me perfectly, with just a hint of spicy pain.

"When?"

"I intended to show you this in twenty years."

"Why that long?"

"So you'd know without a doubt by that point that your feelings for me are real."

I tilted my pelvis so his slow strokes rubbed over my clit. "You didn't order me to love you."

"No."

"But I do anyways."

"I'm glad to hear that, because I'm beyond in love with you. You are literally my everything, Hannah. I can't and won't live without you. I think you're finally beginning to understand just how serious I am about that." A full-body shiver ran through him as I reached down to brush my fingers over where we joined together, my fingers sliding over his cock and my stretched labia. "You have no idea what your touch does to me, how it's better than anything I've ever felt—and I feel it so much."

I closed my eyes, unable to resist the pump and thrust of his body against mine, the tips of my tingling nipples brushing his chest as he worked me with the utmost skill.

"You know," I panted out as he licked the side of my neck. "You didn't have to hypnotize me to enjoy this. You are insanely good in bed."

He rewarded me with faster thrusts that had my body growing more sensitive by the minute. "With you, I wanted nothing left to chance. I had to have you."

"And now that you do have me, what are you going to do with me?"

"Keep you forever, of course."

I sighed in delight as my orgasm cascaded over me like a flurry of sparks, the hollow feeling leaving my chest.

In his own messed-up way, Leo really loved me, and in my own messed-up way, I really loved him. We could probably put a team of therapists' kids through college with all of our issues, but those crazy jagged pieces of both our minds fit perfectly together, becoming something better, stronger.

I wrapped my arms around Leo, the sensation of being completely embraced filling me as another orgasm hovered just out of reach.

"Come on, baby girl, come all over your Daddy."

I did, and I did it with a smile.

Epilogue

Fifteen years later
Leo

On the stage, a dozen chubby little four- and five-year-old girls twirled around in a disorganized circle, their rounded faces intent on their moves.

Our middle daughter, Carla, twirled from one side of the stage to the other, much to her mother's chagrin, and my, along with the audience's, delight. Dressed in a glittering pale jade leotard and matching sparkling tights, Carla beamed a smile at the crowd as she did an odd dance move that utterly lacked any rhythm. Her black pigtails, the same shade as her mother's dark hair, swung with her lurching moves that were an odd combination of tap, ballet, and maybe an aboriginal war dance.

Next to me, Hannah sighed in exasperation while the dance teacher corralled her wayward ballerina. "She must get her dance moves from you."

I didn't dare laugh as I looked over at her seated in a crappy plastic folding chair like the rest of the parents, watching our little dancing dumplings.

That was the name of the dance school.

Dancing Dumplings.

I shit you not.

But Carla had taken one look at the sparkling sign with apple dumplings in tutus on it and decided this was where she belonged.

Next to my always beautiful Hannah, sat our blonde eleven-year-old-going-on-thirty daughter, Tiffany, who was bouncing our fourteen-month-old daughter, Sage, on her lap.

"I don't know, Mom," Tiffany said with a smile, "I still remember the dance you did at Uncle Diego's wedding."

Hannah flushed and I couldn't hold back my chuckle, earning a glare from my wife before she turned back to our too-smart-for-her-own-good daughter. "I was just showing people how to line dance."

"Uh, Mom, usually when people line dance, it's not by themselves."

"I was improvising," Hannah muttered, earning a laugh from both of us.

On the stage, Carla's group was finishing up their dance and they assembled into a ragged line, dropping into awkward curtsies. Well, most of them did. Carla gave everyone a salute. I was really going to have to have a talk with Mark about letting Carla watch war movies with him whenever he babysat the kids.

Then she began to sing the national anthem at the top of her voice, pushing away her teacher when she tried to stop Carla, and I wondered if Ramón, who was recording all of this from the back of the room for Judith and Jose, was pissing himself laughing yet.

One thing my children did not lack was self-esteem. How could my girls believe they were anything but wonderful when they had literally an entire cartel of people who thought they were the cutest things ever? Hannah and I worked hard to keep the girls from being spoiled, but Carla in particular, with her mother's big doe eyes, had learned how to expertly manipulate adults into being her minions. It was quite funny to watch, and it pissed off Hannah that I was not so secretly proud of my middle child's ability to outwit and outmaneuver her Cordova uncles.

Unfortunately, that belief in herself also led to not-so-amusing situations like hijacking the dance recital.

As I shrank down into my seat, the other little girls on stage, a few of them Carla's cousins, began to follow Carla's lead as the teachers stood helplessly aside and followed suit, belting out the next verse.

Then Carla yelled out, "You stand up for the national anthem!"

Hannah covered her face as we stood, along with the rest of the audience, while Carla returned to singing the hell out of the song with all of her considerable, and off-tune, voice.

Grinning down at my wife, we sang along while Tiffany rocked Sage as she smiled up at her big sister.

Slipping my arm around my wife's shoulders, I hugged her close and watched our little rule breaker run the show, already dreading the day when I had three beautiful young women, and the boys who would want to take them away from me.

God help the man who got Carla.

Hannah leaned up, her soft breasts and nicely rounded body pressing into mine. Motherhood had been good to her, giving her womanly curves that I couldn't keep my hands off of. I wanted to have one more child, try one more time for a boy, but she said her baby factory was closed. I still thought I could convince her otherwise.

"I love you," she whispered against my lips while Tiffany made revolted noises.

Hannah and I were an openly affectionate couple, much to our daughter's disgust and my delight.

"I love you too, baby girl."

She leaned up to whisper in my ear, in a voice I could barely hear, "And don't think I'm not blaming you for this somehow. When we get home tonight, you get to wear the butt plug."

"We'll see about that. If you're a good girl, I might—might—let you rim me," I whispered back, the last of the song covering our conversation before the clapping began.

It helped that half the audience was somehow either related to Carla, or were our good friends. Of course, once our girls had started dancing, Ramón's girls had demanded to do the same, then Diego's. Fernando, the lucky fuck, had a pack of little tomboys running around his garage and giving him gray hairs, so he was busy taking them to karate practice and soccer tournaments.

Yep, we were surrounded by little girls, every one of us. That meant our lives were filled with an odd combination of guns and hair bows, assassinations and standing around shooting the shit while our kids got their faces painted at a local fair. We were fucked-up, but we were family, and we'd weather any storm, overcome anything life threw at us, because each and every one of us had amazing wives who loved us with every bit of their formidable hearts...and that made all the difference.

The End

Dear Beloved Reader,

I hope you enjoyed Leo and Hannah's story! If you'd like to read about the other men of the Cordova cartel, please leave a review and let me know. Until then, thank you-as always, for giving me a chance to entertain you. ☺

Ann

About the Author

With over thirty published books, Ann is Queen of the Castle to her wonderful husband and three sons in the mountains of West Virginia. In her past lives she's been an Import Broker, a Communications Specialist, a US Navy Civilian Contractor, a Bartender/Waitress, and an actor at the Michigan Renaissance Festival. She also spent a summer touring with the Grateful Dead-though she will deny to her children that it ever happened.

From a young age she's been fascinated by myths and fairytales, and the romance that was often the center of the story. As Ann grew older and her hormones kicked in, she discovered trashy romance novels. Great at first, but she soon grew tired of the endless stories with a big wonderful emotional buildup to really short and crappy sex. Never a big fan of purple prose, throbbing spears of fleshy pleasure and wet honey pots make her giggle, she sought out books that gave the sex scenes in the story just as much detail and plot as everything else-without using cringe worthy euphemisms. This led her to the wonderful world of Erotic Romance, and she's never looked back.

Now Ann spends her days trying to tune out cartoons playing in the background to get into her 'sexy space' and has accepted that her Muse has a severe case of ADD.

Ann loves to talk with her fans, as long as they realize she's weird and that sarcasm doesn't translate well via text.

Made in the USA
San Bernardino, CA
27 November 2016